the first day of the rest of my life

Books by Cathy Lamb

JULIA'S CHOCOLATES

THE LAST TIME I WAS ME

HENRY'S SISTERS

SUCH A PRETTY FACE

THE FIRST DAY OF THE REST OF MY LIFE

Published by Kensington Publishing Corporation

the first day of the rest of my life

CATHY LAMB

KENSINGTON BOOKS
www.kensingtonbooks.com

KENSINGTON BOOKS are published by

Kensington Publishing Corp.
119 West 40th Street
New York, NY 10018

All Kensington titles, imprints, and distributed lines are available at special quantity discounts for bulk purchases for sales promotion, premiums, fundraising, educational, or institutional use.

Special book excerpts or customized printings can also be created to fit specific needs. For details, write or phone the office of the Kensington Special Sales Manager: Kensington Publishing Corp., 119 West 40th Street, New York, NY 10018. Attn. Special Sales Department. Phone: 1-800-221-2647.

Kensington and the K logo Reg. U.S. Pat. & TM Off.

ISBN-13: 978-0-7582-5938-7
ISBN-10: 0-7582-5938-7

First Kensington Trade Paperback Printing: August 2011
10 9 8 7 6 5 4 3 2 1

Printed in the United States of America

For Rachel, our favorite violinist

ACKNOWLEDGMENTS

A million thank-yous to John Scognamiglio
and Evan Marshall.

An Old Irish Blessing

May the road rise to meet you,
May the wind be always at your back.
May the sun shine warm upon your face,
The rains fall soft upon your fields.
And until we meet again,
May God hold you in the palm of His hand.

1

The Gunshot Anniversary is coming up.

Those six gunshots have echoed throughout my entire life.

They grabbed everyone's attention in the courthouse pretty darn quick, too.

Bang, bang, bang!

There was the expected cacophony of panic with people screaming and diving to the floor, attorneys scattering, the jury ducking, reporters squawking, photographers scrambling for a photo, and the sheriff barreling toward the gunman.

Or, more properly should I say, the gun*woman*.

The gunwoman was my momma.

Marie Elise O'Shea was a well-dressed shooter. She wore her light pink dress with embroidered white daisies circling the trim, matching cotton candy pink heels, red lipstick, liquid black liner that tilted up at the corners, and a yellow ribbon holding back her thick black hair. "Yellow means there's still hope in this pickled, wrinkled, warped world, sugar," she told me. "Yellow means there's a new tomorrow scootin' around the corner, you just wait."

She looked a little weak, a little tired, but still beautiful, innocent even, the gun a strange, black aberration in her firm grip.

Annie and I were the only two people in the courtroom that sunny spring day who didn't move when she started shooting. We knew she would never shoot us.

She was shooting *for* us. Shooting for her daughters, and she had excellent aim. Momma had been raised on a farm in Oregon with fruit trees and rows of lavender and enjoyed target practice as an after-school activity. Some would argue her perfect aim was a good thing, others would argue it was not.

Right before my momma shot off her ladies' gun she said to those three men, in a voice as hard as a chunk of iron, "This is from Big Luke. He's going to escort you to hell. Good-bye." She spread her legs in her cotton candy pink heels so she would have perfect balance, then whipped her gun out from her bra.

Bang, bang, bang. Dead on target. Three more shots to call it good.

Sheriff Ellery knew he did not need to tackle my momma as he would have with any other shooter. He sprinted up to her, sweating, and scolded, "Now, sugar, you shouldn't have done that."

Momma didn't argue with him. She handed over the gun to the puffing, distressed sheriff amidst the utter chaos and declared, "Ellery, I had to. You know they've been threatening to come after my girls as soon as they're loosed from prison and I can't have that. I won't be around to protect them." She held out her wrists for the handcuffs. "Careful, honey. Don't you break my nails. And make sure your wife knows that I will not be able to make her appointment tomorrow for her Cut 'n Blow."

Sheriff Ellery, clearly upset, almost crying, but not because of the missed Cut 'n Blow appointment, snapped the cuffs on. He did not break Momma's nails. His wife was all aflutter about missing Marie Elise's Splendid, Superior Cut 'n Blow. Her niece's wedding was coming up, and the niece's mother, her older sister, who was so hoity-toity, would be there with her "piggly comments," and now who would get her all fixed up to do battle with "that pig-dragon witch? Who? Why couldn't Marie Elise have done the shooting on Monday? She knew I had this wedding!"

Momma went to jail on that sunny spring day and worked her magic on the nails, hair, and makeup of many female convicts. One of them later became the owner of a beauty supply chain, inspired by "the transformation Marie Elise made to my wretched hair and face. She made me believe in me. Me, Birdie Tyson, former delinquent." She named her highest selling shampoo Marie Elise's Pink.

Some say it was my momma's parents' money that got her out of jail because of the supersmart attorneys they hauled on in. Most said it was because the men she shot deserved it and more. But I knew why my momma's life was spared.

It was because of Marie Elise's French Beauty Parlor. Yes, the magic my momma brought to her beauty parlor saved her life.

At least that time it did.

2

"Ladies," I boomed out, my arms spread high in the air, spotlights shining down so bright I could barely see the thousands of Texan women screaming in the audience, "I want you to ask yourselves this question: Do you want to live your life like a mouse—a timid, tepid, squeaking, ineffectual, irritating mouse—or do you want to live your life like Mrs. Spinoza? Which one? *Which one?*"

"Mrs. Spinoza! Spinoza!" thousands of women shouted back at me. "Spinoza!"

"That's right! You want to be a Mrs. Spinoza!" I fisted my hands in victory in the middle of the stage as I concluded my speech. My proper black, boring, expensive business suit and I were projected onto three screens in the auditorium. It was what I thought a life coach who needed armor should wear.

"Spinoza, Spinoza!"

"Ladies, Mrs. Spinoza was fearless. She was adventurous. She was curious. She was a ball-breaking, get out of my way, I'm going to live my life with no boulders in it kind of lady! What are you going to do with your boulders?"

"Crush them, crush them!" they yelled back at me.

"What are you going to do with the mountains in your life?"

"Climb them, climb them!"

"That's right, you're going to climb them! You're going to put your heels on and climb over them! Put your heels on, scream it with me!"

"Put your heels on!" they screamed, a wave of feminine rage, freedom, and defiance. "Put your heels on!"

I strutted across the stage in my heels. Not high-stylin' heels, boring ones. The ones that say: I mean business. "No squeaking, ladies. Speak your mind even if your voice wobbles. Speak up for yourself, no one else will! Don't restrict yourself and the wacky-cool possibilities in your future, and stop allowing others to restrict you! If they don't like the new you, go out and make yourself some new friends, make yourself a new family with people who love to live, to laugh, to have adventures! And stop worrying about what you look like, for heaven's sakes! We've had enough of men telling us how to look, haven't we?"

"Yes. We. Have!" they roared.

"Let your hair down, Texas!" I ripped a rubber band out of my hair and shook loose my dark brown straight hair. It had been mercilessly flat ironed because the curls reminded me of something I tried every day to forget. "Let it dry in the wind while you explore Norway! Let your nails chip and split while you volunteer to dig wells in Africa! Leave your makeup at home when you trek through India! And when you're back in the workforce, put those red high heels on and stride like you mean it! Stride, don't step. Stride! Like you mean it!"

Whooee. Yell and shout. Screams from the bottom of those women's feisty souls.

"Ladies, thank you," I hollered into a massive standing ovation. "Now get out there and live the heel-kicking life your gut tells you to live! Kick your heels!"

I left the stage, the screaming crested, stayed there, deafening, and I was hustled back on. My final words: "Don't forget the O'Shea number one principle!"

I waited for a millisecond, until they shouted it back at me.

"Kick some girly ass, kick some girly ass," they chanted while clapping in sync, as I'd taught them. "*Kick some girly ass!*"

I laughed, waved, left the stage.

I was hustled out of the auditorium, hugged and thanked by the Ladies Power organizers as they insisted I come back next year, and gently shoved into a limo. The limo pulled away before the crowd left.

I leaned back in the seat and started to shake. I shook like someone had turned a blender on high inside my stomach.

I am a life coach, specializing in relationships, mostly for people with vaginas. I tell people what to do with their lives and who to have in it.

And I had told, over a three-day period, a whole bunch of women that they had to take charge of their lives, be adventurous like Mrs. Spinoza, my neighbor for years before she died at the age of ninety-nine at the Great Wall of China, her camera slung around her neck. She had been talking to two young Swedish men about the joys of Russian vodka and toppled right on over. "A death you can be proud of," I said.

I told them not to take any crap, "Live a Crapless Life"; to try new things, "Try New, No Wallowing in the Moldy Old"; how not to feel caged by guilt, remorse, or regret, "Unstrap Your Emotional Corsets"; and to reexamine commitments made decades ago to a life they no longer wanted to lead, "Release Yourself From Your Personal Prison."

I am pathetic.

Emotional crap wraps me like bondage. I am hounded by guilt. Remorse smothers me. I have so many regrets I could lay them end to end and they would cover Uranus. I have an emotional corset over my entire face. In my semielectrocuted mind, I am wallowing in my own personal prison with very wide iron bars, a dirt floor, and no windows.

Here is the truth: I am a lie. I am a lie to others, I am a lie to myself.

I kept shaking.

"You all right, ma'am?" the limo driver said, his brow wrinkled in concern.

"Yes. Fine. Fine. I'm fine."

Sure. Sure I was.

I heard the violin music in my head, a single violinist. I've been hearing violinists and full orchestras my whole life. I don't know why this is, I don't know where the concerts come from, I don't know why no one but me hears them. It's a tricky phenomenon I can't explain. I only know that the violin music is as much a part of my life as my lungs are a part of my breathing.

The violinist was playing Beethoven's *Für Elise*.

How fitting.

Very late that night I flew into Portland, Oregon, drove down a couple of freeways, and returned to the house I live in that I do not like.

It's built like a square spaceship. The lines are smooth and hard, and the furniture's the same way. Modern and edgy, like what you'd see in one of those architectural magazines. In fact, it has been in architectural magazines.

I like the view. I can watch the weather become emotional, but I don't like where I'm standing when I look at it.

Why did I buy it?

Besides the fact that it's exactly, purposefully, totally opposite from the home I grew up in, I bought it so I can prove that I'm someone. I live here because it's an impressive house. It's expensive. Prestigious address. Do I care? Obviously I do. Why? I'm working on that.

My decorator picked all of the hard-edged, oddly shaped furniture. I was not interested in helping.

"Don't you want to shop with me, Madeline?"

"No. I hate shopping."

"Don't you want to look at colors together, designs?"

"No, that would bore me."

"Don't you want to choose the furniture for your own house?"

"No."

"Why not?" She was baffled.

"Because I don't care."

She didn't get it, didn't get me. No surprise. Few people do. I wrote the check, she did the work. I now have a house decorated in angles, planes, corners. It's geometric decorating. You didn't like geometry in school? Me either. And yet I live in geometry.

To fill the cold, detached space, I play my violin. I have

played my violin to fill every cold, detached place in my life since I was a child. I am a rebel violinist and I had a rebel violin teacher from the time I moved to Oregon. I play classical, bluegrass, Texan-style fiddling, Irish reels and waltzes, and swing music.

My violin has small scratches and dents and a bloodstain on the inside. The blood has sunk into the wood, and if you turn it this way and that, it resembles a smashed butterfly. I know it's blood because my grandma made the mistake of answering me truthfully one night when I was a teenager.

We were sitting on her expansive white deck on The Lavender Farm, which Granddad built for her because he knew she loved the view of the rows of lavender. I had just finished practicing Küchler's Concertino in D Major, opus 15 and I asked her about the butterfly spot. In French she said, "Oh, that mark? That is blood."

"*That's blood?*" I answered in French. My grandparents and my momma were from France, and taught Annie and me French. My grandparents also taught us, as they had our momma, German. We are better at French.

Her face shut down. Slammed shut.

"Grandma, blood?" I knew the violin had been my momma's. "How did it get there?"

She waved me off, her jumbo-sized diamond wedding ring flashing. She muttered in German, "I don't know. Silly me. I don't know why I said that."

"But Grandma," I said back to her, in German, "I want to know about the blood."

"No, you don't," she snapped, then seemed to regret her clipped words, her lips tightening. She tucked the waves of her thick white curls back into a ball on top of her head. "It is not blood. It is . . . a stain. I think it is from red grapes."

"Red grapes? How would a red grape get in there?"

"It's a question mark, isn't it?" She patted my hand. "Maybe a peasant with a swirling black cape borrowed the violin from your momma and was playing it by a grapevine and one ripe, juicy grape popped in. Or maybe a falling star knocked the grapes off and they landed in the violin when your mother was dancing in a field with a fawn, a crown of daisies on her head."

As my grandma was an incredibly popular children's author and illustrator, her answer was not surprising. "What about all these other scratches and these dents?" I pointed to them, here, there, everywhere. It was an old violin.

She ran a gentle hand over my cheek, then spoke in French again, her luminescent blue-green eyes filling with tears. "All those marks are a mystery to me. A mystery. Perhaps a grumpy bluebird came down and scratched the violin when we weren't looking. Perhaps a bear's paw made that dent as he danced a jig. Perhaps an elf came and hit it against his knee. All a mystery."

But I knew the marks weren't a mystery to her. I knew she was lying. I knew because her hands shook and she blinked to clear a wall of tears.

"Grandma..." I didn't like to upset my grandma. I loved her dearly. She had saved me, saved us, but I wanted to know about the blood.

"All I know for sure is that I love you, my darling." She kissed my cheeks, four times, back and forth, as the French do. My grandma was slim and trim—she walked five miles a day over the hills of her property—and she always dressed impeccably. Scarves, jewelry, hats on special occasions, heels. She dressed *French*. Even her hands still looked young, especially when she was drawing and painting the swans that graced her children's books, her imagination a free-flowing, curving, color-filled playground.

"Come, let's walk between the lavender rows. We'll drop a few marbles between the plants for magic and I'll tell you a story about a wee swan who always wore pink, not black like all the other swans in her school. She loved the color pink and she loved sparkling shoes for her webbed feet. Now, one day, this swan..."

But lately, long years later, I don't have the same grandma. She has rounded the corner into dementia, and she says things like, "If you go to the left you will die, if you go to the right you will live but they will pull off your arms and legs and run you naked where the swans can't come" or "Pile up, pile down, the black ghosts are coming and we have to hide in the lavender or a barn. Be quiet!"

Always, always, I have known that there are secrets in my family, lies, if you will, loving lies, cover-up lies, but lies all the same. With my grandma's dementia, however, those lies are being exposed, via the scratches, dents, and blood on a violin my momma gave me, who received it from Grandma.

So, in my more brutal moments, I acknowledge this truth: I am a lie. I come from a family of liars. What saves me is that I love the liars.

"She's on the phone again," Georgie told me.

"Tell her I don't want to talk to her." I clenched my teeth and shook my head. I had come to hate the woman on the phone. It wasn't personal. I hated her because of what she was trying to do to my carefully constructed, fragile life and to my sister's carefully constructed, fragile life.

"Ms. O'Shea is not available to speak with you right now, Marlene," Georgie said with firm professionalism.

Georgie is my assistant. She has a dog, Stanley, who barked twice at me, then lifted a paw. I shook it. He barked again. I kneeled and hugged him, the dog's head cuddling into my neck, paws on my shoulders. If I don't hug him, he won't stop barking. When I tried to pull away, he held on tight and wheezed in my ear.

"I said, no," Georgie said. "That is a refusal. A negative. A denial." Her tone clashed with her dyed, snow white hair with pink tips, her lace skirt, and her cowboy boots. She is twenty-five and can wear anything. I look at her and am reminded that I have broken and smashed my momma's cardinal rule on clothing: Don't you dare be a frump. Don't you dare! Let yourself *shine*.

"Why are you having such inner turmoil with the word no?" Georgie went on. "Ms. O'Shea is not available. This is not a wishy-washy philosophical difference that you can play with and manipulate at will. Your spectrum of denial is puzzling me."

I didn't know what a spectrum of denial was. I would ask later.

"Ms. O'Shea has already given you her answer. She does not want to be interviewed for the article. . . . No, she does not have to participate. There is free choice in her spiritual and in her legal reign. . . . No, you are not to call her family, either. Do not contact the Laurents. They are elderly and do not wish to speak to you. Fry me on that one."

I shuddered and took a ragged breath as a sense of wretched doom tripped along my nerves. Stanley squeezed my neck. He is so affectionate.

I had hardly slept. When the sun was still grumpy and tired, I drove to my office in a fancy building in downtown Portland to begin my usual fifteen-hour day. My office has three rooms: the reception area, which is decorated with leather chairs, taupe colored walls, and modern art paintings and sculptures; a conference room with a wall of windows and a long mahogany table for group meetings; and my office, in the corner, with two walls of windows, my thick glass desk with raw edges, a leather V couch over a colorful rug, and more modern art.

I really do not like modern art.

"The family will not talk to you," Georgie said again. "We have already told you no. Release your request from your inner being and go spearhead someone else before I freakin' let you have it."

I had to love Georgie's manner. New wave with a shot of bullying.

"Fine. Go ahead and talk to the kids she grew up with." Georgie tapped the tattoo on her arm. It's a picture of her grandma smoking a cigar. "I can't muzzle everyone in her childhood, but stop unleashing your irritating personality on us."

I froze at that. Marlene was talking to people in my childhood? Who? I thought of one person in particular. What would he say? How would he react? Would he refuse to talk or would he admit the truth, publicly? He'd been on TV two nights ago. . . .

I released Stanley, and he barked in protest, as he was not done with the hug. I ignored him and grabbed the phone from Georgie. "Listen, Marlene, this is the last time. Either you stop calling me or I'll call the police and have you arrested for harassment. Are you getting this? Do not call me, do not e-mail me, do not contact me or my family in any way, shape, or form."

I listened, feeling my fury boil like hot tar as I fought back utter, bleak, white-hot fear.

"We are not cooperating because we don't want the article written." I listened for a moment. "Marlene, if you persist with this article, I will shove legal papers up your ass so fast you won't be able to sit on a toilet for a week, and then I will start on that rag you call a magazine. You will not print anything about my family or our past. You will leave the whole thing alone. You will kill the story because there is no story. None." I hung up.

I stood by Georgie's desk, trembling head to foot. I hate the shakes. I do. And I hate Marlene with a passion. It is not personal.

"Call my attorney again," I told her, breathless. I have a problem with breathing. "Get Keith Stein on the line right now."

"Got it." Georgie picked the phone back up. I liked her. She was smart and loyal. I had given her a very sketchy, brief outline of why Marlene wanted to write the article. She had nodded, taken it in, allowed me not to fill in the blanks that I didn't want to share. She's a confident person and she's okay with blanks.

Stanley barked at me. Twice. I shook his hand, he barked, I hugged him as certain scenes of my past rushed in like a noose, squeezing the life out of my esophagus. I smelled sweat, cigarettes, and a dank shack. I closed my eyes.

Within a minute I was rapid-fire talking to Keith. I've known Keith since high school. He was a bulldog when we were younger and he's a bulldog now with a broad, spiky bite. He owns a megasuccessful law firm and boils people down on a regular basis for breakfast. He enjoys his work. "Shut her down, Keith. I don't care what you have to do, but *shut her down.*"

*   *   *

"I am here to find my inner being. It's here somewhere." She batted her false eyelashes. "I think it might be hiding in my Prada."

"I am here to begin my descent and foray into the world." Her sister tapped her designer shoes. I believe they cost eight hundred dollars.

"I am here to spread my wings and fly. Fly and fly. Fly." The third sister flapped, diamond tennis bracelets flashing.

"Fun and fun!" Adriana laughed.

"Wicked naughty!" Bella giggled.

"Fantabulous!" Carlotta gushed.

I do not like handling three-way coaching sessions.

However, I have made an exception for the Giordano sisters this past year because they are so flamboyant and hilarious, altogether. It's like dealing with three incoming fashion missiles. They each take turns talking, one after another, in alphabetical order. "So we never dominate one another's spirits," Adriana told me. "We each take a turn on the verbal stage of life." Bella sighed. "We like to be in sync with one another, in harmony," Carlotta tittered.

They are of Sicilian descent.

Adriana, Bella, and Carlotta are all unusual women. They are in their thirties, and because of a massive amount of wealth left to them by their father, a jailed mob boss who hid his piles of money, I am quite sure, in several illegal, off-shore bank accounts, they have had the luxury of falling into eccentricity.

Their one-hundred-year-old brick mansion is on a hill with sweeping views of the Willamette River and the city. They have livened the place up by painting the trim purple, adding a purple deck, a purple gazebo, and a myriad of striking steel sculptures and outdoor art all over their property, which has been featured in different newspapers and magazines. In one magazine, the sisters posed in old-fashioned, striped swimsuits and parasols.

On their front lawn alone, they have many organically shaped, neon-colored glass structures that are museum worthy and stunning. One is a shiny purple and blue jellyfish, another is a grouping of tall, twisting corkscrews, and in a back corner are fanciful glass flowers about six feet tall. In their pond, with a fountain in the center, they have colored glass balls with dots and an arc of rainbow-colored glass fish leaping from the water.

Each has a pet cat that comes with them to "life-coaching class" in a specially designed cat basket with the cat's name written on the front.

Princess Anastasia is Adriana's cat. She was wearing a princess outfit in white silk. She even had glittery bracelets on her legs.

Bee La La is Bella's cat. She was dressed as a bee. No explanation necessary.

Candy Stripe belongs to Carlotta. She was dressed as Wonder Woman. Were you expecting a candy cane?

Princess Anastasia made a spitting sound at me.

Bee La La rolled her eyes, I swear she did.

Candy Stripe yawned, took a nap.

The Giordano sisters' momma passed away ten years ago from a heart attack. "Poor Momma, we love you, Momma," they chanted.

"She died of a heart attack when she found out Daddy had a mistress," Adriana said. "Poor Momma, we love you, Momma."

"Poor Momma, we love you, Momma," Bella echoed, then coughed. "Well, there were two mistresses. The first one told Momma about the second mistress because she was so mad that Daddy was cheating on her, too."

Carlotta squirmed. "And the second mistress was so mad she was the *second* mistress and not the first that she burned down the house that Daddy had bought the first mistress. Everybody lived, but the second mistress had to leave the country and go to Sicily."

"Her daddy was from Sicily," Adriana explained patiently. "It's so pretty there. He was in The Family, too. She can't ever come back to America, though." Adriana shook her head, so sad, so sad.

"No, she can't," Bella confirmed. "Not even for shopping! She misses out on Rodeo Drive."

"And the New York shows," Carlotta whined.

"And Vegas!" Adriana moaned. "Such a punishment for a wee fire. She was even insured!"

They all sighed. The unfairness of arson!

"The second mistress loved to gamble. She practically lived at the casinos," Bella explained. "Daddy said she lived at her plastic surgeon's, but he was being grumpy that night. He had a grumpy side."

Another group sigh. That grumpiness their mob boss father displayed! So grumpy!

"And when the first mistress's house was burned down she told Daddy to build her another one or she'd go to the police," Carlotta said. "It made Daddy really grumpy then."

There was a heavy silence.

"She disappeared," Adriana said, tapping her long nails together. "No one knew where she went to. . . ."

Good God.

"We think maybe she went to Baltimore," Bella said, twisting a diamond hoop earring.

Baltimore? I raised an eyebrow.

"Or maybe Boise. Could have been Miami," said Carlotta. She crossed her Jimmy Choo shoes.

I raised both eyebrows.

"I think that she had family in Sacramento. Or maybe it was Baton Rouge," Adriana said.

They all nodded at me.

I nodded back.

"Daddy wouldn't have killed her," Bella said.

"Goodness, no," her sisters agreed. "No."

Good God, again.

"We love Daddy so much! We love you, Daddy!"

I crossed my legs. I was wearing short blue pumps today. Expensive. Dull. No flash compared to theirs, high heels built to rock the fashion world.

Daddy was currently serving a life sentence in a maximum-security prison. I believe it was for a few crimes in the realm of murder, assault, loan sharking, hookers, wire fraud, and tax evasion, but I'm not sure. Some things one does not need to know.

Another group sigh, pitched high at the end. Mob boss daddy never would have killed his mistress for threatening to go to the police. Almost sinful to think such a tawdry thought! Sinful!

"All right, ladies." I cleared my throat, ready to jump into the facade that would follow. "I know that you all are thinking hard about different careers to pursue."

"Yes! Full speed ahead!" Carlotta said, full of cheer, sitting straight up. "A career!"

She said career like this: "Ca *Rear!*"

"Goody!" Adriana said, clapping her hands.

"Working me, working me!" Bella said, wiping a hand across her imaginary sweaty brow.

I wanted to choke. These women didn't want to work. They didn't want careers. They wanted to shop and go to lunch. I eyed their designer clothes, the fur-trimmed coats they didn't need on this warm day, their thousand dollar bags, and their decorated cats.

I got up and opened a wooden chest. "Ladies, you're going to get dressed up in different uniforms and you're going to see which uniform fits you best. I believe this will help you decide in which direction you should go, uh, career wise."

"A costume party!" Carlotta cheered.

"Dress-up time!" Adriana called out. "Outta sight and groovy! We adore you, Madeline. Every time we come to life-coaching class we have so much enlightenment!"

"How come you never come to our parties, naughty girl!" Bella squealed, as she plowed through the chest, her jeweled necklaces falling forward.

"Yes, we invite you all the time. Last weekend we had an all-green party. Everyone wore green and we ate pink food," Carlotta said. "One man wore a black thong and painted his whole body green! He was a green bean, get it?!"

"And the weekend before we had a motorcycle dude party. Wasn't that funny when Charlene Fay drove her Harley into the pool!" Adriana laughed. "She barely missed the glass fish!"

"And last month: Halloween Early party!" Bella said. "We had a King Kong, a banana, Wonder Woman, a condom—that was Paul, who came with his girlfriend, Cal, who was a diaphragm. It was so birth controlly. Environmentally correct!"

I sighed.

"But let's talk about our new Ca *Rears*," Carlotta said. "A Ca *Rear!*"

I knew my sisters, I knew what they wanted to do, I knew what their goal was. Sometimes being a life coach means you offer people direction, encouragement, a plan, goal setting, counseling ... and sometimes you offer them what they need: a laugh.

Ten minutes later we began our "Career Parade."

Adriana swaggered about in a nurse's outfit. She had added her own personal style. She wore her black lace bra with purple trim *over* the white nurse's uniform. She twirled a pink parasol and tottered on Bella's pink heels with cheetah print toes.

Bella model-walked, hips waving, in a blue jumpsuit uniform, a lot like a mechanic might wear, only she had thrown her lace scarf around her shoulders, unzipped the top of the jumpsuit to the waist so her purple camisole showed through, and rolled up the pants legs to her knees to show off Carlotta's knee-high leather boots.

Carlotta was wearing a pink tutu and pink tights and a green silk shirt. To make it more "Carlotta-y," she was wearing all of her jewelry and all of her sisters' jewelry and a black fur hat. She was also wearing Adriana's sage designer heels.

"I love coming to coaching class!" Adriana said. "I love it!"

"You're the best, Madeline," Bella said. "I feel so careerish right now! Don't you, girls?"

"Yes, we have a Ca *Rear!*" Carlotta said.

"I'm a nurse like Mary Poppins!" Adriana said. "Fun and fun!"

"I'm a mechanic for a soft porn show!" Bella said. "Wicked naughty!"

"I'm a ballerina slave for a leprechaun!" Carlotta said. "Fantabulous!"

They pulled their cats out of their baskets—one who spit, one who rolled her eyes, one who *was* asleep—and strutted around my office.

Who knew the world needed nurses who wore black bras over their nurses' uniforms, mechanics in purple camisoles, and ballerina slaves in pink tutus.

Yes, this is my life.

At least the Giordano sisters aren't liars.

"Your next client is here, Madeline," Georgie said. "It's Aurora King. She's got her sparkling pink fairy dress on today. She's wearing a tiara, too. She wasn't wearing a tiara when I met her in Spirit Yoga class and told her about you."

I smothered a laugh. Diane Smith had changed her name to Aurora King so she could be a whole new person. I respected that. I liked whole new people and I liked Diane / Aurora. "She wants to talk about my fairy dust, doesn't she?"

"She says she's seeing it in your aura. In fact, she says she's seeing a threat. A threat to you and your very essence. I'm quoting her. Apparently you have, what is it, Aurora? Okay, she says that there is something lurking. She thinks it's an emotional hurricane with a scary train ride and the Pyrenees Mountains. What else? And a tree with branches that criss and cross and a horse-man."

"Send in the fairy and her dust for my aura. But tell her not to throw glitter at me like last time."

"Don't throw glitter at Madeline," I heard Georgie say as she disconnected.

I opened my door to Aurora.

She threw pink glitter at me.

Two days later I was still picking it out of my hair.

Late that night, completely wiped out from work, I drove up the winding street to my modern house with the geometric decorating that I don't like. I dropped my keys and purse onto a modern, black metal statue shaped like a person with an octagon for a head holding a tray. I slipped off my boring heels and passed my black leather couch—not the cushy type, the hard type. Hanging over it was a light made out of chrome that resembled a giant, spying eye.

I headed to my bedroom with the modern bed frame constructed of shiny steel. I did not open the doors to my closet to put my suit away. I didn't have to, because I have no closet doors in my entire house. Not even my pantry has a door. First thing I did when I bought this house was to take off all the closet and pantry doors everywhere so my mind wouldn't short-circuit every time I wanted to grab a skirt or syrup.

All of my suits are lined up nice and neat, by color, same with my low-heeled shoes, my slippers, my tennis shoes, my sweaters, my ironed blouses. Obsessively neat. Everything is in tight, methodical order. Clearly a control freak jacked up on high octane obsessiveness did this, but I cannot have it any other way. I have to have order.

I have used both closets in my room for clothes, and I hang the hangers about four inches apart. Why? So I can see clear through to the wall behind it. *Clear* through.

Instantly I need to know if any sick, demented people are hiding in my closets, so no doors, and no cramming.

Where did I get this quirk from?

My childhood. Why?

He used to leap out of our closets.

Sherwinn *leaped.*

Right at us.

Boutique Magazine
A Life Coach Tells You How to Live It
By Madeline O'Shea
Vasectomies and You

After particular sessions, I ask my clients if I can print what they've said to me in order to share a tidbit of women's wisdom with other women who might need this tidbit.

My most recent client, we'll call her Tess, agreed. "If I can help one woman out there deal with a man who's afraid he'll never be in heat again like a horny dog if he gets a vasectomy, it'll be worth it."

Tess is five feet one, a hundred pounds, with blond hair that she calls "The Frizz Blast," and, in her words, "outsized brown eyes. I look like a raccoon with blond hair and the teeth of a cow. They stick out, you know. See?"

Here is Tess's story:

"My husband did not want a vasectomy. It was like trying to get a drunk bull to squish through a tire. I am freakin' tired of birth control. The pill makes me vomit and dizzy. Diaphragms are gross and condoms are what you use when you're a teenager rolling around naked in the back of an El Camino. Do I look like a pesky teenager? No, I don't. So I told him he needed to go in and get clipped.

"He acted like I'd asked him to give up his whatsits on a plate with a garnish of pickles and relish. I have given birth to five children, two at one time with the twins, and I have never, ever whined like that man did. But I told him no sex until you're castrated, whack and whack. It took him a week and he finally caved in, but he was pale white, like a ghost, so I trailed after him going, 'Booooo boooo.'

"Anyhow, I had to drug him before we even got to the hospital that morning. A double dose. I had to drag him in like a dead dog. If he could have cupped his jewels with both hands without looking ridiculous, trust me, he would have done it. So I hand him over to the doctor and the doctor claps him on the back like, Buck up, man.

"Honestly, I pushed five kids through something that is normally the width of a grape, and I didn't moan and piss like that. So I'm in the waiting room and I brought a flask of whiskey with me—I needed it after what I'd been through—and I start reading my romance novel and I'm perfectly happy. His mother, Hatchet Face, is with the kids and I am finally alone for the first time in months. Even when I pee the kids come into the bathroom and fight with each other on the bath mat. Anyhow, I am sitting there hoping the vasectomy takes five hours or there's some earthquake-sized complication and we have to be admitted overnight. I mean, wouldn't that be great? I could stay overnight in a hospital! No kids and hopefully my husband would be out cold. But no! The doctor is a man and doesn't understand. Way too quick, and right when I'm in the middle of a hot sex scene, as if I have the energy to think that sex can be hot anymore, the deed is done, he's been sliced and diced. The nurse comes to get me. I wanted to cry when she said my husband was "ready." Darn it, though, I wasn't ready!

"So I trudge to the room and there he is, lying down, his face gluey white. And I let this man get me knocked up five times? This coward? This ghost? 'I think I saw smoke, Tess, and I smelled it,' he whispers, his eyes staring wildly, like he's seen the hounds of hell running around his balls gnashing their teeth. 'There was fire. I think I saw flames. I was *on fire!*' That man got teary eyed over *his testicles.* It's not like they were removed and put in a jar of formaldehyde.

"'You had a vasectomy,' I hiss, pissed off

there weren't complications. I wanted to read my romance! It would have been great if the knife had slipped and we'd had to stay a week in the hospital. That would have been a treat. 'There wasn't any fire or flames,' I tell him real snarky.

'I'm not a man anymore,' he moans.

'Yeah, you're a man.' I roll my eyes. 'You still got your pecker.'

'I'm not a man. . . .'

'If you're not a man, you're not a man, you eunuch, so maybe you won't pester me so much for sex anymore.' I have had sex hundreds of times, Madeline. How many more times do I have to have it?

"So, after a lot of irritating whining, so bad I wanted to smack him, we went home and he lay in bed with an ice pack on his balls, still moaning, and he reminded me of my childhood dog, Frisky. Frisky ran out and chased down kids and bit them, letting out this terrible howl. He would dart out the door before we could stop him. He even had a girlfriend dog that he would visit every once in a while, even though the girlfriend's boyfriend dog chewed him up a couple of times. My mother used to have our neighbor's Saint Bernard chase Frisky down and get him home.

"Anyhow, as soon as my mother got that dog castrated, the ol' balls cut off, he settled right on down. No more gallivanting around, no more cheating with the ladies, no more biting kids on bikes. So that's what I told my husband when he was in bed groaning about the fire and smoke again. I told him about Frisky and said, 'You two got something in common. Now shut up and quit whining.'

"He complained for days from bed. By the fifth day, when he yelled my name three times and I walked back to the bedroom, carrying the baby, the toddler hanging on to my heel, and he whined, 'Can you refill my orange juice? And I need another blanket. I'm chilled. Do you know where my gray socks are? No, not the white ones. I need my gray fishing socks. Can you put them on my feet?' I let him have it. I told him that I'd given birth to five kids. I'd been pregnant for most of our marriage. He never took care of me when I got home from the hospital, even the time I got sick with the flu after the third kid. Didn't even take a day off work to help out, but two weeks later he was able to take six days off to go fishing with his buddies. I hadn't lain in bed for five days after I'd had the kids. In fact, on the second day I was up and taking care of him and everyone else. He never brought me a meal in bed or so much as orange juice. He never brought me socks and put them on my feet. I told him all that and I told him I was sick of his being a baby and I poured an entire pitcher of orange juice on his crotch and told him to get his slack balls out of bed.

"I kicked him out of the house. I packed his suitcase and threw him out and told him to go home to Momma, the Hatchet Face. I threw an ice pack at his head, too, I was so mad. I felt like years of fury were bottled up in me and they all came out. He works eight hours a day, an hour off for lunch, comes home, lies on the couch, and makes derisive comments about how I, 'don't work ... he'd like to stay home all day and watch TV, too ... it's *his* money, not mine. ...'

"I called a lawyer, and the lawyer served him at work, told him what his child support was gonna be for five kids. He came home three days later on his knees after being with his mother, who is a tyrannical dictator. I told him to stay with her for three months because I needed a break from him. The next weekend I dropped all five of the kids off at his mother's house—thank heavens I'm done nursing the baby. I also dropped off all the crap he has stacked in our garage that he refuses to throw away, plus his beer bottle collection and the lights shaped like beer cans. My daughter said his mother left for a hotel by Saturday morning. By Saturday night my husband was crying because the baby wouldn't stop crying, my two-year-old kept fussing, and the other three kids were driving him crazy and wanted to come home to me.

"I had the best three days of my life, Madeline. Can't wait to drop the kids off in two weeks again. He's begging to come back home. *Begging* like a fiend. You know what the lesson here is?

"If you're going to have balls in your life, make sure they're good balls. If I'm going to allow his balls back in my life, there's going to be huge, huge changes. If he doesn't want to make them, he's out. He causes me too much stress. My life is easier, *easier,* Madeline, without him, no question. He's more work than my kids, and he never gives back to me. He takes. Sucks me dry emotionally. I need to go ball-less for a while. The kids and I and none of his balls. And, hey, twice a month, I get free weekends, Friday afternoon to Sunday evening, and every other Wednesday I get three hours to myself. Plus, he's paying through his nose for child support and alimony. Loses more than half his check. Now that I don't have to pay for his gambling and beer runs, I'm way ahead."

Tess left later, and I thought about what she said.

Ladies, you don't *have* to have balls in your life. It's a choice. Remember that. You can be on your own. You can be *very happy* on your own. In fact, much happier than you are now if you're living with a man who sucks the life out of you.

Think on it. Balls or no balls?

I hit send in my e-mail program, which flew my article to the magazine I write for, *Boutique*. It has a huge readership and is growing every day. Good platform for me.

It was very, very late by then, the whole city snoozing, but I was starving so I ate a bunch of fruit, including a mango, an apple, and two bananas, and macaroni and cheese out of a box. I then dug through a pile of mail stacked up in the tray of the black metal man with the octagonal head that freaks me out.

I flipped through a few utility bills, and saw a manila envelope.

It looked so benign, so normal, so boring.

It was not benign, normal, or boring.

I opened it up and stared at the contents, my hands shaking so bad I thought I'd been stricken by palsy. Inside was what I had been expecting, and dreading, and fearing, for a long, long time.

It had found me. It was here.

I dropped all the mail on the floor and ran for the bathroom, my head soon slung over the toilet.

3

~

"The black ghost is flying in soon. He's coming for us. *All of us.*" She tugged on my arm, frantic, eyes wild, her French fast and desperate. "We have to get out of here. We must save the children from the black ghost's wrath."

I stood near the butcher block kitchen table on The Lavender Farm, the morning light pouring through the French doors, as Grandma clutched me. I gave her a hug and answered in French. "Bonjour, Grandma. Sit down. I'll make you some lavender tea."

"No!" she said, grabbing my hands, holding them tight. "No time for tea! Other people are already in their secret rooms and climbing into their teapots. No time for sugar! They're putting lavender in people's mouths until they suffocate."

It is awful to watch someone lose their mind, and Grandma was no different. She would sometimes run from our home screaming, or panting, trying to drag us with her, trying to get us into our pantry where the "secret door" was, or to turn off all the lights and be absolutely silent. She wanted to sleep in the barn. She wanted to sleep in one of the sheds or outbuildings or underneath the apple trees in the orchard. She wanted to hide from "the black ghosts."

Her sleep was sometimes shattered with her own screaming, and she would burst into tears at odd moments and call out in a voice raw and desperate the names of people I didn't know: Avia, Esther, David, Gideon, Goldie—and there was Ismael, who came up often. "Where is Ismael? Is he hiding? I feel him!"

"The black ghosts are gone, Grandma," I said, trying to calm her, knowing her mind was erratic, confused, diseased. "It's okay."

I smiled at Nola, a most wonderful Hispanic woman who worked in my grandparents' grocery stores, named Swans, for thirty-three years, most of it in management. She left as a vice president and now takes care of Grandma, full time, as a favor to Grandma and Granddad, their long-standing friendship, and our family. She lives here at the farmhouse in her own suite. We all love Nola.

"Good morning, Madeline," she said.

"Good morning, Nola."

"Sister," Grandma said earnestly, as she flipped her silk scarf behind her shoulder, "they're using sticks to beat the stars and the violin was dented in the secret room, and they're packing all the cows in tight until they can't breathe. We have to go."

"I have all the sticks, Grandma, and the cows are okay. They're in the field."

She hurried to the window to stare at a couple of cows in the distance. Beyond the French doors lies a land quilt of hills and valleys and forests, and beyond that the blue-purple mountains of the Oregon coast. I don't go to the coast. I don't go to the sea. Neither does Annie.

"The black ghost will tear off our arms and use them for firewood."

Honestly, sometimes Grandma's words are terrifying. "The black ghost is locked away. He's gone."

Grandma put a hand out and ran it through a ray of sun, her jeweled bracelets from Granddad tinkling. She switched to German. "He's locked away?"

I nodded, answered in German. "All gone."

I had arrived at The Lavender Farm an hour before. I couldn't sleep, anyhow, so I left my home at dawn, traveled down the freeways, out through the suburbs, and into the country. My grandparents' white, old-fashioned farmhouse is filled with nooks and crannies and window seats, Grandma's skylighted painting studio, a modernized kitchen with a long granite counter and open shelving, and an island painted blue. A grand piano in the living room takes up a corner, but Annie never plays anymore, though she knows how to make that keyboard sing.

Several paintings of Grandma's swans were hung throughout the house: white swans in boats on a pond playing violins, black twin sister swans twirling parasols, swans crying into lace hankies, swans gathered for picnics of chocolate cake and pears, swans chasing a naughty fox wearing a black burglar mask, swans in tuxes and silky dresses in an orchestra. And, always, sparkling marbles, glittering crystals, mischievous elves, grinning grizzlies, laughing caterpillars, tea-sipping mice, and kite-flying gnomes hidden throughout the paintings, which young readers loved to find.

"Grandma," I said gently. "Look outside. Did you see the lavender? It's going to bloom soon."

"What? Who will bloom?" She tugged at her cashmere sweater. "*Who will bloom?*"

"The lavender." I turned her away from the cows. Grandma could sometimes be distracted by the lavender. "Isn't it beautiful?"

I saw her blue-green eyes soften. "So beautiful. Anton planted those for me. Do you remember?"

"Yes." Anton was my granddad. I didn't remember him planting them. He'd sowed them when my momma was a young girl, replacing plants as they died. The lavender was just always there.

Grandma's eyes teared up and she whispered, "I love you. You are a wonderful sister, Madeline, and I hope you can forgive me for what I did. It was love, love did it to me. It was after the Land of the Swans, I promise. Don't forget your violin." She gets confused about whether I am her sister or her granddaughter. She does not have a sister. She thinks that Annie is her niece. She does not have a niece. We don't correct her anymore. "You must take it with you. It's our history. No more crying. You must be brave or they will stick a spear through your heart and hang you on a wall of fire next to the ogre and the dragon."

I took a deep breath. See, terrifying. "Okay, Grandma, I won't cry."

She patted my cheek. "We will have a new life. The black ghosts can't follow us there. *Ach.* This life. So much pain."

I settled Grandma down, then watched my hand tremble as I poured the hot water over Nola's and Grandma's lavender tea bags in pink-flowered teacups. I often don't breathe right, which causes the trembling. It's not panic attacks or anxiety problems, it's like my breath is stuck in my body behind organs and inside bones. It's been that way since the weather was furious.

Nola, Grandma, and I stared at the rows of lavender in the distance, precise, rolling highways of plants that would soon bloom into brilliant fireworks of blue, pink, purple, and white. Grandma abruptly stood and drew a finger through the condensation on the window. I knew she was drawing a swan.

"There was so much blood that day," Grandma said, her words floating, reminiscing. "Blood. So many other violin people were turned to blood."

I breathed in deep, told myself to be calm.

"And the swans were murdered." She used her fist to make the swan disappear. "They were all murdered. Dead."

I tried to breathe like a normal member of my species. It did not work.

"Play your violin, my sister. Don't mind the scratches from the mountain," Grandma said, her voice still tight, worried. "It always calms me down. Please? It'll calm Ismael down, too."

I didn't know what Ismael she was talking about, but I went to the foyer and grabbed my violin. I played Beethoven's Romance in G major, then I played Massenet's "Méditation" from *Thaïs.*

My grandma closed her eyes and listened, swaying back and forth.

When I was done, I bent to kiss her wrinkled cheek, her gaze off again, lost somewhere, floating through her past, jumping from here to there, helter-skelter, one vision after another, the circuits fried, or closed, or blocked, or dead, her brain slowly killing her.

"Bloody swans," she breathed in French, then swore in German. "Bloody and broken. Their wings sliced off."

My grandparents flip between speaking English, which they were taught by their English governesses from the time they were each three, to French, and German.

And in between all those languages lay their lies and secrets.

I sucked in air like I was drowning.

About thirty minutes later, I saw Annie striding up and over a slight hill toward my grandparents' farmhouse. She'd had a busy night. On one of her calls she helped deliver a foal. I know because she called me on the way home at 1:00 in the morning. She hardly sleeps, like me. It is more comfortable, and we are in more control, when we are awake.

"Hi, Annie," I called out when I heard the front door open.

"Hello, Madeline, how are ya?" Her cowboy boots thunked against the floor. She is the most courageous person I've ever known. She's gorgeous and looks a lot like our momma, with the blue-green eyes of our grandma—but she hides her gorgeousness. No makeup, no frills. She is also slightly off her rocker.

"How are you, Ms. Vet?" I asked, giving her a hug. She hugged me back.

"Haven't had to run from anyone swinging a machete today, so that makes it good. You?"

"Not bad." She knew I wasn't "good." She knew I felt like I was collapsing from the inside out because I was two people, in one, and they were clashing.

"Good morning, Grandma."

"Good morning, Anna." Grandma smiled angelically, as if the fear of minutes ago had never occurred. "You can't bring much when we leave, remember. I will leave all my shoes, and you'll have to wear clothes under your clothes, then your blue coat."

"Okay, Grandma, I'll get the blue coat. Hi, Nola."

Nola smiled back. "Good morning, Annie."

Nola and Annie launched into their usual discussion of the

headlines in the news, as Grandma climbed back into the labyrinths of her mind and I poured lavender tea for Annie.

Annie lives in a blue home she built years ago, about an eighth of a mile away, up the hill from our pond and dock. She is my best friend. I have brown eyes, with gold in 'em, but we both have dark brown hair with, no kidding, a reddish sheen from our Irish, Boston-born-and-bred father. Hardly anyone else ever sees the red, but to us, it's like a beacon. I flatten my hair until it's straight—no curls allowed. Annie pulls her curls back into a tight braid—no curls allowed, either.

After high school Annie went to an Ivy League school. They were impressed with her grades (all As), her SATs (perfect score), her years of karate (black belt) and her awards in that area, her years of archery and awards in that area, her crack shot with a gun, and her awards in that area. She also wields a mean chain saw and can carve anything out of wood including, but not limited to, a pioneer woman with a gun and two kids, a Porsche, two girls on a bench holding tulips, a swan in full flight, high heels, a sea nymph, a cracked violin, a cupcake, Zeus, and—one time, after a bad date in high school—a large penis, which she propped on the guy's lawn.

She also made a carving of a girl named, get this, *Buffy,* who called both Annie and me "ugly, wild freakoid horse monsters," but she made Buffy about a hundred pounds heavier with pimples on her face. She brought it to school five days later.

Buffy wasn't pleased.

Annie graduated with degrees in economics and Arabic. After that...well, it's sketchy. She spent six years in...whatever (undercover) U.S. government agency she joined, of which she does not speak. She spent much of her time in places that precluded her from telling me much about where and what she was doing, and sometimes she would come home with a mashed-up face or another injury.

However, I do know her particular expertise: Explosives.

Now and then she blows up: Houses.

You think our government doesn't train women to explode people/buildings? That would be: Wrong.

When the home of a vicious, demented man who had a dirty, pathetic puppy mill in northern California exploded into Kingdom Come, when Annie was supposedly "vacationing in Fiji, loved the sun," I looked the other way.

When the home of another vicious, demented man who whipped and starved his horses for sport caught fire and turned to a hunk of ash in Washington when Annie was supposedly "vacationing in Fiji, loved the sun," I also looked the other way.

No one was hurt. Annie did not come home with a sunburn.

Annie relates better to animals than people, and she cannot abide abuse of any kind. She decided to be a veterinarian during her "mystery" years. "I saw too many human limbs in places where they shouldn't be, and I decided I wanted to be a part of putting things back together, not destroying them. But I don't want to work with people. I love animals. They don't frighten me, they don't need anything from me but medical care, and they won't hurt or betray me intentionally."

She has a half-blind greyhound with only three legs, who she found limping across the road, named Mr. Legs. She has a mutt who looks like a cross between a beagle, a German shepherd, and a banana named Morning Glory. The dog was so diseased when Annie rescued her from a shelter, anyone else would have put her down.

She has two white, furry dogs she stole from an abusive home, named Door and Window, who were smothered in muck and shaking when she rescued them. She went to the owner's house when he was gone, cut the chains that kept the dogs leashed to a tree 365 days a year, attended to their various life-threatening wounds and infections, and exploded the man's house. The report in the local Washington State newspaper said there was "clearly an electrical wiring problem. These are old homes, code not up to date. . . ."

She also has six cats. One of the cats, named Cat, thinks she is a dog and hangs out with the dogs and eats from their bowls. Another cat, Lisa, is missing an ear and half a tail. Bob is cranky and spitty, Tornado, in my mind, suffers from multiple personality disorders, and Geranium and Oatmeal follow her around like she's the pied piper and meow at her. She meows back.

"You were busy last night," I said as we all warmed our hands on Grandma's pink-flowered teacups. "How's the mother pig?"

"She's doing great. It was Braddock's pig, Stella. You know, the skittish one, always anxious, runs from most people? She shot them right out. She loves her piglets. You're staying tonight, right?"

"Yes, I am."

"Good. I may need help. You can handle the yucky stuff and any animals who bite."

I laughed. "Always a pleasure to go out on your vet runs with you."

I poured everyone more lavender tea and we all chatted the chat of women, the sun rising over the lavender rows; Mt. Hood turning orange and pink, the trees in the distance swaying, dancing their own natural dance; my old, scratched and dented, and well-loved violin in its case propped in the corner.

"I hate the black ghosts," Grandma muttered. "They come in the night and wring the swans' necks."

"Me too," Annie and I said together, quite seriously. We did not like the black ghosts, either; they had spooked through our dreams on many occasions.

I winked at Annie.

We are best friends.

Lavender has an interesting history. It's been around forever. In fact, the rumor around town is that Adam and Eve grabbed it in the Garden of Eden after God told them to get the heck out because Eve, enticed by the naughty snake, ate that luscious apple. It is strange they did not grab more fig leaves to cover their naked selves, but still, the scent of lavender from the garden they were supposed to be guarding was probably not one they wanted to part with. They knew a pretty flower when they saw it.

The word lavender comes from the Latin word *lavare,* which means to wash. The Romans, among all their other brilliant discoveries, used to wash with it. They even brought lavender with them when they invaded and tromped on England one summer for kicks. After fighting the tribes, with a good dose of smashing and killing, somehow that lavender took root in England. It is unlikely that the battle-weary English were grateful for the way this purple plant arrived on their lands, but they came to love it.

The Egyptians were creative and inventive with their lavender. They used it as perfume *and* for mummification. Poor King Tut, that critically sick and hurting child prince, had some in his tomb, although it obviously would have been of no use to him then. My favorite story is about a Hebrew widow named Judith who lived about 550 BC. She wasn't pleased when a temperamental Assyrian general name Holofernes invaded her country by orders from Nebuchadnezzar II, another nut case who was ticked at other countries that did not support him. Judith seduced Holofernes with her charm and a few sprigs of lavender. When he was drunk as a skunk she cut off his head and took it home with her.

I don't know what she did with the head after that.

Perhaps she stuck some lavender in his mouth.

What I do know is that when I arrived at The Lavender Farm, after the gunshots, I spent endless hours in a numbed state, marching up and down those lavender rows searching for peace, tying bouquets together, winding the stems through wreaths made of sticks.

I am still searching for that peace.

At three o'clock that Sunday morning, when it was pitch dark, I sprang out of bed in my old bedroom when Annie burst through the door. I had been asleep for maybe an hour.

"Up and at 'em, Madeline," Annie said. "I need help and my elf helper quit last week."

"That's a negative. No to helping. I can't help. My body won't move." I lay back down and pulled my pillow over my head. It was warm and comfy amidst my fluffy, white down comforter and purple pillows.

"Sleep is overrated, especially when animals need you. I've got a horse giving birth and a very strange farmer suffering from morning sickness who will be of no help. Shovel your ass out of bed."

I groaned.

I moaned.

I ached with fatigue and a dreadful sense of impending doom.

I flipped off the covers and shoveled my ass out of bed.

Horses are part people.

Anyone who has spent time with them knows this. They have their own personalities, problems, fears, issues, strengths, ob-noxiousness, and even humor. They have emotions; they feel love and hate, jealousy and anxiety, friendship and exclusion.

That is why when horses are abused, my sister becomes en-raged. It is why we have fifteen horses on the property, many of whom Annie and I went and got in our horse trailer. With a few of the horses we even had the permission from the abusive/ne-glectful owners to take them. They often limp off the trailer, their bodies broken, half-starved, weakened, diseased, their hair matted and dirty, infections all over. Worse, their spirits are torn and tattered, hanging on by one hoof.

They look like they want to die, as if they've been whipped and starved into a submission that nothing can bring them out of.

But Annie prevents the nothing from swamping them. She knows what it's like to feel the nothing, to feel the bleak de-spondency and despair that drives you to believe that you would be better off dead. She's fought through it.

Annie nurses the horses back to health. They love her. The horses are not riding horses, except for Mr. Pete, who is her horse. They are, Annie says, "in horse retirement. They have a full meal plan and free health insurance. They can run and roll and play all day." They will live on The Lavender Farm until they die.

By 3:30 in the morning we were with Jeremy and Loretta Lou. Jeremy is the man with morning sickness. One might say he has a tad of an obsession with his horse, Loretta Lou. Some might say it's a wee unhealthy.

"It's okay, Loretta Lou, honey, honey oat pie, cupcake, it's okay," Jeremy crooned to his horse. "You push and push and push and I'm right here, baby. Watch your breathing, in and out, in and out, like this, watch me, watch me. Remember what we learned." He breathed in and out, but his breathing was shaky, nervous, agitated. "I'm with you, honey. We'll saddle up and do this together."

The horse neighed once, softly, then continued her agitated walk around the confines of her stall.

"I don't mind telling you," Jeremy said to us, his brow letting sweat flow like a sieve, "I've had a hoofin' bad and terrible time with morning sickness for weeks now. Hoofin' bad time! Morning sickness!"

Jeremy is in love with all his horses and he likes to use horsey language. It makes him feel "included in the family."

"You mentioned your morning sickness a thousand times," Annie said. "I told you to rest, put those big feet of yours up, calm down—"

"Calm down?" He was aghast. "Calm down! Loretta Lou is pregnant! She's going to have a foal! A baby! How can I calm down? I've had problems with my stomach, swollen ankles, I have cravings for avocado, I can eat six at a time, and I wash it down with chocolate milkshakes, I've never liked milkshakes, my digestive system is a mess . . ."

"You'll start to feel better soon, Jeremy," Annie soothed. "Loretta Lou will have her foal—"

He clapped both hands to his face. "I'm a wreck, a wreck! I've had mood swings, tears, rages, then joy, wonderful joy over the baby, I mean the foal, followed by the pits! Pits of low! Of fear! I've had to horseshoe my emotions!"

"You'll be a good father," I said.

Jeremy burst into tears. "Thank you, Madeline, for saying that. I've got my bridles and I'm ready to guide and lead! I hope

I'll be a good father! I hope! But watching Loretta Lou grow and grow, it's been terrible! I've put on ten pounds, too. Right there." He pointed to his stomach. It did bulge. "I'm going to sing to her now."

Jeremy started to sing a lullaby through his semi-hysterical tears as he stroked Loretta Lou's neck. It was surprisingly poignant, the notes clear and crisp, and yet wistful, too. "That always calms her down, always. I sing it every night before she goes to sleep."

"It calmed me down," Annie said, her eyes on the horse.

"It calmed me down, too," I said to Jeremy.

He sang again, and the horse paced. "Loretta Lou, dumpling, you are going to make a wonderful mother." Jeremy wept. "A caring, loving mother, and your baby is lucky to have you. Now, hang on, lady, jump your fear, and we'll have the baby out in a few, and you can begin your mothering. . . ."

I knew that Annie did not think this one-sided conversation strange. She talks to animals, too, only she talks to them as if they're mature humans. I've heard her discuss with dogs, cats, lambs, horses, ferrets, llamas, and pigs the stock market, the political scene in Oregon and the nation, various environmental problems, the value of a military career, volcanoes, poorly fitted bras, cramps, yeast, transgender folks, rock stars, organic foods, and Armageddon.

"I want you to pretend you're in the field, Loretta Lou," Jeremy instructed, still sweating, his face inches from his horse's. "Put yourself in a field of buttercups, that's it, *buttercups,* and clover and hay and some cheesecake, no, not cheesecake, I like cheesecake you don't, but think of that field, go into your pleasant spot, love, your tranquil Zen mode. . . ."

The horse swung her head a few times, stomped a foot, but was otherwise calm. I felt sorry for her. Her stomach was enormous. It looked like, well, it looked like she had a horse in it.

"Sugar lips, you can do it! You can push, darling," Jeremy said. "Breathe in and out, like we've practiced, like we've talked about, stay calm, stay in your pleasant spot, focus, focus. . . ."

Soon Annie's gloved hands were moving under the horse,

while Jeremy kept singing lullabies, his voice cracking as he cried like a baby. "Push, breathe, push, breathe, push!"

I saw two hooves, then two legs, the head of the baby horse, and then the rest of it came right out onto the hay. Annie ripped the sack and declared it a "splendid foal."

"You did it, Loretta Lou! You did it!" Jeremy burst into another torrent of tears, stroking the horse's neck. "You did it, Momma, look at your baby!"

We oohed and aahhed over the foal, which Jeremy named Lou Lou. "Do you like that name, Loretta Lou? How about Lou Lou for your baby girl? Do you? All right, Lou Lou it is!"

Soon, Lou Lou wobbled to her feet, surprisingly quickly, I thought. If I had just been born, I would have wanted to curl up in a ball after having a beer.

"Thank you, Annie. And Loretta Lou thanks you, too, don't you, sweetheart, don't you?" He nuzzled her neck. "Sweetie . . . sweetie . . . sweetie."

I glanced over at Annie. Even in the dim light, I could see her turning white, all blood leaving her face as if it had decided to get outta town. My knees grew weak and spaghetti-like, my heart pumped, my hands tightened into fists.

"Sweetie, you were so brave. . . ."

Annie swayed. I staggered over to her, feeling like I was seeing her from a million miles away and would never reach her as the walls of the barn closed in tight.

She reached out a hand and I held it.

"Sweetie!" Jeremy crooned, then looked up at us, his face alarmed. "Are you two all right? My horsey goodness! Here, sit down, please, rest your saddles; you've been up all night. I'll run in and get you a drink, be right back, stay right there, Loretta Lou, sweetie. . . ."

We sweeties leaned hard against the wall of the barn.

Annie grabbed a nearby bucket and puked.

"I so hate that word," Annie said, wiping the back of her mouth.

"Me too."

I reached for her hand, not the one that she'd wiped across her mouth. I closed my eyes. Annie sighed.

My heart felt like a rock with a giant hand squeezing it tight. I felt her pain, she felt my pain. It was awful.

Sweetie, do this, do that, sweetie, turn this way. Goddammit, sweetie!

Sweetie, if you don't unclench your legs...sweetie, if you want to get home on time, you'll smile...turn over...sweetie, stop crying, for God's sakes, you stupid girl...shit, we gonna be here all afternoon or are you gonna do your job? Sweetie, move your hands out of the way...sweetie, I ain't got time to fool around...if you tell your mother I will put her in a coffin myself, got that.... A giggle followed by, It'll be your fault, you dirty, curly haired girl....

Shut it down, Madeline, I told myself. *Shut it down.*

Shut Sherwinn down and out.

In that barn I tried to shut my own brain down so it didn't implode.

Before I left early the next morning for work, I hiked down to our pond. It's a pretty good size, and Granddad stocks it every year. I spent hours fishing here when I was younger, right next to Annie. Sometimes we took a rowboat out, sometimes we stood on the long dock, fishing poles hanging over the edge. Being at the pond makes you feel like you are in a painting—a meadow here, fir trees there, a picnic table in the distance, cattails and lily pads. Sometimes deer stroll through, coyote, raccoons at night, and there are always birds, chipmunks, and squirrels.

It's quiet, as if you're part of nature and the other part of your life—your work, your commute, your worries—is simply something you do during the rest of the day before you come back and do something really important, like watch the blue heron sail over the water.

Later, as I drove between the pink tulip trees lining the drive that would soon bloom into pink miracles, I missed The Lavender Farm already. That's what our momma had named it, as a girl, because she loved the purple flowers. She and Grandma used to place colorful marbles between the plants for fun, as Annie and I did. I looked back at my grandparents' house, the apple orchard behind it, the forest behind that, a hint of the hills, the blue purple coast mountains, and felt . . . sadness. Deep, aching sadness.

This happens every time I leave, every single time.

I focused on the road ahead. Our past was chasing us as if we were prey. Annie didn't know we were being chased yet. I had hoped to hide it from her, to protect her, but I knew I couldn't for much longer. Annie would feel as if she'd been hit with cinder blocks when she heard about Marlene and her article. My grandma was losing Grandma in the dusty labyrinths of her dying mind, my granddad is losing the love of his life, and I am two people in one, pretending to be someone that I am not, pretending I don't have secrets, pretending that I am not living a lie, every day, a lie.

I thought of that reporter talking to people from my past, the kids, who are now adults, whom I used to run around with in my childhood.

He never knew exactly what was going on until it was over.

I wish I could live with the blue heron.

4

Momma was born in France and plied her magic in Marie Elise's French Beauty Parlor. Decorated in pink, with pink tile floors, light pink walls, and pink swiveling chairs for the ladies, it was the most popular parlor on Cape Cod. "Women like pink. It's feminine and sweet and reminds everyone of pink cupcakes. Come and give your momma a hug. I love you so much, Pink Girls."

There were four crystal chandeliers, lots of mirrors, and a wall full of those dryers that women drop over their heads—all in pink. A large back room with pink fainting couches, called the "resting room," was always filled with women "gathering their womanliness back together and filling themselves with pink strength," my momma said. Coffee and tea, lemon water, pink lemonade, pink divinity cookies, and pink mints made women feel a bit pampered. Momma looked away when the ladies passed bottles back and forth and cackled too loud.

She always wore pink, maybe not all pink all the time, but her outfits always had pink trim, pink lace, a pink collar. She believed in "embracing my womanly femininity."

"Frumpiness is another way of giving in to life, and ladies should never give in," she warned, spraying rose-scented perfume. "Act like a lady who has balls, Pink Girls. Never give in. *Fight*. Fight with everything ya got, and wear your heels. There's nothing like a pair of black stilettos that says you mean business."

Marie Elise's French Beauty Parlor was on the same property as our white house by the sea so it also had a view of incoming weather, a variety of boats, gold and purple streaked sunrises, and moonlight pouring into the waves. It was a miniature of our home, except it had a wraparound front porch painted pink and pink Adirondack chairs. My dad, who everybody called Big Luke, had it built for her. "Your momma wanted to work, but she always wanted to be close to her girls. We love you two most of all." He sniffed the air, the sun glinting off his red-gold hair given to him by his Irish ancestors, the same ancestors that gave Annie and me a red sheen, too. "You both smell like peppermint, did you know that?"

My momma sauntered onto the porch about one second after the peppermint comment in her yellow dress with the wide pink belt, and smiled at him, special-like. When she sashayed upstairs to their bedroom, her hips swaying, our dad made a beeline to follow her, and Annie and I were allowed to watch TV the rest of the night and eat the chocolate mint brownies our dad made for us.

Marie Elise's French Beauty Parlor was open Monday through Saturday. Three other women worked for Momma: Carman, Shell Dee, and Trudy Jo.

Carman was a widow. Her husband, Roy, was killed by a train. We did not talk about why Carman's husband did not get off the tracks with a train screaming its whistle at him. All I know is that they found his arm about a mile down the way by a hardware store and he had gambling debts. I heard her talking to my momma one day.

"He owed Joey Bonnata money, and after he died Joey came to my house with a couple of other men who looked like their faces had been attacked by meat cleavers and told me I had to pay. I poured myself a tequila, sat down on my couch, and told them to take a look around and tell me if they thought I had any money. There were three pails catching the rain that night, a rat ran across the floor, and part of a wall had crumbled down. The four of us ended up talking about what a shit Roy was and Joey gave me three hundred bucks for rent, then sent a team over the next day to fix my roof and my wall. He was a pleasant guy, when he wasn't threatening to shatter my knee. They loved my lemon cake, Marie Elise. You remember my great aunt Tuti? It was her recipe, extra powdered sugar on top, and they *loved it*."

Carman also likes singing love songs while drinking champagne, and bodice ripper romance books to "put my mind at ease and my libido on fire." It seemed like a good blend to me.

Shell Dee and Trudy Jo are sisters. Their grandmother was a recluse who threw rocks at people if they got too close to their house. She lived to be 104. Other than the rock throwing, the woman was sweet as could be.

Shell Dee was interested in the human body, and we were constantly learning about things we did not need to know, like, "Your small intestine is four times as tall as you. Rest your brain on that one for a while!" or "Your eye only weighs about twenty-eight grams. The weight of paper clips, *paper clips!* Inhale that tidbit of anatomical knowledge and sink your teeth in it."

Trudy Jo memorized large swaths of Shakespeare and regaled us with miniperformances while wielding hair dryers and rollers. She believed he was the sexiest man who ever lived. "What a piece of work is a man!" she intoned, and "If music be the food of love, play on." On Shakespeare's birthday, she had a party where we all had to wear Shakespeare-like hats and tights. We toasted William and each took turns reciting parts of his plays.

Shell Dee and Trudy Jo both had husbands and four kids, two of each sex per family. When I knew them, all eight kids were teenagers and hung out like a gang, thick as thieves. Shell Dee said she always knew when her teenagers were lying to her. "Any time they butter up to me, I know they've done something bad and I send them to their rooms immediately until they tell me what the hell they've done and when I can expect the police at my door." Trudy Jo said, "God gave parents teenagers to punish them, so they would be brought to their knees in prayer and would repent for all their own evildoings."

Their kids were always nice to Annie and me and we were in awe of them and their coolness. But they had their quirks. Galen had a penchant for practical jokes. One time he let a pig loose in school, another time a cow. (He later became a clothes designer with his partner, Mark.) Martin had an unhealthy interest in his nose (politician), Steph got into fist fights (state supreme court judge), and Margaret staged a strike at the high school cafeteria because she didn't like the food (famous chef).

Derek, a very clever boy, one time handed out those cardboard placards at a basketball game in town against our chief rival. At his signal, all the kids turned their cards over. They thought they were spelling out "Go Cougars!" Instead, the giant sign read, "You Raiders Have Small Penises!" It caused a riot. (Stand-up comedian. Trust me. You've heard of him.)

Jules was sleeping with her boyfriend by the time she was sixteen, and no matter what her mother did, she "could not control that girl and her libido." Later, Jules married that boyfriend. They're still married, had six kids, and she became a sex therapist. Justin was a top jock and played football (college football coach, who occasionally throws impressive fits on national TV), and Ellie, the baby, was a total math and science nerd and made experiments with beauty parlor lotions and creams combined with dynamite (rocket scientist with NASA).

Annie and I would hang out on the pink fainting couches in the back of the parlor overlooking the sea and do our homework, or sometimes we'd sit in the parlor and listen amidst the clouds of hair spray, the clipping of scissors, the rush of dryers, the chatter of women, the scent of perfume. There was a sign on the pink front door that said, "Marie Elise's is full of secrets. If you share any secrets you've heard inside, you will not be allowed to return."

Secrets stayed inside that pink parlor . . . unless they were already stuff of legend.

Take, for example, the question of who murdered a man in Cape Cod ten years ago. Gordon Annaed was a terrible, obnoxious drunk who groped the ladies and periodically beat people up. He was found with two bullets in his head in the middle of a cornfield one September morning. The ears were ripe.

"Gordon committed suicide," was what people said to the

outside investigators who came through asking questions after the local police gave up trying to solve the crime. "He killed himself."

"He was sneaky like that," Rudy Shwindt said, chewing his tobacco and aiming maybe a little too close to the investigators' shoes. "He was the kind of guy who could put two bullets in his own head."

Recently divorced Develin McKinney said, after she adjusted her blouse to let a bit of cleavage out for the investigators, "Nah, no one murdered that son of a bitch. He had quick fingers. He did it to himself. Boom, boom, boom, like that, two shots, then he died."

The investigators shook their heads, but what could they do? No one talked. Even my friend Carole, who was eight years old, told them, "I saw Mr. Annaed rip off both tails of his two-tailed dog and eat them."

And her sister, Sandy, who was a friend of Annie's, said, "Mr. Annaed had two heads. One comes out in the day, one comes out in the night. That's how he got two bullets in there."

Their brother, Thad, was not to be beat. "I saw the devil go inside him the day before he shot himself. Mr. Annaed stood there and the devil shrieked and poked him with his sword, until his body swallowed him up and he became the devil. That's why his nose was so red. The devil was inside him."

The investigators stared, mouths open, until Thad leaned in super close and yelled, "Boo!"

I heard the investigators jumped back at that, but I don't know if that part is true.

And guess what? No one ever told who killed Mr. Annaed. But I knew. My parents knew. Annie knew. A whole bunch of people knew, including all eight of Trudy Jo's and Shell Dee's kids.

I knew who Lacey Bea Darling was secretly married to, too. One of the ten most wanted men out of Canada, that's who. Apparently he had a love of robbery. No one ever got hurt. They never caught him, but every couple of months Lacey Bea had a bearded visitor for a few days and did not leave her home. We never said anything about it. After all, Lacey Bea runs the annual charity drive for needy families and contributes twenty thousand dollars of her own money. Or his. We didn't know. But it was for the poor! Twenty thousand!

"We need Lacey Bea," my momma told me. "She is the sweetest woman I have ever met."

Who knew that behind that prim exterior and those button-up sweaters lay a woman who loved a convict?

Amidst the secrets, my momma gave advice. I grew up listening to that advice. She never wavered in what she believed was best. She was never vague, she never wobbled, she never hemmed and hawed.

"For heaven's sakes, Marigold. Go back to school and become an accountant." She put the dryer on full blast in front of Marigold's face, her hair whipping back. "You love numbers and money. Now go make some money doing something you love. Quit making those lame, nauseating excuses! Do you want a valuable life or not?"

"Don't be weak about this, Shirley. Stand your ground or your face will soon be ground into the ground. See, like this." My momma lay straight down on the floor in her pink dress, nose to floor. "Don't be ground, Shirley!"

"Why do you always chase bad men, Amethyst? I know why. It's because you don't feel good about yourself. You don't feel good about Amethyst. You don't think you deserve better. You do. You deserve more. Now I am going to spray you with this hair spray until you scream, 'I love Amethyst!' "

"If he hits you again, Tracy, leave. If he comes after you, shoot him." Momma climbed up on a chair and pulled out the ladies gun she kept in a box on a high shelf. "You point it, you shoot. It's that easy." She got in position and Tracy leaped out of her chair and ran to the resting room. Momma shrugged.

The ladies came to Marie Elise's French Beauty Parlor because Momma and crew could transform the frumpiest woman into someone beautiful. They cut, they dyed, they highlighted, they blew it dry, and honestly, sometimes you could barely recognize the lady that came in and the lady that left. Invariably, the ladies had their chins up higher. Magic. Momma's magic.

But those ladies came as much for the advice, yes, ma'am, they did.

No one would have guessed that my kind, passionate, smart, loving momma would be capable of what she did.

But then no one knows what they're capable of doing until their child's very life is at stake.

That is when all mothers fall into themselves and become someone else they do not recognize.

5

When I arrived in the office at eight in the morning, wearing an expensively tailored, deadly dull suit, Georgie was already there, as usual. She was wearing a Japanese-style kimono wrap, jeans, and a peacock feather sticking out from the back of her head.

I wish I could dress with style like Georgie, but then I'd lose my armor.

"I told May to wait for you in your office," she said. "I told her to power up."

"Good. Thanks. I like your peacock feather."

She stroked it. Stanley barked at me. I shook his paw and hugged him.

"The peacock feather reminds me of my particular love of birds," Georgie said.

I could not help but wonder what she would wear if she had a particular love of dolphins.

"The gals who are arranging the Rock Your Womanhood conference in Portland called and they want to talk to you about your opening and closing speeches. They're all atwitter about you being there. I can feel their almost oppressive, hysterical-cheerful dolorophak around me when I talk to them."

I did not know what a "dolorophak" was. I would ask later.

I nodded. I'd been asked to speak at this conference months ago. I agreed to do it. It was a conference for women, with lots of classes and speakers on everything from medical advice to nutrition and exercise, money, emotional health, travel, fashion, career building, starting your own business, makeovers, journaling, crafts, everything. I was the headliner. At first it was going to be held in a conference room downtown, but the number of attendees grew too high. Then it was going to be in a hotel, but that didn't work because more attendees signed up. Now we were at a convention center, huge, with three levels.

"Tell them I'll call soon."

I would call them back and tell them about my speeches. My speeches are filled with lies, as I do not even follow my own advice, which makes me a hypocrite. I know what to tell women to do with their lives, but I have no idea what to do with the workaholism, the fear, and the scraping memories that drive my own.

"So you're still using sex as a weapon, May?"

"Yes, I am," May said. She sat up straight and proud in my leather chair, chin tilted up. "It's a good gun to have in your Vaginal Arsenal."

I nodded, tried not to laugh out loud.

"I have other guns, too." She pointed to her boobs, which had been surgically enhanced—not too much, but enough so that she could "swim in her own sexuality and float through her raging hormones." She calls them The Bouncers.

I stifled another laugh.

"The only way to manage men is through sexual blackmail," she said.

May Shenecko looks like your stereotypical white, blond, wealthy, country-club-attending woman.

She is not stereotypical.

May owns an electrical company. May's Electrical Company: We'll Get You All Charged Up. She employs three other women. They all look about like her. Blond, stacked, sexy. Needless to say, business is booming, and it's not all because of the sexiness. They're good at what they do. They know their electrical stuff.

"You know I'm a life coach, right, May? Not a marriage counselor, not a sex therapist. We've been over this."

"I know. You're a hellaciously good life coach, Madeline. The very best, and you specialize in relationships, so here I am." She saluted me. "I owe my company to you."

"No, you owe your company to yourself. You built it."

"But you showed me all those nature pictures, and I was attracted the most to the picture of the lightning obliterating a tree. We talked about why I liked lightning, and you told me I should be an electrician and it was like I'd been electrocuted in my own head. I've always liked sparks, fire, wires, that sort of stuff. I knew that being an electrician was what I'd want to do for the rest of my life."

I nodded. She had a liking for that photo. I e-mailed it to her and she had it blown up to a five-by-four foot photograph, framed it, and hung it in her office.

"I was about three months from being homeless before I came here, you know. After I finished my schooling and my apprenticeship, I had to work with a bunch of sexist, hairy men with slow-firing brains. Three times The Bouncers and I got into minor fistfights with them, twice I was fired."

It wasn't exactly that simple. They weren't "minor" fistfights. She knocked out three teeth on one co-worker because he continued to make comments about her "tight, sexy ass."

The other co-worker whispered several disgusting suggestions in her ear. He was a married man; he had done it before and she'd warned him, but this time she kickboxed him so hard in the groin he had to be hauled away in an ambulance.

"I believe you almost destroyed one man's left testicle."

She humphed at me. "If he hadn't been lewd, it wouldn't have happened. There would have been no crushing."

True.

"His wife divorced him." She sat up straight. Woman power! United we stand! "No one should stay married to a man who had to have his testicle kickboxed for being sexually creepy." She shook her head, as in, Good for her, and humphed at me again.

"So you told me to start my own business and to wear red

because that's my favorite color. So now I have my own company and we wear red." She stood up. "What do you think of our uniform? I don't think I've ever been wearing it for my O'Shea Reencouragement and Reigniting Sessions."

The uniform was a tight red T-shirt that said, "I'm here to charge you up," tight jeans, and a red belt with rhinestones. "I think men probably get hard-ons looking at you and your employees."

"Probably," she said cheerfully. "All those hard-ons paid for my Porsche. Sal"—Sal is her husband—"he wants to do it in my Porsche. He's built like a truck. He's six foot five. How am I going to do it in there without having my butt pressed against the horn?"

"You know you can go to a marriage counselor for this."

"Screw to death marriage counselors. You're my life coach. Tell me how to fix this problem. Use one of those acronyms you have. How about this acronym? D.I.C.K. Or this acronym, P.E.N.I.S."

"May, I have told you that you should not tell your husband if he mows the lawn and uses the edger he gets sex."

"I don't see a problem with it."

"It's sexual blackmail. You make him earn sex with you. It should be freely given to your husband, when you want to, with a lot of love and hugs, and passion, and he should do the same for you." What was I talking about? I didn't know anything about this stuff. *Noth-ing.*

"He likes it."

"He likes the sexual blackmail?" I swung my foot in its boring low heel and fiddled with a button on my boring suit. My clothes do not attract men, unlike May's getup, which is the way I need to have it.

"Sure he does. I told him if he built me a shed, I'd stay in bed with him for four hours on Sunday dressed like a hooker."

"Did he build you a shed?"

"Duh. Saw, pound, nail, smile, it's up. Gee, Madeline. He can't get something for nothing." She threw up her hands. "It was a great shed, too. I gave him extra"—she winked at me—"attention, down there, because he hung all these hooks for the rakes and shovels and stuff. It's a shed of legends."

What a shed! And it only cost her a few hours!

"Maybe you should surprise him one night and give him a free pass."

Her jaw dropped. "A free pass for sex?"

"Yes. Bring up some chocolate, turn the lights down low, light a candle. That sort of thing." *What sort of thing?*

Her head shook back and forth. "Hell, no, Madeline. Last time I brought in chocolate and beer and Twinkies, he had to re-roof our house."

"He had to re-roof the house for a romantic evening?"

She flipped her hands out like, And what's wrong with that? "Yeah. You think I'm going to put out for nothing? We needed a new roof."

"Did he enjoy his romantic evening?"

She laughed. "Sugar. He re-roofed the house so he got one long night of passion. I even added in the Tiddly Wonder Ropes and Stash 'N Sticks games."

Tiddly Wonder Ropes? Stash 'N Sticks?

"He couldn't even get up the next morning." She clapped her hands once and rocked back and forth with laughter. "He actually begged me to stop. Begged me. He limped down to the couch to watch football and I said, 'Was that worth it to re-roof the roof?' and he said, 'Sugar, I'm never gonna forget it.'"

"Okay, then. What do you have to do for sex from him? Do you have to do some sort of chore before he'll make love to you?"

She laughed, giggled, laughed more, snort-laughed. "You're so funny, Madeline. You crack my funny bone. You have such a dry wit, that's what I'd call it, a droll and *dry* sense of humor. Like a dry martini. You get irony. Not many people get it, but you're an expert."

I resisted laughing out loud. "So what can I help you with today, May?"

"Fire me up, but I don't know how to say this. . . ."

"Spit it out."

"I could, but the idea is still formulating, mixing around in my head. . . ."

"It is a personal issue? A business idea? Please tell me it's a business idea. I don't know what else to say about your sexual blackmailing."

"It's business, pure business. I've got a head for business and you've given me the confidence to know that I can do it. The day when you and I went boating in bikinis in the rain helped, although I don't think that you wearing a bikini over a T-shirt and shorts was fair play, but you're modest, I get it. And when you and I wrote poems about becoming queens and decorated cardboard crowns, that helped, too. I could practically see the crown on my head."

"You can do anything. May, you're a natural leader. You're tough and sharp. You have vision."

"I love it when you talk like that, Madeline. Frickin' love it. Frickin'. Me and The Bouncers dig it."

"So what's the new business idea?"

May pursed her lips together, then stuck her chest out. "The Bouncers." She pointed to her boobs. "The Bouncers and I think I should open another business."

"And that business would be?"

"Bras."

"Bras?"

"Yep. I'm going to make bras and call them The Bouncers." She opened up her bag. "I took the liberty of making you one, Madeline—36C right?"

Man, she knew her breasts. "Yep."

"Here. Try it on."

It was padded. It was lined. I put it on and stared down at my cleavage. It pulled 'em up and stuck 'em together. It was an incredible feat of brassiere engineering. "Wow," I said. "But, I'm confused. You own an electrical company and you want to make bras? Those are two leaps away from each other."

"Not really. The Bouncers get men charged up, electrically

speaking, and The Bouncers will get women charged up, personally speaking."

I could see the electrical connection.

"Yep. That's it. Wow. Your bouncers look a lot better in my bra. You know, Madeline, you're a pretty woman. Sweeping cheekbones, poufy lips, a lot of hair. You cover it up. I don't know why. You gotta get some bounce in your own life. Some sparkle. I'll send you some sparkle. But how do you think The Bouncers will do?"

I grabbed my boobs. "I think you're in business, girlfriend. I think you're in the boob business."

My next client cried. Head in hands, despondent, despairing.

"No one will hire me. No one."

I looked at the young man across from me on my leather couch. It was raining, lightning and thunder. My dad would have said it was Mother Nature throwing a temper tantrum.

"No one will take a risk and let me prove myself." His hands were worn out, his face waaaaay older than twenty-two. He was too skinny.

"I go in, fill out applications, ask to speak to the manager, I start to hope. . . ."

He shook his head, defeated.

"But they get to that one part in the application, and I can see it in their eyes. *I can see it.*"

He crossed and recrossed his roughened work books, dirt on the bottom.

"They don't want me."

His shoulders slumped.

Ramon Pellinsky is from Youth Avenues, a nonprofit for homeless and troubled kids. Ramon's twelve-year-old brother is in the program because their childhood was based in chaos. What did I see in Ramon? Potential.

"I did everything I could, Miss O'Shea. I took college classes when I was there, got a degree, stayed out of trouble, went to the counseling sessions, and when my sentence was over, I got out."

He ran his hands through his brown, not too clean hair.

"How can I be anyone when no one will give me a chance? How can I make a life when I can't even get a job?"

His eyes filled with tears and he did not bother to wipe them away. He had no energy. He was at the bottom. He was drowning.

"Ramon," I said. "Ramon, look at me."

It took a bit for his eyes to meet mine, his shoulders shaking. People, I have found, can't meet your eyes when there's no self-esteem to meet them with. "You said you took online classes in jail and also classes where the professor came in to teach. What did you take?"

"I took everything, Miss O'Shea. Math, science, literature—that was one of my favorites—history. I love books. That's where I go to hide, books. I taught my brother how to hide in books, too. I got my GED, started on the college classes. I took landscape design. Ten classes. I studied all these landscaping books, wrote papers, watched videos, looked at all these gardening magazines and studied them." He paused for a second, looked a shade sheepish. "I like flowers. Sometimes I paint gardens with secret places, you know, a bench in the back, or a gazebo with vines, paths, gates.... If I ever get a house I'm going to have a garden."

I thought for a few quiet seconds. "Tell me about yourself, then tell me why you robbed that bank."

He stood up and paced, back to drowning. "I had to drop out of high school when my mom wouldn't quit drinking and kept disappearing. I worked construction because my younger brother was at home and we were broke. I had a full-time job building houses and doing landscape stuff, like fountains and walls, but I had to bail my mom out of jail because she'd been locked up for driving drunk, again. So I didn't have money for rent and my brother needed all this stuff for football and we didn't have any food, and I got desperate. And I was pissed off and frustrated. No matter how hard I worked at my job, nothing was ever right. Then the construction market started to slow so I took a newspaper delivery job, too. My mom was always passed out or screaming at me and my brother, telling me I was nothing, telling him he was shit. Years of that. Years of her screaming shit."

I closed my eyes on a wave of pain for this guy. Wave of pain. Some people should not parent.

Ramon rolled his shoulders. "I needed five hundred dollars. That was it. Five hundred dollars. So I robbed a bank, got caught, did four years, and now . . . my brother's in foster care because the state took him from my mom when she crashed in a car with him and had meth in there, plus she assaulted someone with a pickax and she's in jail now, but if I can get a job and prove I'm responsible, I can get custody of him instead of visitation only."

He slumped into his chair again. "I have to get my brother back, Miss O'Shea, I have to. He's only twelve."

"Ramon, you can mow and edge a lawn, pick weeds, plant flowers?"

"Sure. Yes. Absolutely."

"These paintings that you make. Can you transfer the painting into reality?"

"You mean, can I look at one of my paintings and take a bunch of dirt and turn it into something cool in someone's front yard?"

"Yes."

Hope peeked through his eyes. "I know I can. I spent hours and hours in prison studying, drawing . . . I even went online and talked to landscapers and gardeners, asked them all sorts of questions. Plus, I know how to work with cement, build brick walls, that sort of thing because of the construction work I was doing before jail. I like being outdoors, Miss O'Shea. I like working in gardens. In fact, I worked in the prison garden."

He was proud of that, I could tell. "Tell me about it."

"We had all kinds of fruits and vegetables, all the time. I built a whole bunch of raised beds, used organic everything, planted seeds and starts. I built a huge grape arbor, a shed with shelves, brick pathways all over the garden, a huge wood deck, a rock wall, a cement patio with a trellis over it. I planted nasturtiums and edible flowers that the cook put on the guys' plates some- times—that's why all the guys in jail called me Flower. Because of the flowers. Even the warden thanked me. He wrote me a rec- ommendation, so did two guards from jail, but no one will hire me."

I thought of the house that I didn't like. Boring grass, dying. Plain. Dirt. "I'll hire you."

He looked shocked. "You will? To do what?" He snapped his fingers. "I could be your janitor. I could be a janitor for this whole building. Can you tell somebody here that I can clean? I did that in jail, too. Cleaned all the time. Cleaned good—corners, too. The guy in charge of the kitchen, Mr. Morriston, he didn't like when I worked in the garden, because he wanted me in the kitchen helping him, every corner, every wall, I cleaned...."

"Nope, nope, and nope. Ramon, you need to shoot for where you want to be, so to speak. Do the Shoot High O'Shea pro- gram."

"The Shoot High O'Shea program? What's that?"

"It means, don't shoot low, shoot high. Shoot for what you want, who you want to be. Ramon, my yard is boring. Only grass, and the grass is dying. Draw out a plan for my yard and we'll work out a price. I'm up in the hills, so if the yard turns out great, I betcha you'll get more business."

He was stunned. "You're hiring me to work on your yard?"

"Yep. Here's my address. Get on up there. Think about it, give me a drawing, and I'll give you a check. How's that?"

"You're kidding."

"No. You have a record, you did something tremendously stupid, and it's going to be hard for you to get a job. So, you're going into business for yourself. You have a pickup, right?"

He nodded. "My uncle died. It was all he had. He willed it to me, along with his tools."

"I'll pay you half up front for working on my yard. Get signs for the sides of your pickup truck advertising Ramon's Land- scaping Services, get cards and flyers printed out, take photos of my yard before and after." I saw his face. "No camera, right? I'll take the photos and give them to you. When you've got some cash, get a Web site up and running."

I scribbled down my address. "You're in business, Ramon. You own Ramon's Landscaping Services. Now get on up to my house and turn it around."

He was starting to grasp the Shoot High program. "So I'm going to be a landscaper?"

"Ramon, you *are* a landscaper. And you have a lawn-mowing business on the side, that's what you tell people."

I saw his chin tilt upward.

"You're also a businessman."

I saw his chest puff a wee bit, the tears drying on his cheeks.

"Pretty soon you'll have employees, and you'll go to clients' houses and you'll bring them paintings of what you're going to do to their yard to transform it, and you'll smile, shake their hands, look them in the eye, be friendly and honest and get every job done on time and done right, because you want every-one to know you're trustworthy and honest. You're going to work harder than any other landscaper in the area and you're going to build your company on the backs of your happy clients."

He nodded, nodded again, his breathing shallow. I could tell he hadn't breathed right in a long time, either. Maybe ever.

"Wow. Me. A businessman!"

"Yep, and a landscaper. Off you go."

Finally, *finally*, on that exhausted, beaten face, I saw a smile. I saw a glimmer in his eyes. I saw hope. Without hope, life is dead. "Thanks, Miss O'Shea. Man, thanks a lot."

"You're welcome."

This wasn't gonna be perfect. He was young, inexperienced. But he had a shimmer of hope. He had a goal. He could do it, he could build from here.

By the time I got home, late that night, there was a painting on a two-by-three-foot canvas of what the front yard of my square spaceship house would look like. A second painting showed my backyard.

I sank down into an Adirondack chair on my back deck.

The paintings themselves were stunning. His clients would want to keep them. Ramon's ideas were in keeping with the lines and modern feel of my house. There was a fountain, brick stairs to the entrance, white and pink cherry trees, a retaining wall, an arbor that mimicked the roofline with a vine growing over it, and layered borders of shrubs and flowers.

I grinned. Darned if I wasn't proud.

Ramon, the ex-con, was in business.

I sent him a check. In the memo part I wrote, "Fear not."

The rest of my week was filled with clients, in particular corporate types, one of whom said his life was so filled with meetings and technological input, he believed he had become an emotionless robot. I told him he was correct and helped him rethink his life. "RTYL," I told him. (Rethink your life.) "Draw a picture of who you want to become." I gave him six feet of butcher paper. He drew a smiling travel writer with a small laptop, multipocketed vest, and camera.

The other was a tightly closeted, repressed gay artist who worked as a CEO. "You're a hypocrite," I told him. "You won't live until you get rid of your lies." I made him stand with me on a table and yell out the truth about himself until he felt comfortable with his truth. He cried when he was done. Good tears.

I counseled a number of homeless/troubled youth (always for free) from Youth Avenues, a nonprofit group that Swans Grocery Stores financially supports with the mission of helping young people, with lousy beginnings because of lousy parents, get their lives on track. When I meet these kids, if I see potential, if they're sober and *want* to go to school, I direct them to a scholarship fund Swans sponsors at our local community college. Free tuition, plus a stipend, and they get to change their lives. If they want to be sober and want treatment, we pay for the treatment, too.

I also went with Granddad to a board meeting for Youth Avenues, a dinner at a fancy downtown hotel, to honor Portland area employees of his stores, attended another charity dinner for a hospital and wrote a huge check, and I wrote a column about lifestyle versus job. Basically: If you were going to be dead in a year, would you want to be where you are? No? *Then what are you waiting for? Don't die with a dead life in back of you!*

On Friday, May sent me a Bouncer. It was a bra with silver sequins sewn over the whole thing, with matching silver-sequined thong underwear.

I had a feeling, from an adult perspective, that my momma would have grabbed that sequined bra and thong, wriggled her curvy hips, and danced around for my dad in them. Annie and I would have been able to eat my dad's chocolate mint brownies and watch TV for hours.

But me? No.

I would not wear it. The Bouncer and thong would not, could not, be worn, as they were not a part of my armor.

I put them back in the box. The box went under my bed.

I could see my momma throwing up her hands in exasperation.

On Saturday morning, about six o'clock, I left for The Lavender Farm. I had been up since four o'clock, anyhow, worrying the deep worry of someone who was being blackmailed. I watched the sun rise through a mist, noted that the mist seemed wistful, said good-bye to octagonal head man, and left.

I drove down my winding hill, past homes that seemed to be built on air, hanging almost completely off cliffs, spindly stilts beneath them, past buildings, high and low, down two freeways, and out into the country. I passed orchards and farms and a big red barn that sells the best apples on the planet. I passed a creaky old grocery store, a cut zinnia business, a church advertising a spaghetti feed, and a café that sells fruit milkshakes.

My granddad was up when I arrived. He believes that "being busy is being productive. Being productive is being useful. Be useful." I waved at him across the field. He was chopping wood. He blew me a kiss, I blew back, then headed for the house. Granddad does not like to be interrupted when he chops wood.

It's his "thinking" time. He gives wood away every year, to all our neighbors. He owns a ton of stores, he's a multimillionaire, and yet every year we troop around in his pickup and unload wood for everyone, more for families who are struggling.

I made orange tea with milk and sugar, and an hour later, on the dot, Grandma rushed in. She was exquisitely dressed, as always—a sparkly brooch in place on her white blouse under a white sweater with jeweled buttons and pressed blue slacks.

"Where is Ismael?" Grandma asked in agitated French. She pointed at a painting she'd created of two swans kissing on a pond. Behind them, the trees were on fire, a red and orange mass of destruction. "Where is he? Is he burning?" She sank into a chair at the table.

"He's not burning." I kissed her on both cheeks, as we always have, as the French do. "But I *still* don't know who Ismael is." I smiled at Nola.

Grandma abruptly stood up and banged her fists on the kitchen table, the huge diamond in her wedding ring catching the light. "Yes, you do! You know who he is! He's your son. How could you not know who he is! Where is he? Is this a joke?"

That hollow place in my stomach, perhaps that empty ache that so wished for children, spread a fire of pain. *Where is my son? I don't have a son. I don't have a daughter. I have no children. I can't even make love to a man.* "It's not a joke, Grandma. Here, I made orange tea, let's have some." I pushed a flowered, almost translucent teacup toward her.

"No!" She banged her clenched fists again on the table, her eyes stricken. "We need to find Ismael and we need to hurry, we need to hurry, we need to hurry. I know where Anna is. She's coming in with the swans, on their backs, to the lily pond. She'll land on the lilies. Do you have her blue coat?"

"No, Grandma, I don't have the blue coat, but I'll get it."

"We have to get the coat and we have to find Ismael. He had blood on him last time. Blood, don't you know, don't you know? *Blood!* We have to find him, carry him, he has to come with us and Anna, too, on the backs of the swans. They'll take us to a new land where the doves talk, not the dogs. It's almost too late. We've waited too long. The black ghosts are coming."

"We'll bring them with us, Grandma." I slung my arm around her shoulders as she banged the table again. Watching someone you love dive deep into dementia is like opening your own heart with an ax. Grandma had gone from being a vibrant, endlessly working, kind, joyful woman who loved painting and drawing illustrations for her books to asking me about a blue coat and my son, Ismael.

"I'm so scared," she whispered, leaning in close to me. "So scared. Everyone is scared. Even your violin is scared. That's how it got the scratch on the back, at the bottom."

"How did it get that scratch?" I knew exactly what scratch she was talking about.

"It happened when we were in the barn. We had to hide it in the hay and it scratched on a nail, don't you remember? We have to kill them if they come for us. Like this!" She picked up the flowered teapot and threw it at the window, glass splintering everywhere. She screamed, slammed her hand to her mouth, then crawled under the table and hid. "Come here, Madeline, get down here before they see you."

Nola darted in, her face worried, followed by Annie, who had just arrived, as I scrambled under the table. They instantly understood what had happened.

"Get down, Madeline! Get down!" Grandma whispered. "Hurry!" I hid under the table with her, and she held my hands with one of hers and with the other she put a finger to her lips and shook her head as in, No talking.

I waited there with her, under the table, aching, saddened, until she whispered, "They're gone, I think. We can run through the garden and hide. We can hide by the lavender."

"Okay, but let's have some tea first."

"Tea won't kill them."

"I know, but we'll have some orange tea first, then run."

"We have to run. Anton's getting the papers. I hear Ismael in my heart. I feel him, do you? He's alive, I know he is, but I can't find him." Her face crumpled. "We're lost from each other." She started to sob, wrenching and raw, old tears and new tears mixed. "I can't find him, Madeline! I've tried! I've tried! Sometimes I've thought I would lose my mind searching for him!"

I rocked her in my arms, bending my head in misery. I can't stand when my grandma cries, and I can't stand her pain, her loss. I can't stand that I know there's truth among the fog, but I can't see the truth.

"Ismael is lost!" she wailed. "Help him! I want him, I want him. . . ."

I hugged her close, then Annie and I settled her into her chair again. Nola poured another cup of tea and added the exact amount of sugar and cream that she liked.

We watched her settle down, the torture gone, the fog still with us.

"I'll drink the tea," she said, this time in German. "But we must run behind the lavender where the fluttering fairies and magical crystals will help us."

"We'll do it," I said. "Call Jess," I whispered to Nola. She nodded at me. Jess was the handyman. He would get someone to come and fix the window.

He could not, unfortunately, call anyone to fix anything else.

I looked at Grandma's painting. The broken glass had not damaged the swans kissing while the trees burned in an inferno of red and orange fire.

Later that afternoon Annie and I made Chinese food with Nola for dinner that night. Nola can cook anything. She has taught us how to make all sorts of American and ethnic foods over the years. Her specialties are Indian and Italian. For desserts, she is outstanding at baking six-layer cakes that will melt your tongue out of your mouth and crepes that you know angels helped her roll.

Nola is fifty-five years old, with dark brown eyes, and three sons who all graduated from Columbia University. They wanted to be together. Granddad and Grandma paid for her sons' educations. She has season tickets to the symphony and the Broadway shows. She has her book group here once a month, and she goes to Gourmet Club. All of her other time, minus vacationing with her sons, is spent at the farm.

Many years ago Nola and her husband paid a "cougar" to take them and their two kids—one a toddler, one a baby—over the Mexican border to America. They were attacked, her husband was shot in the head in front of her and the kids, and she was raped. Nine months later another boy was born. He looked completely different from the other two. She loved all of them, they loved each other.

When Grandma met her, she'd been in the country for a year, working at migrant camps. One night she was running away from one of the men there, who was drunk and dangerous. She burst onto the rainy street, Grandma's car almost hit her, and that was that. Grandma put Nola in the car, took the safety off the gun she had in the glove compartment, and started shooting at the ground and above the head of the drunken jerk until he scuttled off. They went and picked up Nola's boys and brought them to the house. The next day Grandma and Granddad called their longtime attorney and went about getting Nola citizenship. When she was legal, they gave her a job in their stores, where she worked her way up from the back in stock while she learned English, then was promoted to checker, manager, clear through to a vice president. Granddad says no one is better with numbers and money than Nola.

Nola was not only gracious and kind, she worked harder than anyone. She was the one who insisted that she take care of Grandma when Grandma's mind started to snap, crackle, and pop.

"First she took care of me, now I take care of her," Nola said, those dark eyes calm, caring. "As it should be."

Granddad wanted her in the stores, but he wanted her with Grandma more. He still consults her regularly, and she will eventually go back to her vice president's job. But, for now, she has given our family a gift we can never repay: Herself.

You can see why we all love Nola.

* * *

"Now, don't you get frisky with me, young man! There are children here!"

"I'll try not to," Granddad said, so gentle, before bending to kiss Grandma's cheek. "Even though you are irresistible, the star in my galaxy."

Grandma smiled coyly, the candles on our picnic table on the deck flickering in the cool nighttime breeze. "Don't be naughty! Control your passions!"

My granddad lifted Grandma's hand and kissed it, then sat beside her. "I'll control myself, but it is difficult around you, my delightful wife."

Grandma giggled. Granddad makes her giggle. Her mind might be confused, but her love is not. For Granddad, me, Annie, Nola, and all of the people who have been around our family for years—friends, neighbors, long-term employees—Grandma's love has grown for all of us exponentially, as if her last gift is a blast of her enduring adoration. And, for Granddad alone, a blast of passion.

Grandma reached for Granddad's hand, held it between hers, smiled a seductive smile, and said, "Keep your hands to yourself until we're alone! The making love will come later. Me on top tonight!"

Annie and I exchanged smiles. Mr. Legs licked Annie's chin. He was on her lap, his favorite place. Oatmeal and Geranium meowed at her. She meowed back.

"I'll do that, my love," Granddad said, still holding her hand. She snuggled into him as a coyote howled, a horse neighed.

My granddad, Anton Laurent, is tall, like an elegant, lean, plain-talking, semigruff giant with a shock of white hair. He always wears a dapper suit to work, and even when he's in jeans or overalls and thick into the dirt or hay or horse poop on our farm, he always looks formal but friendly.

To me, he is the kindest man I've ever known, besides my dad. My momma married a man like her father. Tonight, though, he looked exhausted and drained. He had aged rapidly in the last six months.

"You look particularly beautiful tonight, Emmanuelle," Granddad said to her, his brown eyes with hints of gold, like my momma's, like mine, softening.

"My heavens, stop!" she fluttered, patting her hair. "Stop that right now, Anton! All this flirting is getting me fired up, up, and away, and we have this lovely dinner to eat first."

She waved her hand at the fried rice, chicken chow mein, orange chicken, and egg rolls that Nola, Annie, and I had spent hours making.

"I will try to resist from any more flirting," Granddad reassured her.

She patted his shoulder. "I know. It's hard for you, always chasing me around, wanting me naked. *Naked!*"

Tonight Grandma was wearing a very flattering red cocktail dress and a diamond teardrop necklace. Nola had told her that Granddad was coming home from a short business trip to his stores, so she dressed up. Nola had even done her hair in a ball on top of her head.

"How was the trip?" Annie asked Granddad after we'd passed the dinner and chopsticks around, Nola had prayed, and Grandma had proposed a toast to "Anton, because he is so good and also yummy in bed."

In the distance Morning Glory howled. She does not like to be all alone without Annie, her mother.

"Wonderful. I have the best employees in the world. The stores in southern Oregon are thriving. Our employees will be pleased with their bonuses and the community will be pleased with the grants we're again able to offer the schools. Enough about me," Granddad said. "Tell me about you all."

Now, Granddad is not the type who takes "We're fine" for an answer. He likes to hear about Annie's animals at home, the animals she's taking care of, and her wood carving with the chain saw. He does not like to hear about her trips to Fiji. "The less I know, the better. Hell, be careful, Annie."

He asks me about my columns, which he reads regularly and comments upon with blunt honesty, my upcoming speech for the Rock Your Womanhood conference, my clients, everything.

He is a man who is interested in others besides himself. He is a miracle.

He talked to Nola and we heard all about her book group. They were reading *Jane Eyre,* and next month it was a Shakespeare play. What magazines was she was reading? The *American Medical Journal.* Where was she going for her summer vacation? New Zealand. The boys were taking her.

"And now, my friend, Emmanuelle, it is time for your bath," Nola said, getting up, as yet another coyote called out and Morning Glory howled from her house. "A hot bath with lavender bath oil."

"Oui!" Grandma said, smiling, as Nola helped her up. She turned and patted Granddad's cheek. "I'll go and get freshened up with strawberries and lavender so my V privates will smell scented." She pointed to her crotch. "Scented like the lavender fields right out here that you planted for me because you're a gentleman and a black ghost slayer." She pointed into the darkness at the lavender fields. "Delicious!"

Granddad's face stilled, tight and taut, when she said the words black ghost slayer.

"I'll be in later, Emmanuelle," Granddad said, his voice low and reassuring. He was never gruff with Grandma. With the rest of us, yes, but not her. "Until then."

She giggled and kissed him on the lips, stroked his shoulder. "You are so handsome. So very handsome!"

"And you are a gorgeous woman. It is an honor to be your husband." Granddad said this with all seriousness because he meant it in all seriousness.

"She would understand," Grandma said, her eyes suddenly intense as she bent to be eye to eye with Granddad. The wind picked up one of her white curls and carried it across her forehead. "We can share you later with her violin."

Granddad nodded as Annie and I exchanged confused glances. So much of what our grandma said lately was confusing, so alarming. When she started to slip initially, she couldn't remember names for certain objects, began getting lost on our property and driving into town. There were some mood swings, nonsensical or roundabout talk. She lost understanding about her life, what had happened yesterday, two weeks ago, but then things had changed. I could almost pinpoint the time. I walked into her bedroom one night a few months ago and she was cradling in her hand a blue glass swan, keening back and forth. She kept saying, as if she'd been hit by a wrenching revelation, "Now I remember. I'll never forget it. You can't take it from me! You can't!"

It was right after that that the talk changed. She started telling part of what Annie and I believe to be her "real" story, mixed with the stories she told in her swan books, with a dollop of horror and violence thrown in. We'd tentatively, gently, asked Granddad about it, and he'd shut down, put us off. "It's something best not talked about. It's in the past and there it will stay."

Mr. Legs shifted positions on Annie, as if he was confused, too.

"Yes." Granddad's eyes, eyes that had seen so much tragedy, so much laughter, were so very tired. "She would understand."

"It's all right. We had to do it . . . and then, love. Between us, love," Grandma said, dropping a kiss on his forehead. "We weren't expecting it, we weren't planning on it, but it came. Like the sunset, like the sunrise, even though the violins weren't matching. Our love came on the backs of swans and blue jays carrying red hearts."

I remembered one of the illustrations my grandma drew for her books. There were swans and blue jays and they were carrying red hearts.

"And we're here now," Grandma said. "Past the barns and hiding in rivers, over the mountains, away from the guns and the work moving rocks, and the no water and the lice, we are here."

"That's right. Enjoy your bath, my love. I'll be with you in a minute," Granddad said.

Grandma smiled, kissed him on the lips. "My V privates will be scented then."

Nola took her arm, smiling, and led Grandma away. I looked up at the sky and saw a star shoot down. The wind picked up a bit, ruffling my hair, my stomach in knots.

In the distance Morning Glory howled again. She does not like to be all alone.

Who does?

Later Granddad put Grandma to bed. I knew their routine.

Nola is in there with them, but she stands back. She's there in case Grandma needs help. She's fallen twice, ended up in the hospital both times, so Nola stays. It's a private moment though, as Nola has told me. "I am quiet. I do not get in the way of their love."

I am in their bedroom when I'm at home. Annie is also. We don't get in the way of their love, either.

Neither Grandma nor Granddad ever looks at us, we are gone to them in the shadows of the dimly lit room. They are in their bedroom, alone together, their nightly routine one they've shared for decades.

Granddad is already in his pajamas, his teeth brushed. He helps Grandma brush her teeth, then takes her hand and settles her in her antique chair in front of her old-fashioned makeup table, complete with an oval mirror and a red rose flowered skirt.

He kneels and carefully smoothes her palms and fingers with lavender lotion, takes out her tortoise shell or pearl clips and hairpins, and brushes out her white curls, which have not lost their lushness.

Next, he gently sits Grandma on their king-sized bed with the lace canopy, and she smiles up at him, that suggestive coyness shining forth. He bends and drops a kiss on her smiling mouth and they smile at each other for long seconds, then she puts her arms straight out, like she's on a cross, and he carefully unbuttons her sweater or her blouse or, like tonight, her fancy dress worn especially for him, and takes it off, folding or hanging it neatly.

She always says, "Take my clothes off. I am yours. We will go to The Land of the Swans together."

There is no modesty as he unsnaps her lacy bra. My grandma, even when I was younger, always wore intricate, lacy bras that my granddad bought for her. Matching underwear, too. One bra, three pairs of matching underwear. She still wears them. He still buys her lacy, sexy bras and underwear because she delights in them. Next Grandma lies back on their bed, a girlish, flirty smile on her face as she watches him pull off her shoes, socks, her pants or her skirt, and underwear.

He slips an elegant nightgown over her head. He has always bought all of my grandma's nightgowns, too, and he spares no expense. He buys her what a lady would wear for a husband who loves her dearly. She wears a pad in her underwear, but she doesn't notice, and I don't think he notices anymore, either; that is not the point.

When he is done, and she is covered in lace and love, he gently pulls her back up, and she says, "My heart, take me to the lake and we'll make love" or "Darling, let's make love by the lavender near the swan." He tucks her in, turns out the light, climbs into bed, and hugs his wife, as they have done for decades, during good times and horrid times, their dreams intertwined, their nightmares shared.

We leave, closing the door softly.

We don't want to interrupt their love.

When everyone else was in bed that night, Annie and I popped popcorn, smothered it in butter, headed back out to the deck, lit pine-scented candles, and wrapped blankets around ourselves. She had returned Mr. Legs, Oatmeal, and Geranium and come back with the gray and white cat, named Cat, who thinks she's a dog and Morning Glory, who is a cross between a beagle, a German shepherd, and a banana.

"What exactly do you think they're hiding?" I drawled. We lay in the wooden chaise lounges and studied the night sky, filled with bright stars, dim stars, and the swirl of the Milky Way.

"I don't know, but they're hiding something." Morning

Glory climbed up on Annie and lay on her chest, followed by Cat, who lay on her ankles.

"A lot of something." I love popcorn. I love the whiteness of it. It's an innocent food. We never had it at the shack, so it makes it innocent, a food with no bad memories, so to speak. "We know they came from France. Momma's one hundred percent French."

We let the silence move between us, liquid, quiet.

"Granddad told me they left before the war," I said. "I think he said that. Didn't he say that?"

"I think so, but, Madeline, I'm not sure. Did he just imply it? I know when someone's lying, been trained on that one, but I was young when I asked my questions, hadn't had the 'how-to-extract-information-from-unwilling-people' classes yet."

I didn't take that one any further. "He said they came to New York, then to Oregon, and he and Grandma sold fruits, pies, French breads, baguettes, stews, soups, and croissants, door to door. They cooked it out of a cruddy house they rented. The roof leaked, the heat was sporadic, and it smelled moldy, but the oven worked, and that's where they cooked."

"Right, and he said the house caught fire on a winter night and burned the kitchen down, including their cooking supplies and their ingredients, and they started over."

I nodded. "That's them. They are not quitters."

The rest is Swan Stores history. They rented a corner of a building outside of Portland. They lived upstairs and sold their food downstairs. "We were dead poor," Granddad had told me, "for a time."

Their flagship store is now located on that corner, tens of thousands of square feet. Fresh local ingredients, French food, great bargains, and bulk items drew crowds, and helpful employees kept them coming back. Swans grew; they expanded, hired, expanded, hired. "We never stopped working," Grandma told me. "Except to take care of your momma."

"They did both say they were born in Germany," Annie said. "And they moved to France as very young children. Their parents were friends, I remember that part. They lived in the same village in Germany, and both families moved together." She tossed two pieces of popcorn up in the air and caught both with her mouth. I was not fooled by her nonchalance. She was trying to puzzle this out with me. "But from there and back, things get fuzzy. I've never liked fuzzy."

Morning Glory whined at her. Annie whined back.

"They'll hardly say anything about France," I said. "They're vague. They change the subject. Who did they used to be? Who were they before they came here? All they will say is that the coffee was better in France, and so was the cheese and chocolate. Everything else is better in America. I asked Grandma about her own family, but she always stopped my questions by saying, 'That was a long time ago. That was when the unicorns and the nymphs ruled the world' or 'It's like a storybook, but the storybook has been read and doesn't need to be re-read.'"

"One time Granddad told me that he and Grandma's parents were gone, and it was just us now. I remember he became quiet after saying that, then he walked away from me, down the hill to the pond, and sat on the dock for a long time. I snuck down and spied on him, and he had his head in his hands. I didn't want to ask him any more questions, because obviously it took him to a very bad place."

"Annie, do you remember how Momma used to cry at odd moments? She would never explain why she was so upset. She'd go outside and watch the waves, she'd speak in French, as if she was talking to someone, and she'd play her violin. Sometimes I'd take my violin out and we'd play together."

"They've been deliberately evasive." Annie tossed up more popcorn. "I spent a number of years in hot, dry countries talking to evasive people, and those two are masters at it." She pet Morning Glory. He panted at her.

"Think we'll ever know what's really there?"

"I don't know. Maybe."

We sat in the liquid silence again and watched the stars while we shoveled innocent buttered popcorn in. One shooting star, two.

"All three of them shared a secret."

"*That* I would bet my house that I don't like on." I reached for Annie's hand and held it. We both had butter on our fingers from the innocent popcorn.

One more star fell through the night. It was now gone.

Dead.

Lavender can be used for love. It has a romantic history.

Cleopatra, that raving feminist, brilliant strategist, and manipulator used it to seduce, it is said, Marc Antony. I hardly doubt she needed help, but being in a bad political position, she can't be blamed for pulling out all the stops.

Lavender was used over a hundred years ago to promote chastity. There are no scientific studies that support any success in this matter. Conversely, the smell of lavender is apparently sexy to men and can help the old guys get it up again. Young women used to stuff lavender in their beds so they could have a rocking good time in the sack, or tuck a few stems between their breasts to attract young gentlemen.

Lavender is also used to heal a broken heart.

So far, it has not worked for me.

Georgie, dressed in a yellow wrappy sort of dress with sunflowers and a perky blue hat, reminded me that I would be on the local TV show *Portland Sunrise* on Friday. "Tracy Shales's assistant called and wants to talk to you."

Stanley barked at me. I got on my haunches, shook his paw. He barked again and I hugged him.

My mind was mush. I had eight million e-mails to plow through and phone calls to return, including one to Janika Jeffs, who was running the Rock Your Womanhood conference. "We are so excited to have you, Madeline. We did a survey, and eighty-five percent of our seven thousand participants are coming because of you! You! You! You you!"

"The assistant wants to review what time you're supposed to be there, makeup, the questions that will be asked of you, all that." Georgie swirled the yellow ties on her dress. "I think this is a good way to forward your spirit to others."

"Thank you. I like to forward my spirit."

"Tracy's got a lot going on right now, swirling trauma and drama," Georgie mused.

"I know." Tracy was in a rather public spat with the station's manager, Thacker Blunt. She was a popular morning show host. Tracy was forty-eight, not thin, and had short brown hair. She was funny, quick, smart, and had fought breast cancer twice and won. She wore a scarf when she hosted the morning show during chemo, and a couple of times she took it right off and there was her bald head. It was a round, shiny, attractive bald head. That woman was roarin' popular.

But when a young, leggy, snooty blonde was invited onto the show to "help her" cohost, Tracy saw the beginning of her demise.

When the young, leggy, snooty blonde named, get this, *Tawni,* was clearly taking over, in a sneaky way, and given more significant stories and the opening greeting, and when eventually Tracy was "reassigned" to a weekend news reporter position, the women of Portland howled.

Very loudly.

Not only her female viewers, and all of the women she knew in the statewide breast cancer organization, to which she had donated time and money, but her church, her walking group, and her neighbors got involved, too, one of whom was the former mayor of the city, another a state senator.

Not pretty.

During those two weeks, the young, leggy, snooty blonde, Tawni, said, *on the air,* when she was interviewing a red-haired fashion designer, "Ladies, if you're a size twelve or above, these clothes aren't for you. They're a no-no. A boo-boo. Isn't that right, Magdalena?" Magdalena, the local fashion designer, looked like she wanted to choke on her turquoise necklace.

"No, absolutely not. These clothes are made for all women, they accentuate curves—" the designer rushed, a gold streak in her hair falling forward.

Tawni smiled, so patronizing. "Designer clothes don't hang right on heavy woman, we know that. But there are alternatives, aren't there, Mags? Stores out there that cater to large women."

Tawni smiled, fake white teeth gleaming, then crossed her thin legs and designer heels.

"And, in fact, even when *I* walk by those stores for biggy women, I've seen things that I like, and I'm a size four! Four! I've seen bright colors, cool belts that can hide those extra cuddle rolls, ladies, and pretty scarves that cover problems on the neck and minimize attention to the face!" She pulled her shoulders back, fake boobs protruding. "Women of all sizes have choices, luckily, and the fatter ones, oops, the *heavier* women, the weight-challenged ones, can look good, too, with some focused, intense, determined attention to detail and material, isn't that right, Mags?" Fake smile, again.

And Magdalena said, pasty white, almost frothing with fear, "My clothes can be worn by everyone, of all sizes. Now let me tell you about these fabrics." She held up a skirt, her hands shaking. "I bought this fabric in India—"

"Come on, now, Mags! You're a size four, too! Do you think your clothes would be flattering on a woman who is a size twelve or fatter? They wouldn't hang right because of the lumps and bumps. Let's not mislead the viewers! Part of being sexy is taking an honest look at yourself and taking action against your own fat." She wiggled her shoulders, then wagged a finger at the camera. "We all have to take responsibility for ourselves! So, hit the gym, ladies!"

Portland Sunrise cut to commercial after Magdalena, the shaking fashion designer, leaned heavily against her chair and went from pasty white to green.

The cacophony of the outrage forced Tawni into an apology. The next morning, a sulky and petulant expression pasted to her condescending face, she whined, "I'm so sorry *if* I offended heavy women." She could barely hide her impatience. "I was trying to point out that designers don't make these clothes for women ... of a certain size. And that we all have a personal responsibility to ourselves and to others who have to look at us to be attractive, not fa—not heavy. But we're all beautiful, right? We're *all* beautiful!" Tawni swung her shoulders back, the protruding fake boobs once again at attention. "Skinny girls, fat women, we're all beautiful on the inside! That's what's important. It's not important if you're bigger than a size eight! What we all have to do as women is bond together!"

The howling reached a deafening pitch, and with Tracy gone and no one watching the show anymore thanks to the women-up-in-arms-rebellion, advertisers pulled their ads quicker than you can say "I hate young, leggy, snooty blondes named Tawni."

Tracy got her full-time job back, Tawni moved to Memphis, the advertisers forked over the cash again, and local and national media covered the event.

Tracy's popularity could not be understated.

But Thacker Blunt, the station manager, by all accounts, was steaming mad. Boiling. Pissed off. By virtue of knowing thousands of people in town, a number of them in the news business, I knew that Thacker was a quack. One of my clients said she was fired from the station because she complained about how he always touched her. She didn't want the legal fight, she did want the wowza "I Will Not Sue You" check, so she moved on. A friendly acquaintance of mine, a newscaster, said that working for Thacker is like facing a firing squad every day, wondering if the bullet will hit your aorta or your co-worker's.

"Tracy got her job back," I said to Georgie.

"She did. The heavenly karmas intervened in that mess. I hated the other host with the fake boobies." She whipped out a mirror to examine the silver sparkles on her eyelids. "I'm glad they sacked her. Even watching her on TV was inviting negative back into my life and bones. When she said that stuff about fat women, my mother sat down and wrote to the station and all the advertisers on that show saying she wasn't going to buy any of their products or watch the station unless they got rid of 'that bitch.' My mother used that language, 'that bitch,' and my mother never swears. She studied to be a nun, you know."

"Yes, I know." I loved Georgie's mother. She dressed in proper blouses and proper slacks and wore a large cross every day over her bosom. She and Georgie could not be more different. They were in love with each other.

"But poor Tracy still has to deal with that manager, and she hates him," Georgie said. "He's sleeping with another woman at the station and he's married and the tramp gal's married."

I shot her a quick look. "How do you know?"

"I know because my best friend, Elizabeth, works there. She's got an entry-level job. She's African American, and she's got these huge, *gigantic* brown eyes, like chocolate drops, and she's this cosmic wonder-girl person, the kindest in the universe, so she's everyone's best friend and they tell her everything. In fact, the gal that Thacker's sleeping with now even told her that Thacker says he's leaving his wife. She says they keep some of their sex toys—and one of the toys is this pink snake, I don't know what that's for, but she says they keep them in the third drawer of his desk. They go to this hotel called The Chateau outside of town every Thursday night and Sunday afternoon. Apparently the girlfriend likes to be spanked. That's what she told Elizabeth. Spanked. With a hand and with Pop-Tarts or licorice. I don't know the connection. That type of weirdness is out of my comfy metaphysical realm."

Spanked. As foreplay? It made me sick, and nervous, and a flashback, appallingly clear and graphic, rolled before my eyes like a movie. I shuddered.

"Yeah, Thacker's creepy. Elizabeth says they have young, sexy women with cleavage and bouncy butts—her words not mine—working there for about four months, then they leave. So, anyhow, call Tracy's assistant. I put her number on your desk with the rest of the eternal messages you receive by this time every morning."

I would.

I tried to get the image of a "spanking" out of my head. The one I remember involved an open palm, a piece of wood, and a whip.

I turned toward my office and shut the door, staring out the windows. It was raining again.

For years I tried to block out my flashbacks when they came for me. I have learned the hard way that I can fight, wrestle, and push them away, but it doesn't work forever. They stay there, planted in my brain, until I run them through. Why is that? Is it trauma? Is it healing? My flashbacks can be triggered by any-thing—a word like spanking, a dilapidated house, two sisters walking together, or someone talking about a beach trip. I don't go to the ocean; neither does Annie, as I've said. Too much was taken by the ocean.

I remembered a spanking. It hurt. It hurt everything in me.

Good God I wish my flashbacks would die.

As a girl, my skin crawled like a thousand red ants were bit-ing my body when I knew that Sherwinn was watching me.

When I watched Sherwinn watching Annie or grabbing her brown curls, those red ants brought out twin fangs.

I thought our highlights glowed like a red aurora borealis over our heads. My momma, my dad, all four of our grand-parents, and that one friend saw it, but no one else noticed, it seemed. The highlights were a gift from our dad, from his Irish ancestry, as much as our toothy smiles were my momma's. My dad's red hair was thick and longish, the hair growing past his collar. My momma cut his hair.

I remember how my dad used to sit in the middle of our sunny yellow kitchen on a pink padded chair, my momma mov-ing around him, slooooowwly, bending to kiss him, rubbing his shoulders. Every few minutes he would swing a giant arm around her and pull her into his lap, and she would laugh and he would kiss her for a long time, her black hair forming a veil between them.

Annie and I would say, "Eeeew, gross!" and we would spin away on our white Mary Janes. I picked up our cat, Bob the Cat, and said to him, "Isn't that gross, Bob the Cat?" but in our hearts we didn't think it was gross.

Momma would take about five times as long cutting his hair as she would cutting anyone else's hair. Every time, when she was done, my dad would swoop her up into his arms, her pink heels flying into the air, and she would laugh, deep and rich, her hair swinging back. Dad would say to us, "Girls, your mother needs a nap. She's quite tired."

Our momma would giggle, he would kiss her again, we would say, "Eeeew, gross!" again, and they would disappear into their bedroom for hours, sometimes not coming out until it was time for dinner. Annie and I didn't mind. When our momma had her "nap," we were allowed to watch all the TV we wanted and pop popcorn on the stove.

Dad would come down first, grin, swing us around in the air, then make hamburgers. Every time. Hamburgers. Ketchup, mustard, lettuce, tomatoes. When Momma came down, always looking happy but sleepy tired, he'd kiss her again and we'd have dinner together on our back deck if it was warm, the waves of the sea a salty backdrop to our house by the sea. After dinner our dad would put on a record and we'd dance... waltzes and freestyle and dance routines. He loved to dance and he loved the sea because of its depth, its personality, its freedom.

He talked about how weather is "emotional," and how as a fisherman, and the owner of O'Shea's Fisheries, he kept a close eye on it. Stormy nights meant the weather was furious. A golden morning meant the weather was calm, waiting for a laugh. A strong wind meant the weather was agitated, worried, or in a hurry. "Weather is a woman and she's got a lot of feelings, so don't mess with her." Annie and I agreed not to mess with Weather.

Sometimes, when I saw my dad looking at me, those green eyes happy and twinkling, like the stars above our sea on a pitch-black night, I'd smile back and he'd recite an Irish poem with a thick Irish brogue.

> In the misty hills of Ireland
> A long, long time ago,
> There lived a lovely Irish lass
> Who loved her father so.
>
> One day he went to fetch some wood,
> But he did not soon return,
> And so his loving daughter's heart
> Was filled with great concern.

She searched for him throughout the day,
And when a fog came in
She wept, for she was fearful
They would never meet again.

Then suddenly, a little band
Of leprechauns came by.
They all were very saddened.
To hear the lovely maiden cry.

They asked if they might have a lock
Of her long and golden hair,
Then tied the silken strands across
A crooked limb with care.

'Twas a magic harp they'd made,
And when the maiden touched each strand,
The music led her father home
Across the misty land.

—Author Unknown

But when I saw Sherwinn watching us, those ants would attack, up and down my back, around my legs. It felt like those red ants were biting me inside, too. It was instinct taking over, I think, every part of me screaming to get away from Sherwinn.
Get Annie and yourself away from Sherwinn.
Hurry! Hurry!

My dad wasn't the only one reciting poetry to me.
He did, too. It was usually about snakes.
He liked snakes.

That night, at home, I picked up the manila envelope again and felt an attack of poor breathing, as if the air were stuck in my kidneys. He wanted $100,000 immediately or he'd release the photos. Of course he did.

How did I know it was a man? Because he misspelled the

words beauty parlor. As in, "I know you from the beauty parlor." He used two t's.

I don't take easily to blackmail. I don't think anyone does.
Damned if you do, damned if you don't.

Impossible situation.

I knew already I wasn't going to play this game, though. I
couldn't.

I knew what would happen if I didn't play.

I knew what would happen if I did.

Both bad results.

Very bad.

But I will not, *I will not,* allow a man to manipulate me, or
my life, again. Not again.

My breath was stuck.

6

You will learn a lot in a pink beauty parlor if you keep your ears open, including, but not limited to, how to get rid of a wart, marriage in all its glories and downfalls, dating, falling in lust versus love, stabbing your ex-boyfriend, all gossip, how men are so proud of their thingies, going broke, getting old, yeast treatments, how Jude Miller's husband has terrible gas, and Carla's boob job—yes, she did have one; that, the ladies knew for sure; why, they went to high school with her and she was flat as a plain pancake then.

The topics of discussion were wide ranging, frequently shouted over hair dryers.

Much of the talk was about men.

When old Mrs. Robisinni bellowed, at the exact moment her hair dryer shut off, "I had better sex with myself than I ever did with my husband," it echoed right through the parlor.

When Rochelle Menks said, "Ladies, how many of you have the art of faking it down to perfection?" and almost all the women raised their hands except for Twyla Thorpe, who said, "I never fake it. I make him keep going till I get my pleasing done," my momma would not explain to me what the ladies were talking about.

When Terralynn Forge said, "Men are like measles," I thought my momma was gonna fall down with laughter.

And when a woman came in who Carman knew was having an affair with the husband of a friend of hers, Carman dyed her brown hair white with black streaks. "Like a reverse skunk," Carman said proudly. "I have always enjoyed skunks. I can't wait to tell Bobbie."

But anytime you have a group of women together, you get fireworks, and Marie Elise's French Beauty Parlor had its fair share of fireworks.

Trudy Jo had a thunderbolt sort of temper. People said she got it from her grandma, who threw rocks. Sometimes Trudy Jo had to go out back and jump up and down and screech if a hair color or highlighting job set her off. She was not allowed to do the hair of Mrs. Berns or Ms. Loyola because twice she swore at their hair. "Dammit, why didn't you suck up that dye, hair?" she shrieked. Or, "You damn curls, I am going to cut you off and shove you up a nose if you don't lie flat! Lie flat! Lie flat!"

Then she dove into Shakespeare. "Cowards may die many times before their deaths, and I am not a coward! Lie flat hair! I will win this fight!"

Shell Dee for some reason liked to get into the thick of the body when she was doing highlights. I don't know why. "Did you know that if your man smokes, his penis can be shortened by an inch? An inch! So there's another reason to hide the cigs, Duffy!" and "Your brain is seventy-eight percent water! Water, not coffee, not beer, water!"

But those sisters did fight. One time Trudy Jo was so mad at Shell Dee, she sprayed hair spray right in her face. For revenge Shell Dee dumped shampoo on Trudy Jo's head. Trudy Jo retaliated with mousse, Shell Dee with cream rinse. It was a mess.

Another time the sisters were fighting because their oldest boys had decided to steal the principal's car and park it in the middle of Main Street about two in the morning after plastering it with pictures of naked ladies they got from a naughty magazine. Each screeched the other's son was "a bad influence" on their son. Trudy Jo threw a roller at her sister, who was giving Mrs. Cornwell a dark rinse at the time to cover up her white hair, and the roller broke the mirror. Mrs. Cornwell did not appreciate glass being added to her hair. She did not leave a tip.

Once a month, on the first Wednesday, my momma, Shell

Dee, Trudy Jo, and Carman had dinner together. The parlor paid for it. "To keep the peace," Momma said. A lot of wine was consumed.

One night Shell Dee danced on top of a bar and started a strip tease before my momma yanked her down. Her husband was not amused that the other men saw her yellow smiley face bra.

Another night Trudy Jo, who had had too many gin and tonics—"her weakness"—took her sister's dare, painted herself bright orange, donned a wig of red curls, and ran through the center of town. She was recognized by many because of her bottom. Everyone said that Trudy Jo had a "wriggly" bottom, and they knew it when they saw it.

One Wednesday night they drove off the Cape, then snuck into a railcar for a "train picnic," they called it, to spice up their usual restaurant scene. The train started to move unexpectedly and they ended up outside of Boston.

People learned quickly that the best day to come in for a perm was not the Thursday after the first Wednesday of the month.

But Marie Elise's French Beauty Parlor thrived. Anyone who went there came out new and improved. That was the goal, my momma said. "If you look special, you feel special." She gave me a kiss on my nose. "You are my special, Pink Girl."

She was my special momma and I loved her to pieces.

In that pink beauty parlor with the crystal chandeliers and gilded mirrors, that's where Annie and I spent the first years of our lives.

We loved it. Loved the women who loved us, loved the conversations, the friendships, we even loved it when Trudy Jo and Shell Dee got in cream rinse fights and when Carman drank champagne and burst into love songs. "*You are my one trrruu-ueee love . . . I cannot liiivvve without you . . .*"

But Annie won't go to beauty parlors again. "I can't go. I won't go. There are some things in life we need to get over, we need to suck it up and deal, but there are some things in life we can't get over and we should quit angsting about it and accept it. I have accepted that I will never walk into a beauty parlor again and the smell of hair spray will always make me miss Momma. Here's the scissors. Start cutting."

If she didn't want hair spray in her life, I got it. Snip snip.

A couple of weeks ago, in the middle of Grandma's kitchen, I cut Annie's hair.

She turned this way and that when I held a mirror up to her.

"I look like a horse."

"No, you don't." I laughed.

She pulled the mirror close to her hair. "Do you think our hair is getting redder as we age?"

I had noticed the same thing. I put my face next to hers and we studied ourselves in the mirror, that red sheen that so very few people could see. "Yes. It is."

"It's like Dad's still with us."

"That Irish blood." How I missed the man with the Irish blood.

"Yep. Probably where I got my temper."

"I'd definitely blame the Irish line for that. You are a spit-fire."

"And you aren't? When you're onstage, you're a volcano."

"Spewing rocks and lava, plumes of ash."

"Definitely the Irish in us."

"Yep," I agreed, but I did not say this: When I'm onstage, I'm a lie.

The man with the Irish blood was huge and had a huge laugh and a huge smile and a huge heart.

When I told him I wanted to be a detective, he bought me a fingerprint kit and we went around town taking people's finger-prints. "You're sharp and you're as determined as a bull dog, Madeline. You'd make an excellent detective." He said that in all seriousness, so I took myself seriously. I could do it because my dad said I could.

When Annie said she wanted to be a doctor, she got a doctor kit and he took her to the café to take people's blood pressure and check people's ears. "Annie, you're a compassionate person and you like learning about the human body. You'd make an excellent doctor." He said that in all seriousness, so she took herself seriously. She could do it because her dad said she could.

When I changed my mind and decided in second grade that I would be the president of the United States, he brought home a podium so I could "practice giving speeches that will rally the American public!" He helped me write my speeches, and when I gave them he draped an American flag around his shoulders and boomed, "Please welcome, the president of the United States of America, Madeline O'Shea!"

When Annie changed her mind and decided she wanted to be a sculptor, he bought her a chunk of clay and they made sculptures together in the garage. "Sculptures are the finest art there is," he told her. "They're reflective of what's going on at that time, in that place, in that artist's mind. They're full of talent and thought and planning. You're going to be a famous sculptor so let's take our time."

And they did.

Our dad made time for us. He had a fishing business and many boats. He had a wife he adored. He had two girls. He made us feel like we were the most important people on the planet. Because to him, we were.

He also loved being of Irish descent and regaled us with sayings and songs.

> May the luck of the Irish possess you.
> May the devil fly off with your worries.
> May God bless you forever and ever.

And . . . May you live to be a hundred years, with one extra year to repent!

We spent a lot of time dancing with our parents. Our dad taught us Irish poems, Irish songs, and Irish jigs. He loved life, he loved us, we knew that. I have carried that love with me my whole life.

7

"Good morning, Madeline." Tracy Shales, the host of *Portland Sunrise,* smiled at me, perky but not annoyingly so.

I could barely move my face. I'd been in makeup and had so much foundation on, I thought it would crack. They'd also straightened my hair.

"You have so much curl," the stylist gushed, wrapping it around her fingers, which gave me the shivers in a very, very bad way. "Let's leave it natural."

"No, thanks." I pulled the curl out of her hands before an avalanche of memories snuffed the life out of me.

She tried again. "But they're sexy, glossy."

"Absolutely no curls." I pulled them from her hand again, my breath getting stuck in my body, somewhere behind my intestines. I did not want curls. Never.

"Good morning, Tracy, thank you for having me." I smiled, and tried not to look directly at the cameras. The audience was filled with women, most between the ages of forty and sixty.

"As Oregon's and America's most loved life coach, we know you're busy, and we appreciate you being here."

"It's a pleasure." I hoped that the makeup would hide my fear. Not my fear of being on a television show, of which I had none, but the fear that lived in my stomach always like a knife-wielding vulture.

"So, Madeline." Tracy leaned toward me. We were in red

chairs facing each other. "Tell us about your work. What do you offer people?"

"I offer them a way to gain back their freakin' sanity."

"What do you mean, freakin' sanity?" She knew, I'd told her about it, we were part of a gig. The Tracy–Madeline gig.

"I mean that women's lives can be Godzilla awful whether through circumstance or lousy choices, and they need to get their sanity back and start living a kick-ass life with adventure and creativity and fun and deeper thought about who they are and where they're going."

"Lousy choices?"

"Sure. I know that will offend a lot of your viewers, Tracy, but it's true. Women often make lousy, blood-sucking, life-draining choices. They screw up. I've screwed up. We all screw up again. *Truth* is what I'm after with my clients. I tell them the truth. If they've made lousy choices, I'm honest. I lay it on the table and say, 'Hey, screwball girl, admit that your choice was so poor, you would have made a better decision if you were tossing back vodka tonics while standing on your head. Now how are you gonna turn this choice around?' Then we go through the steps she needs to take, and if she waffles or is vague, I tell her she needs a slug to the brain, to toughen up, and make those hard choices, even if it drags her bouncy fanny to a place she doesn't want be."

Tracy smiled. She liked an outspoken guest. "Don't be boring," she'd told me.

"My fanny doesn't like to be in a place where it's uncomfortable," Tracy said, wiggling in her seat. The audience laughed.

"No one's fanny likes to be there. We're protective about our fannies. We like our fannies and we don't like change if it's going to require us to rip our fannies apart. I believe in truth, direction, and encouragement. I call it Mind-Splitting Truth, Do-or-Die Direction, and Self-Examining Encouragement."

"Wow. Now that's edgy. Let's try one of those slang things on me."

"Okay, Tracy." I smiled, crossing my legs. Whoodalehoo. This part would be fun. Fun and fun, as Adriana would say.

Tracy and I had planned it *all* out. "How are things going at work?"

"You saw this morning in the makeup room how things are going, Madeline." She allowed a bit of a snip into her voice.

I sure had. After my makeup was done, I went to the bathroom carrying my purse to make sure my monthly curse was all taken care of. As I was coming back in, Thacker Blunt knocked and entered. I stepped back into the shadows so he couldn't see me while he ranted and raved like a sick bull. At the very start of the rant, I thought it would be exciting to whip out my mini, high-tech tape recorder and record him, so I did. When he stomped out I turned off my tape recorder and rejoined Tracy.

We agreed that today was the day to fry her boss like a gasping fish and then boil him alive.

"What I saw today, backstage, is that your boss, Thacker Blunt, the station manager, came in and proceeded to tell you that you had a 'big ass' and threatened to run your big ass out of town if you didn't figure out ways you could be younger and hipper on your show."

"That hurt." Tracy's eyes filled with tears. We had discussed this part. She was to be brave and strong and womanly, but definitely hurt. Almost mortally wounded!

I shoved my laughter back down my throat. "I recorded his diatribe."

"You did?!" Shocked face by Tracy, that brilliant actress!

"Let's listen to the tape so the audience can get an idea of the type of illegal harassment women, and sometimes men, face in the workplace. Folks, this is Thacker Blunt on the other end of the conversation. He's the station manager." I hit play.

The audience leaned forward, eager, a bit confused. The station manager had been recorded? They were playing it live, on air?

"Listen up, Tracy." Thacker's voice was rough and aggressive as it torpedoed around the studio. "This deal with Tawni strained things for me, got things stirred up, and I blame you, and I don't like your part in it."

"My part?" Tracy said.

I glanced at the audience. They were, no kidding, on the edges of their seats.

"Yes, your part." That was Thacker. I nodded at a gal backstage. She had a grudge against Thacker. She flashed a gigantosized photo of him behind us looking smarmy. "You know how you manipulated that situation."

"I didn't do anything to manipulate it," Tracy said.

"Yes, you did. I put Tawni on your show because we needed to appeal to young women and young men. We needed thin, we needed pretty. We needed sexy. Not you, and you kicked her out."

I heard gasps in the audience. Women do not like bimbos who are pushing them out of jobs and marriages.

"I didn't kick her out. The viewers could see that I was being kicked out."

"Look, Tracy. You're getting older. You're too heavy. You're not in style. We need to catch the young ones."

An audience member gasped and shouted, "What a prick!"

The audience at home heard that.

"So you want to fire me because of my age?"

"That's between you, me, and the chair."

"I could sue you for that comment."

"You could, but I would deny that I made it. Your word against mine."

The tension in that studio was thick and getting thicker. Like fury does when it comes alive.

"You're here because all your old, middle-aged menopausal friends called in to the show and saved your ass and Tawni made some unfortunate comments about fat women. I mean, shit, fat women shouldn't be wearing designer clothes. Their rolls make them look like hot dogs. It's gross."

One woman in the audience hissed, "He has a dick like a hot dog!"

The audience at home heard that, too.

"I thought Tawni's comments were rude and inappropriate."

"Who cares what you think? Fat women are fat women. Get the ratings up."

"The ratings are already up, Mr. Brilliant."

"That's the kind of back talk I don't need, dammit. Keep your old mouth shut. Don't tell me how to run my station."

"I don't like you calling me old."

"Don't tell me what to do. I'll tell *you* what to do. You're beneath me."

"I will never be beneath you. That would make me vomit."

There were audible rumblings of that growing fury in the audience, as if fury was becoming one roaring person.

"It would make me vomit, too, Tracy," a man in the audience told Tracy.

The audience at home heard that.

"Don't flatter yourself, Tracy. I'm warning you. You've got a live show in an hour and a half. I've got to go to a meeting across town, but I will watch a copy of your show this afternoon and we'll talk about ways you can reach a younger audience, despite your age, or I'll find a way to run your big ass out of town. *Run it out of town.*"

When the tape was over, the disgust and live fury was heavy in the studio. The only thing that cut through that silence like an ax was one man's slooowwww comment, "I'm gonna run that cowpoke out of town myself with my truck."

I winked at the sound man. He gave me a thumbs-up. Thacker had stolen his girlfriend. I leaned forward and said, "Tracy, you have a hostile work environment here."

"I know I do, but I don't want to have to go to court, hire an attorney. If I did that, I would never be hired again in this field." She dabbed at a tear. Such a brilliant actress!

I nodded sympathetically. "Here's the thing, Tracy. Tawni, the woman Thacker brought on to replace you, was terrifically unpopular with the viewers. But it's my understanding that she was his girlfriend. Is that true?" I knew it to be true. I had made a few calls. Including to Tawni herself, who was still steamin' mad. She'd heard of me, that got me into her confidence. 'He used me,' she'd whined. 'I thought he and I were going to get married! Go to New York together! Have our own show where I would be the host. That's what he said would happen! Now

I'm in Memphis! I'm an assistant to an assistant and my husband left me!"

"I can't comment on their *private* relationship," Tracy said meekly. "I don't want to repeat gossip, even if it's true."

"It's also my understanding that he has another girlfriend working here at this station and they keep their . . . um . . . *toys* . . . shall I say, in the third drawer of his desk."

Elizabeth had, with great fanfare, showed me the drawer today after Georgie called her. Thacker had told Elizabeth, when she was hired, "Ha. I'm movin' up in the world. I have a black on the show now. We need blacks so I don't look racist. Do you know another black who could work here? It doesn't matter if it's a male or female, I need another black. Or a Mexican. Get me one of those. A black or a Mexican."

"Here are your choices, Tracy. One, sue the station. Two, quit, move on with your life. Three, take things as they are. Pray he leaves. Which one will you do?"

"Hmmm." Tracy pretended to think. "Hmmm."

The audience members, those women between the ages of forty and sixty who are tired of taking crap. started voicing their opinions, loudly, until Fury was up and skipping around the room. "Sue him! Don't take that, Tracy. . . . Stand up for us women . . . stand up for yourself . . . woman power . . . prick men shouldn't run the show . . . I'm frothing I'm so mad!"

I snuck a peek at the audience. A frothing woman? Where was that one?

"You know"—Tracy sat up straight, got some fire in her eyes—"I'm sick of this. I'm sick of the girlfriends, the promotions for them because they're young and sexy, sick of the way he treats us women."

"You can't let him get away with it," I said. "Not only for you, but for all of us. What about the sisterhood? Do you want to let another sister be derailed because she's not young and thin enough, or do you want to make sure she gets fairness at work?"

Oh, whooee! The audience voiced their opinions. "He's an

asshole, Tracy.... Sue the station, sue for all of us women.... Girlfriend blondes should not replace other women because they're good in bed."

"Don't be a wimp, Tracy. Don't be walked on." I shook my fist, rallying the troops.

"You're right, I know you're right," she said, thinking deeply, pretending to gather her courage.

I let the pause hang heavy between us and the audience. "Come on, Tracy!" an audience member shouted. "Don't take his abuse! What are you? A woman or a wimp?"

I raised my eyebrows at that one. Nice line.

"Sue for the sisterhood, Tracy!" I cheered. "Women do not need to work in sexually hostile environments. Young girlfriends sleeping with the boss should not replace experienced women because they'll get naked. It's unlawful, it's unethical. It's not right!"

The audience hooted and trilled.

"I think ... I'm going to ..." Tracy drew out the tension. There was scattered applause, encouraging words ... Fury sprinting about.

"I'm going to ..." She tilted her chin up, brave woman, she.

I put both my fists in the air and flung them about, building the tension. "What do you think, audience?"

"Sue sue sue!" they chanted.

"Take no crap, Tracy! You don't want to get to be a ninety-year-old woman and look back and think you were a spaghetti noodle, do you?"

"Sue sue sue!" the audience chanted, ol' Fury blasting away.

"I'm going to ..." Tracy finally stood up, shoulders back, a tough expression on her face.

The audience stood up, too, continuing their chants.

Tracy pounded a fist into the air, then screamed, "I'm going to suuuuueeeee!"

Chaos. I leaped to my feet, arms up in a victory V. The audience went wild. The cameras later showed them on their feet, standing ovation, fists pumping.

"Thatta girl!" I thundered. "Now everyone!" I jumped onto my chair. "Put your fists in the air and yell, 'I am a woman who will take no crap!'"

Tracy and the audience yelled it back to me while Tracy joined me on her chair.

"Louder! You can do better!"

They yelled again, "I am a woman who will take no crap!"

"One more time!"

They hollered, "I am a woman who will take no crap!" Even the men yelled that they were women who would "take no crap." I saw that later on a replay on the news that night. The men bought into it full force, especially the white, middle-aged balding ones.

"I am more than my age!" I boomed.

They echoed it back, deep and passionate.

I grabbed my boobs. "I am more than my bra size!"

They screamed, and they grabbed their boobs. One man had heftier boobs than me.

"I am more than what a man thinks of my ass!"

They full-throttled that one.

"I am me! I am wonderful! I am smart! I kick butt! Say it with me! I. Kick. Butt!"

Whooee!

"I.Kick.Butt!"

"Now come on down here and show Tracy, who has battled cancer twice, who volunteers her time raising money for all sorts of hellaciously good charities, show her that she is one spectacular woman! Come on down, sisters and brothers!"

They poured off the risers, as I cued the sound man and the theme song from *Rocky* pounded the studio.

Da, Da, da, da-da-da, da-da, da, da-da-da . . .

Two men lifted her up on their shoulders, one with the boobs heftier than mine, and the other men and women crowded around and cheered as they paraded a victorious Tracy around the studio, the cameras catching all of it.

*   *   *

Thacker Blunt lost his job.

He didn't even get to return to the studio as the beefy security officers called by corporate blocked his way.

For evidentiary purposes only, the third drawer of his desk was opened by his colleagues with a hammer and a wrench.

This is what they found: Dominatrix kinds of treats. Leather vests. A whip. Handcuffs made of leather. Eatable underwear. A black male thong. Licorice. Condoms. A ballerina outfit. A black ski mask with eyeholes. A pair of red high heels, size 15. Hmmm. Who wore those?

Now, what bad person took photos of all that stuff and passed it around, I don't know. That's not my business. Someone else passed around pictures of Thacker and the young, leggy, snooty blonde, Tawni, and his girlfriend of today, also a young, leggy, snooty blonde. Who did that was also not my business. The often-promoted girlfriend lost her job. That was her business. Perhaps she should not have her married boyfriend wear red high heels.

It was rotten for someone else to take the photos of Thacker all dressed up in drag and whiz those around the office, too.

His wife filed for divorce. Rumor had it that all his stuff was removed from his house and shoved to the street. Then the wife poured gas over the whole pile and set it on fire. The fire made the news. Some said she was dancing around the fire like a witch casting spells, but I don't know if that's true.

The wife was arrested and charged. The charges were dropped.

Tracy's ratings, once again, skyrocketed.

As for me, my profile as a life coach skyrocketed, too.

Whoo-ha. Tracy slugged a home run.

My sisters, together, we have to slug sometimes.

Slug away, sisters, slug away.

I have issues with sex.

I know this.

I know why.

I have tried to get over it. I had a boyfriend in college once.

He couldn't get over my frozen body, the panic in my eyes, the startling lack of enthusiasm.

I didn't blame him. He said once, "I feel like I'm forcing you, and I can't do this again. I can't. I want a woman in my arm who wants to hug me, to kiss me, who wants me. Madeline, I mean, do you not like sex? Are you gay? I feel awful, I do. Do you like me at all?"

I liked him. He was kind and gentle.

No, I wasn't gay. No, I didn't like sex.

I'm a hypocritical life coach who counsels people periodically on their sex lives. A life coach's job isn't technically supposed to be counseling people on sex, but I specialize in relationships in your life, so it comes up on a regular basis. If it's a problem for my clients, it's a problem in their lives. So I address it as best I can if they bring it up.

I had a woman tell me that in the twenty-two years she's been married she's been making love to Jimmy Smits in her head every time instead of her husband. "If I think about my husband, I freeze up." Turns out the guy had the emotional openness of a porcupine, was often cranky, and had a history of lying. No wonder she froze up.

Another client, a man, said that he's too intimidated by his wife to have sex. "She constantly criticizes me about everything, my family, how I haven't been promoted enough, don't make enough money, I've gained too much weight, our neighbors have better cars . . . even during sex, she'll sigh and roll her eyes or not respond, lie there like she wants to get it over with, it's a chore, I'm a chore, and I feel like nothing, nothing, *nothing*."

I met his wife a couple of times in session. She was so cold I almost froze in my chair. Dyed red hair, slender, lots of makeup, perfect, and expensive clothes. She smiled pleasantly, but in the course of my conversation with her I found her to be manipulative, snobby, an expert at mind games, and shallow. Barbie meets a frozen snowwoman meets an "I Am Better Than Everyone" attitude. She refused to work and spent most of her time making herself beautiful. I advised divorce because of her terribleness, the snowwoman part, and he confessed he would rather commit suicide than be married to her for another week. They had no kids, so he divorced her and moved to Bend for the skiing. He's a lot happier now.

Another woman liked having a lot of sex. I don't know where the line of nymphomania starts and ends, but I think she was deep into the nympho side.

"I can't be with only one guy. One stud. I mean, I wear them out. I tell the guys I'm dating that I'm dating other guys. I like sex. I need several studs."

"And you like a lot of it."

"Yes." She smiled, sat up straight. She was wearing an innocent yellow dress and yellow heels. "I love it. I can't think sometimes unless I've had sex."

"No thinking at all?"

"Nope. Brain dries up. I have to have it in the morning before work to get myself together. And I like to have it in the middle of the day if I have a full schedule in the afternoon. An orgasm releases my stress, like a river floating it away."

I nodded, river-like.

"And I like to have it before I go to sleep or I can't sleep. I'm up all night! Is there something wrong with me?"

"Do you feel like something is wrong with you?"

"Sometimes I wonder if I'm addicted to sex, but it's a healthy addiction. I keep my job, I never sleep with anyone I work with, I don't sleep with friends' husbands or boyfriends, or anyone attached at all. But I have a few single men on the side."

"A few?"

She grinned, fiddled with her pearl necklace. "Yes, I love them all. They love me. We have fun. It's not serious. I think of them as my morning, noon, and night orgasms."

"Don't you mean your morning, noon, and night men?"

"No, no, my, no." She grinned again, fiddled with her pearl earrings. She looked so sweet! "They're my orgasms."

"So these men equal orgasms? Do they know that's all they are to you? Is that fair to them? Are they getting hurt in this process? Do they feel used?"

"I'm respectful. I don't look at them and say, 'Hello, Morning

Orgasm! Hello, Lunchtime Orgasm!' It's not like that. We need each other at different times."

"Aren't you at work at noon?"

"Yes, but I leave and meet my afternoon orgasm."

"At his house?"

"No."

"At your house, a hotel?"

"It would be too committed to meet in either place. We usually meet at a Starbucks. In one of the restrooms. Then we have a drink together. I like their sandwiches and their yogurts, too. Then I go back to work."

She smiled.

She's a cardiac surgeon.

She's apparently quite talented.

Amazing what an orgasm can do for a woman.

So I'll tell people what to do about sex.

As if I know what I'm talking about.

I am a hypocrite. I hate that part of myself.

That "other" part.

I thought of the man I used to know who liked snakes. Seeing him on TV awhile ago had brought so much rushing back.

I ignored the voice that told me I was a slut.

"Keith Stein on the phone, Madeline," Georgie called. "And Stanley wishes you a tranquil day."

Stanley barked.

I picked up the phone.

"We can't do anything about the article, Madeline. They're determined to print it. It's the anniversary of the trial. She's interviewing everyone—both judges; some of the jurors; the people in Cape Cod; relatives of Sherwinn, Gavin, and Pauly; even Pauly's son, apparently. And she wants to talk to you, Annie, and your grandparents, as you know."

I felt myself boil once again. I haven't hidden that part of my life, but neither have I talked about it. It happened years ago. It was nationwide news then, but Annie and I were able to slip into life here in Oregon with few people knowing that we were

Marie Elise O'Shea's daughters. By the time we arrived, many months after her trial, the media was no longer interested in us.

Annie wasn't speaking when we arrived in Oregon; she was half-comatose, stuck in her own world, barely moving mentally or physically, certainly not crying, Annie never cries. I was raging, destructive, hurting.

Grandma and Granddad's love, patience, and attention was unending. After tending to the animals here, the sheep, the dogs, and cats, Annie started talking again, and after hundreds of hours of pounding horseback rides, almost obsessive playing of my violin, and the violin in my head playing softly almost nonstop, I began to stop wishing I were dead.

Annie didn't play the piano, though. Not a key. Even though Granddad and Grandma encouraged her to. She refused. "The piano is dead for me."

The thought of dealing with what happened again via a magazine article . . . of reliving it . . . the trials, the gunshots that to this day I *still* hear in my head, Marie Elise's French Beauty Parlor . . . the pain it would bring to my family. I hated that reporter.

I hated her. It's not personal.

Hate kills you.

And I still hated *them*. After all these years, I still hated them.

I felt my rage, hot, simmering, overwhelming, slicing up my breathing into bits.

When I got home, I opened the drawer where I'd flung the manila envelope. There it was. My emotional demise.

Sherwinn pretended he was nice in front of our momma. Gifts of necklaces with heart lockets, or rings with big pink stones from the five-and-dime, hair ribbons, jewelry boxes.

We never believed he was nice. Never.

We never believed he was kind. Never.

Kids can sniff out this type of deceit in adults. They sniff it.

We did believe him when he told us we were bad girls, that he would tell everyone.

We believed him when he said he would kill our momma.

We believed him because he wielded a knife, sometimes under our chins. He pricked me once and I bled. He made me tell my momma I fell from the tree house my dad built us.

I lied to my momma.

Sherwinn appeared normal to many people. He was not normal.

I hesitated at my closet with no doors the next morning. Usually, I pull out yet another suit, my modern armor, and appropriate, sedate jewelry and low-heeled shoes.

When Annie and I were younger, we wore the funniest outfits.

We're only fifteen months apart, and my momma told us once that from a very young age we had "firm opinions" about what we were going to wear. "I never knew what the two of you would walk out in." She kissed us both. "I still don't know what you two are going to wear, but I look forward to it each morning. Your creativity is sunshine to my day."

One year Annie and I decided to wear our gauzy pink ballerina skirts from Grandma every day, no matter what. I was in first grade, she was a kindergartner, and we pirouetted through that year.

Our grizzly bear outfit phase followed that, where we wore only our grizzly bear outfits for two months. The grizzlies were sewn for us by Grandma, and we spent a lot of time growling at each other and "dancing like bears." Each bear had a pink heart on its chest.

When I was in third grade, Annie and I decided to wear glittery pink headbands on Mondays; kimonos on Tuesdays, which we paired with our red cowboy boots; our sequined pink poodle skirts on Wednesdays; our Wonder Woman outfits on Thursdays; and all black with pink tennis shoes on Fridays.

Sometimes the kids giggled, but we didn't care. We were the Pink Girls! Our momma was Marie Elise and our dad was Big Luke! If we were lucky, we'd start a trend and other kids would pick up on our styles.

Before taking us exploring on the beach one time, our dad cut out whales from cardboard and we painted them. Momma pushed strings through the top and we wore them all day long. Even our dad wore a cardboard whale around his neck.

There are photos of Annie and me, standing with our dad wearing hats made out of sticks and wrapped in twine. I am holding Bob the Cat. One sunny day, when the weather was benevolent, we made dresses of white butcher paper and colored flowers with rainbows all over them. We wore only underwear and striped socks beneath. We made a dress for Dad, too.

Style we had. Funny, quirky, never-boring style.

I thought of my suits.

No style.

I thought of my hair.

No style.

I pulled my mercilessly straightened hair back off my face and secured it with a boring clip. My suits, my hair, my discreet, boring jewelry. All armor.

My armor is like my house. It's expensive. It's modern. It's a show. A show to all that I have made it.

It's a battle within, a battle outside.

Every day, a battle. A battle to win, to achieve, to convince myself that I am someone. A battle against the past and what happened, a battle against a maniacal giggle, a cage, and a camera.

Click, click, click.

None of the Giordano sisters' cats were feeling healthy.

"Princess Anastasia feels restless, unsettled," Adriana said, peeking woefully into her cat's basket. Princess Anastasia was wearing a shiny red bow. The red matched Adriana's red, low-necked gown, more appropriate for a ball. She made a spitting sound. The cat, not Adriana.

"Bee La La is sad. The sadness comes upon her sometimes and drags her deep, deep down to where she feels she can't get out and be normal again," Bella said, wringing her hands.

"Poor Bee La La! Am I a bad mother?" Bee La La was wearing a purple bow, which matched Bella's four-inch designer heels. She rolled her eyes at me, I swear she did. The cat, not Bella.

"Candy Stripe is grieving. I don't know why, but she is," Carlotta said, clucking her tongue. "It's loss. It's loneliness, I know it." She petted the napping cat. Candy Stripe was wearing a striped blue and white bow. The blue matched the blue silk sarong wrapped around Carlotta's skinny frame.

I stared at all three ladies sitting around my table. Wealthy. Expensive. Spoiled. Coiffed to within a millimeter of their fake eyelashes.

Lost. Purposeless. Shallow. Bored, but don't get it.

"Ladies, we're going to play 'I Wish'." I handed each one of them a glittery, purple magic wand.

"Your royal highness," Adriana said, bowing at the waist.

"Goody! I love being a princess," Bella said. "Princess me!"

"Sometimes we need to say out loud what we wish to have in life," I said.

"Like one more pair of Jimmy Choos," Carlotta gushed. "The new ones with the dots that look like miniature cheetah paw prints."

"Not exactly," I said. I eyed all of them. We'd had our fun. Let's see what else was behind these ladies. "When you say, 'I wish,' what you're trying to do is go deep. Way deep into your inner desires and dreams. It's the O'Shea Be Honest With Yourself, You Liar plan."

"I understand," Adriana said. "Go deep into our minds and think about what we really wish for, what we really want. Like when we buy our new Porsches next month. Do we all really want to buy the same color? Maybe we should buy different colors."

Bella sucked in her breath.

Carlotta made a squeaking noise.

"To show our personality," Adriana said.

"But," Bella said, "we *are* a personality. We're the Giordano sisters."

"That's right. Adriana, Bella, Carlotta. We're one. We're a unit. The unit," Carlotta said, bewildered.

"But should the unit have different color Porsches? It's a thought, an idea, a bug in our ears," Adriana said, hugging herself tight.

Bella rolled her lips in tight. Carlotta tapped her fingernails together, worried. This was new! Individualism? A rebel among them?

"Thinking beyond the Porsches," I said, before things degenerated, "when you play 'I Wish,' the real goal is to figure out who you are, what you're made of, what you want your future to look like, what you wish *didn't* happen to you, maybe. We're trying to figure out what you want for your life."

"What I want for my life? We're thinking about a pool," Bella said.

"With two curlicue slides!" Carlotta added.

"No, not like that," I said. "Not stuff."

"Hmmm," Adriana said, plucking at her red gown. "Okay! I think I get it. Let's do it, girls! Let's play 'I Wish'!"

Bella gave a cheerleader-type cheer, one leg out, her metallic jumpsuit so shiny.

Carlotta kicked up her black knee-high leather boots. "Hee-haw!"

"All right, I'll start, then I'll skip myself and you three go round and round. Each one of your sentences must start with 'I Wish.' Got it? You can't interrupt each other. You can't add anything. You can't start chatting. Now think, ladies. I wish . . ." I paused, trying to settle my mind. There was so much to wish for. "I wish I understood what my grandma was talking about when she talks about the blood. I wish that her dementia would clear so I would know what happened to her as a young woman."

The sisters gaped at me.

"My!" Adriana said, fingering her fur coat, which she'd folded onto her lap. "I didn't know we were going into . . . *emotions* . . . sadness and all that!"

"I thought we were going to talk about next season's fashion, maybe what restaurant we want to visit during our trip to Paris, or if yellow is too bold for high heels," Bella said.

"Let's go, ladies," I prodded.

I waited in the silence that followed while all three petted their cats. Princess Anastasia made that spitting sound. Bee La La rolled her eyes. Candy Stripe woke up and yawned.

I continued to wait.

Waited more.

"I wish that Favio had delivered that glass sculpture on time. I died waiting for it!" Carlotta said.

"I wish that my manicurist never went on vacation! I miss the butterflies she paints on my nails!" Adriana said.

"I wish that my *favorite* lipstick from Dominique had not been discontinued. I tried to sue them, but my lawyer said it would never work," Bella said.

"I wish I were wearing my pink padded bra." Carlotta grabbed her boobs and stared down at them. "This one doesn't have enough lift, up and in, and I—"

"We should go bra shopping!" Adriana said.

"Excellent!" Bella enthused. "We'll have a Giordano sister bra day and we'll go for a salad and soup and a red wine lunch and we'll—"

I stomped both feet. "No. Stop. Stop being shallow, stop being superficial!"

The three of them sat straight up, as if I'd punched them in their diamond necklaces.

"Stop avoiding depth and sincerity in your conversations. Be honest. Close your eyes, dig deep, bring up what you're upset about, what you worry about. Let go of all this artificial, exhausting prancing about."

They twitched and fidgeted, opened and closed their eyes, tapped their nails, swung their expensive shoes, until they finally settled down.

I waited. I was rather taken aback when I heard Adriana sniffle. Bella wiped a tear. Carlotta brought a hankie out of her purse and blew her nose. "I wish we had had a mom who wasn't always upstairs in bed, drunk. I wish we didn't have so many maids raising us, that she could have done it, made our lunches, met us after school. I wish we weren't screamed at as much as we were. Nothing we did was right."

"Nothing," Adriana said.

"Not a thing," Bella said.

"I wish that Daddy hadn't yelled at her, shoved her against walls, hit her . . ."

"Smashed her face into the sink that time . . ."

"Yanked her down the hall by her hair. . . . She never grew hair there again."

"Held that gun to her head that time by the fireplace . . ."

"I wish that Daddy hadn't lived with us, because he scared Mom so badly she cried all the time."

"I wish he hadn't lived at all."

"I wish he'd died."

Whoa!

"I wish she hadn't had a nervous breakdown."

"I wish she had taken us and run. I wish she had protected us. I wish she would have stood up to him, but she drank too much."

"She drank to drown herself."

"I wish there weren't all those scary men around and that I didn't see Daddy out in the guest house with them and I wish I hadn't heard screams or seen those two bodies dragged out of there and I wish I hadn't read the paper about the men who died and were found in the river, because I remember seeing them at the guest house . . ."

"But before Mom died—"

"Yes, before she died, she told us where the money was, where the accounts were."

"You see"—Adriana held out her wrists—"Diamonds. From Daddy. Sort of. We consider them gifts from Daddy for the yelling, the guns—"

"The embarrassment at school when kids called us Mafia Queens—"

"And how horrible it was when everyone said that Daddy had Quanta's father killed."

"And Anthony's dad, too."

"And maybe Horatio's. We weren't clear on him."

Double whoa.

"You see, Madeline, the more we spend, the more we laugh. Daddy's never getting out of prison. Never," Bella said, for once the fake smile gone, replaced by a steely gaze as she spoke out of turn for the first time. "We send him photos of us with our cars and clothes and boats and fancy vacations. It pisses him off."

"We're spending his money, all of it," Carlotta said, her face tight. "Think of it as our revenge."

Adriana wiped her tears, as did Bella and Carlotta.

I reached for their hands, they reached for mine, and we all held hands together while they cried. Money does not protect from neglect and abuse. It doesn't.

Adriana dug in her purse. "I don't want to play this 'I Wish' game anymore." She opened a box of very spendy chocolates. "These chocolates cost one hundred dollars. Thanks, Daddy!" She dropped it on the table, and they were gone within minutes. They were soft and delicious—thick dark chocolate, white chocolate, peppermint chocolate, lemon-tinged chocolate.

"Thanks, Daddy," Bella muttered. "You fucker."

"Thanks, Daddy," Carlotta said, smashing a fist on the table. "*I hate you.*"

I received another letter. Plain manila envelope.

All three photos were of me alone. I was naked.

I thought of Annie. She had not received a letter, to my knowledge. I laughed, bitterly, like my laugh had gotten stuck in a bottle of rotted limes, thinking that maybe she had gotten letters and hadn't told me. That was a definite possibility. I didn't want Annie to know, and she would feel the same way about me.

I would have to tell her. She would rip out her chain saw and demolish a thick log. She might scream a bit as the wood chips went flying, her roar slashing through the day like hate on super-sonic speed.

I would have to tell Granddad.

He would curl up and wilt, at least on the inside. On the out-side, he'd put his chin up, stand up straight, stuff his ever-present grief for his daughter, son-in-law, and granddaughters back into his spine, and bear it. Next he would throw a consid-erable amount of money into doing whatever it took to hunt down and locate the blackmailer and punish him, all the while comforting us, reassuring us.

My granddad was a *man*, in every sense of the word.

But it wouldn't put an end to all this, I knew that.

I picked up my violin with shaking hands. I practiced Schu-bert's Sonatina in D Major, then, rebel violinist that I am, I played "The Irish Washerwoman" and "Drowsy Maggie," two of my dad's favorite Irish fiddle tunes.

They brought little comfort.

That night, after I lifted my head once again from the porce-lain goddess, I turned off the lights in my modern house that I don't like, lit candles, watched the city lights flicker, and listened to an orchestra playing a Beethoven symphony in my head.

The first time I heard violin music was on my third birthday. I remember hearing a full orchestra when I blew out my candles. I clapped for the music, because I loved it, and everyone thought it was "darling" that I clapped after blowing out my own can-dles.

I realized I was the only one hearing the music when I was about four and on the teeter-totter our dad had built for Annie and me in our backyard. She was three. We went up and down, and each time we were up, the sea stretched way out in front of us. We called it the Sea Saw.

I said to Annie, "Do you like that song?"

She looked at me, puzzled, and said, "What song?"

"That song!"

"There no song!"

"I mean, the music! The violins!"

"There no violins."

"Yes, there is, Annie, listen."

She listened. "I not hear anything."

"Listen, Annie, listen!"

She shook her head. "I like piano." Annie was already playing the piano. She loved it. Our dad taught her.

"Stop being mean, Annie."

"No music, Madeline, only wind. I hear wind, you hear wind?"

I couldn't hear the wind over the violins.

Sometimes it was one violin. It would start and stop, begin again, as if someone was practicing, trying to get every note right. Sometimes I would feel the utter sadness of the musician, the piercing grief, or a freeing happiness. Oftentimes, there were two violins, three violins, more maybe, playing off each other, playing together, sometimes a full orchestra with flutes, clarinets, French horns, oboes, basses, trumpets. There was silence between the pieces, as if the violinist was thinking, or mourning, gathering himself.

As I got older, and continued to practice for long hours, I would often recognize the music, both old and contemporary, but sometimes I knew that the violinist had composed his own work.

I do not hear the music constantly. In fact, I usually don't hear it for more than an hour or two in a twenty-four hour time frame; often I don't hear it for days and days. I can shut it off, too; I'll get distracted, and it will go. Sometimes it's loud, sometimes muted. I'll hear it for a few minutes here and there, maybe in the morning and late evening, or at stressful or joyful times.

It does not interfere with my life in any way. I don't feel that it's an intruder. Rather, I believe it is a comfort to me, a companion, a friend, if that does not make me sound too insane. It is there, and I am there with it. But where is it from? My ancestors? Is it a hereditary thing? A gift? A mini mental illness played out via music? My own mind constantly playing a violin? Is it savant-like? It's extraordinary, there's no doubt about that. Is it from God? A gift from Him? I prefer the latter.

THE FIRST DAY OF THE REST OF MY LIFE 109

I don't know why there are so many secrets around my scratched and dented violin. I don't know why it feels like I am practicing with another violinist, as if we are together, though he or she is invisible. *Why me?*

It is. That's it. It is as it is.

I continued practicing my violin that night, sometimes hearing a lone violinist with me. I played until two in the morning. I went to sleep in my living room, on the floor, thoughts of dank shacks, pepperoni pizza, and sticky hands trolling through my nightmares. In the corners of my dark dreams, the violins soared, dipped, and crashed.

"Although you two both already know about my and your grandma's will, we are here to finalize a few things for when I die in twenty years," Granddad said, then winked at us.

Annie and I smiled, but it was strained. Granddad had needed assistance getting in and out of the car, his body trembling, and walking clearly exhausted him. We had helped him into the law offices of Hernandez and Associates in downtown Portland, a firm of forty-five attorneys, about five minutes from my own office.

Max Hernandez himself, the owner of the law firm, had been waiting eagerly on the sidewalk to help us in. He had offered repeatedly to drive out to The Lavender Farm to make it easier for Granddad, but Granddad had insisted on coming downtown. "I want to see Max's offices again. I'm so proud of that man."

When Max saw Granddad, he enveloped him in a huge hug, Max's face crumpling with emotion that he did not bother to hide. Max's parents had worked for Grandma and Granddad for decades.

"Your grandma and granddad told me," Max confided in me years ago, his voice breaking, "that if I got good grades in high school, they'd put me through any college I could get into. I got straight As. They kept their word. They said it was a gift to my parents. Man, Madeline, my parents cried when I graduated from high school, something they never did. When I graduated from Cornell, they didn't stop crying for days. I was interested in the law, and your grandparents told me to apply to law school. They told me they'd pay for whatever a scholarship wouldn't. They kept their word. When I graduated from law school, my parents didn't stop crying for a week." Max started crying, wiping his eyes. "I love your granddad and your grandma. *Love them.* I'd do anything for them. You know my parents are retired, but he lets them live in that house on your farm for free. Remodeled their kitchen five years ago."

My granddad tapped the shiny, wood table in Max's expansive corner office with the tips of his fingers. "You two know the land is yours, and we have left you both a sum of money that will be paid to you monthly for the rest of your lives."

"We told you not to do that, it's not necessary," I said. "Give it away, Granddad."

"We don't need it," Annie echoed. "My trips to Fiji are at a bargain rate." She winked at me.

When parents die, especially when the children are young, and the parents have life insurance and two successful businesses, the kids become rich overnight. In money, only. In life, in the heart, they become the poorest people.

"My dears, we have been through this before. You know that, for my own mental peace, and for your grandma's mental peace, the peace she would have if she were still fully with us, we must know that for the rest of your lives, no matter what happens, you'll be provided for."

I caught my tears with my fingers. It wasn't the money that made me cry, it was what was behind the money, which was, simply, love.

"Now, we have been lucky in business and with your grandma's books," he said, his face so pale. "Very lucky. We are here today, with our good friend, Max, because you two are the co-executors, and after I die I want the money to continue to be donated to the people and organizations that we give to now." He nodded at Max. "Go ahead."

Max went ahead with a review of our grandparents' money invested in the grocery store chain, land, cash, stock, investments, Grandma's royalties, and so on.

It was quite a list. It was an impressive sum of money. About enough to buy a country.

Then Max discussed the donations that Granddad had outlined we make, when, and in what amount for years into the future. The beneficiaries included, but weren't limited to, a children's cancer association, scholarship money for needy students, an Alzheimer's group, money for libraries and for young students to be exposed to the arts, a sum so generous to Youth Avenues they would be thriving for decades, and a food bank. He had also left money tied up in his businesses for his employees and their children, including full college scholarships.

"Girls," Granddad said, reaching for both of our hands, his eyes suddenly desperate, plaintive, beseeching. "You must continue our legacy of giving, you must promise me that."

"We will," I said.

"You must pay attention to the guidelines, along with Max." His hands shook like fragile birds, scared, out of the nest, unprotected.

"We'll do it, don't worry at all. . . ."

"Not a dollar must be wasted. I must help as many people as I can, even after my death."

The birds intertwined between his fingers, in and out.

"We'll carry on your legacy. . . ."

He abruptly got up. Annie, Max, and I immediately stood to help him, but he waved us away, the birds dismissive, and hobbled toward the windows.

"Granddad," Annie said. "We're your grandchildren, we're *you*. We'll do as you ask. Please, Granddad, it makes me upset when I see you upset."

"Every detail, Mr. Laurent," Max said, honesty ringing every note in his voice. "Every detail. I will handle it personally with Annie and Madeline. You know I owe you everything, sir."

The shaky, fragile birds came to rest on the windows, still, for a moment, as Granddad said, almost to himself, "I must atone. Even after I die. I must atone."

Annie, Max, and I stopped, as if a wall of ice had suddenly appeared between us and him, unrelenting. *He must atone?*

"You must atone?" Annie said. "For what? For what must you atone?"

Granddad's eyes were fixed on the skyscrapers and beyond, not seeing anything, and I knew he was somewhere we couldn't go, couldn't join him. It reminded me of the place my momma used to go when she played her violin outside and spoke to someone in French.

"For what, Granddad?" Annie persevered. "What do you need to atone for?"

"But nothing I can do will atone for what I did," he whispered. "Nothing." The fragile birds went to his head, pressing against his temples. "I hope God grants me forgiveness, because I do not deserve it."

"Granddad!" Annie said.

"Sir!" Max begged, distraught.

"Granddad, God will forgive you anything, you're wonderful." *What was going on?*

At that he whipped around, so quick for a very old man. "No, I am not wonderful." His face twisted, flushed. "No, I am not wonderful. I am an awful man. A terrible man. I am not a man by any definition. I am unworthy, I am a betrayer, I am a traitor—" He stopped, his lips slamming together, his eyes not with us any longer, focused once again somewhere else, a land of pain.

"No, sir!" Max argued.

I opened my mouth but could not respond. Annie made a choking sound.

"Granddad, please, what are you talking about? What?" Annie said. "You've never hurt anyone in your entire life, ever—"

He held up a hand. Stop. "Yes." His voice gentled, defeated. "Yes, I have. I don't want to speak of it, but my whole life . . . *my whole life . . .*"

We were stunned to see tears streaming from his tired, despairing eyes. "My whole life I have tried to atone for my unforgiveable act, a desperate act in desperate times. It has followed me, like a curse, as it should. I have not had one moment's peace, not one moment's rest, and I don't deserve it. I am ashamed, so ashamed. It is your job, Annie, Madeline, Max, to make sure that my atonement is complete. You will do that, yes?"

We all nodded, exchanging horrified glances, as a tiny iceberg melted down my spine. For the life of me, I had no idea what he needed to atone for, but I knew Annie and I would go to our own graves knowing we had done what our grandparents had wanted us to do with their fortune.

He slumped into a chair, the birds clasped together tightly in front of him, quiet, not fluttering, dead now.

He would say nothing more, not a word, as the three of us rushed to him, kneeled, anguished, the wall of ice between us.

One thing was clear, though: Our granddad was tortured. Absolutely tortured.

I know what it's like to be tortured by guilt. In fact, guilt stalks me, like some black leopard intent on its prey, and I am the prey.

Why the guilt? Because I didn't protect Annie.

I was twelve years old. Rationally, I know I can't blame myself, I know that.

But, you see, what the head knows and what the heart accepts are two different things.

I was the big sister. I was responsible for her. I should have used a knife. I should have run away with her.

Click, click, click.

I should have, I should have, I should have.

"You're trying to get me tipsy so you can take advantage of my innocence," Grandma said to Granddad as he opened a bottle of wine.

"I would never do that, my darling," he said, winking at her.

"I know, sexy man." She waved her hand, a ruby bracelet from Granddad dwarfing her slender wrist. "But I wish you would!" She was wearing a purple ball gown, her hair curling down to her shoulders, her makeup exquisite. She had donned a pretty good push-up bra, too, and her cleavage was up and out there.

"You look radiant, Grandma," I told her honestly.

"I do it for him," she whispered to me, one hand half covering her mouth, although the three of us could hear her clear as a tolling bell. "I dress up for my husband. Isn't he handsome? He makes me tingle."

"He sure is, Grandma."

"You minx!" Grandma said to Granddad. "You're irresistible!"

Nola had made us her famous calzone and fruit salad, then left for her book group. Annie and I set the dining room table with Grandma's china with the tiny blue flowers, lit about ten tea candles, and took the red roses that Granddad had bought Grandma, trimmed them down, and spread them amidst three crystal vases.

On the wall was one of Grandma's longest paintings. It was a family of black swans, all at dinner at a polished table exactly like ours, with a chandelier exactly like ours, wearing their finest, most shimmery clothes. They were eating stacks of pancakes. Two swans were leaning together, collapsed in their laugher; two others were clearly arguing, one brandishing a pancake on a fork; and one boy swan had thrown a pancake at his sister swan. There were grandparent swans and two twin baby girl swans in high chairs. That painting was in one of her most popular children's books ever.

While Grandma tittered and giggled while she ate her calzone, Granddad, Annie, and I talked about the farm, the two coyotes Granddad had seen on his morning walk, how the gazebo needed another coat of white paint, the rainbow that had arched over the hills, Annie's work with a farmer who had llamas, and Granddad's stores—they were opening three more this year.

Afterward, Granddad kissed all of us. "It's been a long day. I'm going to go and lie down, ladies."

Grandma turned her cheek up for his kiss and winked at him,

so coy. "I'll be in in a minute, dear, don't you worry. Can you wait?"

"Yes, my darling."

"I won't be long." She blew him another kiss. "My fires are on fire!"

I smothered a chuckle, and Annie did the same.

"But I'm always on fire for you," she went on. "Ever since I was a young lady, I knew you were the man for me. Tall, passionate . . ." She giggled and whispered, "Sexy!"

"Thank you, Emmanuelle," Granddad said, as he bowed slightly.

"My flames are leaping, my libido is on high, my lust surrounds me," Grandma went on with that sweet, vacant smile. "But only for you, the man I have slept with thousands of times. Your touch still stirs me." She patted her heart, and then, turning a bit, as if to hide her movements from Annie and I, she pointed to the nether regions of her crossed legs. "Right here, too," she declared.

I smothered another chuckle. They were so dear. Their love passionate, unending, dedicated.

My granddad smiled again, his smart eyes softening. He loved my grandma to the core, as my dad had loved my momma. Grandma was expressing what she'd always expressed to him, only when she was sane she knew to do it privately. But still, who was around? Only his beloved granddaughters who knew, and understood, this love they had together.

She pointed again. "In the private spot! I still have it for you, and I'm going to let you take a peek in a few minutes."

Granddad kissed both her cheeks, his hands cupping her smiling face. "I'd like that peek. Thank you, my dear."

"Anything for you, my protector, my friend, my lover!" She glanced at us, halfway covered her mouth and whispered to our granddad, "You are a marvelous lover! Marvelous and creative and—"

Apparently that was a tad bit too graphic for our proper granddad, because he kissed her on the mouth as she smiled, and he said, "You all enjoy your evening."

"Good night, Granddad," Annie and I called. Annie had been in Fiji recently. There were still half-moon circles under her eyes. I'd asked her how her trip was. "It was explosive," she'd told me.

About four states away a breeder, a man notorious for the horrendous conditions in his kennels, had lost his house. Apparently the heating system blew up and the house was blasted to bits. Strange that it blew up as that state was having a heat wave. . . .

"Good night, lover!" Grandma said. "I looovee you!"

After Granddad left, Grandma turned to us and said, matter-of-factly, "He doesn't know that I know about the other family and the candles that killed them. We had candles, too. From my parents when we left Germany, and from my grandparents who left Russia. The other family had candles, too."

"What other family?" Annie asked, dropping a chunk of bread.

"I remember them. They were a nice family. A father, a mother, a young girl and boy, a teenage girl. Like us. It was them, they were supposed to go." She took her finger and outlined one of the blue flowers on the china.

Annie raised her eyebrows at me, while I felt the blood rush down my body like a flood was carrying it away and putting it in my feet.

"Where were they supposed to go?" I asked.

"They were supposed to go to the Land of the Swans, not us. Not us. He doesn't know I know. It's a secret. I didn't know until afterward." Her voice crackled, and I knew her mood was changing rapidly.

"What secret, Grandma?"

She gazed at me with two types of vacant expressions. One said, "I don't know what's going on anymore," and the other said, "This memory is for me only. You're not in it, you can't come in."

"There's a lot of secrets." She wiped the tears off her cheeks as they spurted and ran over the lines of age on her face. "And they're all sad, they're all sad! I can't bear it." She thumped her heart. "I can't bear it! And he, he has had to live with this! Eating him up. Eating him!"

I took a deep breath, and so did Annie; I heard it. This was exactly what Granddad had talked about today at Max's.

I reached out a hand and held hers. "It's okay, Grandma, it's okay."

"No, it's not okay," she argued, her head wobbling. "It's not okay. Nothing is okay. They're gone. Everybody's gone. They're all gone. Your violin knows it. I can see the death on your violin."

"Would you like to go and walk by the lavender tonight? I'll play my violin for you?"

"No, no, I don't. I can't be happy by the lavender or by the palaces or the leprechauns, I can't."

"Why, Grandma? Why can't you be happy?"

"Because . . ." She burst into broken sobs, her slim shoulders shaking. "You know why."

"No, I don't know why." I wasn't sure I wanted to know. Was this real? Was it true?

"You know why I can't be happy."

"Tell me again."

She spoke through her wrenching, terrible sobs. "I can't be happy"—she leaned over her china plate with the tiny blue flowers and wrenched out, her old voice breaking—"because he left them there and he knew they would die."

The blood finished pooling at my feet. Annie made a choking sound.

"He left them there to die. Shot and burned or smashed."

Shot and burned or smashed?

"They died, or we died. But I didn't know, only he knew. He was a husband then. There were no more swans to take them off. The swans were gone by then."

I sagged. What on earth was Grandma talking about?

"We ran away. We ran away as fast as we could. Run, run, run, escape. Use the wings to go over the mountains! Bring her violin! Don't smash it!" She threw her hands in the air, then wrapped them around her thin body. "Wipe the blood off! It's all over."

She rocked back and forth, back and forth, back and forth.

"Yes, we killed them. Them for us. The candles burned their throats black."

"Who, Grandma? Who did you kill?" Surely, she wasn't serious. She was a storyteller, a gifted storyteller.

"Black and crispy were their throats! Run! Run! You have to get away from the candles or they'll set fire to your castle and the drawbridge will be ash and you will be incinerated!"

Good Lord.

"Good-bye. Good-bye, you are gone." She picked up her teacup, turned it over, and placed both hands over it. "No breath in them. Dead."

After Annie and I watched our granddad put Grandma to bed, not interfering in their love at all, I took a walk to the gazebo, carrying my violin, the moon shining down intermittently through the clouds. My dad would say it was a shy moon tonight. I caught glimpses of stars here and there, the Big Dipper, the Little Dipper, all familiar friends that my dad had introduced to me at our house by the sea.

I lay on the built-in benches in the gazebo, listening. I didn't hear any violin soloists that night, or an orchestra, only crickets, an owl, some rustling in the bushes, a dog barking over the hill, a cat fight, and cooing.

I opened my violin case, then drew a finger down the strings and onto the butterfly stain inside, thinking about what Grandma had said.

The violin was my momma's, which she said belonged to her momma. It was she who taught me how to play the violin at our house by the sea, sometimes inside, sometimes outside on our porch, the churning waves as background music. I learned on a quarter size, then half, then three quarter, as I grew.

When my momma ceremoniously gave me her violin, and bought herself a new one, she said, in French, in a vague, nostalgic way, "Ismael and I used to play together, now you and I can play together, Pink Girl." Then she closed her mouth tight, and I knew she instantly regretted saying what she had, like my grandma years later.

I asked, "Who is Ismael?" and Momma shook her head. "Who is Ismael?" I asked again, and she put her hand on my shoulder, her eyes filling with tears, and whispered, "Not now, Madeline. I will tell you later, but not now."

"Why not now?"

"Because now is not the time. The story is not to be told yet."

"Stories shouldn't be told?"

"Some stories are not to be told for years, until the listener is ready and the storyteller can tell it properly."

"What does 'tell it properly' mean?"

"It means . . ." She stared over my head at the waves crashing against the sand. "It means a story should be told when you can tell it honestly with truth everywhere, in every nook and corner of the story. I will tell you the story later, when you are not so young; then you can tell it to your children when they are ready, so no one in our family ever forgets."

"Forgets what, Momma?" I whispered, scared, watchful, knowing as only kids can know there was black stickiness behind her words.

"So that no one forgets who we are, who we were."

"But, what do you mean, *who we were?*"

She kissed the top of my head. "That is enough for now, darling. Let's begin."

And we began, like that, playing together by the sea, the clouds rolling through, mysterious and gray, over the waves, the waves sputtering and cresting, the notes of our violins spinning between them. Our favorite piece was Bach's Double Violin Concerto.

I have often brushed my fingers over the butterfly stain of blood inside the violin. Where did it come from? How? When?

This is one thing I know: A violin should have no blood on it. None.

8

~

"The reason women want their hair to look perfect is because that's one thing they can have control over in their lives," Momma told me as she painted my nails in one of the pink swivel chairs in Marie Elise's French Beauty Parlor, the sun glittering off the chandeliers.

"Now when Graciella came in here the other day complaining, I couldn't help her control her mother-in-law, who threw out all her sexy negligees and put in place granny-styled pajamas and prayed at a church dinner in front of two hundred people that God would 'turn her daughter-in-law away from being a sex maniac into a God-fearing servant to her husband,' but I can trim four inches off her length to give her hair fullness."

I nodded at Momma. She was wearing a slim pink skirt, black heels, and a black, short-sleeved sweater. I was wearing a pink skirt, black shoes, and a black, short-sleeved sweater, too. Annie was, too. We were the O'Shea Pink Girls!

"And I can't help Jessie Liz control her child, Shoney, who is dead set on painting pictures of naked ladies on any bare wall he can find in town, but I can help her tame and control those red curls. And I can't help LaShonda control her addiction to buying bras. She doesn't know why she needs so many bras, sixty-one at last count, and I don't either, but I can take some bulk out of that black frizzy hair."

"She looked a lot better when she left."

"She sure did. She felt like a lady."

"You used your magic, Momma."

My momma laughed. "Love is magic. Don't you forget it." She kissed my nose.

One of the best examples of my momma's magic was Maggie Gee's grandmother.

Maggie Gee's grandmother lived with poor Maggie Gee. The grandmother was a fiery, explosive, tiny woman who wore only black, including a long, black lace mantilla. She was from Germany and sometimes spat at people. People said she was still in mourning for her husband, but he'd been dead twenty years, and it was rumored she'd run him over with a tractor, so I didn't know what to make of that.

Grandmother Schiller refused to get her hair done. "I like this way! No touch, no touch!" It was gray, stringy, and wound up on the top of her head like a cylinder. Grandmother Schiller insisted on decorating her hair with plastic flowers and tiny green plastic gnomes.

She refused to shower more than once a week. "I get sick from water! Sick! Blech!" She threw plates when she was upset, so Maggie had to buy only plastic plates.

"Help me, Marie Elise," she begged my momma. "If I have to look for one more day at that *thing* she has on top of her head, my spleen will pop open. It reminds me of a twirled-up squirrel." She clasped her face with both hands. "Do you think the woman will live forever? I can't bear it."

So Maggie literally dragged Grandmother Schiller into the beauty parlor one day when Annie and I were doing our homework.

"Help me, Marie Elise," she called out, panting, straining, Grandmother Schiller's black heels stuck in the ground. "I've got Grandmother! I've got her! Help!"

My momma, in her pink heels, swayed on over, her black hair waving down her back, smile welcoming, makeup perfect. Her cheeks looked extra rosy, but I had been told that my dad had picked her up for lunch, so I figured that put the blush in her cheeks. "Love puts blush in your cheeks," she'd told Annie and me many times. "Plus, your dad and I had a nap. That always makes us feel better."

We nodded our heads, taking in that serious note of wisdom: Naps and love equal blush in your cheeks.

"Hello, Mrs. Schiller!" Momma called out to the black-clad, wrinkled, disagreeable woman with a pile of twirled-up squirrel on her head.

"Ack! Ack!" Grandmother Schiller threw her purse on the floor as Maggie heaved her in the door, her own hair a frazzled wreck. "Bad granddaughter!" she said, pointing, as if we couldn't find Maggie on our own. "Bad granddaughter. She here stab me with scissor. Stab me!" She mimicked stabbing herself in the face with scissors.

Maggie held tight to her grandmother, a pathetic, begging expression on her face.

"Mrs. Schiller, no one is here to stab you with the scissors," Momma said. "We're here to help you with a new hairdo."

Grandmother Schiller said, "Bah! I no want hairdo! I got hairdo! Here, my hairdo!" She pointed to her twirled squirrel. "She take my flowers!" She pointed to Maggie Gee again, with grand accusation. "Where my gnome?"

Grandmother Schiller picked up her purse and smacked Maggie. On the second swing, Maggie ducked.

My momma did not like violence. "Mrs. Schiller!" she said, her voice firm, authoritative. "You will stop that this instant."

Grandmother Schiller froze. "She stole gnome!"

"You will not hit!" Momma pulled herself up to her full height. "Stand up and act like a lady."

Grandmother Schiller's eyes widened. "I a lady."

"You're not acting like one. When you are in Marie Elise's French Beauty Parlor you will act like a lady."

Grandmother Schiller grumbled. She mumbled. She let go of her very bad granddaughter. "I not get cut hair. You no stab my hair with scissors! Snip, snip, no snip snip."

"Yes, I am going to snip your hair," Momma said.

"I say no!"

"I say yes, Mrs. Schiller. You look awful."

Mrs. Schiller's mouth fell open.

"Your hair is a mess. It's not sexy. You need a modern look."

"I not sexy?" Grandmother Schiller raised her eyebrows toward the squirrel. "Hair like this, many years growing."

"Exactly. And those years are over. This"—my momma lifted the mantilla and ran a hand through Grandmother Schiller's hair—"is a disgrace. Come." She pointed to her pink chair. "I'll fix it."

Grandmother Schiller muttered something, low and guttural, and Momma answered in German.

Grandmother Schiller turned in surprise, said a few more sentences. Momma answered, clipped, with her I-Know-What-Is-Best tone.

Then, to the cataclysmic relief of her exhausted, bad granddaughter, Grandmother Schiller nodded and plopped her tiny self and the twirled squirrel into the pink chair.

"Mrs. Schiller." Momma took off the black lace mantilla. "We're going to help you get control of this mess on your head. If you get control of your hair, you'll get control of your life."

"Ya. Control." She pointed her index finger up. "I got control bad granddaughter. She stole my gnome. Where the gnome! He good luck."

My momma unwound that twirled squirrel hair until it hung about five feet long, almost as tall as Mrs. Schiller, then she took her scissors and cut about four and a half feet off with a couple of snip-snips.

Grandmother Schiller yelled, "Ack!"

Maggie Gee spent the whole time in the resting room on a pink fainting couch. She had two coffees with tons of cream, lemon water, almost all the mints, and half a bottle of wine that Estelle Mosher brought in with her to celebrate her eighty-eighth birthday.

Maggie Gee couldn't even speak when she saw her grandmother about an hour and a half later.

Mrs. Schiller spun around in front of her granddaughter, her hair dyed a lovely white color, shaped into a thick bell, cupping her face. My momma had told her, in German, "No more plastic flowers because they're tacky. No more gnomes because people will think you're insane. No more being rude to Maggie. She loves you and you don't want to lose her love forever, do you?"

Grandmother gasped. "Ack! No, no! I no lose her love. That bad."

"Splendid. I will see you in six weeks for a trim."

"Ya. I see you in six weeks, Marie Elise. Ya. Thank you." She spoke in German, then turned to her granddaughter. "You good granddaughter. Ya. I think that." Then she took Maggie Gee's face, turned it this way and that, and kissed her. "Now I so pretty. Just like you."

My dad died in inky darkness.

The storm stampeded across the ocean like it was being chased by Mother Nature on a rampage. It gathered speed, it gathered might, it gathered the lives of eight men on two different fishing boats, and threw them into the swirling wind and the pounding waves, as if they were nothing. As if they were not loved and adored, hugged at night and kissed in the morning.

My dad would have fought against the boiling water, the waves as tall as buildings, and the wind that whipped up the ocean into a frothing, furious, deadly caldron. He would have struggled, he would have battled, he would have tried to save the other men.

And, in the end, when the water yanked him down beneath the freezing waves and held him there, he would have thought of us.

He would have thought of my momma, of Annie and me, his Pink Girls.

Would he have seen us on the porch of our house by the sea or on the cliffs waiting for him? Would he have seen my momma, swaying in pink, smiling, her arms wrapped around his neck? Would he have seen us in our grizzly bear outfits, our tutus, our homemade stick hats? Would he have thought of us all dancing around the house to rock music, to Bach, to jazz, to country-western, he and Annie on the piano, my momma and I with our violins?

When the golden light from heaven grew brighter and brighter and he fought, harder and harder, against the walls of waves, would he, at one point, give in? No, he never would have, not for a minute, not until that golden light surrounded him and gently lifted his collapsed, drowned soul up through the stormy, raging clouds, the sky splitting thunder and cracking lightning, to a calmer place, a place of peace.

The night of that soul-sucking storm we had no peace. My momma did not leave the cliff that overlooked the sea by our home. She stood straight and tall, wearing a pink shawl, the shawl billowing out behind her in the wind until it was too soaked to move, waiting for a light from her husband's fishing boat.

My momma waited all night and into the morning light. She knew.

Annie and I waited on our covered porch, sometimes venturing out through blustering winds and sideways rain to see her, to beg her to come in, to hold her hand, to plead with her, and she refused. "Go back inside, darlings," she'd tell us, her voice raised over the thunder. She walked with us, back inside, then returned to waiting on the cliff, where she prayed and begged, that pink shawl like sodden loneliness.

When Sheriff Ellery drove up the drive at dawn, got heavily out of his car, wiped the tears from his face, and lumbered toward my momma with her pink shawl, she didn't say a word to him. She didn't look at him.

He caught her when she collapsed and carried her back into the house.

My momma was never truly happy again after losing my dad.

That storm took my dad's life, then it took our joy, laughter, and love and swept it out over the ocean, way, way out deep, and drowned it as surely as if we'd been caught up in the same speeding whirlpool and spun down to the floor of the ocean with him.

His memorial service was packed. Against each pew a fishing pole leaned. His coffin was covered in a wreath over a fishing net. Grown, hardened men cried when they spoke of my dad, Big Luke, their best friend. He had listened, he had pulled them out of trouble, encouraged them, bought them a beer, whacked them on the side of the head when they weren't being "family men." They would miss him forever.

On his headstone, underneath his name, Luke O'Shea, my momma had these words carved, as she knew he loved them:

> Scatter me not to the restless winds
> Nor toss my ashes to the sea.
> Remember now those years gone by
> When loving gifts I gave to thee.
> Remember now the happy times
> The family ties are shared.
> Don't leave my resting place unmarked
> As though you never cared.
> Deny me not one final gift
> For all who came to see.
> A simple lasting proof that says
> I loved and you loved me.
>
> D.H. CRAMER

It wasn't long after that, maybe a few months, when she started to have the headaches. We knew they were from missing Dad.

We knew that.

Why? Annie and I had headaches sometimes, too, from not sleeping, from crying that we couldn't stop, crying that went on and on. It was immediately after my dad died that I started having trouble breathing right, as if the air was stopped up here and there in my body, ragged and chopped, and it was a struggle to get air everywhere at the right time.

Sometimes Momma couldn't stop crying, either, even when she was making our lunches, or painting our nails, or making paper art with us. When we played our violins, her tears got on the strings. She had to go to bed for long hours while her friends and our neighbors and our grandparents took care of us.

She would get up and cry more, buckets and buckets of tears.

So we knew the headaches were from the crying.

We were wrong about that.

Wrong that the headaches were from crying.

9

On Sunday evening I went out on my deck, the lights of the city flickering, and had some green tea. It's supposed to be good for you. So are Brussels sprouts, beets, cauliflower, wheat germ, and pumpkin seeds, but who eats that crap? Not me. Life's too short to eat Brussels sprouts, that's what I think. Whenever I see lists of healthy foods that nutritionists want us to eat, I want to stick my fingers down my throat. Come on, food researchers and dieticians. Do you think Americans are going to start adding beets to their meal plans? If I wanted to eat kale, spinach, and figs, I'd turn myself into a rabbit.

When I finished the green tea, I ate half a box of chocolates. They were so much better.

Boutique Magazine
A Life Coach Tells You How to Live It
By Madeline O'Shea
Pap Smears

On Friday I got my pap smear.
To say that I don't like getting pap smears is like saying I don't like hanging upside down from my heels in an underground dungeon in Saudi Arabia being whipped because my hair

showed in public. Not to equate the two, but you get the gist.

There are a myriad of reasons for my almost pathological distaste for this particular medical infringement, but I do it, anyway.

Why? For my health.

In my doctor's office, I slip into the blue and white cotton sheath thing. The back opens so my bottom is out and about, wriggling on its own, my boobs unfettered by a bra. I read the gossip magazines while perched up on that brown padded table, something I never do, because it is a waste of time and because the women look eerily, intimidatingly perfect. They are not perfect. *Anyone* with an army of professionally trained stylists, the exact lighting, and a Photoshop crew can look wowza, trust me on this one. Still. The magazine women make other women feel ugly.

My doctor looks a bit like a crane. He is a benevolent crane, tall and lanky, with eyes like a giraffe, if a giraffe had blue eyes. Dr. Crane ambles in on spindly legs and we chitchat, but it is not long before he is asking me to lie back, spread 'em, and put my feet in cold, silver stirrups. One day those stirrups will come to life and grab the feet of many a startled woman, I kid you not.

"You're going to have to slide to the edge of the table," Dr. Crane says, and he laughs. I imagine his crane wings spreading out behind him.

"No." I am lying down, but I don't yet feel like hanging my bare butt over the edge of a table so my lotus flower can be explored with cold, metal salad tongs and pokey things.

He laughs. "Come on, Madeline, this won't hurt." He snaps on gloves.

I am sweating.

The nurse and the doctor wriggle me on down. The nurse has muscles.

"Let's put your feet in the stirrups now, Madeline," Dr. Crane says, like a cheerleader. "You can do it!"

"Let's stab forks into my body first," I tell him. "That sounds more relaxing."

He laughs, he lifts my knees, I bring them down, he brings them up and puts my heels in the stirrups. I squeeze my knees together, tight, like a clamp. A vagina clamp.

Dr. Crane laughs. Then he and the smiling nurse start using the pap language. "Pass me the spatula," he says cheerily, joking about the speculum.

The spatula? I think of something that flips pancakes.

He asks for some other tool, too. It sounds like he's asking for an Inserter. He shows me this groovy long thing that is going to do the job. He's so excited about his new vaginal toy. It is plasticky and definitely doesn't belong in *me*. Maybe *you*. But not *me*. I slam my knees shut again.

"I don't think I need a pap," I tell him, and try to get up.

Dr. Crane thinks I'm so funny! "Aw, come on, now, it's not so bad!"

The nurse smiles and pushes me down again.

"If someone wanted to look up your thingie with a spatula, you wouldn't like it, either, buddy."

Dr. Crane laughs again.

My knees are shaking. I stare up at the

ceiling. Please tell me why doctors have not gotten smart enough to create a "woman's ceiling," where there are pictures of Jimmy Smits, so that you can gaze at him when a doctor is using a spatula and salad tongs on your lotus flower. Surely this would be more relaxing than counting ceiling holes?

"I need Jimmy Smits," I whisper.

Dr. Crane laughs.

"Me too!" the chipper nurse chips out.

"No, I'm serious. I need Jimmy Smits."

"I'll warm things up!" Dr. Crane says, still so cheerful even though he spends much of his day peering up women's woo-woos. "No one wants them cold! No one wants anything icy there!"

The salad tongs do their job, up and up, until I think they'll poke out my nose.

The doctor is using a miniflashlight to peer up my lotus flower. "It looks splendid in there!"

For heaven's sakes.

Next it is time for test-tube-like things and cotton swabs and, drum roll, my favorite: The pelvic exam! Think: Gloves!

You might wonder what my pap smear has to do with my telling you how to get your act together. Ladies, your health is your business. Your health is your top priority. If you're not healthy everything falls apart: Your body, your mental outlook, your attitude, your job, your marriage, your relationship with kids and family. Your sex life. Save your sex life at all costs.

So, from me, the meanest life coach in the world, get your "health-act" together. Get *you* together. You can't plan for your future, focus

on a promotion, get creative ideas, or start a
new business if your health is in shambles.
Exercise that bod. Eat healthy stuff. Get your
pap smear.

And if you can get Jimmy Smits to come
with you and hang from the ceiling while
smiling, all the better. If not, bring a picture of
his face and hold it above your head when the
doctor is using a flashlight and a pancake
flipper on your lotus flower.

"I'm alone. I'm always alone."

I nodded my head at A'isha Heinbrenner and tried to ignore
the sad rain streaming down the windows of my office. Darn the
rain. It was hiding my view and I like to be able to see far out. It
makes me feel less trapped, which helps me breathe like a normal human. "And are you lonely, or are you okay with being
alone?"

Her brow furrowed. "I've recently divorced my husband
after thirty years, my five kids are all over the States working or
going to college, my sister and I are estranged, my brother is in
Alaska. I'm alone. I'm fifty-two and I'm alone."

She stared at me. She was sort of frumpy. Worn out. Probably
wanted to lose twenty pounds. Her hair was short, a dull color,
lots of gray. No makeup.

"Are you lonely?"

"Sometimes I think I should be lonely because I'm alone,
right?"

"No, not necessarily."

"It's been a curious time."

"How?"

"I have spent the last thirty years taking care of people. My
husband, my kids, my parents as they were dying, my father-in-
law. I worked ten hours a day as a high school teacher. Now I'm
retired and I have a pension. All those years of teaching with the

low salary earned me a pension. Every month, the check comes. The house is mine, and paid off, so I put it in savings."

"How do you feel with your family all over the place, the estrangement with your sister?"

"The truth is my sister always caused me stress. She has personal problems, constantly, of her own making. She's been married four times, one husband worse than the others; she's had affairs, traumas, health issues—she's exhausting. She hasn't talked to me in six months, and it's been a relaxing time for me. I had no idea how strung up I was on her problems."

"What about your kids?"

"I love my kids. But I'm worn out. Raising five kids isn't easy."

"And your ex? How do you feel about him?"

She thought. "I wasn't in love with him the last twenty-three years of our marriage. He was an alcoholic. He'd come home, have dinner, and drink until he passed out. He was a benign drunk, but it's tough to be in love with a man when there's a whiskey bottle between you. There's no truth with whiskey. We were together. I had accepted that he would never change. I accepted I was in a marriage by myself. I made myself happy, content, built a life for myself without him."

"So you accepted the emptiness. You accepted the aloneness. You dealt with it. But your acceptance was another form of dying. You accepted that you would never have enough, and it corroded you."

"Yes. It did." She nodded her head. "I was corroded. Surviving. On my own."

"Let's continue working on your Individual Life-Force plan. What do you want to be doing in six months, a year, five years? What are you going to do to bring out your life force, your reason for being, your reason for not only living but for thriving, for lusting after life?"

A'isha thought for a long time. I like silences between my clients and me. It gives their brains time to work.

"I want to find myself."

"That sounds like a plan."

"I want to find out who A'isha is, on her own."

"Excellent. How will you do that?"

Another silence.

"I don't know. What do you think, Madeline?"

"I think you should travel, by yourself, internationally."

She thought again. More silence, and she nodded. Her eyes lit up, a wee bit of that dullness, the dullness we all get when life disappoints way too much, receding.

"I think you're right."

"Absolutely I'm right. You need change. Drastic, utter change."

"Tell me what country I should go to first."

"Scotland. I like the way they talk."

A'isha's brow furrowed again. We had ourselves another silence. She sat up straight, blinked a few times, as if coming out of a trance, or as if she was coming out of a marriage that had slung the lust for life clean out of her body and through a window. "All right. It's Scotland." She smiled, tentatively.

"Three weeks."

"Three weeks it is." She inhaled, the inhale was shaky, but I dare say that light was growing in her eyes.

"You'll be uncomfortable at first, A'isha, nervous. Accept it. Be okay with it. Make reservations, one week in each of three new places. Book beautiful places to stay. Bring books, notebooks, colored pencils. Imagine. Dream. Hike. Think. Paint. Explore."

We sat in our silence again. "I think I'm off to Scotland."

"A'isha, you didn't answer my question. You kept saying that you're alone all the time. Are you lonely?"

We had one more silence. I love reflective people. She rolled her shoulders, like she was throwing something off of them, perhaps a past that had had no A'isha in it. "You know, Madeline, I'm not. I'm not lonely at all. It's bothered me that I'm not lonely, because I thought that I should be. But I'm not. Alone means I'm with myself. Alone means I answer to myself, I do what I want for, literally, the first time in my life. Alone means that I can think what I want. It means I'm not burdened with the constancy of doing things for others. It means that I don't have to manage my husband, his moods, his thoughtlessness, the trap of marriage. I felt like I was always deflecting the hurts he casually threw my way through neglect, through not wanting to know the real me, through not helping me. That's exhausting, you know, being in a relationship that you constantly have to protect your heart from. It's numbing."

"It is, indeed."

"So, Madeline, no, I'm not lonely, I am alone. And it is, absolutely, positively"—she smiled wider here—"fantastic."

I winked at her. "Send me a postcard. When you get back we'll plan some more."

"I'll send you a kilt."

"You do that."

"I'm going to Scotland." There was wonder in her voice. "Maybe I'll go to Faerie Glen and make a wish."

"Make several wishes."

"Maybe I'll drink some Scotch whiskey."

"Save the bottle as a souvenir."

"Maybe I'll listen to Scottish music."

"Buy a CD, it'll bring back the memories."

She called me from the airport three days later. "You didn't think I'd do it, did you?"

I told her the truth. "I knew you would. And I knew you'd leave soon, before you chickened out."

She laughed. "You know the inside of my freedom-seeking mind, don't you? See ya, Madeline, and thanks."

"See ya, A'isha, and you're welcome."

I couldn't believe what Ramon had done to my yard already. Brick steps climbed from the sidewalk to the front door, in a sort of zigzag fashion, a rock wall was halfway built along the front, and he'd laid sod so I had green where beige and brown used to be.

I walked around, in awe, before fumbling in my purse for my keys.

As soon as I walked in, I instantly felt like I was in a gigantic, cold, ultramodern tomb.

I so don't like my house.

I dropped my purse and my briefcase, tossed my keys to the freaky black metal statue with the octagonal head, and dumped myself into a stiff, modern leather chair that was completely unlike my dad's comfy, poufy leather chair.

Why did I feel so cold in my own home?

Why did I feel like a visitor?

Why did I feel like I had to be quiet here, as if I couldn't talk, or move?

Why did I feel like I couldn't breathe in my own home? Why did I feel like I had to hide, as if I was an imposter, a fake, an interloper, a burglar, even?

Why is that?

And, if I feel this way, why am I still here?

"Greetings, Madeline."

"Hi, Georgie." I'd been in the office since six in the morning. I moved one client folder over, replaced it with another, clicked on my e-mail, and decided the forty new e-mails and twenty-three phone calls that had come in that morning could wait. I had already talked to Janika Jeffs, the head honcho organizing the Rock Your Womanhood conference. "Can't wait, Madeline, we *can't wait* to hear your closing night speech! I'm rockin', I'm rockin' already!"

"Aurora King is here," Georgie said over the phone.

"I'll bet she's wearing the yellow fairy dress today."

"Yes, she is," Georgie said. "How did you know? Wait. You have unrealized psychic abilities, don't you? I knew you were in touch with your inner self. Anyhow, Aurora says her spirit is light and flowing on a stream of goodwill."

"Superb. Her tiara in place?"

"Tilted perfectly. She wears the tiara to remind herself that she is a princess. What, Aurora? She wants me to tell you that she feels some black around the edges of your aura. What, Aurora? She says she sees red. She says it's mysterious blood.

What? She sees a fire. A ball of fire. By that same tree with the branches that criss and cross. What else, Aurora? A heavily armed airport and a senator who has to resign."

"I'm wearing a black suit and black heels. I think my underwear has red trim. Tell her that's what she's seeing. There are skyscraping-sized trees in Portland. I looked at a plane today. I don't know about the senator. You know I think politicians are drivel slobber." I continued to shift papers. Where was my draft for my speech? I'd been working on that in the wee hours. . . .

"I don't think she is talking about your boring black heels."

I was not offended. "Did you say boring black heels?"

"Yes, I did."

I heard Stanley bark.

"I have offered to go shopping with you, Madeline, so we can touch your fashionista, wake her up."

"My inner fashionista died a long time ago." Yep, the fashionista died in a shack. "Plus, I wear suits because I'm a professional."

"You wear suits because you are not in touch with the creative side of your spirit. You are unwilling to release her into a welcoming spectrum world."

I didn't know what a welcoming spectrum world was. I would ask later. "There's no inner spirit in me that wants a release."

"Yes, there is. You have to meditate to bring her out, coax some color and flavor into your wardrobe to reflect the complexity of the spirit."

"I'll try to get the spirit out tonight. Maybe she'll attack my frumpiness. Send Aurora King in and tell her not to throw glitter at me again."

"Don't throw glitter at Madeline," I heard Georgie say before she disconnected.

I opened my door to Aurora King and closed my eyes when I saw her hand swing up.

She threw yellow glitter at me.

Two days later I was still picking it out of my hair.

*   *   *

Corky Goshofsky was next up.

"You are not succeeding because you are blaming everyone else for your failures," I said, twirling a pen in my fingers.

"What?" Corky's voice sounded like a machete on sandpaper. Ugh. She rearranged her significant, interesting bottom on one of my chairs.

This is an odd thing to say, but Corky has a butt that has a life of its own. When she walks, one cheek goes up, wiggles at the top like piled-up Jell-O, then sags while the next cheek does the up, wiggle, and Jell-O thing.

"You are not succeeding because you are blaming everyone else for your failures." I wanted to eat a burrito for lunch. Extra cheese and avocado.

Corky glared at me, crossing her arms. "People are always talking behind my back. No one gives me a break. When I work in groups I can't help it if I get frustrated with slow people. I speak up when I have an opinion, and they don't want to hear it, even though they know they're wrong and I'm right."

"Your personality is also a huge barrier to your success."

"What do you mean by that?" The words came out like verbal bullets. *Pow, pow, pow.*

"You're abrasive, offensive, and difficult. You come off as superior and condescending."

"This is the third session I've paid for, Madeline, and I'm not coming here to listen to you take their side."

"Then you can go."

That took her aback. "What?"

"You can go. You came here because I'm a life coach and I help people with their relationships and their lives. I can't help you with your life, with all the problems you're having at work and home, if I'm not honest with you, so here's the truth. You're obnoxious."

She sputtered. She bopped up and down in her seat on that interesting bottom, her graying, curly brown hair bouncing. "I am not!"

"Yes, you are. You have to learn how to like Corky. You don't like her at all, do you?"

She sputtered. The sputtering sounded like: Blind denial.

"Yes, I do! I'm smart! I'm successful! I have a bunch of money and a huge house and a Lexus!"

"You have much of that because you received an inheritance. You've been fired from three jobs in three years. You complain that your Lexus is too low to the ground, and all this is beside the point." I waved a hand in the air. "You have got to do something to learn how to like yourself, and when you like yourself, you'll be able to like others—"

"I don't like other people because they're rude, uncouth and judgmental, and social idiots—"

"You don't like all those people because you don't like yourself. Pure and simple. Look here, Corky." I leaned my elbows on my knees. I would add hot sauce to my burrito. "You need a Bash 'em in the Brains O'Shea Reality Check. You have to re-do Corky. You need a makeover physically so you'll like yourself. You need to join one of those diet places and a gym, because you have to get your health together before you collapse. You need to walk every night so you can be in nature. Notice leaves, trees, spiders, obsessive-compulsive squirrels and chipmunks, stuff like that. Get your hair done at a salon. That'll give you a lift you won't believe."

"I don't like the outside! I don't like nature! I don't want to be in it!"

"I'm sure nature doesn't like you, either, but she's willing to put up with you in hopes for a better tomorrow. Now, for your personality fix, you need to chill. Relax. Quit attacking people. Compliment them. Be sincerely interested in their lives. Volunteer, if you can be well behaved, so you can get a picture of what other people's lives are like who are not on your same socioeconomic ladder. Your complaints and incessant whining will seem ridiculously petty, and hopefully you will shut up at that point. Honestly, there are teenagers who are homeless, kids in prostitution, and others starving tonight. They'd trade places with you in a minute. Spend time reading to open up that clamped-down brain of yours, have adventures to get yourself out of your rut, go to a play so you can be interesting. Be someone people want to talk to. Right now, your entire conversation is filled with what I call Roaring Shit Negatives and Corrosive Complaints. No wonder you have no friends."

"How dare you say that, you skinny moronic twit." She was purple with rage.

"I dare because you've paid me money to be honest. I will have to deny being a twit." The twit wanted lemonade with her burrito, too.

"I've paid a lot of money!"

"I charge you extra because you're a pain in the butt." I ignored her shocked look. "You need to change so the rest of the world does not have to put up with your critical, narcissistic personality anymore. It's unfair, Corky. No one should be allowed to ruin someone else's day. That should be a law."

She hauled her interesting bottom up and grabbed her chair, and her face, which resembled a purple sponge, scrunched in fury. I leaped behind the couch, and she tossed that chair with a bad word following closely behind it like a tail.

Luckily, the chair did not break any windows. I am up high in this building, after all.

"Bitch!" she screamed.

"I thought I was a twit."

Georgie popped in with Stanley at her heels. He barked. "Can I help with this degenerating emotional situation before it reaches a galaxy-sized disaster?" Georgie said, quite calmly through a sucker she had in her mouth.

"Nope," I said.

"Bitch!" Corky twisted and reached for another chair. Her bottom wiggled at me.

"If you do the things I told you, Corky, people won't hate you so much."

"Double bitch!" she screamed again.

I did not tell her that she should have screamed "Triple bitch," not "Double bitch," as I dove beneath my desk when another chair went flying.

"You're not doing what I said," I called out, singsongy.

"Should I grab her?" Georgie asked. She was wearing a short

jean jacket over a purple tube top and a floaty black skirt with ruffles and black ankle high boots. "Should I hold her against her will and cap the volcanic emotional rocks bursting forth?"

"Triple bitch!" Corky threw another chair. I ducked once again.

She was out of chairs. I grabbed one of the chairs that had been thrown, scooted around the desk, dropped it right in front of her, then darted back behind my desk. "Go ahead and throw it again, Corky!"

She picked up the chair and pitched it. "Straight-haired, spindly legged snot!"

I scrambled out and brought her another chair, then hustled back behind my desk.

That chair broke on my desk.

"Tight-assed, stuck-up, know-it-all!"

Even though she called me "tight ass," I didn't think it was time to tell her about her wiggly Jell-O bottom. I scooted out a third time, handed her another chair, and darted behind the desk. "One more time, Corky."

"Arggghhh!" She tossed that chair and it split, too.

"Okay, you've had your temper tantrum, Corky. Now go home and think about what I said. Meditate. Yoga-ize yourself. Slap your cheeks. Whatever it takes."

"I'll never think!"

"Never?"

"No, never! I'll never think!" She was shaking all over.

Georgie said, "Wrap yourself in your spiritual nature as you leave. Think pleasant thoughts. Think of waterfalls, rivers, streams, a naked man. Think of a naked man. That's what I do to calm my spirit."

I glanced at Georgie while keeping a close eye on the chair thrower. Eye candy. Georgie used men as eye candy for inner peace.

Corky turned to huff out, but first she kicked my wall and threw a metal side table. Stanley barked at her. Twice. He did not raise his paw, he did not want a hug. "I'm going to sue you, you liar, you silly-headed creep, you poop!"

Poop? I was a poop?

She blushed redder. I knew she regretted saying the word poop. It sounded so poopy.

"My pleasure," I called out. "Call my attorney, Keith Stein, directly. He's in the book."

"You're going to regret this!"

"You're not. You're going to go home and fume and rant and rave until everyone around you is literally running when they see you lumbering their way, and you're finally going to have a Herculean breakdown and cry your eyes out, and three days later you're going to call me and make an appointment."

"Never! I'll never make an appointment with you again. You don't know anything. I don't know why you're all famous and everyone thinks you know it all, you know-it-all-poop."

"Think about what I said," I said. Maybe I'd have two burritos.

Georgie sucked on her sucker. She is such a noisy sucker sucker. "Thinking can cause different philosophical and metaphysical thought processes to grow stronger, making you more one with the intelligence in the universe."

"I'll never think!" Corky declared again, red, sweaty, quivering. "Never!"

When she finally waddled out, Georgie said, "She's vowed to never think. That's a first."

"Sure is. Make sure you charge her for the chairs she broke. Three hundred dollars each, at least."

"Okeydokey." I heard Stanley bark. Twice.

I went over and shook his hand, then hugged him. "Sorry about that, Stanley. Let it go."

"He doesn't like conflict," Georgie said.

"You're going to have to get used to it, Stanley. Life's a conflict."

Georgie rolled her eyes. "How about that shopping trip?"

I read an article about him in the *New York Times* that night. He was also in the *Boston Globe,* the *San Francisco Chronicle,* and so on. I cut them out, studied what he said, how he said it.

I wasn't stalking him. Or spying on him.

I was merely keeping track of him and his life. That's why I have a manila envelope full of his photos, articles, etcetera, which I peek at when the moon is high and feeling romantic.

I did not have tears in my eyes for any other reason than a bit of dust had gotten through a window in the house that I live in that I don't like.

A bit of dust.

10

I remember when we met Sherwinn.

Momma, Annie, and I were walking down the main street of our town near the ocean. Momma was wearing a purple and pink flowered dress and a wicker hat with a pink flower in it, her hair flowing down her back, like a black, feathered wing.

Annie and I were in matching blue jean shorts and matching pink T-shirts with butterflies. We were going to the ice-cream saloon. At that point, we loved ice cream. Chocolate mint, chocolate fudge, rainbow, and our favorite, peppermint, because it was pink.

"Whooaa," Sherwinn drawled, stopping right in his tracks on the sidewalk and ogling Momma. "Lady, you are the finest looking woman I have seen in years."

My momma gave him a hint of a smile. She wasn't feeling "as bright and white as daisies," as she put it to us, what with her headaches from crying and all.

"I had no idea the Cape produced such beautiful, can I say, *sexy* women."

Sherwinn was tall, muscled, and good looking, with all the right words for a lonely widow. To many people, he would appear perfectly normal. He had moved to town to work in the fishing industry and had that tough-guy attitude so many women find irresistible, to their own peril. "If I had known that you were here, I would have moved sooner than I did. That was my loss, but we can always turn it into a gain."

My momma said, "Heard it before, slick, and it's not going to work," but she smiled and he smiled back and he knew he had her. He had her. Like a gang of tarantulas, he had her.

Will you, Marie Elise O'Shea, have Sherwinn Barnes to be your husband? Will you love him, comfort and keep him, and forsaking all others remain true to him as long as you both shall live?

Theirs was a short, intense romance. Lots of dates, lots of intensity, enough so my momma's brain whirled. Sherwinn spent money on her that my momma found out later wasn't his money. As an adult, I understood what my momma temporarily liked about Sherwinn. She liked feeling alive again. She liked shedding the grief of losing my dad twenty months prior. She liked all of Sherwinn's attention. He was a charismatic, compelling force, with that possessive, I'm-in-control sexiness. My momma, fighting fatigue, her headaches, her grief, her aloneness, couldn't think straight, couldn't put up a fight against Sherwinn's overwhelming, take-charge personality.

And I know something else, something I shouldn't know. My momma was the last of the virgins. She did not have relations with my dad until she was married. They only dated six months, after meeting their senior year of college in Boston, but he was a looker and, as my momma told me later, "I could barely restrain myself, darlin', around your dad. That's why we didn't wait long to marry. I wanted that white dress and I wanted it to mean something."

Will you, Sherwinn Barnes, have Marie Elise O'Shea to be your wife? Will you love her, comfort and keep her, and forsaking all others remain true to her as long as you both shall live?

One night, I got up to get myself another slice of my momma's French silk chocolate pie and I saw my momma and Sherwinn under a tree. I saw them rolling, I saw what they were doing, and I closed my eyes and ran upstairs, sickened.

The next day, my momma cried all day, and the next day, too.

On the third day, she was engaged to marry Sherwinn. Now why a grown woman would feel compelled to marry a man simply because she'd had relations with him is something I don't understand. But that incident under the tree, combined with the force of Sherwinn's personality, well, it was a tornado that swept her up, up, and away.

Almost two years after our dad died, she married Sherwinn in the backyard of our house by the sea. My dad's parents weren't there. The grief of losing their only child had overwhelmed them and they died six months apart, starting three months after my dad died. Though I was not as close to them as I was to my momma's parents, it was two more losses.

My momma was pale on her wedding morning, withdrawn. Sherwinn was grinning, happy as could be. His family consisted of his father, who got sloshy drunk and had to be hauled off by my dad's relatives, a younger brother who had been released from the state pen two weeks before, and another who ambled in and hit on no fewer than three clients of Marie Elise's French Beauty Parlor.

The night before the wedding, after the rehearsal dinner, I heard my grandparents talking to my momma on the porch. They spoke German.

"Honey, please don't, it's not too late to back out . . . what do you find attractive about this man . . . he resembles a good-looking possum with the education of a rancid pig . . . he might be sexy, Marie Elise, but there needs to be more . . . I don't understand . . . we don't understand, dammit . . . no, we don't like him, we can't pinpoint what it is, but there's something there, a gut feeling, it's killing me, something's off, damn off . . . what about the children . . . now, don't cry, Marie Elise, chin up, shoulders back, let's fix this ruckus of a problem and send him off on his merry way . . . we know you've been lonely, we know you miss Luke, we do, too, sugar . . . this is not the answer, it's a rat hole . . . for God's sakes, Marie Elise, *what are you doing?*"

The talk degenerated from there, my granddad clearly furious and baffled as to why my momma would marry Sherwinn, and my grandma tried to cajole her daughter with gentle persuasion, but my momma wouldn't listen. For once in her life, she wouldn't listen to her parents. Later, we would blame our momma's insidious grief and her medical issues for her colossal lack of judgment.

After the wedding, Grandma and Granddad called Annie and me to chat by phone, they sent cookies and gifts, but that fight with my momma was so bad, we didn't see them again for what seemed like, to us as children, forever. Maybe momma told them not to come. Maybe they didn't want to be around Sherwinn. But whatever it was, we felt abandoned by two of the people we loved best in the world.

Later, after what happened, they both apologized, their agony over not seeing what was happening to Annie and me, bringing them to their knees.

With this ring I thee wed, and all my worldly goods I thee endow. In sickness and in health, in poverty or in wealth . . .

The next day, the wedding day, it rained like someone had taken a machete to the turbulent clouds massed over Massachusetts and dumped all the rain in one place.

The wedding was moved indoors. The caterers burned the steaks Sherwinn insisted on. The minister came late because Shell Dee's and Trudy Jo's sons dismantled the minister's engine so he wouldn't make it. When he arrived, after running to the house, he said to my momma, "Are you *sure,* Marie Elise? Very sure?"

Dr. Rubenstein and his wife were in a minor car accident on the way over. Two mirrors fell off the walls and broke. Carman saw a black cat run across the grass.

And still, in our living room, my momma said, I do. Yes.

Interestingly enough, she did not change her last name. "We're the O'Shea girls, that's never going to change."

Sherwinn's eyes, from the moment he was in our house, moved all the way up and down my body, like a serpent. He snapped my bra strap when my momma wasn't looking, wound my curls around his fingers and pulled. He patted my butt when he could, telling me not to be a "bad girl" and to obey him. "I'm your father now, Madeline. As long as you do what I say, we'll get along."

He could hardly quit hugging Annie, dragging her onto his lap and cuddling her.

But never when my momma was looking.

Oh, no, when my momma was around, he was careful. Fatherly.

He touched our momma. He'd hold her close, squishing her chest against his. He'd grab her boobs. He was always slipping a hand over my momma's body, as if her body were his drug. She'd slap his hands away and say, "Not in front of the girls." He'd come up from behind and grind himself against her.

Pretty soon the grind was on us.

. . . till death do us part.

Death did part my momma and Sherwinn.

Death parted Annie and me, physically, from Sherwinn.

But his demented spirit, the crimes he and they committed against us, that hasn't left. It's like I have Sherwinn still with me, still controlling part of my mind that I have tried to snatch back from his evil psychosis my whole life.

11

I dreaded telling Granddad and Annie about the article Marlene was writing, as much as I would dread being run over by a pack of raging rhinos. But it was coming down the pike, and though Keith was throwing legal bombs the publisher's way, he had no ground to stand on, and we both knew it. If I didn't tell them, someone else would, like Marlene, or they'd hear of it when that blasted article was published.

In addition, in the last blackmail letter I had received, one of the photographs, of Annie and me, had been torn up into about five pieces. I got the point. Pay up, or our lives would be ripped apart.

I would not pay up, even though my air seemed to be hiding behind my organs, not swirling through my lungs as it should. I would not be threatened by any man, or woman, ever again in my life. I would not be told what to do. I would not be a victim again.

I waited on the deck of the farmhouse with Annie until Granddad and Grandma finished their stroll through the lavender plants, the late-afternoon sun breaking through the clouds. The day seemed cheerful but ominous. Foreboding.

I could see them in the distance, Grandma smiling, sometimes turning and stroking Granddad's cheek, his smile warm, if not tinged with sadness. Watching Granddad deal with Grandma's dementia had been so painful I thought my guts would split.

"Here we go, Emmanuelle," Granddad said gently, as they walked up the steps to the deck. He looked pale and exhausted. "Let's take a nap."

My grandma smiled at him, coquettishly. "A nap?" She winked at him. "I'll do it, Anton, let's go and take a nap." She glanced over at us, then put a hand over her mouth and giggled. "You mind your mouth! Keep this to ourselves!"

He kissed her cheek and said, "You're right, let's keep it to ourselves." He put an arm around her waist. "I'll be right back," he told Annie and me.

Grandma turned around. "It will be awhile, dear. He doesn't believe in rushing these things." She said in French, "He's a pistol. And the pistol has a certain ... dance, shall we say? A certain rhythm. *Boom, boom, boom.*"

I laughed.

She added, also in French, to Granddad, "I love your rhythm. Rhythm me, handsome."

I watched as they hobbled into the house, Nola opening the door for them.

They both thanked her, and Grandma kissed her cheek. "I love you, Nola."

"I love you, too, Emmanuelle. You are my best friend."

Nola followed Grandma inside. She would not interfere with their love.

About thirty minutes later, Granddad came out and joined us on the porch swing. I knew he had helped her to lie down, brought a comforter up and over her body, then hugged her until she went to sleep. "I have to have Anton's arms around me in bed, or the nightmares come," she'd told me. "He battles those nightmares away from me. Sometimes with a gun! Sometimes with a knife! Sometimes he hides me." Then she whispered, "Sometimes he puts me in a barn or a shed or under a house and I stay quiet. Shhh. I am quiet. Shhh. Quiet so we're not captured and filleted like a fish."

I held Granddad's hand as we swung back and forth. His hand was cold. I didn't want to tell him what I had to say.

"Granddad, I've said it before, I'm gonna say it again,"

Annie said, handing him a glass of lemonade. "You need to go
to the doctor—"

"I'm fine."

He wasn't fine. We knew he wasn't fine.

He brought his other hand up to his forehead and stroked it.
Something was killing him, not just physically, but mentally. It
was the atonement guilt he'd spoken about at Max's.

"You don't look fine."

"Thank you, Madeline. You know how to make an old man
feel older still, downright cadaver-like."

"Any chance you'll go to see Dr. Rubenstein?"

"I will not be going to the doctor. I don't want to be shot, cut
open, forced to swallow vile pills, X-rayed, poked or prodded,
or told what to do."

"Granddad, something isn't right," Annie said. "I'm not a
medical genius, but I see it. You've got a pretty gray sheen to
you."

"That's my makeup," he joked. "I chose the wrong color.
Girls, all is right in terms of the pattern of my life, of your
grandma's life. We're old people. We're getting closer to death. I
have had a long, long life, and I'm ready to go, but I won't go, I
refuse to go"—he raised his voice, as if instructing God—"until
after your grandma. I will care for her until she is no longer with
us."

I pushed my eyelids down so I wouldn't make a mess of myself. See what I mean about their love?

"We love you, we need you," Annie said. "Dr. Rubenstein
could help—"

"And I love you girls, with all my heart, with all my being."
He lifted my hand, then Annie's, and kissed them. "You are
everything to your grandma and me. Everything." His voice
caught on his tears.

"Then stay with us, find out what's wrong."

"Nothing's wrong. I am old. Old people die."

"Something is . . ."

"Do you think that I, at my age, would treat anything that
was wrong with me? I'm not going to do chemo. I'm not even

sure I'd consent to an operation, with the risks of problems afterward, recovery, the pain. There's very little I'd choose to fix. I don't want to do the treatment. I don't want to spend my last days ill, in a hospital, doctors and nurses flurrying around like hyperactive bugs, bothering me."

What do you do with an older relative who is completely sane who won't go to a doctor? Drag him there? Override his decision? Take charge? Take over his life? No. Not if he's still with it, still able to make reasonable, cognitive choices.

Even as I fought off panicky grief at the very thought of losing my granddad, I understood him. If I were his age, would I want to be at the mercy of the medical establishment and perhaps lengthen my life but lose the quality?

"This is not a group decision," Granddad said. "I am not a group. I make my own decisions. I will not listen to your arguments."

"Okay, Granddad," I said, holding his frail hand with both of mine, knowing I was going to cause him grave pain but also knowing I had to do it. "There's something else I have to talk to you and Annie about."

When I was done, Granddad was white. Annie was rigid, staring straight ahead.

The sad part was that I had told them only half of the problem. I hadn't had the heart to tell them about the blackmailing or the photos with the two girls wearing vapid, defeated expressions, dressed in slutty outfits made from leather.

Click, click, click.

Lavender has medicinal uses.

Some say it can help with everything from fungal infections, migraines, aches and pains, insomnia, depression, anxiety, impotence, gas, and gum problems.

There is no conclusive research stating that lavender can whittle away at memories best left forgotten forever.

Annie did not want to talk about our conversation the next day. I accompanied her on a vet call to an alpaca farm, after she'd been on two calls already. One for a cow, one for a horse named Gotcha Baby. The alpaca farm is owned by Bertie Schouten.

Alpacas are beautiful animals. They seem to me to be a cross between Santa Claus's beard, a horse, and a centaur with the black eyes of wet gumdrops.

Annie and I were there because Bertie Schouten said one of his alpacas, named Brad How, was sick.

"He's uh . . . he's uh . . . uh . . . he's under the weather," Bertie told us when we got to his house. Bertie's house was designed by his architect brother, Eric Schouten. It's open and bright with windows and glass doors everywhere. "It's not enough that I live in the country," Bertie told me one time. "My brother wanted the country inside my house. He wanted me living amidst all these hills and trees and rabbits and chipmunks and mountain lions running around here. I can almost feel the grass under my butt when I sleep. Look at these walls of windows. If I saw a bear outside I'd probably start running in the other direction and plow right through a sheet of glass to get away and bust my head open."

Bertie is supersmart. He went to MIT. He flies in and out quite a bit, so he hires Annie to take care of his alpacas when he's gone. We're not sure where he goes, he's very vague, but he has come back with a couple of not-so-fun diseases, his face has been mangled up a few times, an arm broken, and a leg smashed, so the guy is probably in and out of some third world countries getting in fights.

"He's in Special Ops," Annie told me, cracking her gum. "Highly trained, on-contract. He's like Tom Cruise in one of his movies only he loves Alpacas. He's a strange guy."

"Brad How is coughing, too," Bertie said, his face happy and shining with good glee. "But come on in first, I have lunch ready. You ladies need to sit down and take a break. How's your shoulder, Annie? Better?"

"It's fine," she drawled. Annie had mentioned she scratched it in the woods on a horseback ride.

"Lunch'll be great," I said. I turned to Annie and grabbed her elbow as she hesitated. She was wearing jeans and a green tank top. Her arms are so built up with muscle she looks like a Barbie doll—Ken, the Barbie doll, not dimwitted Barbie the Barbie doll. Annie might look slender all dressed, but she is wiry and hard and gives her punching bag hell every night for about an hour.

Bertie opened the door wide. "I have your favorite soup, Annie, that artichoke chicken that you love from the café, plus a fresh shrimp and avocado salad from Darren's Deli, those fluffy rolls from Chitty Chang's bakery, and a fresh green salad. I went over to Sally's and got some of her lettuce. I know you love her arugula."

Annie managed a tight smile.

"And I bought a chocolate cheesecake. I know you like chocolate cheesecake, Annie."

Such an eager beaver.

"Yum," I said, pinching Annie's elbow

She managed another tight smile. I saw her swallow hard. I pulled her inside.

"I've got the table set outside on the deck, Annie," Bertie said, so delighted to have Annie for lunch. "I know you like the view. The weather's perfect today. We'll eat, and when you're ready we'll go and see Brad How."

"You are so thoughtful, Bertie," I said. "This is my favorite vet call of the day."

It was the only call of the day that I was going on. The only one I'd been invited on so far. Truth was, every time that Bertie called because an alpaca was sick, Annie made me come.

Why?

Because Bertie is in love with Annie. He can hardly think he's so in love with her, and she needs me as a buffer.

"Here, Annie," Bertie said, pulling out a chair for her. Annie sat down, still silent, and he handed her a yellow cloth napkin. Cloth napkins. Can you imagine? A man who understands the value of a cloth napkin?

I sat down and Bertie poured both of us raspberry lemonade. You might think that Bertie was very unattractive, like a sumo wrestler with two heads and a tail, which is why Annie won't date him.

Or you might think that he has a terrible personality, perhaps psychotic or clingy controlly or deadly boring, which would explain why Annie won't date him.

Perhaps it has crossed your mind that maybe Bertie has been married many times and has many bratty children and a leech-sucking momma, which would explain why Annie won't date him.

"I hope you like it, Annie," he said. "You, too, Madeline," he added as an afterthought.

She smiled tightly. She swallowed hard.

None of those assumptions would be true.

Bertie is perfect. He's tall, lanky, and strong with longish blond hair and rimmed glasses. He wears manly man sorts of clothes. He's never been married, no kids. I've met his mother and father, and if I could adopt them, I would. His two sisters and two brothers live in the area, and they are so funny I wet my pants one time I was laughing so hard.

"I bought you some of that peanut brittle you like from Elga's, when I was on the East Coast. I'll bring it over later."

See? He would bring peanut brittle over later. He wouldn't give it to her now, no, he needed an excuse to drop by her house.

"Thank you," she said tightly. I kicked her under the table. "That's nice."

Bertie's face fell at her tone. He cleared his throat. He sat down, eying her, with more hope than he should have.

Bertie told me once that Annie was the most beautiful woman he knew. No matter how Annie has tried to play down her looks, she can't hide perfect bone structure, puffy lips, huge eyes the color of a twirling blue-green sea, and hair that is thick and dark.

But it's not her physical beauty he loves.

"Annie understands people, Madeline," he'd told me. "She is one of the only people I know who is able to look past the surface and see people, see what's inside. She can talk about anything, but she listens, too. No one listens anymore, but she does and she's so damn smart. She's gentle with everyone. I can relax around her. Sort of. I mean, I can hardly think when I'm with her. I want to talk to her, and make her laugh." He put his head in his hands. "I've tried everything, Madeline. I asked her to go to a play with me in Portland, out on my boat, to a barbeque with my family, out to dinner and breakfast and lunch, even brunch. She won't go. She doesn't like me, does she?"

I patted his shoulder.

Annie liked him. Everyone liked Bertie. What was not to like?

But Annie couldn't . . . get involved.

She never had. We, together, can't.

She had tried, I had tried, but men make us feel physically ill when they touch us.

"I'm not gay," she'd told me, years ago, as we sat together overlooking the rows of lavender plants, yellow raincoats on as Oregon's almost constant winter drizzle drizzled over our hoods. "I'm not attracted to women."

I put an arm around her shoulder. "Me either. I don't want to touch a breast. I don't want to touch my own breasts that much."

"And I sure as heck don't need another vagina in my life."

"No, no to another vagina."

"And I don't need another woman in my home with hormonal mood swings."

"Or cramps."

"Or yeast."

"No yeast. For heaven's sakes, why did God make vaginal yeast possible?"

"Mistake. It was a mistake. He had a whoops. Probably got sidetracked, we all do."

We pondered that, God getting sidetracked.

"But I think about having sex with a man and all I can see is . . ." Annie whispered out a terrible mutual flashback in a few succinct words, the bad dream we'd lived through barreling in in Technicolor.

"I can't do it. I can't have a man touching me." She ran her hands over her arms, as if they were suddenly crawling.

"I feel the same." A mental image of the snake lover popped into my mind. The snake lover could touch me, but only him.

"I've accepted that I can't change this part of myself, Madeline. No can do. I have a blue house here in the country. I see Grandma and Granddad and you all the time. When I'm not with my animals I work on my rose garden, or fire up the ol' chain saw, punch my boxing bag, go to Fiji, walk. I read, I listen to music. That's enough. It's more than most people have, and I'm sick of trying to be someone I know I'm not and can't be. That relationship, with a man, is not going to happen for me."

Those three men had robbed my sister and me of much of ourselves, as surely as if some phantom wielding a scythe had burst through the ceiling of hell and carved us inside out and thrown our guts into a bonfire.

"I get it, Annie."

"Any feeling or desire I might have had to be with a man, have a husband, was killed. Slaughtered by him and his sick friends. If only I had been trained in knife fighting or grenade throwing then."

"My rage about them comes like a rush, like a train, and either I am bowled over by it or I come up swinging. I can't predict when it'll come, but when it does it's like I'm gone and the rage is replacing me. Do you think the rage will ever go away?"

"I don't know, Madeline, I don't know. Shit. Why do you think I'm so good at attacking wood with my chain saw?"

In that drizzle we watched the sun go down, right over the bluish purple coast range in the distance, the lavender swaying ever so gently under the rain.

So a relationship with the eager Bertie wasn't going to happen.

We ate lunch and Bertie and I talked. Annie entered the conversation sporadically, and she even smiled several times. Each time she did I saw Bertie's face light up, like the sun was feeling a burst of delight, a spurt of joy.

But when his hand and her hand accidentally touched as they

reached for the same bowl, Annie's hand jerked away and the sun on Bertie's face went down.

"Come here, Brad How," Annie murmured to the alpaca after lunch, standing in the middle of the corral among six other alpacas. "Come here, my friend."

I didn't think the alpaca was sick.

In fact, I knew he wasn't sick. If he was sick, Bertie would have separated the animal from the others. He knew to do that. He had simply forgotten to do it, because he was lovesick.

Brad How looked perfectly healthy. He even ran about, had tons of energy, nuzzled Annie.

It was all a ruse.

All an excuse for the lovesick Bertie to have yet another few hours with the love of his life, my sister, Annie, who was haunted by a shack of a house, a camera, and men who had perversion coursing through their arteries, like the rest of us have blood. Annie couldn't love a man because of the clawed demons that sprung from the murkiest recesses of her mind. That's what caused my rage.

My rage was eating me.

In my head I heard an orchestra warming up. Eventually they played Aaron Copland's *Appalachian Spring* and Nikolai Rimsky-Korsakov's *Capriccio Espagnol*. Totally opposite pieces.

Stunning.

"I remember where that long, skinny scratch came from, Madeline," my grandma said the next morning, running a finger down the back of my violin.

"You do? Where?" Grandma and I swung on the porch swing, the sun poking over the hills, red, fluffy blankets wrapped around our shoulders. Grandma had asked me to "fiddle it out," and I played "The Arkansas Traveler" and "Ragtime Annie" while she clapped her hands, then asked for the violin.

"That scratch happened when we were playing in the gardens by the swan pond. You were playing a song for the unicorns! Do you remember that? How colorful the gardens were! All the grass to run on and the trees! Old, so tall, the branches wide enough to hide tiny tree dwarfs here and there, chatting yellow cats and singing peacocks. . . ."

I smiled, my heart aching a smidge. I had so loved my grandma's stories when I was younger. She would pretend there were tiny angels hiding between the purple lavender flowers or miniature villages filled with frogs riding bikes and chasing butterflies. She would point to an outbuilding and tell me there was a silver staircase made of stars leading down, down, down into the earth where a pile of colorful jewels was guarded by a jealous witch.

Even when I was a teenager, my childhood a catastrophic wreck, her imaginative stories took Annie and me away from the harsh reality of the charred ruin of our lives.

"That sounds like a fantasy garden," I said.

"It was!" She patted her white hair, up in a sophisticated chignon. She was wearing her diamonds that morning, with a red sweater and beige slacks. "There were fountains and pathways, flowers blooming everywhere in pots and in the trees! Do you remember the swans on the pond, Madeline? We named them Queen, King, Prince, and Princess! And the stories we told! How they turned into kings, queens, princes, and princesses at night and danced across the pond on ice skates when you and I were sleeping."

"Were they good dancers?" I sunk into my grandma's storytelling. There is comfort in hearing stories from the same beloved person again and again, even if that person is sitting beside you, awash in dementia and needing twenty-four-hour care.

"Yes, most elegant, with tuxedos and gold dresses, crowns, jewels. The orchestra was there, too. Mother and Father had their orchestra friends over all the time, you remember, for impromptu concerts. They all brought their instruments out on the patio and they would play, Father on his violin in his silvery chair, and all their children would run around and laugh and chase each other and the fairies would come out and light the way on the paths of lavender with their glittery wings. Now, do you remember where this scratch came from?" She touched the scratch on my violin with her finger.

I shook my head, and she cupped my cheek.

"It was so funny! You were running with your violin, around and around the pond, and you ran to give Father a hug, and you tripped over a cello—it was owned by a renowned cellist—and you fell on the patio and that's how it scratched. The Tinkerbells had to pick you up. It was brand new, too! Mother and Father had given it to you for your birthday."

There was her past, her authentic history, mixed in with a few Tinkerbells.

"But then they came!" Grandma said, shoving my hand away. "They shot their ghost guns and they set the house on fire! All of the paintings, the staircase, Mother's dresses, Father's tuxedos, the instruments, they burned it all after the murders."

"Grandma," I said hurriedly, as she started shouting and stood up, shaking her fist through the mist of the morning and cursing in French, then German. "It's okay, Grandma. I'm right here. It's me, Madeline."

"They came with their ghost guns and you jumped from the sky and hid under the boat with the boy with the blood, but the swans, they grew and grew, and protected you from the black ghosts!"

I felt like I'd been stabbed in the gut. "What?"

Her eyes went blank, blanker than they already were. She was lost in her own turbulent memories. She balled her hands into fists and jammed them together, slipping into German. "I hate them! I curse them! They did it! They put hate in themselves and killed and he couldn't walk! No walking! But he had a gun. And she did, too! She shot, too! For protection! For love!" She hit her fists together, hard, swore again, then the fight left her, in a rush, as if it ran out through her feet, and she sank back onto the swing. "I miss them, don't you, Madeline? I always miss them. The fairies couldn't save them with their glittery wings. The pelicans who served tea couldn't get through the gates to help. The flamingos tried to fly in but they were shot, too. Pink and dead. Even the mice with the hats were smashed by black boots. There was no more magic."

"Grandma, I—"

"It was all gone, Madeline, remember? Like that. Burned. The ashes fell down. Even the swans were burned down to their beaks. That was all that was left of the swans."

My dear grandma, the woman who could weave a story from the wind and the curve of a flower petal, started to cry. "Down to their beaks. There was no honk left."

I held her close, rocked her back and forth, shaken. Her past was shaking me, the honks were shaking me, and somewhere between the shots and the honks, there was the truth.

I received yet another e-mail from Marlene, the reporter I hated. It wasn't personal.

"I would still like to interview you for this article, Madeline. I know you don't want to do it. I know you've asked for privacy, and I understand your request. I do. But please know that this is an opportunity for you to share what you remember about your mother. I would like your input, and Annie's, and I would like to talk to your grandparents. There's some confusion for me, and I'm hoping you can clear it up. I've looked up your grandparents and I have a few questions. . . ."

Can you confirm that your grandma was born in Holland before moving to France as a young girl?

Holland?

She wasn't born in Holland.

Can you confirm that your grandma was one of eight children and her parents' names were Solomon and Yentl Levine?

Grandma was an only child. I don't know her parents' names. I don't know if I've ever known them. It was part of a past she mostly refused to talk about.

Can you confirm that your grandfather's parents' names were Shani and Tomer Laurent and their family has lived in France for hundreds of years?

My grandparents were born in Germany, then moved to France when they were very young children. Their parents were born in Germany, while *their* parents on both sides were born in Russia. . . . I didn't know their names, either. . . .

Can you confirm that your grandfather had two brothers, Meyer and Sagi?

My granddad did not have any brothers.

In doing a little research, I am very confused about something else, too. If you could call me, perhaps you could clear things up.

I was confused about all the questions.

I deleted the message and called Keith Stein.

"We're about done, Madeline. There's nothing I can do here." He cleared his throat. "You need to prepare yourself. You need to prepare your sister and your granddad. I know your grandma has dementia, but she's a smart lady, so keep the newspapers and Marlene's magazine away from her."

"The newspapers? Plural?"

"The newspapers, plural. I think they'll run with this, too. It'll die down, Madeline, trust me, but it was an enormous case years ago, and as you know, people have always been curious about what happened to you and Annie. Your granddad fended them off for a long time when you were kids, but with your popularity growing . . . this is one more twist that they'll be interested in."

I was a twist. Annie and I were a twist. Our momma was a twist.

I thought of my momma. Her maiden name had been Marie Elise Laurent. What a beautiful name.

My granddad's name is Anton Laurent. My grandma's name is Emmanuelle Laurent. Her maiden name was . . . her maiden name was . . . what was her maiden name again?

Holland? Where did Marlene get Holland?

12

～

Sherwinn did not waste much time after he married our momma on a day when mirrors broke, a storm blew in, and the steaks burned to turn our lives into a torture chamber.

"Come and sit on my lap, Madeline," he told me, winding his fingers around the curls of my hair. Of course he couldn't see the red in it.

"No, it's okay."

My momma had already gone to bed, the fatigue catching up to her. "I am wilting like a lazy yellow tulip," she'd said, her skin pale. We didn't know then what was growing in her head.

"Right here, right now." He patted his lap. He was sitting in the leather chair my dad always sat in. I used to climb on my dad's lap all the time, Annie and I together, and he would read one story after another to us. He especially liked stories about boats, fish, and fishermen. Sometimes he'd make up stories about brave fisherwomen who caught more fish than all the fishermen—striped fish, polka-dot fish, pink fish, fish the size of our house by the sea. "Women can talk to fish and the fish listen," my dad told us. "There are magic fish out there, Pink Girls. Magic fish." We'd giggle and he'd wriggle his eyebrows at us.

"Get over here, Madeline." Sherwinn's voice hardened, but he kept it down so my momma wouldn't hear. "Get over here right this damn minute."

"No, I don't want to." I felt a cold snake of fear swirling around my spine.

Annie was upstairs doing homework. I'd tried to go upstairs as soon as Sherwinn came home from the bar, but he hadn't let me. He'd had me make him a turkey, lettuce, and pickle sandwich and he'd watched me the whole time. "Add more ketchup. For blood." He'd giggled.

"Yes, right now. Don't be a bad girl."

"No." The snake twisted around my spine and stopped up all my breath in my back.

Sherwinn got up from my dad's leather chair, smiled that sick, scary smile at me, then took his muscled arm and swept all my homework off the table and onto the floor, even my pink pencil box my momma bought me and my pink folder for my spelling words. He picked me up out of the chair and flung me over his back.

I struggled, and he laughed, bringing me down on his lap in my dad's chair, one meaty hand over my mouth.

When I kept struggling, he yanked my curls back and hissed like a demon. "Shut up, Madeline. I'm going to give you a checkup because you're a dirty girl." He let go of my mouth and put a hand on my neck.

"I don't want a checkup. Dr. Dorn does my checkups." The freezing cold snake kept slithering.

"I'm going to do it. That geeky doctor doesn't know what to check for, but I do." He grinned at me again. "Don't say a word, Madeline, not a word," he hissed in my ear. "You have to be quiet for your checkup. Be a good girl. You want to be a good girl, don't you?"

I nodded, panicky.

"Your momma needs you to be a good girl. No one likes a bad girl. No one wants to be with a bad girl. No one wants to live with a bad girl. You be good and don't cause your momma or me any problems, you got that? I don't want to tell your momma you're a bad girl because then you couldn't live with us."

"I'm not a bad girl," I protested, fighting back tears. The snake bit my spine.

"Not yet, you're not. Now hold still so I can check you."

I struggled and he pulled back on my curls, wrapping them around his fingers, as if he enjoyed it, my neck snapping back.

"No checking, no checking . . . I don't want you to check me. I'm healthy!"

He pulled my hair again, and I felt some of it rip from the roots of my scalp.

"I said to be good," he hissed. "Be good, you short bitch."

Hot tears flowed out of my eyes and my nose started to run.

"Momma," I pleaded, my voice cracking. "Momma!"

Sherwinn slapped a hand to my mouth. "Shut your face." He laughed, low and husky, with a high-pitched corkscrew at the end.

That corkscrew shook my whole paralyzed body as his hands, Sherwinn's beefy, sweaty, sticky hands, "checked me," from the top of my head, over my shoulders, down my chest, between my legs, up between my legs, and over my butt when he flipped me over, my face staring at our wood floors. When he was done he gripped the curls of my hair. "Did you like that, Madeline?"

He made my head nod up and down, then giggled.

I have no idea how long this went on. I have no idea if it was five minutes or five hours.

What I do remember is going still, every bone going still, even the cold snake stilled, as my mind left me, I know it did. It left so that it could save me from those cascading pits of emotional destruction, and all I could hear was violin music—sweet, piercing, haunting violin music—as I was checked.

My hell began.

In the morning Sherwinn smirked at me, and when my momma wasn't looking, he snuck up on me in the bathroom when I was brushing my teeth with cinnamon toothpaste and whispered, "We'll have more fun tonight."

I vomited in the sink, the red toothpaste mixed with streaks and smears.

He laughed, with that sick corkscrew at the end, then ripped my hair back. "If you tell your mother what happened, I'll do to her what I did to Mickey."

I wiped my mouth, panicking again, tears rushing to my eyes. "What do you mean?" I coughed. "What did you do to Mickey?"

He giggled again.

Mickey was my hamster. My dad had given Annie and me hamsters about a week before he died.

I ran out of the bathroom and peered in Mickey's cage. His body looked funny, like he'd been squished, like he was a hamster pancake. He used to be fluffy and plump, now he looked so . . . thin.

"Mickey?" I said, my voice weak, shaking, the vomit scent circling around me. "Mickey?" I opened the cage and stuck my hand in, stroked his furry body. "Mickey!"

I put my head back and howled.

Mickey was dead.

Sherwinn had killed my Mickey.

I hardly remember the next few days of unrelenting misery and fear.

The only thing I remember is that a full orchestra—cellos, clarinets, French horns, bassoons, trombones, tubas, violins, trumpets—was blaring in my head and it never let up, it never let me go, it never left me.

Some people would say that hearing an orchestra meant that I was teetering, at least somewhat, into craziness. Others would say it was brilliance, not necessarily healthy brilliance.

I would argue that the only thing that kept me sane was that orchestra.

The only thing.

After Sherwinn killed Mickey, I sat like a mummy at school.

I didn't do my work. I stared.

I didn't play at recess with my friends. I stood against the wall of the school.

I didn't talk. I hunkered down, numb.

My teacher, Mrs. Rodriquez, asked me what was wrong, and all I could see was Mickey, dead in his cage.

"What is it, honey?"

I had loved that hamster.

"Can you tell me? Are you sick?"

If I told, Momma would die.

"Honey, do you want to go to the nurse's office and lie down?"

My dad was dead.

"You can go home and rest if you want. I can call your mother at the beauty parlor and she can come and get you."

My momma couldn't know. She would become a person pancake, like my hamster. I shook.

"No, I'm fine," I said. "I'm fine."

Fine. I wasn't fine. I was dying.

I stuck as close as I could to Annie.

Not for me, for her.

He wasn't doing the same thing to Annie, was he?

Please let it be only me. I hugged Annie close, even though I suddenly believed I was dirty. Yucky. Bad. Such a bad girl. Sherwinn's hands were sticky and hot and mean and they made me dirty. I could feel their dirt on me even in the shower, even though I scrubbed and scrubbed. I could feel that dirt and shame. It never washed away. Overnight I remember feeling that I wasn't good enough anymore. I didn't have the vocabulary to explain how I felt, but as an adult, I named it: I was shamed and unworthy.

But Annie, with her luminescent blue-green eyes and her clean, chocolate brown hair with the red Irish sheen, she was innocent and sweet and kind. I didn't even want her to know what happened to me. I didn't want anyone to know. I was so humiliated I could hardly lift my head. And Sherwinn kept telling me that he hoped I wouldn't be a bad girl.

"Bad girls get in even worse trouble than Mickey," he told me after he left my bedroom one night. He'd put his lips on mine and stuck his tongue in my mouth. My body ached. It hurt where he'd touched me, rubbed me with his sweaty hands.

Two days later, Teresa was dead.

Annie picked up her hamster in her small hands and ran out into the yard, screaming.

I turned to Sherwinn, shocked, horrified.

He smiled at me. "She's a bad girl, too," he whispered. "As bad as you."

13

"Thank you for joining us this morning, Madeline."

"Thanks for asking me to be here." I spoke into the microphone, adjusted the headphones over my ears, and smiled across the table at Conner Mills, Portland's most popular radio show announcer.

White haired, six foot six inches tall, gruff and blunt, the man had a heart of gold and came to see me at my office because he secretly knitted baby booties and wanted my help in building his confidence and "Grabbing His Gumption," my slang, to get out there and sell them. "I know I could market these, Madeline. I'm up all night making them, see here, I'm so careful with my stitches."

The baby booties were not normal pink and blue baby booties. They were frogs, pigs, salamanders, worms, cows, cats, pigs. But the booties didn't match. You chose two animals for your baby. "Kids like animals, right?" he said. "They can have a polar bear on one foot and a giraffe on the other."

He had a point. Why limit the animals in your life?

"I'm thinking about making them for adults, too. I made them for myself and my wife. She likes wearing one dolphin because she likes swimming and one giraffe because she likes friendly eyes. Me, I wear a jaguar on my right foot because I like to think I'm fast and a gorilla on my left because I like bananas. See? You can personalize your feet animals. What do you think?"

"I think it's brilliant. I'll take a cat and a gargoyle."

"A gargoyle? Hey. I can do it."

"One animal purrs at you, the other eats you, Conner."

All traces of animal baby booties were gone that morning at the radio station. The man was a pro. Work was work. Do it right or don't do it at all.

"People," he said into his microphone. "Madeline O'Shea lives here with us. She's an Oregonian, graduated from Beaverton High, and is the nation's most popular life coach. She's a weekly columnist for the popular magazine *Boutique*. 'A Life Coach Tells You How to Live It' is filled with advice from The O'Shea Principles, and any conference she speaks at sells out within hours. She's a life coach who specializes in relationships, but Americans go to her for advice about every aspect of their lives from jobs, career paths, and marriage to enlightenment, fulfillment, and integrating a meaningful life into the life they're living."

Yes, I advise people, I thought, but I rarely follow my own advice. Should I announce that on air? "Yeah, I sling out O'Shea Principles and quotes but I am a lost cause." Should I say that? Should I say that I'm a lie? It's exhausting being a lie.

"Tell us how you got started, Madeline."

"I was getting a degree in counseling, but I wasn't doing very well in my classes because I spent so much time playing my violin in the university's orchestra. I also stood on the street corner and played my violin for money for a few hours a day. Anyhow, I started writing an advice column for the university's newspaper because it paid twenty dollars. Soon it was picked up by other newspapers and syndicated. Grew from there. I took on clients. I was asked to speak at various events, small ones, then larger. I started writing my column in *Boutique*."

"You were young when you started advising people on how to live their lives."

I was young when I started *listening* to advice. My momma in her pink beauty parlor was an overflowing fountain of it.

"I gave them the truth, Conner. I was young and blunt and saw through all the bull-arky that surrounded their lives and their relationships. I showed them a path out. Here's how to deal with an ass at work, here's how to widen your life, here's why you gotta get rid of that person. I added acronyms like D.O.N.'T. B.E.A.W.U.S.S. and I was in business."

Yes, I was young. At first I counseled a lot of young people. Then they brought their parents in. Grief, the gunshots, the trials, all of that made me waaaay more mature than I should have been. And I was angry, I was not sympathetic to whiners or sulkers, and I swatted my clients' sorry butts more times than I can count. Funny enough, they bought into my tyrannical tirades.

"Your career is blazing hot and getting hotter, Madeline. Why do you think people need life coaches?"

I did not say, "Because they need someone to hold their hands when they launch their animal booties." I said, "People need life coaches because life is a freakin' mess."

Conner laughed. "It sure is."

"I can only compare life to being shot from a cannon into the middle of space and being bombarded by all sorts of debris—pieces of satellites and shuttles, asteroids, shooting stars, maybe an alien spaceship. We're hit all the time and sometimes we can't find Earth. We can't even find the Milky Way galaxy. We're lost. Running around, dodging this and that, trying not to get hurt or killed, and all the while we're looking for home. That's how life is. It's a meteor shower. People call me to help them get recentered, to help them with their life relationships, whether it's work or personal, so they can get back out there and do the three Fs."

"What are the Fs?" He knew what they were. We had discussed them at length when discussing piggies.

I winked at him, and he chuckled. "The three Fs stand for fight, fortitude, and forgiveness. We all have to get out there and fight. Fact is, life feels like a fight sometimes. You have to fight for your job, your promotion. Sometimes you have to fight with your mechanic who thinks it's okay to charge a woman twice as much as a man. Women have to show their balls, no other way around it."

Conner slammed his mouth shut so he wouldn't laugh.

"You have to fight for yourself, surround yourself with good people, positive people, so the negative spiders at the bottom of the barrel don't bite you. You have to have fortitude, strength. Don't whine. Don't feel sorry for yourself. Don't pity yourself. On any day I can tell you that there are, literally, billions of people on this planet having a worse day than you. And forgiveness is to forgive people who have wronged you and let it go, and forgive yourself, and let it go. So three F it, Conner."

"With the three Fs in mind, we'll have our first caller on the air. He doesn't want to give his name, but he wants to know what you think of open marriages because he wants to be in one."

"Hello," I said pleasantly.

"Hi, *Mad-e-line!* Wow. Sweet. Awesome. Thanks for taking my call. I saw a photograph of you and can I say that you are gorgeous?"

"You could say that, but we're not on topic, are we? Would you tell a man that he was gorgeous? No. Okay, so you want to be in an open marriage. Are you in one now?"

"Geez...uh...blunt question there....I'm married...yeah."

"I hate when people are vague. Are you in an open marriage now?"

"Uh. Boy, uh, my wife isn't in an open marriage, but I think I want to embrace that lifestyle...."

"Which means you're cheating on your wife, do I about have it?"

Conner's expression was stamped with surprise.

Dead silence. Dead. "Uh. Ah. That's a hard question....I've met someone, but...I...I still love my wife."

"But you're sleeping with two women, right, and you want me to condone this?"

Conner mouthed to me, "How did you know?"

The caller's voice came out spindly, winded. "I'm, professionally speaking, I uh, I just was wondering what you think of open marriages."

"You don't have an open marriage. You are cheating on your wife."

I heard him suck in his breath.

"You are a slug. You are a dishonest cheat. You are cheating your wife, your kids, your marriage vows, and you're cheating this woman you're with, although I don't care about her because she knows you're married, so that makes her a hormone-flashing slug."

He coughed, sputtered, his voice pitched. "Yeah . . . she knows. . . . We met at work and we can't control our feelings for each other. You can't stop yourself from falling in love, can you? But I still want my wife and the kids. . . . This gal is only for me, you know, to give me some relief, to help me get through my day, to offer sex and fun."

"Yeah, bite me, you creep. You're a liar. Your morals are in the mud. No, they're beneath the mud. They are in a swamp of infested termites. This is not an open marriage. What do I think of open marriages? I think open marriages work until you realize that your partner is boinking someone else and has a whole secret other life without you and is comparing your performance, and the size of your thingie, with her new partner's. I think open marriages are slimy and crude and beneath all of us. Kind of like you." I looked up at the phone number on the reader board and the name of the caller. "Okay, Korbin Berndale of Southeast Portland, I hope I've answered your question."

I disconnected the call. Conner said, "Thank you, Madeline!"

I winked at Conner. He laughed back. I had high hopes that his booties would sell. Monsters and chickens together! Zebras and King Kong!

"We'll go to commercial and be back with Ned, who hates his in-laws, particularly his father-in-law who is constantly putting him down. This is Conner Mills for KBAM." We took our earphones off. "Madeline, you gotta get your own radio show. You'd sizzle the wires off the damn poles."

After leaving the radio station, I walked back to my office. On the way I passed a major chain bookstore. In the windows were his books.

I wouldn't buy them.

I had an idea of what they were about, because I'd read the reviews, but I couldn't go there, couldn't read them.

He was famous for those books. He was a professor at a college. He lived on acreage in Massachusetts. He traveled. He wrote.

He knew. He knew what happened.

After we left Cape Cod, he tried to keep in contact. Letters, postcards, drawings. I never replied.

As adults, letters, e-mails, a postcard arrived, infrequent, friendly, cheerful, nonthreatening.

I shut down.

I thought of him often.

But I would not respond.

He was coming to Portland to speak.

I would not go and see him.

I wouldn't call him.

I couldn't.

Torey Oh growled at me.

"Good," I said. "Do it again."

He growled deep, flicked his tail. The long, brownish tail was attached to the back of his suit. It was not a real tail.

"Once more, with feeling. Growl! Grrr!"

He growled, arched his claws up, then hissed.

"Motivating, Torey. That was motivating."

Deep-throated roar, scarily threatening.

"Outstanding. I think we're making progress."

"You do?" Torey settled on the floor, cross legged, and I joined him. Good thing I was wearing a blue suit jacket and pants, not one of my dull skirts.

I adjusted my armor. He wrapped his tail around his lap.

"Good releasing of your animalistic emotions," I said. "And I like your suit."

"Thanks. I got it from the tailor's. I think this charcoal color matches with my tail, don't you? The fabric of the suit, versus the fluffiness of the tail, but I think the tail is making a statement, too."

"What is the statement of this particular tail?" I crossed my legs.

"The statement is"—he flicked his hands up and down, as if he was playing the drums—"The statement is: Animals."

"I like animals. How is your company coming along?"

"Rippin' like a raptor."

"Rippin'?"

"Yeah, we're all on board. Got a growly woman named Geraldine in charge. Vice president is Foresty Green. That's not her birth name," he hastened to add. "Her birth name is Cybil, but she didn't like that name, so she changed it."

"I can see why."

"Foresty is groovin' in my vision. See, all the profits are going toward organizations that help animals." He stroked his tail.

I nodded. "I like animals."

"Me too. Can I ask you something?"

"Shoot."

"Will this make me happy?" He stroked his tail.

I thought about that. "Torey, you've been coming here to chat for a year."

He nodded.

"First you came in your designer suits, and we talked, and I knew you were hiding something."

"Yeah, you sniffed that out like a fox."

"So we got to the center of you, and why you like the tails."

"Because my dad always pulled the tails of our dogs so hard." He sniffled.

"Yes." I tried not to think of my hamster.

"He pulled them till they screamed and whimpered." He whimpered, his face started to crumple, and he brought his tail up to hide it. His father seriously damaged him.

"Right. And, Torey." I barked at him, softly, until he snapped back out of that memory. "You admitted you wore tails to relax and now you bring them with you here."

"I like to do that. You make me feel normal, Madeline, not like I'm a crazy badger."

"Is it important to you to feel normal?"

He thought about that. "I don't know...." He blinked rapidly. "I don't know if that's important. Is it?"

"It's only important if you feel it is, but then you have to figure out why on earth it would be important to you, Torey Oh, to feel normal."

He barked, twice, like a question, and I knew I'd given him something to think about.

"And what is normal? What is normal to you?" I asked.

He stroked his tail, confused.

I whimpered like a dog. "You took that terrible experience with your father, you left home at seventeen, put yourself through college, started a business with technology stuff I don't understand, and you're a millionaire. You're only twenty-eight. You're amazingly successful, Torey, I have no idea why you wouldn't embrace being you."

"Because I wasn't sure if being me was good enough."

I felt like I was sagging into myself. *Not good enough.* I have been fighting to be "good enough" my whole life. When I wore pink, I was good enough. After Momma died, I never wore it again. I glared at my brown heels. Not good enough.

"Torey, you are good enough. You are more than good enough. You are fantastic."

Two tears ran down his handsome, angular face. He wiped them with his tail. "I feel like I'm trying to prove it to myself, but it's not here"—he pounded his chest—"in the doggy heart." He made a sad dog sound.

"What have we done so far, Torey, to make you feel good enough, safe, joyful?"

"You made me get a hobby." His face brightened. "You said try snorkeling so I could see a whole new world in the water, with fish and turtles, so I went to Maui three times. I saw fish that looked like they were wrapped in plaid, rainbow fish, fish with fins that looked like feathers, and the hugest turtle ever." He paddled his arms as if he were a fish, then became more animated. "You told me to get out of that dingy apartment I had and buy a house that was pretty and had views so I could have vision and think into the heavens. I liked that line. Think into the heavens." He barked, happily.

Torey and a team of contractors had restored his whole, gracious 1920s home to the period. It was painted yellow with white trim on the outside, yellow and white walls on the inside. The kitchen, the wide wood floors, the box ceilings, the built-ins, the shelving, and the fireplaces were all lovingly repaired, sanded, painted, and designed so you felt that twenties homey splendor.

"I still feel safe there. Lots of land, on a hill, not too big or lonely. It feels like history. The family who built it had a horse farm. I like horses." He flicked his tail. "Neigh!"

"I told you to get another interest outside of work so you could bond with people, make friends."

"And I did!" He pounded his tail, bopping up and down with excitement. "I volunteer at the humane society, and I revamped their computers and I walk the dogs. Now I have friends who love animals, too."

"So, Torey, you own a company, you volunteer, you love to snorkel, you have friends. You donate money all the time, so you're a giver. You're continually asking me if one thing or another is going to make you happy."

"Yes."

I leaned over and patted his tail. "Take it, Torey. Take this, take all you have, and be grateful for it, be humble, and accept that you're happy."

"I am?"

"Yes, Torey. You're happy."

He looked quizzical, confused, then a smile formed.

"Torey, your happiness is right here. This is it. *This is happy.* When you look back at your life as an old man, you're going to say, 'That was one of the best times of my life.' This is 'that' time. Embrace it. You don't need to look around further. Sometimes we miss happy because we're always looking for something else. We worry, we give in to fear, we compare ourselves to others, we're planning and plotting, but happiness is here, it's a choice, day to day."

Then why wasn't I happy?

He swirled his furry tail, his smile growing. He barked at me, I barked back, then meowed, then he reached over our curled-up legs and hugged me.

He wrapped his tail around my waist.

I received another manila envelope.

I didn't want to open it. I fought it, fought the bile threatening to form a whirlpool and choke off my breath, but in the end, with numb hands and a resigned, numb mind, I slid the note and the photos out. Ah, yes. He was furious. He wanted the money, didn't I know he would release these pictures shortly and my entire life would be nothing? He spelled nothing as nuthin. He also misspelled pictures. He spelled it pitchers.

A genius.

A conscienceless genius.

I stared at the black-and-white, gritty, trashy, annihilating photos but tried to block the impact of them.

It was impossible. I remember that day. I remember everything, even that I heard Beethoven, Symphony no. 6, *Pastoral,* in my head. A lovely piece, triumphant piece, as Annie and I descended into black muck.

The photos slipped to the floor from fingers that had lost their grip as I leaned against the tight leather couch that I don't like.

14

Sherwinn was "visiting" me at night.

Women said that Sherwinn was movie star good looking, but his face, hard edged and with a scar over his eye, scared the tar out of me. "You want me to take off my shirt so you can feel my chest, sweetie?"

"No." I trembled all over.

"Yes, you do, sweetie. You want to touch me. It's okay. Women have always been all over me. My aunt, she was all over me when I was eleven damn years old."

Something changed in the blankness of his eyes. Something flashed, evil and sick and livid with anger.

"I was eleven and she was twenty-two. Twenty-two!" he shouted. He pounded the wall above my head. My momma was out with Carman, Shell Dee, and Trudy Jo. They'd gone roller skating. I had begged her not to go. She'd hugged and kissed me, and left.

"She'd come into my bedroom every night and take off my pajamas. They were my train pajamas, I remember that. Trains! And she'd get on top of me and make me touch her breasts, her hips, that furry area between a woman's legs—you'll get that, too, sweetie. For hours she'd be in there with me." He slammed my head against the wall, the pain splintering through my brain. "Every night. Until one night, I hid a knife between the mattresses and I stabbed her in the leg. She hit me when I did that, but she didn't ever come again." He giggled, his mood changing lightning quick.

He brought his gun in to show me one night and placed it under my chin while wrapping my curls around his other hand. "Do you know what happens when a trigger is pulled under someone's chin?"

I whimpered, then wet the bed, my breathing shallow, weak.

"The person's brains go right out the back of their head. They shoot right out, like mush. Like oatmeal. Do you like oatmeal brains, Madeline? No? Then you do as I say, got that? I'm going to go to bed now and make your momma remember why she married me. She likes it, you know." He twisted the gun under my chin. "Be good, Madeline."

The pee soaked the mattress.

The next day Annie and I asked our momma if Annie could put her bed in my room. I wanted to protect Annie, and I wanted to protect myself at night. Over Sherwinn's vehement protests— "They aren't babies, they should have separate rooms . . . how are they going to study if they're together . . . they got to learn independence . . . those two are like twins . . . too attached . . . it's friggin' weird . . ."—she said yes, and we moved the bed in. Before we went to sleep that night, and every night thereafter, we moved the dresser and the desk in front of our door.

This didn't always work, though. As soon as our momma headed to bed, often early because of her headaches, we grabbed snacks, water, all of our homework, and told her to come in and give us a kiss good night. When she left we shoved the dresser and desk in front of the door, believing we were safe. But we weren't. Twice Sherwinn was there, hiding in our closet.

The doors opened, slowly, quietly, his eyes maniacal, that grin splayed on his face, like the devil rousing himself from hell, and our torture would begin.

Why do I have no closet doors?

Now you know.

Sherwinn's friends, Pauly Gyrt and Gavin Samson, came over a lot, almost always when our momma was at the beauty parlor.

They would watch me, their eyes slithering up and down, like snails on high speed. But when Annie walked into the room, their tongues almost fell out of their mouths. Even I could tell she was gorgeous with her thick hair and those blue-green, murky eyes. She was the pretty sister. That prettiness was her downfall.

Gavin was an assistant night manager at a factory and Pauly worked as a manager of a photo shop. He was divorced and had one son, Sam. The first time he saw us he wiped a fist over his slobbery lips, burped, and said he wanted "to photograph you two pretty, sexy, young girls."

Sherwinn giggled.

Gavin rubbed the waistband of his pants, his forehead soon sweaty.

Pauly reached into his backpack and showed us a book filled with statues of naked people. He lurched toward us, his bowling ball stomach preceding the rest of him. "Do you know what art is, girls? That's art. Do you like art? You don't need to be embarrassed about being naked. Naked is art. See, all these famous artists made sculptures of naked people. They used models who were naked for their art. The models were famous. Like the models today. They were lucky." He eyed Annie and me, and burped again. "Do you girls want to be models?"

"No," I said.

"I'm not going to do that," Annie said.

Sherwinn giggled, glanced at his creepy friends, and nodded. I was a child, but I didn't like that nod. I knew it meant something bad for us.

Sherwinn blocked the family room door when we turned to run. He grinned for a second, then laughed, superdeep, a laugh that had been brought in by red demons.

"Sure you want to be models," Gavin said. "You'll be famous then. Like the girls in the magazine."

"See?" Pauly said, burping again. We shook our heads as the stench from his burp surrounded us.

"See all those girls? They're models, like you're gonna be. We'll take some pictures of you. It'll be great. I got my camera."

He took a complicated-looking camera out of his dirty backpack. "Smile!"

We did not smile.

"Smile!" Gavin said again, his voice edgy.

We did not smile.

Annie said, "Can we go now?"

"No, smile!" Gavin yelled.

We did not smile.

"Goddammit, do what Gavin says!" Sherwinn yelled. In two long steps he was before us, his hands in our curls, yanking our heads together. "You put a goddamn smile on your goddamn faces right now or I'm gonna cause you a problem in a place you ain't never had a problem in before!"

Annie burst into tears, as did I.

"Goddammit!" Sherwinn roared again. He grabbed the front of our pink dresses and shook us hard, our heads flopping back and forth, then leaned in close and whispered, "Smile." He stuck his fingers in both of our mouths and pulled back the corners, hard, so our mouths felt like they were ripping.

Pauly said, "Back off, Sherwinn, you don't want to bruise them, their mother . . ."

"Fuck off, Pauly," Sherwinn roared.

Bob the Cat, our gray, ten-year-old cat, wandered in and Sherwinn giggled. He picked her up and threw her across the room. Annie and I screamed as she crumpled to the ground. "You tell your momma and I'm gonna do to your momma what I did to Bob the Cat. Got it? Do you want that to happen to your momma?"

We stared, shocked, at the crumpled body of our cat. She meowed, softly, weakly.

"Do you want that to happen to your momma?"

Bob the Cat tried to get up, but she collapsed.

"Are you fuckin' deaf?"

Bob the Cat lifted her head, then it flopped back down.

"No," I whispered. "No, we don't."

We didn't.

We loved our momma.

As we darted from the room, I grabbed Bob the Cat. Bob the Cat's tail waved, then sagged.

She lived. She never stopped limping.

That about sums us up, too.

We lived, but we never stopped limping.

15

Corky, the chair thrower, stomped into my office later that day at two o'clock.

I did not get up from my desk, for self-protection. I waved my hand so she would sit in the new chairs in front of it.

She glared at me. I watched her carefully. I definitely wanted to flop behind my desk if she flew off into a Corky-style temper tantrum again.

"Madeline," she said.

"Yes."

"You weren't very nice."

"I'm not here to be nice."

"You said some mean things."

"You should have heard them years ago from someone. It would have made your life easier."

"You were harsh."

"Deal with it."

Her face got all scrunchy, and she bawled and snuffled, head down on my desk, shoulders heaving, hands wrapped tight around herself.

I stood and patted her back. "We'll get through this, Corky. Hey. How about if we get out the giant wooden blocks and talk about how each one of the blocks is representative of your life and how we're going to get rid of some of the heavy blocks and add some positive blocks. What do you say?"

Her shoulders shook, up and down.

"There, there, Corky. You'll be okay."

"But everyone hhhhh-h-hates me," she stuttered through a deluge of tears.

"Yep. They do. Currently. You've been obnoxious for a long time. But we'll change that. Your relationships are gonna change. No throwing my chairs again, though, please. I don't want any blood on my suit. It might stain."

She nodded her defeated head.

That evening, about eight o'clock, darkness blackening my windows, I checked my calendar. It wasn't long before the Rock Your Womanhood conference. I would be speaking before thousands of women. If it went over with a bang, it would be huge for my career.

What did I feel? *Sadness.* Overwhelming sadness. It didn't take a genius to know why I was feeling that heavy sadness, either. The life I was leading, on so many fronts, was collapsing around me like I was standing in a black hole.

Marlene's article would rip my past and the gunshots right into the open again. She clearly was onto something about my grandparents. The photos would resurface. They would be printed and distributed. My grandparents were not who I thought they were, which meant my momma wasn't, which meant that I am not, either. I don't like my home. I don't like my car. I don't like my clothes. I don't even think I like the city.

I am two people. The public Madeline O'Shea, flamboyant and confident, who inspires people, mostly those with vaginas, to grab life, shake it around, and sling it in a new direction, and the other me who cowers, likes to be alone with my seriously unbalanced mind, doesn't trust, battles near-crippling fear and sadness, and has problems breathing because the air gets stuck under my armpit or in my stomach, or around the corner from my spleen.

I am a lie.

This lie scrapes against my quaking soul every day.

I have no more business advising people what to do with

their lives, or their relationships, than I have advising NASA how to build a spaceship to Alien Monster Land.

I am unqualified for my job. I am unqualified to give any advice.

I am unqualified.

Period.

Someone was outside my window.

I froze in bed, petrified, and yet . . . I was *ready to fight*, ready to hit, ready to swing the bat I kept under the bed, or wield the knife I kept in my dresser or shoot the gun in my nightstand.

I would fight. I was ready. I would not let any man come and hurt me again. The rage that is barely tamped down in my tightly strung body roared to life.

I heard the noise again, closer to my window, slunk out of bed, dropped to the floor, pulled my gun from my nightstand, pressed myself against the wall, and peered out through the warm fuzz of morning sunshine to see . . . Ramon. Hard-working, focused Ramon who wanted to live with his brother full time. He was hauling a mongo-sized rock in a wheelbarrow.

I sagged in relief, put the safety on the gun, dropped the gun in the nightstand, told my breath to work with me here, *work with me*. How I wished I'd had a gun as a child.

I pulled on my robe and headed outside.

"Hi, Ramon," I called.

He stopped what he was doing, turned, and smiled. And in that smile, one of the few smiles I'd ever seen from him, I saw what we all need, what we all can't live without, what we can't dream or plan or love without: Hope.

"Hi, Miss O'Shea."

"I love what you've done. I love it."

"You do?" He was vulnerable, so very vulnerable, and desperately needed my approval.

"It's incredible."

"You think?" His voice wobbled. He was still such a kid.

"Yeah, I think. It's incredible."

He smiled again, then bent his head and tried to hide a couple of tears. "Thanks, Miss O'Shea. Thank you."

I patted his shoulder. "Ramon, thank you. I have a present for you, wait a second."

I went inside and got the gift certificate. It was to an automobile sign painting business. "Now you can get Ramon's Landscaping Services painted on your truck."

He gaped. He didn't hide those pesky tears again. He hugged me.

Annie called me that night at two in the morning. I'd been in bed for about five minutes, after working until midnight. I'd been hearing Mendelssohn's Concerto in my head, subdued and muted, for about an hour, which inspired me to play my violin on my deck. I'd hoped it would soothe my screaming nerve endings.

Annie was in the back of an ambulance. "They think he's had a heart attack, Madeline." Her voice was calm, but I heard the pain.

As she'd told me years before, "Grandma and Granddad love us beyond life itself. I think it's the only reason I haven't killed myself. Had I not had Grandma and Granddad and you, after losing Mom and Dad, I would not have stayed on this planet. God gave me a gift with explosives, and I would have used them to self-destruct. I think He still would have let me into heaven, given our circumstances. There's no need in heaven for explosives, unless there's a Red Sea and it needs to be parted again. I think God's only going to do that once, though. Like the talking burning bush. That was a one-time deal, too."

"I'm coming," I said, already jumping into my clothes. "Annie, I'll be right there."

"It was a heart attack," Dr. Rubenstein said to us in the hospital hallway, his white coat too tight for a body built like a linebacker. "He needs twenty-four-hour care."

"We'll get it for him," Annie said.

"No problem," I said. "We'll set things up. We have round-the-clock care for Grandma. We'll add another person for Granddad. Plus, Annie is three minutes away, and I'll move in."

Dr. Rubenstein nodded. He was the son of two other Dr. Rubensteins, both of whom were my grandparents' best friends. His father had been our granddad's doctor before he and his wife retired and moved to Arizona. They still talked on the phone weekly and were even at my momma's wedding and trial in Massachusetts. Dr. Rubenstein Jr. had kind eyes, like his father. There was a picture behind him. It was his wife and six kids, all adopted from other countries.

"Unfortunately, this heart attack, the stress on his body, will obviously exacerbate his other underlying conditions."

"What?" Annie asked.

"I'm sorry?" I asked, brushing my furiously flattened hair back from my face, my hand shaking. Seeing Granddad lying out on a gurney, doctors and nurses rushing around him, Annie leaning against a wall, gray with worry, had turned my world upside down with a sucker punch.

"What other conditions does he have, Dr. Rubenstein?"

Dr. Rubenstein blinked at us, his eyes huge behind his glasses. "You don't know?"

"No, we don't," Annie said.

He hesitated. "I don't understand. He hasn't talked to you about this?"

"About what?" Annie asked. She was standing tight, preparing for a blow, but her face was calm, militarily calm.

Dr. Rubenstein sighed. We were next of kin, Granddad's wife had dementia, and we would be providing his care.

"He has prostate cancer."

What?

"What do you mean prostate cancer?" Annie said. I felt her shock zing through my own.

Dr. Rubenstein twirled a pen in his hands, his eyes so kind. "He has prostate cancer, heart disease, arthritis, and now with the heart attack . . . I believe he is willing himself to live for your grandma."

Prostate cancer? Heart disease? Arthritis? *What?*

"Willing himself to live, you mean...you mean...what you're saying is...are you sure...you're saying he's *dying?*" I asked, feeling a chill spread, head to foot, as if someone had dumped ice into my head through a slit.

"He's told you nothing?" Dr. Rubenstein eyes blinked owlishly behind his glasses. "This generation. So secretive. They buck up and take it, don't share their problems, believe that they should handle everything themselves, independent, brave—"

"Nothing. He told us nothing."

"I'm not surprised, in a way," Dr. Rubenstein said, taking off his glasses and rubbing his eyes. "This group fights. They know how to fight, which is what your granddad is doing now. They'll do things their own way, though, and they don't like interference. Especially your granddad. He wouldn't want to burden you girls."

"Dr. Rubenstein," Annie said, "is he...what is...Madeline, I can't say it. You say it."

I tried to get a breath, which was hard for me, as usual, especially now when I felt like curling up with my arms over my head. "How much time does he have?"

"It's hard to say. The prostate cancer isn't what I would predict would kill him. He could have that for years. It's the heart disease that's the issue. Anyone else, someone who wasn't your granddad, I'd say they could go at any time. But your granddad, maybe not. He may still have some time, I'd bet on it, and I'm not a gambler."

"How...how much time?" I felt grief riding into my body, like a thief, black and mean.

"Impossible to know. Impossible. I'm sorry, Annie, I'm sorry, Madeline." His voice squeaked as tears flooded his eyes. "I love your granddad, your grandma, too. I'll be with you on this, the whole way through."

We nodded at him, through the shatter of pain.

There were good men on the planet. He was one of them. I gave Dr. Rubenstein a hug. I pretended not to notice when he wiped his tears.

My granddad and grandma were dearly loved by many people.

I don't like mysteries. I don't like secrets. I don't like unanswered questions. I don't like the unpredictable. I don't like surprises.

Annie and I sat on a couch in the hospital in a waiting area. We held hands. Outside, dawn was arriving, soft and sweet. I see dawn often, as I wake up early, whatever is on my mind yanking me out of sleep.

This dawn had new meaning for me, though. This was the dawn of a whole new time.

A time of death.

That's what it was. The sun was rising, our granddad's life was ebbing. We would not be the same again.

Would we know his mystery before he died? His secrets? I didn't know.

I squeezed Annie's hand as I heard a full orchestra burst into Beethoven's *Eroica* Symphony.

"She's hanging birds."

"She's what?"

"She's hanging birds," Annie said.

Annie and I peered around the corner of our grandma and granddad's master bedroom suite.

Yep. She was hanging birds, and humming while doing so.

The walls of their bedroom were painted light blue, the ceiling and trim white. There were two sets of French doors and windows that framed a panoramic view. Furniture they bought decades ago, still polished often, and Grandma's makeup table, with the oval mirror and red rose flowered skirt, added authentic charm and history.

A rather naughty painting of two swans hung on the wall facing their king-sized bed with the lace canopy. The woman swan was in a blue negligee, the man swan was in . . . nothing but a black top hat. They were in bed, their wings holding champagne glasses clinking together, smiling at each other. Over their heads was another painting, of a woman swan, wearing nothing, her "hip" curving into the air, cleavage showing beneath a wing. The words "You Are My Home. I Love You" were painted across the top.

Grandma painted it for Granddad on one of their anniversaries.

"Look," Annie whispered to me.

Grandma was sitting on her Persian rug, a box of Christmas ornaments open. Every ornament in that box was a bird ornament. Red feathered birds with black beaks, tiny yellow birds with orange feet, even pink birds. They were hand-carved, hand-painted, glass blown, realistic or fantasy-types of birds with swirling plumes and wispy tails, peacocks, pelicans, flamingos, cranes, and blue jays in Santa hats. And swans, so many swans, of all shapes and sizes.

She hummed a piece by Chopin as she strung twine through the hoops of the ornaments, her voice rising and falling. Nola stood by and we said hello. It was apparently her job to take the birds, hung with twine, and staple them to the ceiling. They had been busy. There were birds all over.

"It's like we're living in a flock of very strange, sparkly, funny birds. I have always wanted to be a bird," Annie said mildly. "A bird with a wing full of miniature grenades."

"She is insistent sometimes," Nola said, those warm, lovely eyes tender. "Determined. This is how she was before all this. No one could stop your grandma. She was a steamroller. A gentle French steamroller in high heels and high fashion, but still a steamroller."

"Nola, go and take a break. We'll stay with her." I gave her a hug, and so did Annie.

"Hello, Grandma," I said gently.

She turned around from her seat on the floor, her face alighting when she saw it was us. In French she said, "How wonderful to see you! Hello, Anna. Hello, Madeline. Look who's here, Nola. It's my sister and my niece!"

I tried not to sniffle. It's heartbreaking when someone you have loved forever is floundering in the rolling mists of dementia. "Hi, Grandma." Annie and I settled next to her amidst a mass of birds with feathers, beads, sequins, and wooden bodies.

"Look what I'm doing!" Grandma held up a bird carved of wood with goggle eyes and limp feathers. "Anna made this for me."

I looked at the wood bird. No, Annie hadn't made it for her. I checked the bottom for a date. There it was. Our momma made it for her when she was a girl.

"This is my favorite one," Grandma gushed to Annie. She held it to her chest. "My favorite one. You were always such a wonderful artist, Anna, wonderful! You have so many talents, especially with your violin. You are a talented violin player and a beautiful person." She ran her hand over Annie's cheek. "Most importantly, you are beautiful inside."

I wiped a tear as Annie glanced away, but I saw her jaw working. We're fortunate, really. Grandma is often so confused about us, who we are, and she could have turned into a terrible, grumpy person, but no. Her essentials, that sweetness, that kindness, the love, all there still, but jumbled up.

"And, Madeline!" she said, her smile broadening. "Gorgeous and talented, the butterfly amidst all of us moths. We're all plain next to you, all dry and shriveled compared to the brightness of your light." She handed us twine and extra scissors. "Here, you can help me. I'm doing this for you, Anna. This is all for you, because we had to let your birds go. I'm sorry, honey." She leaned over and kissed Annie on both cheeks. "They would have starved to death in their cages but outside, maybe the birds could run away, hide, have a chance to hop again!"

Grandma turned a pure white bird with gold-tipped wings in her hands. All the birds had gone on our Christmas trees in past years.

"We let them go in the park, don't you remember, Anna? You were there, Madeline. It was before the accident. That was terrible. The accident." Grandma dropped the white bird in her lap, her eyes traveling backwards in time. She switched to German. "That was terrible! Right before! You know, it was right before! How could that happen?" She covered her face, shuddering.

"Grandma, honey," I said, hugging her close. Annie linked an arm over mine and patted Grandma's knee. We have learned with the swift mood changes to simply comfort. "It's okay."

She was back into French. "How can you say that? How can you say that? It wasn't okay. It's never been okay." She grabbed a blue bird, glitter all over its body. "This will make you happy, Anna. It's like you're getting your birds back again. I can't give you Ismael back, but I can give you your birds."

"Ismael?" Annie asked. "Who is Ismael?"

Grandma whipped around. "You've forgotten, Anna? How could you?" She clapped a hand to her mouth. "You were very young. Very young. But don't you remember going to the park with Ismael? To ice cream? To the museums? Don't you remember his smile? He loved you so much, Anna. He carved you animals out of wood. Don't you have those anymore?"

Annie shook her head. "I don't think so, Grandma."

Grandma's face fell and she jumped back into German. "That's right. I remember now. We had to leave them. We had to leave them before we ran with blood on our hands. We were late, late, late!" Her shoulders sagged. "I still miss Ismael. I will always miss him, but I feel him." She tapped her heart. "I feel him here."

"Madeline," Annie said, her voice quiet, "how 'bout you go and get your violin. Play her a tune."

I scooted out of the room, brought my violin in, and played Corelli's La Folia, then switched to "Lark in the Morning," my fingers flying, for a little variety.

Within minutes, all sign of tears and grief were gone. Grandma clapped when I finished, then came over and stroked the violin. "Do you see this scratch in the back?"

I nodded.

In German she said, "That's where the knife hit. Right there. We were hiding the knife in it, but it nicked it on the way out. He killed three men with that knife. Right here." She pointed to her stomach, then her heart, then her pelvic area. "If he hadn't we all would have died. They tried to betray us, when we were in the barn before the long walk. Black ghosts. They had to die or we would die—you, too, Anna. You had to live. We love you. I held one of them down, kicked the other when he tried to get up until he didn't move." She went to her dresser and picked up a large photo frame of Granddad. "He saved me, and he saved you, Anna." She touched Granddad's face with the tip of her finger. "He had to kill to do it, but he did it. He did it for his family so one day we could go to the Land of the Swans."

I leaned against the bed, my mouth hung open. I told myself to shut it. Annie sank into a rocking chair.

"I love him." Grandma sighed. "I always did. Even after I knew what he did. I couldn't help myself. He did it for me. For you, Anna, for us. Someone in our family had to live." She stroked the picture again. "Someone had to live. They put the other birds in a prison, hurt them, tore out their feathers and plucked out their hearts and ripped off their feet and snapped off their beaks."

After that pronouncement, Grandma went back to stringing her birds. "Come, come. Aren't you going to help free the birds?"

Yes, we were going to help, even if our hands trembled while we freed the birds.

"I love birds!" Grandma said, with grand exuberance. She threw one up in the air. It was wooden so it didn't break. "Fly! Be free! Don't get cooked in the fires!"

We visited Granddad at the hospital the next day. We stayed for hours. Most of the time he was asleep, so we watched him sleep.

He woke up and saw Annie and me hovering over him, like mother hens.

"Not dead yet, girls," he rasped out. "Not dead yet."

"No, not yet," Annie drawled. "It would help if you could get some color in your cheeks, though. I'll buy some blush."

"Superb." He closed his eyes again. "I would like some of that shadow stuff you ladies put on. Longer lashes . . . red lipstick. I'm sure it will liven up my coloring nicely."

"Don't forget that we can tattoo your eyebrows for you, too."

"Ah, my greatest wish, fulfilled."

We laughed. "How are you?"

Granddad smiled. "I'm still tickin'."

"Tickin' and clickin' and everything else," I told him.

"How's your grandma?'

We assured him she was fine. We did not mention the hanging of the birds or the killings.

He sighed, then seemed to sink into the pillow, his face so pasty white. It is crushing, and humbling, to be in a hospital with someone who may not live long.

"Girls, in case . . ." He took a deep breath, and I saw him tilt his chin up. "In case, I don't make it—"

"You're gonna make it, Granddad," Annie clipped, jaw tight. "You'll make it."

He grabbed her hand on one side of the bed, mine on the other. "Sometimes it is your turn to go, and it may be mine, so I want to tell you." His chin wobbled and I clamped down on my own cry. There was so much vulnerability in that wobble. "I must tell you that I am sorry. I am sorry."

"What are you sorry for, Granddad? There's nothing I know of to be sorry for. You're the best," I rushed. "We love you."

"I am sorry for what I did. I am sorry that what I did years ago may affect you now. I am sorry for the pain it will cause you. I am sorry for the pain it caused your mother. I am sorry." Tears trickled out of his eyes.

"Sorry for what?" Annie asked. "We know there are secrets, Granddad, we get it, but, hell, we don't know what's truth here. Honesty might be a good option."

His eyes filled with tears. "I cannot stand to see the hate in your eyes, the shame, the disappointment, when you find out who I was. I cannot stand it. I cannot stand myself. It has followed me my entire life. Like a shadow. Like a crow that caws at me. Like death." He laughed, but it was mirthless. "I have been stalked by death, stalked by ghosts my entire life."

"Why, Granddad? What happened?" He was shrinking into himself before our eyes.

"What happened is that I sinned most grievously. It is unforgiveable. I am unforgiveable. It was a bad time. All I could see was myself, my family. Your mother. Nothing mattered, nothing else. We were hunted. We were going to die. . . ."

Exhausted, he put a trembling hand to his forehead and looked at the ceiling. "Sorry," he whispered, as if he were not with us anymore. "A million times, I am sorry."

He sighed again, then fell back into a deep sleep, where his apologies could be heard only by him alone.

Annie and I locked glances.

"He's sorry," I said, baffled. "What the heck is going on?" I felt everything colliding, all at once. "I don't know what's going on here. I don't get it."

"I hate surprises," Annie muttered. "Hate 'em. And I don't think I'm going to like what we find out with this one."

We sat with our granddad, holding his hands, for another hour, then drove home, through the city streets, the traffic, the noise, down the freeway, into the country, out to The Lavender Farm with the drive lined by tulip trees, the lavender waiting to bloom, and a passel of Annie's animals that had all been diseased or injured when she found them.

Injured and diseased animals and people. Not much difference.

On Sunday afternoon we brought Granddad home. When he hobbled into his master suite on a walker, he found it covered in birds hanging from the ceiling.

He hardly showed any surprise at all. Grandma floated to him, arms out, the kimono she wore a blaze of red. It was see-through. Beneath it she was wearing a red negligee with a push-up bra. "Isn't it beautiful, Anton? So flighty! So wing-y! We have Anna's birds back! The ones that we freed!"

"It is beautiful, Emmanuelle." He put an arm around her shoulders.

"Anton!" Grandma said. "Let's go to the park soon and watch the birds and swans before they come and fry them all to death, or starve them with typhoid and sick dragons. Can we?"

She twirled around under her birds, her face glowing, her blue-green eyes vague but peaceful.

"I do believe a stroll in the park is exactly what I need," Granddad said. The man looked like he could barely stand up. He leaned heavily on his walker. We got him into bed, then fed them both dinner later on. Grandma insisted on wearing a different purple negligee that she stored in her "Sexy Drawer," as she called it.

So there was Granddad, exhausted, recovering from a heart attack and a range of other medical problems, and next to him was Grandma, in her sexy, purple negligee, the bodice cut to her navel, smiling coyly and whispering, "Wait until they turn out the lights, Anton! I'm going to give you a night to remember! Would you like to be on top?"

"Thanks for moving in, Madeline," Annie said as we sat drinking wine on the dock that night, our feet hanging over the ledge. "It'll be good to have your advice when I'm whacking at my wood carvings with a chain saw."

"I'm happy to. I'm actually looking forward to it." That was the truth. In fact, the more I thought about living in my childhood room with my white bedspread and piles of purple pillows, the peaked ceiling and window seat, the better I felt.

I wanted to be with Grandma and Granddad. They had been with me when I wanted to curl up tight and die as a younger person, I would be with them now and I would be with Annie. Taking care of dying parents or grandparents should never be left to only one child. It is too much.

I snapped opened my violin case and pulled out my violin, a gift from my mother to me, from her mother to her, with all its dents and scratches each, apparently, with a story behind it. I wish Annie still wanted to play the piano. Not that we could have dragged a piano out here to the dock, but it would have been nice to strum some strings and bang some keys together.

The moon shone through wandering clouds onto the water as I practiced Bach's Concerto in A minor, then threw in a Texas-style fiddle tune, "Beaumont Rag," to move my mood to a better place.

Annie said, "Tomorrow I'm going to carve a swan."

I nodded, put my violin away.

"The swan is going to have a knife in its mouth. For protection. Everyone needs protection." She swung her feet, in and out. "I wished I'd had a knife."

I knew what she was referring to. Not having a knife was part of the reason Annie's a little off her rocker.

"A sharp one," she said.

I heard a fish flop in the water, then another.

"One with a jagged edge."

"Got it, Annie."

The fish flopped again.

"I think I'll carve a cape on the swan, too."

"A super hero swan, then?"

"Yep. Super Hero Susan Swan."

Later that night, in my own bedroom, a bouquet of dried lavender on my nightstand, I stared at the ceiling. I thought of my granddad, who was in the good-bye years of his life, his health slipping away, my grandma's mind jumbled up. I would miss them when they were gone. I would miss them as I miss my parents. The grief I have for my parents seems to be unending, controlled, but unending, because the bare truth is that if you are fortunate enough to be born to loving parents, as I was, you know that no one, *no one*, will ever love you as much as they do. That love is not replaceable. My parents were never replaceable.

I miss them every day.

When I was done staring at the ceiling, I slept.

In my nightmares Sherwinn was on the back of a vulture. He giggled. The vulture flew right toward me, his beak ripping me in two before setting me on fire.

Too bad Super Hero Susan Swan wasn't there. She could have saved me.

16

Lavender is soothing. It's used in perfumes and massage oil, bouquets, wreaths, eye pillows, sachets, potpourri, essential oils, and topiaries.

Momma, Annie, and I made all sorts of crafts using lavender with Grandma when we visited from Cape Cod during the summers. We made lavender wreaths and sachets, sewing the purple silky material by hand, tiny stitches like Grandma showed me, then dropping in the lavender buds. We cut lavender and arranged the stems in vases throughout the house as the sun's rays tumbled down.

Our momma played her violin, and our dad sang Irish songs and recited poems in the gazebo overlooking the rows, his deep voice soaring and snappy. To my momma he once recited "My Dark Haired Girl," by Samuel Lover:

> My dark-hair'd girl, thy ringlets deck,
> In silken curl, thy graceful neck;
> Thy neck is like the swan, and fair as the pearl,
> And light as air the step is of my dark-haired girl.
>
> My dark-haired girl, upon thy lip
> The dainty bee might wish to sip;
> For thy lip it is the rose, and thy teeth they are pearl,
> And diamond is the eye of my dark-haired girl!

My dark-haired girl, I've promised thee,
And thou thy faith hast given to me,
And oh, I would not change for the crown of an earl
The pride of being loved by my dark-hair'd girl!

He grabbed her afterward, leaned her over his arm, and planted a smackeroo on her lips while Grandma and Granddad and Annie and I laughed and clapped.

When we arrived to live with them permanently, damaged and destroyed, Annie not speaking, I lost deep in my head listening to the violins, Grandma always had new crafts for us, often using lavender. She'd take us on strolls through the rows and we'd drop those sparkly marbles here and there, "For the gnomes . . . for the good white witches." This time, though, she used the lavender to keep our young, battered minds from being blown to dust under a hurricane of trauma.

Lavender is soothing. But it cannot protect anyone from the quicksand and swamps of life.

Sherwinn picked Annie and me up from school on a Friday. I remember it was a Friday because every Friday we had spaghetti and brownies for lunch. I loved the school's spaghetti and brownies. We could buy lunch only one day a week. The other days Momma packed us tiny sandwiches, croissants, quiche, cheese, potato or carrot soup, cheese crepes, and pink cookies or tarts.

Sherwinn told us to "get in the damn truck," then drove us to Pauly's house.

Pauly's house was a shack outside of town. The home slouched like a dead armadillo, the porch sliding off, weeds two feet high, surely a metaphor for what was happening to us. Behind it was a mammoth oak tree, its branches curving and bending and stretching, leaves blowing. I wanted to climb that tree and hide.

"Go inside," Sherwinn said, menacing and huge beside us. I was panicked down to my toes. I reached for Annie's hand.

"No," Annie said, her voice loud. "Take us to the beauty parlor. Momma knows we're coming."

Sherwinn laughed. "I told her I was taking you all out to ice cream. She's resting at home, anyhow. She didn't feel good."

I didn't feel good, either. My momma's headaches were worse, she slept a lot, my dad was dead, and Sherwinn was here. "We don't want to go in."

"Too bad," Sherwinn whispered.

As if on cue, Annie and I turned to run. We got about three feet before Sherwinn lifted us up by the collars of our pink dresses, spun us around, and tossed us through the air. We landed with a thump in the weeds, near the oak tree, as if we were hardly better than they were, hardly better than the green nuisances, the air, and our innocence, rushing right out of our bodies.

Annie didn't move. "Annie!" I shrieked, crawling over to her and pushing her curls out of her face. "Annie!" She opened her eyes, dazed.

"Are you okay?"

She tried to sit up, and I put my trembling arms around her.

I felt, rather than saw, Gavin and Pauly sauntering over, as Sherwinn prodded us with his boot. "You girls quit fakin' it and get up."

"We're gonna have a modeling session," Pauly said. He ran a hand through my hair, and I pulled my head away, then slapped at his hand. "Dark hair. That's good." He didn't see the red. Someone like him would never see it. "Models pose in all kinds of positions. Like queens, you know? You'll be famous. You girls are gonna be famous all over the world."

I pulled away. "I don't want to be famous."

Pauly laughed, a smoker's laugh, heavy and polluted, his bowling ball stomach heaving.

Gavin scratched his crotch, started to sweat.

Sherwinn said, "Too bad. You're gonna be slut models. You first, Annie. You look like your mommy, you know that? You're a short Marie Elise, except for those bluish eyes ya got." He grabbed Annie and yanked her in by her collar, her arms and legs flailing. I leaped for her, but I was too late. Gavin grabbed one side of me, Pauly the other, my legs spread, my arms spread, my pink dress up to my waist, as they trudged up through the weeds, those nuisances, up to the porch that was sliding off the shack's frame.

I struggled, I kicked, I yelled. Annie tried to stand up and fight Sherwinn, but she was no match for him. He hauled her up into midair and socked her in the stomach. When she doubled over, he slung her over his shoulder and stomped up the steps.

"Annie!" I screamed. "Annie!" I kicked again, smashed Pauly in the face, and freed a foot. Gavin wrapped his hairy, smelly arms around me, his breath a mix of beer and rancid rot, sliding down my throat.

We were shoved into Pauly's house, a house that reeked of old pizza, beer, cigarettes, stale air, and pungent, soul-sucking moral depravity.

We fought, we argued, we begged. It didn't help at all.

Pauly got out his camera, yelled at his red-haired, fifteen-year-old son, Sam, to "take a fucking walk" when he got home from school, and took photos. Sherwinn backed up his threats with his fists, Gavin "got ready," so to speak, and we were photographed.

Sherwinn wrestled the pink sundresses right off us, buttons flying. We tried to cover ourselves with our small hands as hysteria took hold. It didn't work. Our underwear went arching into the air after that.

We were girls, girls who wore pictures of lions on our T-shirts, sparkly nail polish, red jeans, and flowers in our hair. We were photographed without clothes on.

They thought it would be cute if we still wore our white socks with the lace trim and our white Mary Jane shoes.

"You're models," Pauly told us, swiping a hand across the front of his pants. "Sexy models."

Gavin scratched, sweated.

Sherwinn wrapped his fingers through our curls. "They're gonna love the curls, aren't they?" he asked Gavin and Pauly. Those creepy men nodded. Pauly burped.

They told us where to sit, where to stand. We cried and cried, buckets of searing tears, our little girl bodies, only starting to grow into womanhood, rocking back and forth, horrified, *shamed.*

Those men didn't care. They didn't care about tears at all.

They didn't care that we were mentally ruined.

Click, click, click.

The next time we were there, I heard the violin music in my head. "Do you hear that, Annie?" I whispered to her. It was snowing. There was snow on the branches of the oak tree. We'd watched it get whiter and whiter while we were trapped in the shack. We were freezing. We were starving. We both were eating far less than we used to. Our exhaustion was a sheer, straight line to emotional death. "Do you hear that? The violins? Don't you hear them?"

"I don't hear anything. I want to go home."

I wanted that, too. I wanted home. It never came soon enough.

The violins came to me, though, soothing. Soothing in the sickness of my shame.

We were taken to the shack often after that.

One time I said, my voice weak and wobbly, "What are you doing with the photos?"

They laughed and laughed.

Pauly said, through his smoker's cough, "We've started a business."

Gavin said, so sweaty, "A model business. Naked models."

Sherwinn smirked. "It's a nationwide business. You girls are getting very popular."

I didn't want to be popular. Annie didn't want to be popular.

Sherwinn threw a pop can at my head when I said, "I hate you, Sherwinn."

I stared at the oak tree that afternoon. I wanted to be in the branches, far and away, up in the sky with the weather that my dad told me had emotions. Whenever we were at the shack the weather was scared.

Sometimes I saw my dad behind my closed lids when we were there.

Always he was crying, his head in his hands, his broad shoulders slumped, body heaving with grief.

I wanted to comfort him. I wanted to hug him, to climb on his lap and hear his stories about fisherwomen who caught striped fish, polka-dot fish, pink fish, fish the size of our house by the sea.

I wanted my dad.

But he was dead.

17

"**A** man named Steve Shepherd called," Georgie said, Stanley beside her. "Called about an hour ago. Had a manly man voice. I know who he is."

I leaned back in my chair, that name wrapping itself around me, warm and snug, filled with fishing trips and canoeing and lace ribbons. At the same time, I instantly struggled to find enough air. It seemed to be hiding in my nether regions.

Stanley skipped over and barked at me. I shook his paw. He barked again. I hugged him. He barked when I pulled away. I lifted him up and put him on my lap. He kissed me. I did not kiss him back.

"He's that wicked awesome author. I've read all his books." Georgie rubbed her upper arm, near the tattoo of her grandma smoking a cigar. "I told you to read them. They make me cry and laugh. . . . It's this whole series, you know, starting with *The Girl in Pink,* that's the title. He met her when they were kids, and every book is a new chapter in their lives, but he's got this creative, wacky angle where their lives are parallel, and sometimes tragic, sometimes funny, and there's this third element there. It's like magic, but not magic, and they never quite make it together. . . ."

I sagged in my chair as Stanley kissed me again.

"Why is he calling you, do you know? Do you know him? I've seen a photo of him and he's cute. Not like hot cute, not sexy cute, but you know, adorable cute, like you can squeeze him and match your soul with his and fly around and be happy together . . . and he's romantic, I mean, what testosterone driven male ape is romantic? He gets women's drifts, their currents."

What is a woman's drift? A current?

"Do you know him?"

"A long time ago I did."

"You should know him again, wrap yourselves together. He's got a field of goodwill around him. Read his books, then you can see into his mind."

Yes, I knew him. I knew Steve Shepherd.

He liked snakes. Frogs, too.

After Annie, Steve Shepherd was my second best friend when I was a kid.

Our parents were also friends and neighbors. The Shepherds had a house down the road, a long rambly thing that overlooked the ocean. There were a ton of photos of us together, as babies in yellow seats on the backs of our mommas' bikes, as toddlers with life jackets on sailboats, in school plays dressed as pilgrims, in matching Halloween outfits. One year we were fruits with Annie, another year we were the three Musketeers, the next year the three blind mice.

He was tall and thin and lanky like a giraffe, and a star on the youth basketball team, partly because he was the tallest one there. He had blue eyes and always smiled at me, and he smelled like the ocean, pine trees, butterscotch, and a hint of spring.

We passed notes in math class that made me laugh so hard, I had tears running down my face. We drew pictures of our math teacher. Sometimes we dressed him as a woman, a monkey, a turtle. Together, he and Annie and I and lots of other noisy friends got together and we all ran around, house to house. Steve always said, "Let's be friends with everyone, but Madeline, you're my best friend."

We poked our skin with needles, rubbed the blood together, and became blood friends. "Now we're best friends for life, right, Madeline?" he asked.

He even tried to protect me from Sherwinn.

"Lemme tell you something, Madeline," Sherwinn said one

afternoon after I pulled on my pink penguin T-shirt and yanked on my flowered jeans with hands that shook with humiliation and free-ranging fear. "If you tell anyone about this, not only is your momma gonna be like Teresa and Mickey, I'm gonna send the photos to Steve."

I'm sure my face showed my devastation, because Sherwinn said, "You thought I didn't know about your boyfriend? Think I'm that dumb?" He smirked at me, his eyes wandering over my body. "You wouldn't like for Steve to see those photos, would you? Then he'll know what I know: That you're a dirty, bad girl. That you do bad things with men. That you're not a sweet and innocent girl anymore. Do you want me to show him this photo?" He held up a photo of me. Pauly was on top of me. My face was looking at the camera. I had a dog collar around my neck. "What about this one?" He held up a photo of me with Gavin. I will not describe it.

I lost it, my hands to my face, the despair that was now my constant companion welling up, swirling around, forcing all the breath out of me in my pink penguin T-shirt.

Sherwinn ripped my hands away from my face. "You want Steve to know what you look like naked? You want him to see the bruises you got when you weren't being good? You want him to see you with us doing bad girl things in those red high heels? You want him to see a close-up shot of your privates? No, you don't." He leaned in to whisper in my ear, "Keep your trap shut. Keep Annie's trap shut, and you can be friends with your Steve. But one word and he knows you're trash, he knows you're a slut. Got that, bad girl? You got that?"

I nodded. I got it.

I got that I didn't want to live anymore.

Two days later I saw Sherwinn talking to Steve at the hardware store. When Sherwinn sauntered off, a smile lurking creepily, I hurried over to Steve.

"What . . . ," I said, then choked on my fear. "Steve, what . . ." I choked again. "What did Sherwinn say to you?"

He smiled at me—Steve always smiled at me; he said I was buttered popcorn to him, his favorite—but something in his blue eyes showed worry and unsteady confusion. "He said that you were a great daughter to have, that you did what you were told, that you were obedient. That's what he said, that you're obedient, and he said that one day he's going to give me a present. I asked him what kind of a present." His face clouded again. He was young but he knew something was off. He felt it. "He said that I'm supposed to ask you what kind of present I'm going to get from him."

Everything in front of me went blurry, like I was in a bottle, by myself, stuck in there, trapped, and blackish, bacteria-ridden water was filling it, funneling down my throat.

"So, Madeline, what kind of a present is it? Madeline, are you okay?" He stepped in closer. "Do you like Sherwinn? Because I don't like him. There's something about him, something scary and creepy and gross. I don't like him. Do you want to come to my house after school from now on? You can bring Annie."

I don't remember fainting. Later, Mrs. Coonstock said that Steve caught me, held me, yelled for someone to call my momma.

The only thing I remember feeling as I drowned in the bottle was that I would never, ever get out of that bottle. Steve's face, crinkling in distress, grew smaller and smaller. I wanted to reach for him, hold him, but that infected water was drowning me.

My dad would have gotten me out of that bottle, I knew that. He would have swam down, holding his breath, and pulled me to the surface. Steve would have done the same thing, if he could.

I saw my dad again that night when I was trying to sleep, Annie beside me, a dresser in front of our door.

Our dad was crying. Our strong, tough dad was crying.

I heard a piece by Mozart in my head and I held on to it as I would hang on to a cliff if I was over the edge, a frothing river filled with alligators below, ready to shred my skin.

I kept playing my violin, alone and with Momma.

Annie, though, quit playing piano for months, and then she quit altogether. Why? Because Sherwinn snuck up on her one night and whispered something that made her drop her hands from the keys and stare straight ahead.

Sherwinn giggled.

What did he say? "Annie. Naked. Piano. Photo."

Click, click, click.

The next day Steve brought me purple tulips because he knew they were my favorites. He wrapped them with a lace ribbon. He put them in a silver pail. I still have the lace and the pail. He baked Annie and me chocolate chip cookies with his mom in the shape of Mickey Mouse. He put the cookies in an old-fashioned blue and white flowered tin. I still have the tin. The next day he gave me a dinosaur that he put together with rocks and hot glue with the help of his mother. I still have the dinosaur. He gave me a red ribbon because "you have brown hair, but there's red in it, too, all over. It's like it's magic. Red magic."

So, yes, I knew Steve Shepherd.

We had been best friends.

He was coming to Portland on his book tour, another blockbuster he'd written. A movie was being made.

I would not call him back.

I couldn't.

I made Grandma and Granddad breakfast a couple of days later. Whole wheat blueberry pancakes, scrambled eggs, and orange juice. I brought it to them on a tray while they were still in bed under a flock of birds.

I did knock first. No need to surprise those two and their possible naked acrobatics.

"Thank you, Madeline!" Grandma gushed. She was wearing a light blue lacy negligee with a see-through lacy robe over it. "We'll need the energy for later, won't we, darling?" She elbowed my granddad, sitting up in bed next to her. He smiled wearily at me.

She giggled. "Only the birds and swans can watch!"

"That sounds lovely, Grandma," I said, winking at my granddad. He winked back. Always the gentleman.

"It will be." She leaned over and kissed Granddad on the cheek.

"Thank you, my love," he told her.

"He's a randy man! But you have to keep your man happy in the you-know-where." She pointed at my granddad's crotch. "He's a romantic swan, but goodness, insatiable in the bedroom! He wants me all the time, but then look at me." She pointed to her chest. "I can't help that these breasts make him think naughty thoughts, can I?"

"You sure can't, Grandma. Those are God given."

"God given! Thank you, God!" she shouted. "Anton loves these breasts. Naughty man!" She leaned over and kissed him on the lips.

I chatted a bit, then left for work, so glad I was coming back to The Lavender Farm that night and not to the metal man with an octagonal head.

My first client was a man who wanted a career change. He'd been an inventor. He was a multimillionaire. He'd finally retired from his last job four weeks ago and was "bored out of my mind. Bah! Sitting with old men, boring! Golfing, boring! Hanging around the house, boring! My wife hates when I'm there all day, and I hate it, too. Boring! Retirement, boring!"

"What do you love doing?"

He thought about that for half a second. "Airplanes! Old airplanes!" He always spoke with exclamation marks. "My hobby is building toy airplanes. I do it for hours, every day. The wife thinks I'm crazy. Got 'em all stacked up on custom-made shelves...."

"Want a business doing that? You could sell what you have online or people could order a toy airplane from you and you could personalize it. Name it the *Cassandra*, the *Bryan*, the *Muhammad*. Whatever they want, paint it in their favorite colors. You know how to market, you've done that for years...."

He thought about that, thumped his walker. "Ha-hum! I think you've got an idea there, Madeline, young woman. That's an idea! It's not boring! No boredom there! I could have a toy airplane business. Hell, young woman, you've given me new life!"

He shuffled out. "Never too late to take on a new business, that's what I always say!"

"Go kick some ass."

"Ha-hum! Yep. I'm an ass kicker. Still got my ass, so I'll kick others' asses."

Al Dover is ninety-three years old.

The next week he sent me an exquisitely detailed toy airplane about three feet long. It was incredible. I hung it by the windows of my office.

Al named it the *Madeline*.

Within two weeks I saw them hanging in the windows of a toy store. A week later they were gone. I called Al. "They sold out, by damn! Sold out! I gotta get crackin'! Crackin'!"

Later that day one of my clients, Shelby Edwards, cancelled. I was her one allowed call from the police station. She is a politician. "Yep, Madeline, can't make it to my appointment. Been arrested for embezzling. You were right. I should have done something honest. That's confidential, right?"

"It's confidential, but you have broken O'Shea's Principle Number One: If you are dumb enough to commit a crime you will go to jail. Before you go to jail, you will be plagued by guilt, fear, and the sneaking suspicion that you are a loser. Bad mistake, Shelby. I'll visit in jail. No charge."

"Gee, thanks, Madeline. You're a sport. Can you run by my house—key's under the purple flower pot—and get my cat?"

I would, I did. I gave the cat to my neighbor, Alex, whose own cat died at the age of twenty-two of what Alex says was "earwax."

To my next client I said, "Quit your job."

"You're serious?" Hope spread on that handsome face.

"Yep."

Hayward is an attorney who wants out. What sane attorney doesn't want out? Would you want to fight and argue all day with people with massive egos, not to mention the incessant

stress of trials and reams of hideously boring briefs and deposi-
tions?

We looked at his finances. I told him to quit and go to the police academy and become a police officer because he'd always
wanted to do it, ever since he was six and got a water gun for
his birthday.

"You think I can do it?"

Hope was taking hold of Hayward. "I know you can do it.
Your student loans are paid off. Your house has a reasonable
mortgage. No credit card debt. And you're miserable. Quit, Officer Hayward. You're gonna look hot in a uniform, anyhow.
Totally hot. Maybe you'll get a date for once."

He sagged in relief. "I needed someone to tell me I'm not
crazy for doing this."

"You'd be crazy to stay where you are."

He rubbed his eyes. "One of my clients was arrested today
for embezzlement."

I thought of Shelby, but I did not laugh, no, I did not.

"She didn't even call me. I heard it from a police contact. Embezzlement. She's guilty, I know she is, and she does, too. And I
don't want to defend her. I can't do it. She's got a public position, too."

I nodded. This was not the first time one of my clients alluded
to another.

"You're miserable, right, Hayward?"

"I could not be more miserable."

"Buddy, you could crash and die tomorrow and if you're
lying on the pavement, staring at the sky, and a meteor of white
light is rushing toward you, I can guarantee you're going to
wish you had followed O'Shea's Live or Maggot Rot Principle."

"Which is?"

"You can die any day, any time. Live your life with meaning
and joy, or allow yourself to rot with maggots on the inside until
you come to a point where you wish the maggots would eat
your liver so you could cut out early."

"You never mince words, do you?" He grinned back at me.
Hope had wrapped around Hayward. Yes, it had.

"No point. I could die tomorrow. Why be vague?"

"I could do this."

"You will do this. Go get your uniform. Come visit me when you're wearing it and try to get a date. Off you go, officer."

"Hello, cat sisters!" I said. "Meow!"

I had spent a lot of time thinking about the Giordano sisters. They are the most shallow women I have ever met in my entire life. They spend hours on their makeup and clothes. They spend fortunes on themselves. If they gave up spending money for one day, they could feed part of a third world country. The excess kills me, here.

And yet, they're so darn likeable.

So what did they need? Depth. Purpose. A reason to be on the planet. Underneath the furs and manicured nails and silk and Ferraris, they were cats who needed to be needed.

"Hello, darling!" Adriana called out, sweeping through my office carrying Princess Anastasia, white gloves to her elbows, a white silk dress and a white hat at a jaunty angle. The cat was wearing a white bow and a white skirt. She looked bored and embarrassed. When she saw me staring at her, she made a spitting sound.

"Sweeeeeeetheart!" Bella sang, holding all consonants. She was wearing a red hat with an impressive diameter and a two-foot-long red feather. She had on red gloves, a matching red dress, and heels. Her cat, Bee La La, had a red bow around her neck and a red cape. She rolled her eyes, I swear she did.

"We're here for our life coach session, sweetie!" Carlotta announced. She had on a purple hat with one of those black nets that halfway cover the face and a purple ensemble with flared pants and a jacket. You guessed it. Candy Stripe wore a purple bow and a silky dress. She yawned. Such a sleepy cat.

Ah. They were playing the part of European socialites. How dandy!

"Ladies, we're going to be cats today."

They sat straight up—the ladies, not the cats.

"Cats!" Adriana exclaimed. "That sounds fun and scratchy." She put her claws out and elegantly scratched the air.

"I'm a slinky cat," Bella said, standing up and stretching like a cat, her diamond bracelets glittering on her arm.

"I'm a ferocious cat," Carlotta said. She hissed and hissed. "Meow!"

I told Georgie to come on in. She was ready to go. Georgie's hobby is makeup. She and I used face paints to turn the ladies into cats, then I had them get in their cat outfits, which I'd rented for them.

"Fun and fun!"

"Wicked naughty!"

"Fantabulous!"

"Now we're going to do something cat worthy. Come with me, cats."

We left my building and went to a local coffee shop. The ladies meowed at people staring at them. I had each one of them buy one hundred dollars worth of ten-dollar coffee cards and let them loose.

"Be good cats. Find people who look like they need some loving meowing in their lives and hand them a gift card with your paw. No cat hissing!"

They were shocked, then puzzled, finally excited. They meowed at each other, rolled their whiskers, flicked their tails.

They returned later, exhausted, thrilled.

"That was the best thing I've done in my life!" Bella said. "The best! I couldn't believe people's faces when we gave them the coffee cards. They looked so surprised, then so grateful. I gave one to a teenager sitting against a building. She looked like she'd been there forever and was melting into the wall."

"One woman cried, she cried!" Carlotta meowed, then burst into tears.

"Meow!" Adriana threw her arms up and let 'em rip.

"Tears! Meow!" Bella buried her head in her arms, her back heaving. "Meow tears!"

When they left I heard "Sweet Georgia Brown" in my head.

It was appropriate.

The cats left with a renewed sense of purpose outside their Jimmy Choo shoe collections. Within a minute Georgie called me.

"Madeline, Aurora King is here. She told me that your aura is very, very black. She's seeing a crash, a change, a reckoning for you. What, Aurora? Okay. She says not to be alarmed, but she sees you naked, emotionally naked, and there's a plane, too, plus a crowd of people, palm trees, a lush garden. What else? She says the number seven, twenty-eight, a pink handcuff. Don't ask, Madeline."

I tried not to roll my eyes. "What is she wearing?"

"She's in purple today. Lots of tulle and fluff, a wand. She's clearly in tune with her inner fairy."

"Tell her not to throw glitter at me."

"Will do. Don't throw glitter at Madeline," I heard Georgie say as she rang off.

I opened my door to Aurora King and closed my eyes when I saw her hand swing up.

She threw purple glitter at me.

Two days later I was still picking it out of my hair.

I was not surprised to get another blackmail letter in a manila envelope when I swung by my house later that week to get the mail. Using letters from magazines, he had misspelled the word regret. He spelled it with two t's. As in, I would "regrett" it if I didn't pay up.

I tossed the manila envelope back on octagonal head-man and headed out of the city.

I didn't know what I would do with this blackmailing deal, but I knew what I wouldn't do: Pay up.

When I reached The Lavender Farm, I had dinner with Nola, who was smiling gently; Granddad, who looked beyond exhausted; and Grandma, who was painting a four-foot-tall mother swan who was clearly, frantically, looking for her baby swan. The baby swan was stuck in the thorns of blackberry bushes, a mean wolf with bared teeth beside him. It gave me a shiver.

I cleaned up the dishes, watched as Granddad lovingly got

Grandma ready for bed, said good night, then grabbed my violin and headed for the gazebo to meet Annie. I swung my violin to my shoulder and practiced some Texan-style fiddling while Annie sat there, quiet.

I figured I knew what had triggered the blackmail letters and photographs in the manila envelopes. It was that reporter, Marlene, who I do hate, though it is not personal. She was snooping around on the Cape and word had gotten out about the article she was writing. Apparently it had gotten out to my blackmailer who was, undoubtedly, vermin scum.

I had kept in contact with Carman, Trudy Jo, and Shell Dee over the years, who had together bought the beauty parlor. I was told that no one would talk to Marlene, that she had been asked to leave three bed and breakfasts when the owners found out who she was. Even the hotel was suddenly "booked solid, for weeks, nope, no rooms." This was the off-season. There were plenty of rooms.

As Shell Dee's daughter Jules told me, "No one wants to hear about this story again, and we sure don't want to hurt you and Annie. You two—" She paused and her voice caught. "You two have been through enough. Losing Big Luke, he was my father's best friend, you know, your pink-loving mother, my mother still misses her every day, you know, what happened to you girls. I still cry . . . cry . . . cry about it, you know." She burst into tears, then started making that braying donkey sound she always made when she lost it. "You know!"

Mrs. White, Carman's sister and my fifth-grade teacher, called, too. "No one's talked, hon, but she's digging, and she had a fancy-pants investigator-type guy with her, and it's all coming out, but we won't give her a lamb's shake of the tail, honey, don't you worry. How are you, honey? All famous now, aren't you? I still miss your momma. . . ."

And the mayor called, an older gentleman. "Big Luke and I, we went way back, and I'm doing what I can to protect his girls. I told the reporter to leave. I threatened her, told her she wasn't welcome here, and she got two attorneys out here and they 'bout buried me in paperwork and lawsuits. Used the words harassment and discrimination. As if that's gonna get me all riled up. Couldn't find a place to stay so she started sleeping in her car."

He sighed.

"Too bad when she left the car to take a shower at Rick's Gym, it was towed and dumped in the lake. She found it when she saw the bumper sticking up. Patty told Howie to weight it, but heck, didn't work. Howie has always had a problem with his listening skills, remember that, Mad?"

Marlene had recently called Annie for the article, which about made my blood boil and fly out of my skin. Annie told her that if she called her again she would "firebomb your house and turn it into a ball of flames."

The reporter hung up after saying, "That's not very nice," to which Annie said, "Neither is trying to write a story that will rip open the lives of my sister, me, and our grandparents, one of whom has recently had a heart attack, the other who has dementia. Even with dementia, she deserves her dignity. Now you have a choice. Don't write the story or forfeit your house. Which is it?"

The reporter said, "I'm writing an honest story."

And Annie said, "And I am honestly going to burn your house down."

Annie was not kidding, but I told her she could not burn the house down. Nope. Never. Don't.

"Why not? I know what I'm doing. There won't be any evidence." Her brows came together, puzzled. She is a little off her rocker. She stroked Tornado, the cat with multiple personalities.

"Because you threatened her. If her house burns, she'll point the finger at you."

"Then I'll have one of my buddies do it."

"No, you won't. You'll end up in jail."

She thought about that. "I would not like jail. I would not be able to take care of all my animals. Door and Chair need me." She meowed at Oatmeal, who meowed back.

"That's true."

Annie winked at me. "I'll firebomb her car then."

"It's in the lake." I rolled my eyes, and Annie gave me a hug, then wiped a lone tear from my cheek. "We'll be okay."

"This is going to be a mess."

She nodded, then lifted her chin. Tough. She is tough. Toughened up as kids, further toughened by her work with one of our government's agencies. Toughened up as she exploded things to kingdom come in faraway lands.

Someone had a stack of nasty photos of Annie and me. Marlene had clearly, inadvertently alerted them to the article by asking about us. They, or he, probably had no idea whom I had grown up to be, but when they did, they thought they could cash in. They probably looked me up, saw the business I have, the speaking engagements, the columns, and deduced that I have money, which I do.

Has that money, or my inherited money, saved me from pain in my life?

Not at all.

Truth: I'd toss everything I had off the Broadway Bridge, every penny, to have my parents alive today.

The blackmailer wanted $300,000 in cash. Of course he did.

I heard my old friend, Vivaldi, in my head that night, the notes soaring up and around the hills and valleys and out across the coast range, and the faraway ocean, the weather peaceful, a storm brewing madly underneath the placid clouds.

Granddad was still so weak, but it was the bleakness in his eyes that caused me grave worry, although not a complaint left his lips. All he would say is, "The old ticker gave me a hiccup. That's it." Or, "I don't know what all this damn fuss is about." Or, "Stop mother henning me. Do I look like a chicken?" Or, "Medicines. I think they make me sicker than if I did nothing at all."

But he wanted to talk about the article. "Madeline, my dear," he said one night after a dinner of seafood pasta and Caesar salad, his voice raspy. "This reporter."

"Yes." I reached for his hand across the kitchen table, feeling nauseated at the thought of that article. See what stress does? It makes you physically ill.

"You said this reporter is researching the trials, what my daughter did in court...." His voice trailed off. Anytime my granddad, tough, weathered, strong, brought up my momma, he would cry. Sometimes it was only his eyes flooding, other times he had to leave the room for a few minutes.

I waited.

"I know she's writing about what happened to you and Annie. Does she—" Another pause. "Does she have the photos in hand?"

"I would think that she's seen them, Granddad." I hadn't asked. I didn't even want to know. It made me feel like my stomach was grinding rocks. I thought of my young self. I wanted to protect my young self—my old self, too. I wanted to protect Annie. "I don't know how, but Sherwinn mailed them out. It probably wouldn't take much to get ahold of them. Journalists are tenacious."

He ran both of his hands over his face. "I'm so sorry, my love."

"I am, too. I wish she would leave it alone, not drag this whole thing out. Annie's carved a King Kong and she's working on a shark if that tells you a bit about her mood."

Granddad cleared his throat. "Honey, I have to ask you another question. Is there anything else this reporter is writing about?"

I remembered Marlene's questions, the questions that had plagued me.

Can you confirm that your grandma was born in Holland before moving to France as a young girl? Can you confirm that your grandma was one of eight children and her parents' names were Solomon and Yentl Levine? Can you confirm that your grandfather's parents' names were Shani and Tomer Laurent and their family has lived in France for hundreds of years? Can you confirm that your grandfather had two brothers, Meyer and Sagi? In doing a little research, I am very confused about some-

thing else, too. If you could call me, perhaps you could clear things up.

"I'm confused. I don't understand but..." I told him the questions Marlene had asked me.

Granddad's face dropped into his old, age-spotted hands. "That's it then," he whispered. "That's it."

I could hardly speak. My granddad had rarely appeared defeated in my whole life. Watching him grieve over my dad, even as a child, I knew he was broken. When he was at the hospital with Annie and me and he realized the abuse we'd suffered, I saw his devastation again. During my momma's trial, the night before the jury came back, same thing. His worry had almost killed him, and when he could not rescue my momma, that bleak, raw grief swallowed him.

And now. He'd had another blow. A hammer blow. "What's wrong, Granddad? Granddad, please. What is it?"

He shook his head, his broad shoulders caving in.

"Why did she ask that, about Holland? Your parents' names aren't Shani and Tomer. You don't have brothers. She's obviously confused and for some reason is researching another family for an article about Momma, but I have no idea why."

"Dear God," he said, his words raspy. "*Dear God.*"

"Dear God, *what?*" I pleaded. I was getting so tired of not understanding whatever my grandparents were hiding from me. I'd had enough lies in my life and they were all scraping me bloody. "Please tell me."

He turned pale—a sickly, pale color—and whispered, as if to himself, "It will all come out. She'll find it. She probably already has. She knows."

"Please, Granddad . . . there's so many secrets in our family. Annie and I have asked you questions a number of times, especially since Grandma started living in the past, but you keep putting us off. I think we need to know at this point. We need to know why you've buried your own history."

He hugged me close, then rasped out, "Very soon, I will tell you, Madeline." Then he muttered, in French, "I will have to, or she will do it."

I buried my head in his shoulder. Marlene was unearthing so much, too much, forcing us all into a place we didn't want to be. How can one person do that to another? We were children then, yet here she was, ripping our past out into the open, tearing our lives apart, as if she had every moral and ethical right to do so. As if she had every right to ruin us one more time. She had all the control. She had control over me, over my own family. She wanted to write the article and damn the consequences to us. I felt that fury scalding my stomach, the rage that always simmered.

"God help us," Granddad muttered. I lifted a shaking hand to his cheek and wiped away a tear.

His tears poured over my hand, the drops hot, despairing.

"I love you, Granddad, I love you."

"And I you," he choked out. "And I you."

But I knew this: My hand was being forced, and his would be forced, too.

Grandma and Granddad saved us in many ways. Their love, attention, kindness, and compassion never wavered.

When we first came to live with Grandma and Granddad, Annie and I would often sleep in their room. In an alcove, where Granddad used to have his desk, they fit in a queen-sized bed for us. Covered in a yellow, poufy, flowered bedspread and an abundance of yellow pillows with lace, it was our haven. Our nightmares were on lower drive in that room, but if we did wake up, terrified and screaming, or if Annie tried to climb out a window, or fling herself through the French doors, or if she tried to hide under their bed, or started throwing books while screaming, Grandma and Granddad were there to soothe her, to hug those night terrors away.

And if I woke up in a rage, furious, flustered from being hit with a vision of Sherwinn, or a whip, or a run-down shack that smelled like must and lust, Grandma knew it right away. She would comfort me with her magical stories of swans, and as soon as dawn crested over the mountains, we'd be slinging saddles over horses, galloping on the trails around the property, the violinist in my head playing something fast paced, angry, as if he were being chased, too.

"You girls are always welcome," Granddad told us, when we were adults. "Life gets hard, and if you want to come back and sleep in the same room as your Grandma and me, you can. Some people might think it strange, I think it normal. Fortunately, I haven't worried about what anyone thinks of me since I was eight, anyhow. I love you, girls."

But in our high school years Annie and I both went into self-destruction mode. This is not atypical for people who have experienced abuse and who have endured the traumas we have. We started partying, experimenting, trying to drown ourselves in stuff we shouldn't have been in but reached for, anyhow. We never snuck out to clubs to go dancing, though. No way. Annie and I don't dance.

Grandma and Granddad found out about our rebelliousness. I distinctly remember both of them charging into a house where we were at a party, no parents home, inebriated. He was in a tux, she in a silk, flowing black dress. They had been at a fancy dinner, where they'd donated money to a drug rehabilitation center, ironically enough, because they strongly believed in "second chances." They hauled our asses out of there so quick, it felt like we were flying.

After some rapid, supersonic detective work, where they found out that Annie and I had been lying about our whereabouts and what we'd been doing, and we'd been skipping school, those two went on hyperoverdrive.

Since we had proven ourselves "irresponsible," they came to school *with us*. Granddad went class to class with me for a day, and Grandma went with Annie. The next day they switched. They even sat with us at lunch. We drove there and back with them after our sports or after-school activities, like my violin lessons. It was *humiliating*.

My award-winning violin teacher, Jeanine Emros, who was also a rebel violinist, like me, was pleased to have them with us at my weekly two-hour lesson. "Lovely people," she said.

"Now, we'll work on your classical pieces, then a bit of blue-grass to shake things up, shall we?"

From our after-school activities, we went to work in the stores. We got home at ten at night, and we did homework, under their watchful eyes. On weekends, we worked at the stores starting at six in the morning, basically moving boxes and sweeping floors and cleaning bathrooms. When we got home, we worked on the farm. We were exhausted, but we did not get into trouble anymore. We didn't have the energy.

One afternoon, six weeks after the punishment began, Annie and I lay between the rows of lavender, wiped out. Our grand-parents scooted right up that hill to scold us. "Up you go, ladies. Laziness and slothfulness is a sin! Idle hands will make trouble!"

Annie said, "I give up."

I said, "I surrender. You win."

Our grandparents hugged us close. "You were out of control. We had to step in to get control. . . . We love you, that's why we played it tough. . . . If you weren't going to follow the rules, we were going to follow you until you did. We love you."

Annie and I nodded, we got it. We understood.

We expected to be invited in for a huge celebratory dinner, you know, a "Now we're all getting along" type of thing. "Hooray for family! Hooray for our girls who have seen the light!"

Nope.

"There are berries to pick in the south field," Grandma said.

"When you're done there, the barn needs to be cleaned out. Cut some lavender to sell in the stores. You two need to make more wreaths. At least fifty," Granddad said. "Up you go."

They worked our bones to brittle ends, but we did not get in any more trouble. They dragged us through the danger zone of despair, until we were able to fight the despair on our own.

They literally, physically, saved us.

They'd lied to us about their past. Lied by omission.

But I loved them. I loved the liars with all my heart and soul.

18

My momma's brain tumor was discovered on a bustling Friday at Marie Elise's French Beauty Parlor. Every pink swivel chair was taken, a head warmed under every dryer, and on every pink fainting couch lay a chatting woman. The curling irons curled, the nails were polished, the hair was dyed, highlighted, washed, rinsed, cream rinsed, and cut, the talk was quick, the laughter a pleasant staccato rhythm.

Annie and I were serving cookies on trays to the women lying on the pink fainting couches while they passed a bottle of wine back and forth. We frosted them with pink icing and added Red Hots in the shapes of smiles. We were also serving pink lemonade. Not only could we avoid Sherwinn all day when we were at the beauty parlor, Momma paid us five dollars at the end of the day. Not bad.

I listened to the women chat back and forth, as two violinists played a piece by Bach in my head, not loudly.

"I swear my gas is worse today than it was two years ago. It's got to be my age. Excuse me, again! . . . I cannot control my Lillianne, she and that boyfriend sneaking out to meet at night, why, he has long, shaggy hair, he's a dreadful hippie . . . my anxiety got the best of me yesterday . . . did you see *One Life to Live* yesterday on TV? The guest doctor is enough to get my engine running . . . I have not had sex in five years. Five long years. I think if I did, my orgasm might give me a heart attack . . . I'm going to buy a poodle. Better a poodle than a man . . . do they have whorehouses that women can go to and buy a man for an afternoon? . . . darn it, I forgot to buy sugar . . . have you tasted Ed's cinnamon rolls? He's going to win again at the bake-off, I know it, beats me every year . . . I think I saw Tessa and Yvonne holding hands the other day, they've been living together for thirty years now, they must be the best of friends . . . did you see how Jessie Liz's son painted another picture of a naked woman on the back of Ed's Groceries? All the men sneak back to look at it. . . ."

Everyone took our cookies. "My goodness, aren't these delicious! Did you girls make them?"

We did. We had made them with our momma the night before. She had a headache in the afternoon and said her eyes felt funny, so she took a nap, then we baked together, sifting flour, measuring sugar, cracking eggs, dropping in red food dye. We snuck Red Hots.

Sherwinn was out of the house. We didn't care where he was, so for a minute we could pretend he did not exist. It was just us and our momma in our sun-filled kitchen with the window that overlooked our sea, the sun shining down on the frothing waves with a friendly smile.

"Yummy! You girls, bring us a couple more, please. Do you girls have a tip jar? I want to pay you for these scrumptious cookies!"

We were pleased with the idea of a tip. Why, we could go downtown then and buy nail polish and sparkly eye shadow or flowers for Momma.

The corners of Annie's mouth tipped up, she so rarely smiled anymore.

"Gracious God!"

"What happened?"

"Marie Elise! Marie Elise! Call for an ambulance, hurry, hurry! *Hurry!*"

Annie and I dropped our trays with the pink cookies and rushed to our momma. She lay on the floor writhing, twisting, shaking, her eyes blank, like she wasn't there, her back arching up and down.

"Get the girls out," Mrs. Grasher ordered as she bent over our momma. She was a nurse and I heard her say, "She's having a seizure. . . ."

The women hustled us out the door, even as we fought to stay, as we called to her, "Momma, Momma, Momma," the pitched screech of the siren petrifying.

What was going on? Was our momma dying? Would we have *no* parents? Help our momma! Help!

Outside Annie and I hugged each other, and the ladies who had pushed us out the door wrapped their arms around us as we wailed in fear.

"I am sorry, my loves, my dearest grandchildren," Grandma told us two nights later, holding us close together on her lap in our living room. She and Granddad had flown in immediately on a private jet. She was dressed impeccably, black slacks, silk shirt, a purple scarf, sparkling jewelry, her wedding ring heavy on her finger. Her clothes directly contrasted with the raw, aching pain in her blue-green eyes, so like Annie's. "I am so sorry, beloveds. Your momma has a brain tumor."

The tumor was inoperable. They would treat it, they would pray.

Our momma walked into our house by the sea about a week after she'd had her seizure. She was wearing a pink dress with a flared skirt and had her hand under Granddad's crooked elbow. When she saw us, her face wreathed into smiles. "Pink Girls!" she yelled, and flung out her arms.

We were inundated with exquisite meals and treats from everyone in our town, and people were in our home all the time, trying to help or visiting. Our grandparents moved in, without even asking Sherwinn, which I heard him complaining about. "This is my house. I am in charge. I'm the man. You didn't ask, Marie Elise, for my permission."

I wasn't surprised to hear my momma say, "They're moving in. If you don't like it, move out."

Sherwinn slammed out of the house that night, the door rattling the rafters, and I dropped to my knees and prayed that he would never come back. The prayers were not answered.

Annie and I loved all the people in our home. We did not love that our momma had a brain tumor—that part frightened us so much our bones knocked together. We saw Sherwinn glaring at us and we ignored him, shaking inside, but we could be brave on the outside, because we felt safe with our grandparents around, safe with all the friends.

As for our momma?

We saw her sobbing sometimes in the kitchen, her shoulders shaking, when she thought she was alone. We saw her bent over in the garden, her hands to her face. We saw her staring out at the sea from our deck, rocking herself. We heard the notes of her violin floating back to us on the wind as she stood on the cliff, her mouth moving, as if she was talking to someone.

But, in front of us, she was all smiles, hugging and loving us, baking all sorts of French desserts like Clafoutis aux Cerises, chocolate ganache, chocolate truffles, crème brûlée, crème caramel, and pumpkin soufflés. She cut way down on her hours at the parlor, so she was home when we got home from school if she wasn't at a doctor's appointment or the hospital.

She wore pinks, reds, yellows. She used yellow ribbons for hope to hold back her hair. She told everyone, "I'm gonna beat this, you watch me . . . No, I never ask, 'Why did this have to happen to me? *Why not me?* You won't hear any whining out of my mouth . . . don't you look gorgeous today, Gretchen . . . I can volunteer at Quilting Sunday, that would be my cup of tea, I'll bring my Pink Girls . . . God's got His arms around me, I can feel them . . . I am so fortunate to have you all in my life . . . you made me dinner, again? Sheri, aren't you the best? Gregor Stein! You made me my favorite banana bread, aren't you dear?"

Sherwinn's true colors started to show to our momma. He wanted a warm woman in bed and he wanted hot meals and he liked that our momma had a comfy home by the sea and money to boot and daughters to hurt. But he didn't like all the attention she was getting. He didn't like that there were people around all the time, so he couldn't get at us. He didn't like that he had only been married a few months and already he had an inconvenience on his hands.

"Can we not talk about your tumor, Marie Elise, I'm sick of

that topic ... dammit, you haven't made my breakfast ... no, I can't drive you to the doctor, I have plans for today ... somebody's gotta work since you aren't workin' as much as you used to ... shit."

Sherwinn's attitude, his lack of caring and help, infuriated our momma, I could tell, and they started having some rip-roaring fights, which exhausted her.

There was one thing she took action on, though. When Sherwinn was gone, two attorneys came to our house. One was Jack Shears, a friend of my dad's, another was Melanie Cho, who was a friend of my dad's in high school. Our momma was in bed and Jack, Melanie, and our grandparents went up to her bedroom and shut the door. Annie and I knew that a shut door meant we should listen in.

"We have to make this airtight so my girls get every cent of my money. It is your job to make sure that this happens, Jack, Melanie," Momma said, her voice only above a whisper from being worn down by her tumor. "I love those Pink Girls."

She outlined the money that our dad had left her. She made sure that her will gave us, her girls, that money, including the money that our dad's parents had left to Momma. The house and all the possessions would go to us. Our momma had been smart enough to sign a pre nup with Sherwinn, and that pre nup came into play.

And, most importantly, she was adamant about who we were to live with when she was gone. "Madeline and Annie are to live with my parents. Sherwinn is not to gain custody."

Annie and I sagged against each other. We did not want our momma to die, but can you imagine, two innocent girls, in deathly fear that if their momma dies, they will be handed over to a child molester?

Over the next couple of months Momma's health declined and improved. She was hospitalized often, slept for hours, and was in and out of doctors' offices. We dove onto the same waves of emotions that people go through when fighting a terminal illness: Hope and despair and around again. She fought back nausea and vomiting and exhaustion.

But, when she was well, she held out her arms and the three of us danced a waltz on the grass near our house by the sea.

Her friends were her anchors.

"We're all wearing pink," Trudy Jo said. "To give your momma encouragement." She switched over to Shakespeare, the "real man" in her life. "And thus I clothe my naked villainy . . . They did make love to this employment . . . unsex me here."

I put my hand over my mouth. I didn't know what "unsex me" meant.

Carman burst into song, her champagne glass held reverently high. "For your mother, honey." She cleared her throat. "My friend, my forever friend. . . ."

"We bought your momma a pink robe, pink slippers with feathers, and two sets of pink jammies," Shell Dee said, "so her body will be comfortable. Here's some interesting facts about the skin that covers our bodies: The average person, man or woman, has about, get this, twenty-one feet of skin! At the end of the year about one-point-six pounds of skin has flaked off! Disgusting! Think of all that dead skin flaking off billions of people on this earth. In fact, when there's dust in your home, it's mostly skin that's leaving your body!"

Ugh.

We begged our grandparents not to leave, but a few weeks after the diagnosis, they had to. Grandma had books due, Grand-dad had the stores, and Momma had temporarily stabilized and seemed to be responding extraordinarily well to treatment. I could tell that our granddad and grandma hated Sherwinn, and they talked to our momma about their dislike, Grandma especially being blunt in calling him a "crude, white trash orangutan" and Granddad calling him "a pure asshole. Let my attorney handle the divorce for you, honey," but my momma couldn't do it then. Too much. A tumor in her head and a divorce?

The three of them had one enormous strike against them, though: They could not imagine the crime that Sherwinn was committing. It was not in their repertoire. It is not in any sane, kind person's repertoire. Kind, sane people don't do that type of thing.

Once they left, Sherwinn, Pauly, and Gavin started in on us again.

We shut down, Sherwinn's threats to kill our momma and make it look like it was part of her "damn brain tumor" solidifying us into rigid, semidead girls. "I didn't sign up to be married to a sickie and a weakling," he shouted as he shoved us back into the shack as an orchestra playing Mozart blasted through my mind, blocking out the rest of what he said.

He lurked around us, like slimy pollution. Behind her back he once wielded a knife, a warning to us not to tell. He put a dead mouse on my dresser and held one finger up to his mouth and said, "Shhh, Madeline." He showed Annie a picture of a woman's corpse, and giggled.

Sherwinn was a nightmare we lived with every day, and while our momma fought for her life, we fought for our lives, too.

Click, click, click.

What do I blame for my momma's mistake in bringing Sherwinn into our lives? I blame her brain tumor. It was clearly growing before she even met Sherwinn, and I think it affected her judgment. I blame her entrenched loneliness after my dad died. I blame Sherwinn's captivating, deceitful personality that swept my momma off her feet. I blame the mysterious grief she carried with her that I never understood, the tears that fell down her face when she played her violin and spoke in French, as if reaching for someone, a hand out in despair.

I could hate my momma for bringing Sherwinn into our lives. I could hate her for being blind to his demented personality and what was happening to us in her own home. But the truth is, he only lived with us for a few months. When she found out what they did, she killed all three of them.

Even so, could I hate my momma for bringing total emotional devastation to Annie and me?

I could.

But I didn't. Why? Because I loved her so very, very much.

Marie Elise Laurent was the best momma on the planet.

19

We live in a freewheeling, free-dealing country. We are rabid about our rights.

I get it.

I am a born and bred American. I love America, and I love my rights.

But I take issue on our "rights" to pornography. People say others have the right to view whatever they want in the privacy of their own homes, on their computers, in their mailbox, and so on.

Okay. I hear that.

But aside from the fact that pornography corrodes minds, fills them with human depravity and filthy sexual images, intrudes on marriages and relationships, causes pornographic addictions to disgusting and demeaning images of women, and promotes violence, we have to think about the people whose photos are being shot.

Now, I am not overly concerned about the American porn star who is *an adult* and making millions every year. I don't like what she's doing, I don't like her choice for her own mental health and safety, and I don't like the result and how many millions of men and women will be panting and slobbering while watching her videos. I don't like that she's choosing to be a catalyst for millions of men to mentally and physically jack off. I don't like that she's doing something that addicts millions of men and boys, and some women, to porn, and how that twists their minds into morasses of tarry, moral-less messes.

Argue all you want, but you're watching someone else naked, having sex, or doing something atrocious and your mind is getting all hyped up about it. It's disgusting.

However. The porn star making millions in America who retires to the country to run a horse farm is not the norm. The norm is millions of young people, mostly very young girls, many, if not most, underage, being forced into this hellacious business. Think that naked woman in the video having something disgusting done to her appears young?

She is.

She's probably some poor Eastern European fourteen-year-old girl who has been whipped off the streets and forced into this sickness.

Think the long-haired Asian woman who's on top of that hairy white man has the body of a child?

That's because *she is a child*. She was taken from her parents and told she was going to work as a maid in someone's house in a city in China. She is not working as a maid. She is working as a sex slave.

Think that boy in that homosexual position looks like he's about five? He is. *He is five.* He should be in kindergarten painting a picture of a spider with furry feet.

See that blond girl? She's American. She's from California. That man with her? *That is her father* and you are watching that girl getting raped while her father films it. Over and over.

I wonder if rancid people who view porn ever take the time to stare into the "actors'" eyes? Do they? Probably not. It's not what they're looking for, and they don't want to know the harsh truth of what their vomitous addiction is doing to someone else.

They are repulsive people. Do not try to tell me they are not. *They are repulsive.*

Pornography is a scourge on this planet. It is a soul-stripping business that profits, mainly, off helpless, powerless, scared-to-death young people who are forced to do things that most of us wouldn't even do in our bedroom. They are imprisoned and they literally can't leave or they will be shot, attacked, or beaten till their faces are smeared into glue.

They are children. They are kids. They should be out kicking a ball, buying lip gloss, or swimming in the city pool. If they are no longer technically children, they are in their twenties, probably being forced into it, maybe under threat of losing their lives, and have drug and alcohol problems that make them unable to function, and think, like a normal person.

Folks, there is nothing redeeming about pornography. *Nothing.* If I could take it away forever, I would.

And it is my fervent hope that when the men—and it's mostly men—who promote and watch this trash die, and hopefully it will be a bone-crushing, painful death, and they look God in the face and are asked to explain to God why they forced His innocent, sweet children into that squalid pit, that they finally realize the destruction they have wreaked.

I would not want to be them. I would not want to look God in the eye and tell Him I promoted porn. I can only hope that when these sickening monsters are tossed down to hell that Satan himself has a bonfire crackling and steel rods ready.

Welcome to hell, he'll cackle, and they'll catch on fire and burn. But they won't die. They'll live to burn again. Every day. For eternity.

To pay them back for the burning they did here on Earth.

I wish my rage would go away.

I also wish I could breathe like a normal member of the human species.

That night I made chicken burritos with mango salsa and avocado strips for Grandma, Granddad, Nola, and Annie.

Afterward I helped get Grandma to her bedroom. Annie and I left when Granddad tucked Grandma into bed, spending extra time smoothing lavender lotion into her hands. Right before we shut the door we heard her say, "Anton! You send me to the heavens!"

And our granddad, such a gentleman, said sweetly, "And you do the same for me, my love."

"I like heaven!" she piped up. "Right between my legs!"

On Thursday night, as I lay in my bed surrounded by purple pillows, the closet obsessively neat so I could see straight through to the wall, I heard Grandma open the door to my room and run on tiptoe to my bed. She said, in French and English, with only three words in German, "I will save your daughter for you. I will raise her as my own. We will walk over the mountains. We will escape." She kissed me on the forehead. "Good-bye, my sister."

The last three words, she said in German, "Good-bye, my sister."

I leaned my head back. *Good-bye, my sister? I will save your daughter? We will walk over the mountains?* What in hell was Grandma talking about? I was so tired of their secrets.

"Anton has the papers, and we are leaving. I don't know how I can live without you, sister. My heart is breaking. I can't live without you. How do I do this? How?" She burst into tears, her shoulders shaking.

"It's okay, Grandma, it's me. Madeline." I sat up and wrapped my arms around her.

"I will take your violin for Anna. There is a scratch in the back. It happened when we ran from the black ghosts, away from the stars on the backs of ostriches. Only a skinny scratch, made by, perhaps, a tiny gopher wearing an apron. The notes are still good."

The door opened and Granddad came in. "Hello, Madeline," he said, his voice soft, understanding, the voice that had steadied me my whole life.

"Hi, Granddad," I said.

She turned to him. "I can't leave Madeline, I can't leave Ismael. I can't leave them. I won't—"

"They are with God now, Emmanuelle." My granddad's voice split, pain racking every word. He sat down next to her on my bed and linked an arm around her tiny shoulders.

"I want to check, I want to make sure. The doctor said he's dying, but I want to check...."

"He's dead." My granddad's voice choked. "Come with me, come with me, Emmanuelle, back to bed."

"They are dead, and we go, we live. It is not fair. Why us? Why do we live? For my sister, she is more deserving."

"No," he said. "It is not fair. I don't want to go, but we must save ourselves. We must save Anna. Come. Let's go and sit near the lavender plants."

My grandma stilled. "The lavender is ready? It is purple and white and there are magic marbles in between the plants next to the tiny swans?"

"Yes, the lavender is ready and there are marbles already there. The swans flew in."

"The miniature swans with yellow magic beaks? All right." She wiped the tears off her face. "If you're sure. I feel Ismael, still. I hear him, I see him, I know he's here." She tapped her heart. "How can he be gone?"

"He is gone." My granddad bent his head and kissed my grandma on the forehead. "But you and I will see Madeline and Ismael and Anna again."

"When?" She turned her tear streaked face to his, her hands on his chest. "I want to see them."

"Soon, I feel, very soon, my love. We will see them again."

"I want to see them! Let's go to the lavender. But call me Dynah."

What? Call me Dynah?

"I'll do that," Granddad croaked out.

"And I'll call you by your real name, Abe." She stroked his jaw. "Abe. My love, Abe."

What? I'll call you Abe?

He nodded. "I think it's time."

"Yes, it's time."

Grandma reached around and patted my granddad on the bottom, her mood changing lightning quick. She smiled coquettishly at him, then winked.

They had spoken in French, then switched to German halfway through their conversation.

I caught my granddad's eye and this time, I saw it. I saw his exhaustion, his resignation, his understanding that this could not go on any longer.

He would tell me.

He would tell me soon.

He was done with his secret.

"I can't believe it, but she bombed us with her persistence this morning." Georgie stuck a silver butterfly clip in her hair. The wings bounced. She had sprayed the ends of her platinum hair red. She was wearing a red dress and red boots today.

"Who?" But I knew who.

"Marlene, that reporter."

"You're kidding." Marlene was the type of person with tunnel ambition. Nothing mattered except that ambition, that story, her byline. Nothing. And if someone had to get trampled in her quest for her raging ambition, too bad.

"I told that female warlock that her spirit needed to be realigned so she didn't hurt people, bother people, get in the way of the flow of their own life chart."

I raised an eyebrow. I didn't know what a life chart was. I would ask later.

"And I told her that she was not only harassing you, but she was harassing me, too, because I kept having to rouse myself to deal with someone who was breaking the rhythm of my body functions, which was causing gas."

"Okeydoke. Gas. How did she respond?"

"She said in that quiet voice of hers, 'Does Madeline know that if she participates in the article, she can control this somewhat? She can give her input, address the issues, the past?'"

"And I said, 'Madeline is the smartest woman I know. She knows all of that and she has chosen to disregard your efforts to intrude upon her life and now I am withdrawing my blessing.' That's what I told her."

"You withdrew your blessing?"

"Yes, I did."

"Good. And you hung up?"

"No, because she got in some questions lickety-split quick." I listened intently as Georgie told me what Marlene had asked, all questions having to do with my and Annie's nightmares, a hole like molten steel singeing my stomach.

"Did you hang up after that, Georgie?"

"I did, but first I told her to screw herself with a pencil."

"Ah. Lovely. What did she say?"

"She said she would prefer not to do that."

"And you said?"

"'Good-bye. You have no blessings and now your day will be cursed.'"

Later that evening, my mind spinning, I stared west out the windows.

What should we expect out of life? What is reasonable?

What is right? What is selfish? What is outlandish? When we have a dream for our lives and it crashes and incinerates, is it worth the disappointment?

Should we embrace tragedy as we do gifts?

How?

How would that look for me? How would I embrace what happened to Annie and me?

What good came out of it? Not much that I can see, although I wish something would.

And, if there was good out of it—that I can relate to people's tragedies better because I've lived it, that I understand their tears and grief, their fears and terrors, that I have risen above that abuse and built a life—are those skills good enough to obliterate the bad? The long-term damage it did to us? The death of my momma?

No.

I would rather not have gone through what Annie and I and our family did.

I would be a different person, that is true. I would not be riddled with jagged nerves and breath that gets wrapped around my organs and bones and stuck before it can fill my lungs. But I had moved forward, in many ways.

When we move forward through the muck, isn't that, right there, a huge accomplishment?

I watched the sun set, the sky growing pink, yellow, orange, then blue, darker blue.

Today was leaving, tomorrow would come.

I wondered if I had the courage, the guts, to make my tomorrow different from today, or if I would simply plow through it as I have forever done.

Should I plow through?

When would I be done plowing? Would it ever end?

When do I start living without the plow?

20

On a Monday, after a snowy weekend, Annie passed out at school. The teacher flipped, and then moved quickly into hysteria, because when she shook Annie, Annie didn't move. Other teachers raced in, followed by the principal and the paramedics.

I was out at recess. That day, instead of clinging to the wall in shame, I was playing wall ball under the covered area. My friend, Joyce Brown, sprinted over to me, her pigtails flying, and said, "Madeline, run! It's Annie! She's going away in the ambulance!"

My feet flew as I ran with Joyce and two other friends. When I reached her, I saw Annie on a stretcher with an oxygen mask and started screaming. I grabbed the stretcher and wouldn't let go.

"Madeline," the principal, Mrs. Jett, insisted, her hair falling out of her bun, "stay here with me, honey, stay here."

"No," I screamed. "No!" I jumped on the stretcher and held her tight, pushing hands away, until they gave up and put both of us into the ambulance. "Annie! Annie!"

The siren wailed into the morning, down the street in town, even reaching Marie Elise's French Beauty Parlor where Momma received a call that one of her beloved girls had passed out and the other beloved girl was emotionally disintegrating.

Momma dropped the dye she was using to color Mrs. Ellerton's hair and, with her black apron on, she and Carman flew out of the beauty parlor and into the disastrous, harsh truth of Momma's life and the demon-plagued lives of her children.

About an hour after arriving at the hospital, I pretended I was asleep in the bed next to Annie's so I could hear everything the doctors were telling my momma, Carman, Trudy Jo, and Shell Dee. Sheriff Ellery was there, along with two of his deputies and nurses. Annie was still woozy, not all together.

Momma sunk into a chair after hugging and kissing Annie and me, too dizzy with shock to stand anymore.

I could tell by the doctor's tone, a man who had been fishing with my dad many times, that he was gravely troubled, but he was taking things slow, one thing at a time. "Annie and Madeline are way too thin," Dr. Hayes said. "Have you seen them without clothes on recently?"

"No, no, I haven't—" Our momma wrung her hands. "I thought they were . . . I thought they weren't eating as much because of my illness, because they were upset. They cry, they hug me all the time. But I've tried to get them to eat, I've tried, dear Lord, I have tried."

She had tried. She made us breakfast every morning. Pancakes cut into the shapes of dogs and cats. Oatmeal with brown sugar. Scrambled eggs she arranged into a smile. We couldn't eat. Hard to eat when the man who stuck a pencil in your bottom, chalk in your mouth, and a ruler in your hand for a naked "Back To School" porno shoot was sitting across the table smirking at you.

"Do they eat lunch?"

Yes, some. Whatever we could choke down, plus a lollipop for the walk home. "For energy," Momma had told us, squeezing our cheeks.

"They're at school. I can't watch them eat there, but I do pack them a good lunch."

Her lunches were delicious. The envy of all. Whenever I opened my lunch sack, I tasted my momma's love.

"I don't understand . . . I don't understand . . ." Our momma's makeup was smeared down her face, her hair a mess. Carman tried to smooth it. Shell Dee handed her another tissue.

"Marie Elise," Dr. Hayes said, "after giving Annie an IV for fluids, we did a full exam."

I did not miss the harsh tone of the doctor's voice.

"Yes, what's wrong? What is it?"

From my bed, I saw my momma's face crumple.

"First I need to ask, where did the bruises and burns come from?"

My momma, Carman, Shell Dee, and Trudy Jo gasped.

Carman said, "Dear Lord in heaven."

Shell Dee said, "My God."

Trudy Jo said, "Jesus help us!"

"*What?*" Momma whispered. She had already been pale, but now she was the same color as the white wall. "What bruises? What burns? Where?"

I knew what bruises and burns. Overwhelming guilt and shame torpedoed me. I was dirty. I was bad. I was a slutty girl. Now Momma would know.

And Annie, my little sister. I was supposed to protect her, but I couldn't do it. I had tried! I had pleaded with Sherwinn, Pauly, and Gavin. I had fought for her. The last time I fought for her, Sherwinn shoved me in a big dog cage in the back room and locked it shut.

Carman and Shell Dee helped my momma up from her chair, as she could no longer walk. Even from my bed, through half-shut eyes, I could see my momma's body rocking back and forth, her balance gone the second she saw her beloved daughters in hospital beds. The sheriff and his deputies, the nurses and other doctors crowded around Annie, who was still asleep.

The doctor gently pulled the sheet back. My momma peered down at Annie's beaten, bruised, burned, emaciated, naked body. My body looked the same. Carman, Shell Dee, and Trudy Jo released raw, primal moans. Sheriff Ellery semishouted, "Holy mother of God." One deputy moaned and said, "Aw shit, Big Luke would kill if he saw this." A nurse gasped and covered her mouth.

My momma took one look and passed straight out.

* * *

When my momma crumpled backwards, I sat up and screamed, believing she was dead. The attention was then on both of us, doctors and nurses rushing to help before my momma was wheeled out on a stretcher.

"Madeline," Dr. Hayes said. "I think we need to examine you, too, don't we?"

I shook my head. I said no, I didn't want to. They lifted the back of my shirt, anyhow, then the front.

I saw the grim looks on Dr. Hayes's face and on the faces of the nurses.

Did they think I was bad? They did, didn't they! It was my fault! I wrapped my arms around my knees.

One of the nurses held my hand. "I'm sorry, child. I'm sorry this happened to you."

The other nurse hugged me. "How about a Popsicle, honey?"

Carman, Trudy Jo, and Shell Dee crowded around, hugging me, snuffling. Sheriff Ellery and the other officers stood against the wall, along with the doctors and nurses.

Carman said, "Who did this? I will kill him."

Trudy Jo said, "This is killing me to see this, killing me."

I was so ashamed.

"Who did this?" Shell Dee said, kissing me on the forehead. "You can tell us."

I felt so guilty.

"You need to tell us. This bad person needs to be punished."

If I told, everyone would see the photographs! They would think I wanted to do them! They would think that I should have told to protect Annie! They would think I was a slutty, bad girl with curly hair—that's what Sherwinn called me. "A slutty, bad girl with curly hair." Momma would be so upset with me.

Click, click, click.

"This isn't your fault, you know that, right, hon?" Shell Dee said. "This is a bad person's fault. Whisper me his name."

I was tempted. I glanced over at Annie's bed. She was so tiny, so fragile, I thought she was dead when she was on the stretcher.

"No." My voice cracked, the hot tears finally coming. "No, I can't."

"But why?" Carman said. "We love you. We want to know who hurt you."

"If I tell," I whispered, a vision in my head of *that knife*, "he'll kill Momma."

A tense, electric silence shot through the room.

"No, honey," Sheriff Ellery said, standing beside my bed. "He won't. We're all here. We'll keep her safe."

"He'll kill her like he killed our hamsters! He killed Teresa and Mickey. He'll kill Annie, too, and me. That's what he said. That's why I didn't tell before!" I heard my voice pitch, high, all raggedy. "That's why!"

"But now is the time to tell," Sheriff Ellery said. I heard a cold anger in his voice, but I didn't think he was angry at me, because he held my hand. "Help us here, so we can help you."

"I can't tell!" I put my arms over my head.

Shell Dee held me close. "The only way to keep you and Annie safe, my love, is if you tell us who did this."

"No!" I said, broken and backed into a black, depressed corner.

"Yes," Sheriff Ellery said, his voice becoming very stern. "Madeline. We need the name. We need it now."

Sheriff Ellery had always been so chatty with me, smiling ear to ear, but that day he stood tall, in uniform, gun strapped to his side, and he looked imposing, intimidating. Later he told me he was sorry if he had scared me in the hospital. "The only way to help you, Madeline, was to go after the men who did this to you. They needed to be locked up, like animals, before they knew you were in the hospital and tried to make a run for it. I hope you'll forgive me for scaring you."

Sheriff Ellery fixed me with his stare. "Right now, young lady. I'm not leaving until I have that name."

I glanced over at Annie, a tiny lump in the bed, her head to one side. I knew what was under that sheet. I knew what was under my sheet. I didn't want this to happen to us ever again. "Will you keep them away from Momma and Annie?"

"You bet I will," Sheriff Ellery said. He was very mad.

"Me too, Madeline," one of the officers said.

"We'll make sure of it," the other officer said.

One more time I peeked at the tiny lump of Annie. If I didn't tell, she might die, anyhow. That's what I got down to: If I didn't tell, Annie might die from the abuse.

I told. I uttered those three names, then from somewhere in the hospital, someone started shrieking. Shriek, shriek, shriek. I didn't know it was me for a long time.

Sheriff Ellery wasted no time. He assembled a team from neighboring towns, and the team surrounded Pauly's house. He'd thought to bring a fire trunk, which was very smart. As soon as Sherwinn, Gavin, and Pauly realized they were surrounded, they tried to set the armadillo-slouching shack on fire.

It only partially worked.

Many of the photos were turned to ash, but not all of them. All of the ones that were left were collected by the police.

Sherwinn, Pauly, and Gavin were drunk, and stoned, so therefore easy to apprehend, which was unfortunate, as I heard Sheriff Ellery tell Granddad later, who flew in immediately with Grandma, "If they'd put up a fight, sir, we would have been able to shoot them on the spot. I would have enjoyed that. Yes, I would have enjoyed doing my part to eliminate scum from the earth."

All three men were read their rights, arrested, and later charged with multiple offenses.

The police collected all of the photos of Annie and me, the whips, the cages, the outfits, the wigs, the school supplies. I was told that the police had to take turns going outside to breathe, they were so furious. Their wives/girlfriends/sisters all went to Marie Elise's Beauty Parlor and news got out quick.

I was a bad girl.

"Can you tell us what happened, honey?" Sheriff Ellery asked me the next day. His face was red and tight, bags from lack of sleep under his eyes. Big guy, big heart.

"No," I said, snuggling into my momma on the hospital bed. In many ways, she didn't look like my momma. No makeup, her skin grayish, thick black hair down and messy, clothes rumpled, mouth tight. "I can't."

The doctors were in our hospital room, but there were a couple of police officers, too, and men in suits, who I later found out were attorneys. I had been fed, hydrated through tubes, and for the first time since Sherwinn bulldozed our lives and began his attacks, with my momma's and my grandma's arms wrapped around me, the imprint of their kisses on my forehead, I slept peacefully.

"Sherwinn, Pauly, and Gavin are all in jail, so you can tell us," Sheriff Ellery said. "They won't hurt you again."

Even their names scared me, and I pulled the sheet over my head. "No, I can't tell you."

"Sugar, Sherwinn's going to prison for a long time," Sheriff Ellery said. "So are Pauly and Gavin."

"A long time isn't forever," I said, pulling the sheet down and glaring at the sheriff. "It isn't forever! That means they'll come back out!"

I knew I'd hit a nerve, because Granddad turned away, his back bent, and Momma covered her face with a trembling hand.

Grandma said, those blue-green eyes pleading, "You must tell what happened to you. They will go to jail, but we need to make sure that they have to stay a long time, that they're punished. We don't want them to hurt another girl, do we? We must protect the next girl."

I thought about that. I thought about my girlfriends at school, Theo, Jackie, Stella. I thought about Trudy Jo's and Shell Dee's daughters. I thought about the two-year-old girl who lived across the lake who always hugged me when she saw me and called me "Mad." I did not want this to happen to my friends. And I wanted them to go to jail!

Most of all, I thought about Annie. I looked at her under the blankets, still sleeping, a small and skinny lump. . . .

"He had a knife," I started, instantly angry, scared, shamed once again. I closed my eyes so I wouldn't have to look at their faces when I told. "And pliers. And cigarettes . . ."

Over an hour later, when I was done, and I opened my eyes, one of the attorneys had his head in his hands. Sheriff Ellery's eyes were so swollen he could hardly see when he left.

Grandma was weeping, my momma looked half dead, my granddad, his shoulders down, head bent, glared out the window of the hospital.

Click, click, click.

The nurse gave me a Popsicle. It was green.

I woke up in the middle of the night, one bright star white and glowing, its light reaching my hospital bed. Granddad heard me and came immediately to sit by me. He kissed me on both cheeks, held my hand.

"I'm here, Madeline," he whispered. "You are safe. Go back to sleep."

I closed my eyes and let sleep sneak on in and take me to oblivion, but before sleep could claim me completely, I heard my granddad, strong and indomitable, dissolve into heaving sobs. I am sure he thought I could not hear him.

"I am sorry, my granddaughter, I am sorry," he whispered. "I failed you, too, Madeline, and I am sorry. I should have protected you, insisted you come and live with us on The Lavender Farm. I am so sorry, I didn't know, I didn't know. . . ."

Two hours later I woke up again and watched my granddad standing near the window, his shoulders slumped, his head bent, his life shattered.

When we left the hospital and went home, there were many changes in our house by the sea.

Everything of Sherwinn's had been taken away, including his truck, which was later found exploded to the shell in a field. Pauly's truck was in a lake, and Gavin's car had been smashed by a tractor. "By accident," Shell Dee's husband told us.

"These types of things happen sometimes. Bad wiring," Trudy Jo's husband said.

"Babies." My momma wept. "I am so sorry. So very sorry. This is my fault. Please forgive me. Forgive me." We heard her say it a hundred times.

Annie wasn't speaking still, but eventually we started to heal, our grandparents' and our momma's love, attention, and care helping us every day.

My momma never, ever forgave herself. Not for a minute, not for a second.

Her apology to us? Those gunshots, as strange as it sounds.

21

〜

"Tilt your head up, Madeline . . . to the left . . . turn to the side . . . too much . . . back . . . there we go." The photographer shifted from one place to the next as I sat in my leather chair in my office. My smile froze, the *click, click, click* sending me to places I didn't want to be. I felt myself start to sweat.

"Smile, please, Madeline," the reporter, Quinn, asked me. She was young. She was in a brown suit. She wore horn-rimmed glasses I bet she didn't need but sported them, anyhow, to look smart.

"I'm smiling." I quit smiling.

"No, you're not. Lift up the corners of your mouth."

I rolled my eyes. "Are you ready, Arnie? I'm going to smile." I pulled on the buttons of my black suit, crossed one leg over another, and tried not to rip my boring black heels off my feet and hurdle them.

Click, click, click.

I smiled, teeth showing, for ten seconds. "That's it." I quit smiling, stood up, the sweat rolling down my back.

"What?" Arnie said, surprised.

"We're done." My body wanted to heave and my breath was stuck in my toes, not moving.

Quinn and Arnie exchanged baffled looks.

"But, but, but—" Quinn stuttered.

"What you got is good enough. One of those photos will work." I wiped the sweat off my brow.

"Okay. We'll wrap it up. Thanks, Madeline." Arnie bent to put all his fancy gear away.

"Have a seat, Quinn." I gestured to my leather couch. "I'll be right back. "

I went to the bathroom in the hallway and splashed cold water on my face, ran it over my wrists, jumped up and down to move the air stuck in my toes, then leaned heavily on the sink.

I so hate cameras. After the Cape, Annie and I refused to have our pictures taken, even at school. My grandma had to call in on picture day and tell them we were sick. We ended up making crafts with lavender on those days, hanging lavender bouquets upside down in the kitchen to dry, or riding our horses.

No photos for us.

Click, click, click.

"Okay, Madeline," Quinn said. "As you know, we're doing an article on you to coincide with the Rock Your Womanhood conference coming up here in Portland, a huge event. So, my first question is . . ."

And we were off.

Q: What advice do you have for women, in general?

A: Don't screw up your life. Seriously. *Think.* Make sound, rational, unemotional decisions. Do not delude yourself into making a bad one. Men will try to drag you into poor choices. Don't let them. Don't spend a bunch of self-centered time study-ing the latest self-help book or new-wave religion to figure your-self out. Remember that *most* of the time you spend wallowing in "I don't know what to do with my life," or whining, is self-centered. Reach outside yourself. Help others, go back to school, travel, work hard, love hard, nurture healthy relation-ships, save money, and stay out of debt so your finances don't give you a heart attack.

Q: What advice do you have for men, in general?

A: Same advice. But I'll add one more piece: Don't be a dick.

Q: I know you specialize in relationships, so what's the worst mistake people make about marriage?

A: That it's gonna be a blast. It's not. It's gonna be a pain in the butt sometimes and you will look at your partner and say to yourself, "What was I thinking?" Trust me, he's thinking the same thing about you sometimes, too. So, in your mystification, go back to bed, roll around naked, take yourselves out for a pizza and beer, and get on with it. Work to keep your spouse in love with you. Don't look for your spouse to fill all your needs. That's impossible and unfair. Get interests and hobbies outside your marriage. No need to be locked at the hip. Have new adventures together, laugh, give each other one compliment a day. Fight fair and remember that the person who is meanest during the fight, even if they win, always loses. They shut the other person down. The shut-down person will eventually leave.

Q: My sister and I don't get along.

A: What's the question?

Q: What can we do to be closer?

A: Be nice?

Q: No, really.

A: That really was my answer. Some sisters are best friends, lovey-dovey. A lot aren't. Quit forcing yourself to try to be close to someone when it's not working. You may never be close to your sister. Accept it. Call on birthdays and holidays, send cards or flowers, let her know you love her. Keep conversations short, noncontroversial. Don't compete with your sister, don't compare, don't make snide remarks while smiling, don't tell her she looks tired, don't manipulate each other, don't be passive-aggressive—that's so annoying and people hate it. Embrace what you love about her, toss the rest, and be okay with not spending time with people, even family, who you just don't like.

Q: You talk a lot about fulfillment. How should women find fulfillment?

A: A grateful heart goes a long, long way. Look around. What are you happy that you have? Be grateful for your health, be grateful you're not being eaten by maggots in a coffin. Be grateful for your kids, ripe tomatoes, rainy book reading days, two legs, cherry blossoms, campfires, friends. You will, if you're lucky, be ninety-one day. Make sure you can look back on your life and say, "I did that...I did that, too...I tried...I loved... I adventured...I dared...I sang and danced...I was kind and compassionate and honest. Have morals and stick to them. Do not hold yourself back. The person you are at ninety will hate you for not living more fully right now, in your youth. Buy a vibrator. And don't wear ugly bras. Yuck. No beige. Never wear a beige bra.

Q: Is there a man in your life?

A: Hundreds. They're called clients.

Q: A special man?

A: No.

Q: What's your dream date?

A: A hot bath. Alone.

Q: Truthfully?

A: Yes. Men give me headaches.

Q: Advice to young women entering the workforce?

A: If you must work for corporate America, do not let it kill your soul. Do not base your confidence solely on your job. Have a huge life outside of work, so work is only part of you, not all of you. If you hate your job but must keep it, start stockpiling money, or working a second job, or work your dream job on the side, so one day you can release yourself from your corporate bondage.

Q: What's your advice for women who are sandwiched between aging parents and teenagers?

A: Get drunk.

Q: You're not serious.

A: Of course not. That would be stupid. Only stupid people get drunk. Get a massage. A long one with those hot rocks and lotions that smell like pine trees. If there's a massage oil that smells like wine, get that one. Don't drink the wine oil. Know that this time of your life will pass. Teenagers are going to be difficult, accept that fact, accept that your perfect child will make perfectly awful choices and will most likely lie to you.

Know it's coming. As for your parents, care for them, check up
on them, keep to a schedule if possible. Hire a housekeeper, hire
a lawn guy, take the pressure off yourself, and let your stan-
dards down. Treat yourself as your own cool best friend or you
will fall apart. Most importantly, remember this: If you're doing
your best, it is good enough. It truly is good enough.

Q: What's happiness look like?

A: It's moments. A moment in a forest. A moment holding
someone's hand. A moment of quiet. It's ridiculous to chase
down happiness as if it's prey and you're the predator, and if
you can just catch it, bite down on it, you'll be there. That's un-
true. Happiness, most often, is a choice. Make the choice to sit,
breathe, and be in that moment.

The reporter left after I gave her advice about her job (how to
deal with jealous female co-workers), her mother (bipolar), her
boyfriend (troubled). "You're the best, Madeline. I would love
to be you when I'm older."

"Super. Then there will be two of us. I will call you Madeline
O'Shea Number Two."

Happiness is in moments. Where the heck did I get that?

Georgie stuck her head in. "Aurora King is early today."

"Good. Tell her to go outside and toss glitter at unsuspecting
people because I don't want any in my hair today."

"I'll do that."

"What is she wearing?"

"Green. Lots of fluff. She says that your aura is steely. Rigid.
As if you're preparing for collapse but you don't know it yet so
you're holding yourself tight—tight to your spirit, but the spirit
is unleashing itself. She sees exposure wrapped around your
fiber, that's her wording. She sees a piano and hankies and a
spotlight and there's a bit of purple around the edges for sex. I
don't know if that means purple sex, but I doubt it. I doubt the
part about the sex for you, too. Remember I said I'd take you
shopping any time."

"Send Aurora King in and tell her not to throw glitter at me again."

"Don't throw glitter at Madeline," I heard Georgie say as she rang off.

I opened my door to Aurora King and closed my eyes when I saw her hand swing up.

She threw green glitter at me.

Two days later I was still picking it out of my hair.

I wrote my column, which centered on choosing a career based on what you loved doing as a child. "Find Your Child, Talk to Her" was what I titled it. "Get a picture of yourself when you were a child. Ask that child, 'What do you like to do? What are your hobbies? What are you interested in? Where do you like to go on weekends? What are you curious about? What makes you laugh? Who do you like hanging out with?' Take that info and think about it. Shake it up, spin it around. How can you apply that to your own life. . . ."

I answered a ton of e-mails, some from the Rock Your Womanhood chiefs, others from people on a couple of charity boards I sit on, and I took calls from a few hysterical clients. One client, Janice, quit her job in a grand way: She had a banner made that read, "Omar, you have a small dick," and strung it across her boss's office when he was at a meeting.

"Do you want me to show you the banner, Madeline?" she'd asked eagerly. She was in a bar. She'd had too much scotch, that was clear. "I want you to call a cab and go home, Janice. I want you to walk by the river tomorrow until you can't take another step. I want you to drink coffee and read a book. Tomorrow night, start journaling. Write down the O'Shea Make a Change plan we talked about. Start job shopping the next day, when you're not hung over. This time, find something you like and believe in."

"But it was true. Omar did have a small dick."

"How do you know?"

"My friend is his ex-girlfriend. She said it was the size of her middle finger."

Lovely image.

"Avoid making banners at your next job."

When I was finally done, my brain fizzling, at eleven o'clock that night, I decided to stay at my own home. I actually drove by my spaceship house initially and had to back up when I passed the corner. My jaw fell open as I stared at what Ramon had done.

A long, elegant, arborlike structure had been built across the front of my property, parallel to the sidewalk on top of the rock wall. The arbor's lines matched the lines of my modern house, and it was . . . stupendous.

That would be the word for it—*stupendous.*

I parked my car, scrambled out, and gaped.

My neighbor, Roth Hamil, wandered over. He always walks his dogs at night. Like me, he has insomnia. He's a proctologist. I would be up all night, too, if my day consisted of rectums. "Incredible, isn't it?"

I nodded, speechless.

"He's building a deck in my backyard when he's done. I'm second."

"What do you mean, you're second?"

"Walt and Cherry got him before me. Then it's my turn. George and Darren get him after me, then Pho and Stephanie."

"You've all hired him?" I felt this soft, warm glow.

"Sure have. We've been watching him transform your yard. He's got a lot of work now. Good man, he is. Good man."

I nodded.

"He told me about the robbery. He told all of us."

"We all make mistakes," I said. "It was a desperate situation. Lousy home life. He was a kid, trying to help his brother. He paid his time in jail, now he's trying to get his life back."

Roth nodded. "We men are a flawed species. We don't think right. He's gotta forgive himself and move on."

"Yep."

"So, while he's forgiving himself, he's gonna build me a deck." He rocked back on his heels. "I can't wait."

I made a call the next day to Keith Stein, the lawyer bulldog, and explained the situation with Ramon and his brother. Bull-dog lawyer understood. His childhood had consisted of a drunken father and a mother who disappeared when he was in kindergarten. She was in charge of planning the class Christmas party and when she didn't show up with the cake and party games he knew she'd taken off. "The other kids blamed me for having no party. It was terrible. What was worse was watching my momma before then, and knowing, absolutely knowing, that she was going to leave me. I knew it. Hell, yeah, I'll help Ramon. Give me his number and I'll call later this morning."

"Send me the bill."

"I'll discount it."

I called Ramon next. "I love it."

"You do? That was a daring move architecturally and I knew that, but I thought your house should make a statement, you know? I'm going to plant three clematis. They'll all meet and you'll have this draping vine all over it. It's gonna be awesome."

"It's incredible." I listened. "Where are you?"

"We're at the science museum."

"Who's 'we'?"

"My brother and I."

I did not miss the joy in his voice.

"Once a week I get to take him out and we're going to do something to make us smarter. This week it's the science museum. Thanks, Madeline, for the check. I got the cards printed up that you said I should. You gotta see my truck. That sign you paid for is awesome sweet."

"There's a man named Keith Stein who's going to call you. He's an attorney. He'll help you get custody of your brother."

I heard silence.

"Ramon? Are you there? Are you there?"

"Madeline," he said, his words all wobbly. "Man, I am never going to be able to thank you enough, lady, never."

Grandma's second-story, white-walled studio, with two sky-lights, faces west. Her easels, paints, pencils, canvases, and all other painting and drawing supplies, including several tables, a rocking chair, and a huge island with multiple cubby holes in the center, fill the bright space. She loves coming up every day to paint.

She doesn't always finish her work anymore. The head of a swan, no neck or body, was carefully painted in the middle of one canvas. On another, there was a bold outline of half a blue jay, a tear in one eye. In a third, a yellow bird with a blue bandana around its neck teetered on the edge of a building. It had no wings. Some of her other paintings, the paintings that will live in children's hearts forever through her books, were carefully wrapped, hung on the walls, or propped on built-in shelves. Others had been auctioned off at various charity events for thousands and thousands of dollars.

"Let's get ourselves a little privacy, Madeline, Annie," Granddad said the next rainy Saturday afternoon. We knew what he meant. He needed to talk to us away from Grandma, while Nola and she were baking ladyfingers downstairs.

We settled in three chairs in front of the French doors that led to the small deck. I could tell he was trying to rally himself, as if he were waiting for all his bones and muscles and even his soul, to line up and speak. "I need to tell you how your mother, your grandma, and I got out of France."

I sagged, with relief and dread. "You said you left before World War II started," I said. "I think I remember you saying that." Hadn't he said that?

He closed his eyes.

"Isn't that right, Granddad?" Annie asked, her braid over her shoulder.

Looking at him, I thought he was painfully dying before my eyes, maybe not physically at that second, although that was a definite risk, but spiritually.

"They were forged." He clasped his hands tight together, his eyes way off in the distance, staring at the rain weeping on our lavender plants. "The papers were forged."

I glanced at Annie, feeling my breath get stuck somewhere in my left arm. I tried to suck in some oxygen. "What was forged?"

"They were forged for a family that I knew, with the help of someone from one of the embassies in France. The family had a mother and father, a teenage daughter, a young daughter, and a young son. Their family was like mine. I didn't know them well, but the father told me one day that he had the forged papers. He was trying to help me, trying to help us get out, too."

He put a hand to his eyes and rubbed them.

"You needed help getting out of France?" I asked.

"Granddad, why did you need help?" Annie asked.

He sighed, his voice cracking. "Because I knew I couldn't do it on my own. It was almost impossible."

"I thought you flew out of Paris, went to New York, didn't like New York, flew to Oregon. Didn't you?" Did I assume it, as a younger person, and as I aged accepted it as fact? Maybe he hadn't mentioned a plane at all. . . .

He laughed. There was zero humor in it. "No, that was not true."

"Not true?" Annie asked. "So what the heck is true? You may be old, but I'm not above using some truth-gathering maneuvers on you at this point."

What is true? Those words wrapped around my neck and squeezed. What is true? What is true in my life, *at all,* at this point?

"Jews could not simply leave after France was invaded and the detentions began."

"Jews?" Annie and I said together, shocked.

"What do you mean *Jews couldn't leave?*" Annie asked.

"I mean, my dear, that your grandma and I, and your mother, are Jewish. You two are half Jewish."

I tried to speak, no words came out.

Annie tried to speak, no words came out.

The rain seemed to be seeping through the windows and wrapping a cold coat around me. "What are you talking about?" I whispered, although the pieces were falling rapidly into place, finally making a tragic sort of sense.

"We could not easily leave France because the Germans marched right into Paris and took over. With the cooperation of the government and millions of French people, the Jews were stuck, and Hitler and the Nazis tried to obliterate us. A whole race of people. He wanted us gone. So many people decided that was the best solution. So many."

"Good God," I muttered.

Annie clenched her jaw so the scream wouldn't come out.

"We were trapped in France. Trapped. I had a grocery store, but that was ransacked and taken from me, so we had no money coming in. Your grandma's parents weren't well. We wanted to leave sooner, but we couldn't, she refused to leave, even though her parents begged her to get out. Then Jews were rounded up, captured, arrested, dumped in trains used for cattle, sent to work camps and death camps. We had to escape. We had to outsmart the Nazis."

I didn't even know where to start with my questions, didn't even know where to go.

"I was young, I was desperate, I was trying to save my family. There were five of us. Five to save, plus her parents."

Can a brain explode from overload? "What do you mean, there were five of you?"

He turned his head then, to look at Annie and me, and that's when those old, kind eyes filled with tears. "There were more of us," he whispered. "More in our family. So many, many more, but they're gone now."

"I don't—" Annie started.

"Can you start over, Granddad? I'm lost—"

"I think I need this slower," Annie said.

"Who are the five?" I asked. "I thought there were three. You. Grandma. Momma."

"There were more than that. But we were Jews, and I never—"

Grandma sailed into the studio then, arms outstretched like a swan. Annie and I jumped with surprise; we hadn't heard her come up the steps. She was wearing a black, lacy negligee with lace trim and three-inch-high black mules. "Darling," she said, smiling at Granddad. She strolled toward him, bent to kiss his lips, and gave him an eyeful of her bosom. "Were you playing hide-and-seek?" She turned and kissed Annie and me on both cheeks. "Lovely sister, lovely niece. I love you."

She turned to the painting with the yellow bird with no wings. "I heard you talking." She picked up a paintbrush, squished out black paint, and right over the wingless bird she started painting. "You were talking about this, weren't you?"

She drew one thick, black crooked line, then another, until a swastika covered the yellow bird with no wings.

I gasped, stricken.

Granddad groaned.

Grandma pointed at it with the paintbrush, her face drawn tight, angry now. "I hate that crooked cross. I hate it. I hate that it's twisted. It scares me so I will fix it because of the hate. I hate you, crooked cross!" She growled at it, then turned again and started painting. Soon the black swastika turned into the body of a black swan with fluffy feathers. She added wings, a graceful neck, an orange beak. From swastika to swan, with an arch of purple orchids over its head. Though I was stunned by what Granddad had told us, what Grandma had done, part of me was still in awe of her immense artistic talent.

"There. That is so much better. Swans over death. Swans over blood. Swans eat the cross. This is a black swan." She turned and smiled at all of us, then set the brushes down. "I think it's time you came to bed and enjoyed this." She put out an elegant hand and ran it from head to toe, then shimmied her chest at Granddad. "Right this minute. Come on in, darling, with me and the nymphs. I won't take no for an answer. Men need sex or their brains dissolve. Sex loosens up their ligaments and bones. But not one bone! One bone is hard!" She giggled.

"Later, girls," Granddad said. "I will tell you more, later."

He smiled at us, weakly, then kissed us on both cheeks, like the French do.

We kissed him back, on shocked automatic.

Lavender is a plant with a long history of protection. Frightened people wore it to protect them from the plague in Europe.

Grave diggers slipped it into their gloves so they wouldn't be contaminated by the dead person's disease. Mothers placed it in their children's clothes to keep evil away. A dot of lavender oil could keep the spirits away from you, and a cross of lavender brought God into the house.

Yes, lavender was thought to add peace and safety to a person's life.

I have been surrounded by lavender for years.

It's blue and purple, and all shades in between, and when Grandma told me her tales about the swans soaring over a field full of lavender and giving rides to sword-wielding turtles and squirrels wearing cowboy hats, I thought I'd been transported to fairy land.

But protection?

No. It has never worked for me.

"I put a poster up," she said.

"You put a poster up?" Annie asked her, raising her eyebrows.

"Yes, I wrote LOST at the top."

I eyed the young woman, the daughter of the llama owner. Mother and daughter looked a lot alike. The mother had had her daughter when she was nineteen but decided early motherhood wasn't going to stop her from becoming what she desired to be above all else: A llama owner.

The mother's name was Amelia, the daughter's name was Amelia Lyn. They both had long brown braids, bangs, and wore plaid shirts and jeans. There was no father, because Amelia had had a fling during spring break in Mexico when she was attending an elite private college in California and didn't know who he was. She moved into family housing, finished school, became an accountant, and got her llamas.

"So, Amelia Lyn." I hooked my boot on the bottom rung of the wood fence surrounding the llamas. "You put up a LOST poster because you lost your pet possum when you were playing with her outside."

"I thought she would only wander around in nature, you

know, as usual. She's a good possum and likes to be near me."
Her brow wrinkled. She was puzzled about this possum. Puzzled! "I turned around for a second because Jason called me on
the phone. He's my boyfriend. We're not together now, or on
the weekend, but on Tuesday we were together, but not by that
evening, Wednesday we were on again, but then we broke up
last night . . ."

"And what happened to the possum?" I asked.

"She was gone. Gone." She twisted her brown tail-braid. "I
wonder if she was kidnapped or abducted."

Or eaten, I thought, but did not say it aloud. Amelia Lyn
would not like the image of her eaten possum.

"I'm her mother so I'm worried," Amelia Lyn said worriedly.

"You don't look like a possum's mother," Annie drawled.

Amelia laughed. "She's the possum's mother, as I am the
mother, along with Amelia Lyn, of our five llamas."

"Got it," Annie and I said together.

We were here on their farm so Annie could vaccinate the llamas and do a general check, but we got caught up in the drama
of a lost, possibly kidnapped or abducted possum.

"I put a picture of Beth on the LOST poster and wrote, 'Lost:
Pet Possum. Her Name Is Beth.' "

"And no one has found her?" How surprising!

"Not yet," Amelia Lyn said, "but on the poster I also wrote,
'Don't try to pick her up. She might bite.' Beth only lets me or
Mom hold her. She's particular like that. She's particular about
a lot of things. She likes to be held like this"—she crossed her
arms—"her food has to be cut up, her pink pillow in the left-hand corner, and she sulks, too. Gets in her cage, won't come
out if she thinks I haven't been paying enough attention to her.
She'll sometimes nip at me, too, you know, but when she's in a
better mood, she'll sit on my shoulder. She's afraid of strangers
and might bite if someone tries to pick her up."

"That would be very bad. Do you think there's a lot of people out there who would pick up a possum?" Annie said, in all
seriousness.

Amelia Lyn pondered that one. "Not a lot. Some. But not a lot."

"If someone saw the poster of Beth and later saw a possum, how would they know it was Beth?" I asked. "They could be chasing down a native possum who was in a bad mood, vicious, defensive, hormonal, etcetera."

"If people look at the picture, Madeline," Amelia Lyn said, only smothering her teenage disgust a bit, "then they would know which possum was Beth and which one wasn't, you know? I mean, come on. Beth has a distinctive look. Her nose is more pointy, she has longer whiskers, her paws are a light gray. She's not like other possums. And, too, if you call her name, she always puts her head up and that's how people would know. I wrote that on the poster, too. 'Call her name, Beth, and if she puts her head up, that's her.' "

I nodded and tried to be sage. "Do you want people to call you, then, if they spot her?"

"Yep. Call me and I'll come and get her. I have her pink pillow in her cage, her favorite foods are flowers, bread and honey, grapes, and a plum. I'll put her toys in, too. She'll crawl right in the cage when she sees it."

Annie and I nodded.

"Do you think I'll find Beth?" Amelia Lyn asked, hands on hips.

"I don't know," Annie said, ever the realist. "She could have met a gang of other possums and decided to hang with them."

"Have you tried whistling to her? Calling her name? Singing her favorite song?" I said. Annie rolled her eyes at me. The Amelias didn't see it.

Amelia Lyn looked like she was about to cry.

"We'll help you look for her," I said.

"You will?" She brightened.

"Sure," Annie said. "Let me take care of the llamas first."

The Amelias nodded and we went to work. One llama was half brown and white, one white, one spotted, and two others were black. They were all named after rock stars: Elton John. Jon Bon Jovi. Cyndi Lauper. Sting. Pat Benatar. Annie weighed the llamas, one spit at her, and checked their bodies for growths or tumors or bumps. She gave them a dewormer mixed with apple-sauce using a syringe and took a peek at their teeth and jaws.

Llamas are adorable, I will admit this. They look like a cross between a camel without a hump, sheep, minigiraffes because of the neck, sheepdogs, and people. It's in their eyes, the people part, and in their personalities. They are curious, smart, social, and don't spit as much as one would think. Amelia and Amelia Lyn use them for 4–H. They are pampered and spoiled on this farm.

"I think the gang is looking good," Annie said to Amelia when we were done. The gang wandered over to say hi.

"Don't say that so loud," Amelia said. "They'll become arrogant. Snotty."

I laughed.

Amelia seemed baffled by my laughter. Baffled!

"I won't say it again," Annie said. "But they are looking good."

"Shhh," Amelia whispered.

"Will you help me find Beth now?" Amelia Lyn asked, running to us. She'd been checking for Beth out in the field behind their barn. No luck. Maybe she should put up a LOST possum poster in the field and one of the deer would tell her where Beth was hiding out for a few days, or a coyote would admit to eating her.

"We'll give it a shot," I said, and winked at Annie. She knew what I meant. If a possum got too close to me, especially if it made hissing sounds, I'd shoot it.

Together we hunted around the sheds and the barn, under the decks, in the shrubbery, behind the tall pine trees, in an abandoned car, etc., etc. At one point, I kicked a bunch of wood crates stacked high in an outbuilding.

I am not kidding, a possum ran out. Annie and I didn't move.

"Beth!" Amelia Lyn called. "Beth!"

That creature, no kidding, stopped and put her head up. Amelia Lyn ran to her tearfully, picked her up, and, I am also not kidding, kissed Beth on the mouth.

Sheesh.

Possum lovers. You never know what they'll do next.

"I'll be going to Fiji again soon," Annie told me on the drive to The Lavender Farm that afternoon. We had stopped off to check on a sheep named Parrot and a dog named Captain Cook, which was owned by a man who made his living as a pirate. "Argh!" he had shouted at us, brandishing a knife, his patch in place, a red and white striped shirt stretched across his gut.

Quick as a wink Annie had him up against a wall, elbow in his throat, the knife in her hand and pointed toward him. "Tony, don't you ever wag a knife in my face again, you got that?"

He was hurtin' so he groaned out a yes. We left with Tony's pumpkin cake, which was delicious. It was in the shape of a pirate's head.

"Off to Fiji?" I said, watching the farmland, the fields, and the orchards roll by. "Need a break? A tan?"

"Yes, I need a break, so to speak."

"I worry about you when you're in Fiji."

"I worry about what happens to four-legged animals if I don't go to Fiji."

"You need to be careful."

"I'm always careful."

"Will you be retiring from your trips to Fiji anytime soon?"

"Doubt it."

"Perhaps you could try another country?"

"No."

"Aren't you worried that someone with handcuffs will some-day catch you on your trips to Fiji?"

"No."

"Why?"

"I can't concern myself with that. I need to do what's right for Fiji."

"Got it."

We rode in silence, then Annie asked, "How are you doing?"

"I'm okay."

I knew what we were talking about. Granddad's revelations. That article. What happened to us. I still saw no reason to tell her about the blackmail. We're so close and yet this horrible, tragic, sick thing is hanging between us. I love Annie with all my heart, and she loves me. In many ways, I will never be closer to her than I am to anyone else. On the other hand, we saw each other in these twisted positions, being hurt and humiliated, and we've hardly talked about it, ever. What was there to say? *Gee whiz. That was a bad spot, wasn't it? Cup of tea?*

"I'm fine," I said again, as if to reassure myself.

We rode in silence.

"You're not fine."

"Neither are you, Annie."

We rode farther, in silence.

"You're right. I'm not fine, Madeline."

She pulled into our driveway, lined with the pink tulip trees that Granddad had planted for Grandma. We drove past the house, past the rows of lavender, the barn, the apple orchards, the place where the summer vegetable garden would be, and up through the forest to the highest point of our property. We both got out of the truck and went to sit on a wrought iron bench we'd brought up years ago. We sat side by side, our straight hair mingling in the breeze, our shoulders pressed together.

Ahead of us, the whole valley spread out, the topography fascinating. In some places it was raining, in others, sunshine laced through the clouds. If only I could sew the picture of that valley into a quilt and somehow stitch in all the emotions of weather. . . .

"Everything's coming down pretty quick here," she said.

"Yep." It was an understatement. We liked understatements. It kept a menacing world at bay.

"Who knows what the reporter has, but my guess is that she's got the whole story."

"Nailed down." I tucked my hair behind my ear as a cool, subdued breeze meandered by.

"She called me again."

"Damn and damn again." I hated that Marlene had control over my life, that she could wield my past over my head, swing it around, and lob it like a bomb. "She's a pit bull with a pretty voice."

"We will not be able to hide from our past anymore."

"We will definitely lose our privacy."

"The photographs will probably be sent everywhere. Famous life coach and sister, Ivy League veterinarian . . . nude. In heels. A rope. A sailor hat. A fake snake. A naked man."

"Completely likely." I felt a shiver wrap tight around me.

"And, you, Madeline, with your career, this is gonna be ugly."

"Yep."

I thought about that. The conference, the speech, my clients. "We'll be exposed."

"That's the word for it, exposed."

"It'll feel like we're naked again." I could cry. I reached for Annie's hand. She held it. I knew she felt like crying, but she wouldn't. Annie never cried. "And what we learned from Granddad, today, that could be in the article, too."

"Possibly. She asked me about Holland, as you told me she asked you."

"She's got something. I don't know what, I don't get it, but she's got something."

The breeze blew our hair together. It was a pleasant, friendly breeze.

"Madeline, I'm tired of hiding."

"What do you mean?"

"I mean"—she took a deep breath—"we knew this day was coming."

I had known that. "We've been dreading it."

"Yes, we have. But dreading it kept it a secret, kept it as a hidden shame, when we were not responsible for it, we didn't ask for it. We were victims of a criminal attack as children. There is no shame for us in that. We've been running from it ever since. When we were kids we naturally wanted to protect ourselves. Part of me, even with my cache of explosives, wants to protect the girl I was. The girl who wore tutus and grizzly bear outfits and sequined poodle skirts. But running is not in my nature." She tucked a strand of hair back. "I'm sick of it."

After being in the city, the silence of the country is soft. Your brain can finally de-sizzle, wander around, fly, soar over hills and grassy fields, through cornstalks, around flower beds, over a coyote or a raccoon, and around the moon and back. Nothing gets in the way, so to speak, of thinking, and I was thinking very deeply.

"I'm exhausted from the run."

"Me too, Madeline. I can't run anymore. I've crossed the finish line. I am done."

"I'm done, too. I can't live like this." My lies, my cover-ups, my fear, it was all strangling me. "I'm with you at the finish line. I won't run anymore, either."

The pleasant, friendly breeze blew our hair together again, our shoulders touching, the weather parading across that quilted landscape.

"I think I have an idea of how we should handle this magazine article without exploding Marlene's home," Annie said.

Later Annie and I turned on her outdoor lights and I watched her fire up her chain saw and attack a piece of wood. It would morph into a pirate. She is so talented.

The next morning she left for Fiji. She wasn't gone long.

A few days later I read about a house that had caught fire in the middle of the night in California. The owner was not home.

Firefighters were very disturbed to find an outbuilding filled with roaming, aggressive pit bulls, and other pit bulls in cages. Many of them had festering wounds, missing fur, sawed-down teeth, bite marks. Others were too thin, limping, sick. Dog-fighting paraphernalia was also found.

The home was owned by a man who owned a string of chain stores.

He was arrested for animal abuse and neglect. It made front page news.

"We don't know yet what started the fire," the fire marshal said. "It appears to be faulty wiring. Although the home is new, so the electrical work should have been up to date. Still, faulty wiring is the likely culprit based on what we found. . . ."

22

Prison was not a happy place for Sherwinn, Pauly, and Gavin. They were sent to a prison off the Cape, and the other prisoners beat Sherwinn and his co-devils to a pulp the first, second, and third days they were there. My dad had a high school buddy incarcerated because he was convicted of running an organized drug ring, and he used his organizing skills to schedule regular beat-up times for all three of them.

Sherwinn and crew ended up in the jail's hospital. They had multiple broken bones and lacerations, some of which were made with a knife, others with a brick, and they had testicle problems that were caused by "groin crunchers." I do not know what a "groin cruncher" weapon looks like. I bet it hurt. Apparently there was also a "titty squisher" weapon used on them and a "concussion inducer."

"The warden," Carman told my momma one afternoon when it poured like the clouds had been saving rain since Noah and his ark sailed off, "is my uncle, honey. He told me that he didn't give a muskrat's ass if those freak-asses were taken apart with a crowbar and planted in the back garden of the prison as fertilizer, but he didn't want it happening on his watch. He's got six daughters to put through college or marry off and he needs the job. No offense, honey. He told me to tell you that he's very sorry. Very sorry, and they would have made good fertilizer, his words."

She hugged my momma, and when she saw me hiding around

the corner in our house by the sea, she hugged me, tighter and warmer the more I shook. "Baby, I pray for you every day. I love you so much, Madeline." I tried to hug her back, but I was shaking too much. "Madeline, darling, darlin'. Now you stop. You're making me cry and my mascara is smearing! What the heck—" She burst into tears. "Let me sing you a love song."

I feel like I've been shaking in one way or another my whole life, but the shaking is mostly contained inside me, locked up with my bad breathing skills. Honestly, since the day that Sherwinn came after Annie and me, I don't think I've stopped shaking.

News of the photographs of Annie and me swirled around the Cape, and though most people were very kind, and we were deluged with stuffed animals, pretty new clothes, and dinners that would feed us for months, there were a few people who blamed us.

Yep, they blamed the victims. *Blamed the victims,* two young girls who enjoyed playing jacks and hopscotch.

In a few warped minds, in some twisted, sick way, we had "enjoyed the attention," or "cooperated," or were, "rebellious, uncontrollable youths . . . always dressed in pink like that!"

Mrs. Tilda Smith, a customer of Momma's with a bottom the size of Arkansas, felt we had "asked for it."

"Obviously they wanted to be a part of that filth, or they would have walked right out that door and away from those cameras! Wild girls! Wild! Marie Elise simply isn't up to raising her children with good morals. Why, what would you expect from a woman like that? Always in heels! Always dressed up in skirts and that *eyeliner*, so la-di-da French, thinks she's better than us!"

Jealousy of one woman over another has caused Herculean damage over the years, hasn't it? Cavewomen were probably slugging each other over who had the best furs or the most teeth.

Trudy Jo told me later that Momma heard what Tilda Smith was saying about her daughters.

"Your momma was so mad, she kept slamming her brushes and combs down, and she scrubbed Angela Peacock's head so hard when she was washing it, I'm sure Angela thought she was getting a brain massage instead of a Marie Elise's Magically Excellent Shampoo, Cut, and Blow Dry."

Trudy Jo shook her head. "But your momma, me, Carman, and Shell Dee thought up a plan to take revenge. Your momma named it the Revenge and Vengeance Pink and Red Attack. She was so pleasant to Tilda at first. She swiveled the chair around, and Tilda wriggled her cannonball cheeks into the seat. Have you ever noticed her bottom? It's like a thing unto itself, her pants so tight the dimples show in her cheeks. Anyhow, I heard your momma say hello, and Tilda said, 'I can't wait to tell you what Bianca's up to again. I was up late last night, watching for burglars with my binoculars, and I saw who she had over!'

"I stood right close to your momma as she mixed up the dye," Trudy Jo said, "because I wanted to be part of the action, part of your momma's magic, and hoo-hee. Your momma was so magic that day. She turned Tilda away from the mirror and slopped all that dye on Tilda's head—it's shaped like a pyramid, that probably explains her stupidity—and she made sure it was good and in. Then your momma stood in front of her and said, 'Tilda, I hear from a number of women that you've been lying about my girls.' Now, Tilda, in that chair, she looks like she's going to choke on her fat chins. 'I don't know what you're talking about, Marie Elsie,' she squeaks. 'I think you do,' your momma says. 'You've been telling people that my daughters wanted to be in those photographs.'

"Now Tilda's face goes all red and the other girls in the shop made sure all the dryers are off so it's quiet. Pretty soon the ladies in the resting room are in there, too, because ladies sniff out fights, like they can sniff out burned marshmallows. Your momma is brandishing not one but two pairs of scissors in her hands, and she starts swinging them around like knives.

"'Tsk-tsk! Marie Elise,' Tilda says in this squeaky voice because everyone's glaring at her and you can feel those women's fury. 'At any time your girls could have told you, and that would have been that. They could have run away. But they didn't. They stayed and went back again. I can't help thinking they liked it.' She wriggled her bottom in the chair, her face all red, and I thought of Shakespeare's, 'How sharper than a serpent's tooth' and she is 'the portrait of a blinking idiot.' I thought your momma was going to pop. She couldn't even speak for a minute. She turned and stabbed, I mean, she *stabbed*, the scissors into her work station, then whipped around and trapped Tilda in the swivel chair, her arms on the handles.

" 'My girls,' your momma said in the meanest voice I've ever heard out of that darling woman's mouth, 'my girls did what they did to protect my life. They are heroes, and here you are with your triangular-shaped head and your blubbery stomach telling everyone in town that they wanted to be a part of it. That they wanted to be attacked. How could you? *How could you?*'

" 'Maybe . . .' Tilda choked out, 'it's because you always wear fancy clothes, always in pink, and heels, and I think your girls got that from you and they might . . . might want . . . a man's attention. . . .'

"Your momma," Trudy Jo said, laughing, "she swiveled that chair around so fast that Tilda and her dimply bottom went sprawling, and she leaped and stood over her and shoved her pink heel deep into Tilda's flabby stomach and said, 'I feel like squishing you, Tilda. I do. I could do it.' The Reighton triplets, you know those ladies, they're the three oldest triplets on the East Coast, they started yelling, 'Squish her, squish her, squish her!' and one said, 'Mean women gotta go!' to which her sisters chanted, 'Gotta go, gotta go!'

"Your momma leaned down and said, 'Look, you gigantically bottomed, squid-faced idiot. You are to leave this parlor right now. You are never to come back. If you ever set foot in this parlor again, I will shoot you. Do you have that? Has that sunk in through the fat? And if you don't tell everyone in this town that you lied about my sweet girls because you are a jealous, demented woman, I will sue you for defamation of character and I will take everything you have, you pitiful slug.'"

Trudy Jo was enjoying the story, I could tell. She clapped her hands and rocked onto her toes.

"Sugar, your momma was in a pink and red mood that day. Tilda's hair came out pink and red. One side red, one pink." Trudy Jo sighed. "The Reighton triplets clapped their hands and started a cheer. 'One side red, one side pink, you are a pig, Tilda, and you stink!' "

Trudy Jo laughed. "Tilda screamed and ran out. But I have to tell you the best part. When Tilda was leaving with her pink and red hair, your momma grabbed a bottle of green spray paint that Shell Dee confiscated from her son Derek when he was helping Jessie Liz's boy, Shoney, paint another outline of a naked woman on the back of Hal's Hardware. She sprayed a line of green right down that woman's back and swore at her."

I gasped. "My momma swore?"

"She called her a bitch. A mean, *skunky* green bitch."

I gasped again. "My momma never swears."

"I know, sugar, but she did that day. She screamed it, screamed it!" Trudy Jo fisted her hands above her head in victory. "Everyone clapped! It was a wonderful day at Marie Elise's French Beauty Parlor. Your momma showed that her magic extends to revenge and vengeance. The triplets did a victory dance."

I giggled. A tight and captured giggle, but it was a giggle. It was one of very few giggles at that time, but I enjoyed it.

I loved my momma so much.

"Happy dagger!" Trudy Jo said, up on her toes and using a quote from her favorite man. "Asses are made to bear, and so are you, Tilda!"

Steve kept trying to talk to me, but I ran away from him.

"Madeline, what's wrong? Madeline!" he'd yell, chasing after me until he caught up. "Why can't we be friends? I won't hurt you, like they did. I'll never hurt you. Don't you want to go to the lake and chase frogs? Don't you want to draw together anymore? I brought you a chocolate." He opened his hand. My favorite chocolate, only slightly melted, was in his palm.

"I don't want to be friends with you anymore." That was a lie, I wanted to be friends with Steve, but I couldn't. I was dirty. I was ashamed. I was mentally screwed up, emotionally ripped. Steve knew about the photos, I knew he knew, and I couldn't be with him. He was clean and innocent, and I was in bad pictures and had done bad things.

"Get away from me, Steve!"

"But . . . but why?" His voice was strangled. He didn't bother to hide the tears in those blue eyes.

"Because I don't like you anymore."

"You don't?" he whispered, so upset. "You don't like me?"

"No, I don't. Get away from me." I ran off as fast as I could. He ran after me, too, calling my name, pleading with me, but I pushed him away one more time, both of us crying, and I ran off again, blinded by tears.

It was so hard to run, I wet my pants, I still remember the feel of that hot urine searing my legs, like defeat. I remember that.

Steve and I were never friends again, even though he has tried, off and on, throughout all these years to contact me. He has not done it in a stalkerish sort of way, but a friendly, funny, how are you doing sort of way.

Some say that young people cannot be in love, they cannot know love, that they *believe* they are in love, but they are not. It is passion only, infatuation. This is false. They can fall in love. They are in love, and their love is intense and real.

I was twelve years old and this is what I knew about Steve: He was my best friend next to Annie. I trusted him, believed in him. He made me laugh. I was happy when I was with him. I could see a future with him. I had daydreams about him, giggled when I thought of kissing him or holding his hand. Those loves we have when we are young are true, and deep, and those people stay in our hearts, and there they last forever.

Steve has been there forever.

Not long after Sherwinn, Pauly, and Gavin went to jail we received the first of several letters.

The first one appeared on our doorstep early one morning at our house by the sea, when the clouds were angry.

It was brief, it was terrifying.

It said, "Sweetie, drop the charges or the girls will die." It was smeared all over with something red. It was blood.

I found the letter after I caught my momma, who dropped to the floor in a dead faint.

My momma called the police. Sheriff Ellery was livid. He called the warden, Carman's uncle. Sherwinn, Pauly, and Gavin all ended up in isolation for weeks after that. But Sherwin and crew had accomplished their mission: They had scared the liver out of all of us.

How did the letter get there? I figured it was Sam, Pauly's son, who had snuck peeps at us through the window of the shack and dropped his pants and underwear two times in front of us while his father laughed.

"They aren't going to get off, Marie Elise," the prosecuting attorney, Arthur Benning, said. "But they won't stay in jail that long."

My momma, my grandparents, and Arthur were downstairs at our kitchen table late one blustery frightened night as Annie and I crouched against a wall, our flowered nightgowns over our knees as we listened, hidden by the shadows.

"What do you mean they won't stay in jail *that long?*" My momma's voice sharpened to steel strength. She dropped the ice pack she'd been holding to her head, her tumor stretching, growing.

"He means, honey," Granddad said, his voice seared with barely contained rage, "that Sherwinn, Pauly, and Gavin will go to jail, but they won't die there. They're coming out."

"That's correct," Arthur said. He was about fifty and a former marine. His back was rigidly straight, all the time. He was an iron wall with a head.

"What?" My momma gasped. "I thought when the judge saw their past records, when he understood what they did to my girls, they would go to jail for decades!"

"No, they won't," Arthur said. "I'm sorry. They're going to jail for years, Marie Elise, mark my words on that, but one day they'll get out. It might be seven years, five, maybe less, but they will get out. This is not a life sentence they're looking at."

Momma listed the crimes that had been committed against us, her voice razor sharp.

"I don't agree with it, Marie Elise," Arthur said. "I'm telling you the reality here."

"They'll come and get the girls. Sherwinn will, I know he will. My girls will never be safe. They'll *never be safe.*"

In the shadows Annie and I clutched each other, trembling.

"Marie Elise," Grandma said, reassuring, "you'll come and live with us on the farm. We'll put up an electric fence, we'll hire guards, we'll track them through an investigative agency, we'll get restraining orders—"

"That's not going to do it!" our momma said, screechy, pounding the table. "It won't keep him from them. I know it won't. He's psychotic . . . he'll come after them. He'll hurt the girls, he may well kill them, I know he will."

No one argued with her.

Why? Because they knew Sherwinn, knew the truth. Knew him. *He would come for us.*

My momma wasn't worried about herself. She never said, "They'll come and kill me," because she knew she'd be dead. That was her reality.

Annie and I cowered in that threatening, black shadow, sickened by fear. I heard my granddad swear, followed by my grandma's useless comfort, before Momma dissolved into broken, choked gasps.

"I'm not going to let him do this to them," I heard my momma weep. "I won't. I will take care of this and I will protect my girls. I will protect Madeline and Annie."

She did protect us.

That, she did.

If my dad had been around he would have protected us.

I closed my eyes and saw him. He was still crying.

* * *

That night I snuck downstairs in my flowered nightgown, the stars scared, cowering behind the clouds. I watched my momma staring at the fire and saw an expression on her face I'd never seen before—intense, focused, restrained.

When I squiggled a bit, she turned to me, her tense mouth turning upward into a smile. One has to understand her position at that moment in life. Her beloved husband had drowned. She had a brain tumor that was inoperable. She was going to die young. Her daughters had been abused and photographed. The criminals had threatened to kill us.

"Momma?"

"Come here, my love," she said, her voice soft, melodious. I sat on her lap and she hugged me close and spoke in French, her face softening. "You are my heart, my daughter, my everything, you and your sister, and I love you both so much." She kissed my forehead. "I will protect you always, Madeline, and Annie, too. I didn't before"—her voice caught as her tears mixed with mine—"but I will not fail you again. Never again."

"You didn't fail us, Momma. We love you. You didn't know. We didn't tell you."

She didn't hear me. As the fire flickered across her face and around the shadows, her eyes were seeing something else. "I didn't protect you girls. I didn't protect the family. Family is all there is, my daughter. All there is. Family is what God gave us to get through life. I will protect you, and Annie, I promise you."

My momma's decision? In order for her girls to be safe forever, Sherwinn, Pauly, and Gavin would have to die. She did not believe she could control them, and she was right. She did not believe her daughters could live in peace, in safety, be guaranteed a life that would see them holding their own grandchildren, without them dead. In her head she had failed us and she would not fail us again. She did not see any other way around it.

Frankly, even now, as an adult, I don't see another way around it, either.

Some people do not belong on this planet with the rest of us.

* * *

Steve waited a week after our last tearful conversation when I told him I didn't want to be friends before he dropped off terrariums for Annie and me with all kinds of plants and rocks and plastic frogs. I dropped tears into the terrarium.

When I went back to school, Arty Painter made the mistake of saying to me, "Hey, can I see you in your naked pictures, Madeline? I want to see your boobies."

Steve was right behind me and he whipped around so fast, he blurred. He pounded the tar out of that kid. Steve was suspended for three days, over his parents' loud protests. Arty was suspended for a week. No one would sit with Arty at lunch for weeks. Steve made him apologize to me.

Arty was so upset, he blubbered his way through "I'm sorry." Arty's parents called to apologize and brought my momma a side of beef for winter.

Another boy, Runi Saleh said, "Is your boyfriend Sherwinn? Did you do it with him? You had sex!" Steve knocked both his front teeth clean out, blood spurting all over the playground in gushes.

Steve was suspended for three days, over his parents' loud protests. Runi was suspended for a week.

Runi's father wrote my momma an apology and built us an upraised flower bed and planted one hundred bulbs with his son.

One more classmate, Daphne, the daughter of Tilda Smith, she of the pyramid head, which is why she is so stupid, and cannonball bottom, said, "You did bad things with men. I would never do that. You're bad now. You're not a virgin. You can't wear a white wedding dress."

Steve found out and he isolated her so fast she didn't know what hit. No one would talk to her, and her friends walked away when she approached them.

Her mother never apologized.

But that was that. I wasn't teased at school anymore, and neither was Annie.

It is amazing what one popular kid like Steve can do.

But Steve and I, we weren't friends again. He kept sending

gifts—a frog in a fish tank and flowers he pressed between books and glued to cards. He drew a picture of him and me together, fishing, a light cloud of "red magic" encircling my head, because he saw so clearly the gift from my Irish dad.

I still have the picture.

But I was emotionally dead. It was too late.

The trial made everything worse.

23

About a month before I was to give my speech at the Rock Your Womanhood conference at the convention center, I received a bouquet of purple tulips in a clear, curving, glass vase. At the bottom of the vase were a bunch of heart-shaped, glass rocks in a rainbow of colors.

The card read, "Good luck, Madeline. Steve Shepherd."

There were at least twenty-four tulips.

They were very pretty.

They were my favorite flower.

He remembered.

I sniffled.

What to do? What to do with a boy named Steve Shepherd who grew up to be a man named Steve Shepherd?

What would happen if I called him?

Later, when I swung by my house to pick up mail, I pulled out the envelope I had with photos and articles about him. I pulled out my wallet, too, and stared at the photo of him and me and Annie, when we were kids, standing at the lake fishing with our poles. I held those photos for a long time.

I wouldn't call him.

I couldn't.

I was still too dirty.

"The Giordano sisters are here," Georgie said. "They're looking quite cat-ish today."

"Prepare for a meowing good time and send them in." I stood up and pulled at my gray skirt with my hands, slipped my arms into my suit jacket, and patted my hair, which had been flat ironed until not a curl would dare show itself. I was in my armor. I don't like my armor.

The cats entered. They had outdone themselves. The sisters were dressed in world-class cat outfits, head to toe, their makeup like a feline from *Cats* on Broadway.

"Madellllliiiine!" Adriana sang out, hands up in cat claws as she scratched the air. "You have given us purpose!" She was a black cat with white paws. "Fun and fun!"

"Direction!" Bella said, twirling her tail. She was a golden cat. "Wicked naughty!"

"Goals!" Carlotta said, twisting a whisker. She was a striped gray tabby cat. "Fantabulous!"

"And to celebrate!" Adriana enthused.

"To embrace you and the wisdom you have brought into our lives!" Bella yelled.

"To thank you for what you've done for us!" Carlotta sang out.

"We have a present."

"A gift from the heart."

"We're including you in the gift you've given us. Ready, ladies?"

And with no further ado, they opened a large black bag and pulled out a fourth, yes, a fourth, cat costume.

"What's that for?" I asked.

"Today, Madeline, you're going with us! We're doing good cat deeds. You're going to be an English shorthair, and we've brought the makeup, too!"

"I'm going to be a cat?"

"Yes! Meow meow!" Bella said. "We heard of a woman named Makeesha who's battling lymphoma, and we're going to her office building to give her a gift!"

"A gift? What are you giving her?" I envisioned a basket with goodies.

"It's a cruise! We're sending Makeesha Jefferson on a cruise with her best friend!"

I did not think I looked bad as an English shorthair. With all the cat makeup on, no one could recognize me, Madeline the Cat. The sisters had a limo and chauffeur out front. The limo dropped us off at the pink building. We took the elevator up to the twenty-seventh floor. The receptionist was in on our Good Cat Deed, and he laughed and led us to the conference room, where Makeesha sat with a bunch of other businesspeople. She had an embroidered blue scarf wrapped around her head, but I did not miss the exhaustion, the lack of hope, the despair.

"Meow!" we all declared. "Meow!"

We gave a lot of those uptight businesspeople a shock, but no one was more shocked than Makeesha when we presented her with plane tickets, cruise line tickets, and a thousand dollars for spending money. Twelve days, the Bahamas. First class.

She burst into tears.

The uptight businesspeople cried, too.

Meow!

Honestly, I heard a violinist in my head.

Yep. It was "Memory." From *Cats*.

That night, around eleven p.m., I sat on the deck at The Lavender Farm and watched the lights of farmhouses tucked into the hills shine on and off.

I am swamped in work, buried under an avalanche of Things To Do.

I work to blind myself from realities I don't like. I get it. I need the oblivion that work brings. I need the recognition so I can prove to myself that I am Someone Important, that I am not a bad girl, a dirty girl, a slutty girl, but someone who deserves respect and does not belong in a shack that smells like smoke and looks like a dying armadillo.

I have fought since the *click, click, click* part of my life to believe that *I am someone worthy*. I still fight for it.

I have surrounded myself with expensive "stuff" to prove it to myself, too. It hasn't worked.

But now, someone else, some stranger with ambition named Marlene, had control over my life and what was going to happen in it. I have a visceral, instinctive reaction when I feel anyone is trying to control any part of my life.

The most personal, destructive disaster of my life, of Annie's life, was in someone else's hands.

I could not have that.

I heard again Annie's words. What she'd told me to do.

I heard Momma next, so clear it was as if I were back in the pink beauty parlor with hair spray, pink nail polish, glittering chandeliers, and cookies with pink icing and Red Hots.

Take control.

You can't take control of anyone else, or anything else, in this world besides yourself, sugar, but you can take control of you. So do it, then sit down and make sure your nails are polished, your heels on, your hair styled. There is no excuse for frumpiness.

I thought of my suits. My momma would not have liked my suits.

She would like it, however, if I took control.

Yes, I was done.

Early evening the next day, Annie and I climbed into Granddad's black pickup truck and he drove us to the top of the hill. As usual, we sat on the same wrought iron bench we'd sat on for years to admire the land quilt in front of us, the golden lollipop to the west heading down over the mountains.

"How are you feeling, Granddad?" I asked.

"I'm fine, dammit." He took a deep but ragged breath. "Fine, dammit."

"Dammit," I said. "I'm glad you're damn fine."

He glanced at me. I interpreted the glance. Exasperated, but he loved me.

"It's good to be damn fine," Annie said. "For example, Fiji was damn fine."

Granddad rolled his eyes. "Fiji was fine," he muttered. He was a law-abiding man, but he was a realist and knew he could not stop that particular granddaughter. I chuckled.

We watched the leaves ruffle, the trees sway, a hawk glide, and I heard the faintest notes of Haydn's Symphony no. 39 in G Minor in the back of my head.

We waited Granddad out, as was our plan.

"I believe I owe you girls more information," he said.

"That'd be good," Annie said.

"Please," I said.

"It's not pleasant, and I know it will hurt you girls." He brought a hand up and pressed on his eyelids. "I tried to put my past, our past, behind us. I didn't want to think about it. It hurt too much and it wasn't anyone's damn business. Plus, you girls went through so much as children, why add more pain to your lives? More confusion? More secrets? I wanted to protect you. I wanted you to start your lives over, here, at The Lavender Farm, with us, and to heal. What good would it do to tell you things you didn't need to know? I wanted it all buried."

I don't like that word, buried.

"Buried pasts have a way of sneaking out of their coffins, don't they?" Annie said.

"Yes. And it's coming out of that coffin now. I can't protect you anymore from my history." He dropped his hand, and said in French, "I am cornered. This reporter has cornered me. And, perhaps, it is all best, anyhow. Best for you to know."

"Know what, Granddad?" Annie leaned forward.

"The truth may explain things for you, offer you clarity about your mother, about Grandma and me. You'll know what Grandma is talking about now. It won't make things easier when you listen to her—in fact, I think it will cause you great pain—but you'll understand the context. You will, however, probably not wish to speak to me again, and I understand."

I felt the breath in my body still, stuck again, holding on to itself. "That would never happen, Granddad."

"Never," Annie said. "We love you."

"The Nazis marched into a quiet Paris," my granddad said,

his voice so weary, as if he hadn't heard our reassurances. "People had fled, or were fleeing, or hiding, hunkered down. We needed to flee, too." He took a deep breath. "It would be more accurate to say that we needed to escape."

Escape. They needed to escape because they were being hunted.

"Doctors, mothers, musicians, artists, scientists, grandparents. We all had to escape, or die." His bitterness was not lost on me. "Hitler was a psychopath, but he could not have done what he did without the help and agreement of millions of people, all of whom did nothing, nothing, save for a fraction of them, to help us. So we Jews were on the run. We were fighting to exist."

His fists clenched, then he sagged, as if the anger rose, then dissipated again, too exhausted to hold on to after so many decades of futility.

"But we were late getting out. We stayed far longer in Paris than we should have. We had to. Your grandma's mother, Frieda, was terminally ill. Her liver was failing. She was yellow. Her husband, Eli, was ill, too. He had had polio as a child, and a different form of it had returned. He was in a wheelchair, and moving him would have been almost impossible. Like I told you before, they begged us to go without them. I didn't want to leave them, neither did Madeline or your grandma. I loved them, but I was desperate. Desperate to get my family out, to get the ones out who might live to see the next year."

"Madeline?" I asked. "Who was Madeline?"

Granddad took a deep, trembly breath, his whole chest shaking. He reached out his hands, hands that never seemed to stop trembling anymore, and said, "My dear granddaughters. Madeline was your grandma."

No, she wasn't. That was my first thought. *No, she wasn't. Grandma is our grandma. Emmanuelle Laurent is our Grandma.*

"What?" Annie asked. "What do you mean?"

Granddad held his eyes shut tight for a second. "Your grandma, Emmanuelle Laurent, is the grandma of your heart. She is the grandma whom you love and who loves you. She cared for you, she would give her life for you, that I know for sure. But she is not your direct, biological grandma."

Neither Annie nor I could speak for long, long seconds.

"What—*what are you talking about?*" I asked.

"Your biological grandma's name was Madeline. You, my dear"—he nodded at me—"you were named by your mother for your grandma. Your mother named you after her mother. Madeline is the sister of your grandma Emmanuelle."

"I'm lost," Annie said, her face pale.

"This is too confusing," I said. Too much.

"Your grandma, your beautiful grandma, is my second wife."

"Your *second* wife?" I asked.

"Yes. I was married to her sister, Madeline, when we were barely twenty."

He was married to Grandma's sister?

"But . . . what happened to her? What happened to your . . ." I could barely see it. "What happened to your first wife? To Madeline?"

His eyes closed, like he'd been hit, then opened to focus on the ruffling leaves, the swaying trees, the hawk that was back up after stabbing the mouse. . . .

"She died. . . ." Granddad's jaw clenched and his eyes swam in tears. Amidst my utter confusion, I was struck that after all this time, Granddad still cried for a woman he had loved and lost decades ago.

"She died right before we were to escape."

Oh, my God. "Granddad, I am so sorry," I whispered.

"Shit," Annie said. "And hell."

He wiped his face and sunk back on the bench, exhausted already, overwhelmed.

"How did she die?" I asked.

He coughed, cleared his throat. "She died a few hours after she jumped."

She jumped? "She jumped from where?"

"She jumped from the second story of her parents' home in Paris."

I felt like I'd been slugged in the chest with a hammer.

Annie stilled, tight, tense.

"Why . . ." I envisioned a woman leaping from a second-story window. "Why did she jump?"

Granddad sighed, his shoulders slumping. "She jumped because she was trying to escape."

"From . . . ," Annie asked, but she knew, and I knew, too.

"The Nazis were coming." Granddad's voice crackled.

Like locusts, like hate on feet, like death. He and his family were human targets. Human Jewish targets.

"Granddad," I said, then stopped, fighting back a rush of despair.

"Oh, my God." Annie didn't cry because she never did, but I knew she felt this pain. "Oh, my God."

"Madeline and Emmanuelle's parents had been tipped off by a neighbor. He was a bookseller, and he learned from someone else who was passing notes back and forth to him through the books that the Nazis were coming to arrest all of us in our homes. When, we didn't know, but it would be soon, so we packed and tried to prepare."

Granddad put his elbows on his knees and leaned forward. "It is like yesterday," he whispered. "As if these other years, these decades, have not happened. I can see everything. I can hear their boots, the screams, that guttural shouting, the smell of fear. It was rampant, it invaded every corner of Paris. I wasn't there at your grandma's parents' house that evening when the Nazis came, shouting, demanding, threatening. Their parents, Madeline and Emmanuelle's parents, how shall I say it? They *stalled* them." He laughed, so bitterly. "They stalled them so she could escape."

"How did they stall the Nazis? I thought they were sick?"

"Their father had a gun. Eli could barely stand. He spent most of his time in that wheelchair, but he stood when the Nazis came in, five of them, and he shot off his old rifle before he himself was shot dead. They turned on your great-grandma, on Frieda, and she had a gun, too. She was so ill, but she raised that gun in shaking hands and pulled the trigger. She was killed instantly by returning gunfire."

I envisioned that—a man, a *real man*, protecting his family, barely able to stand, but stand he did, knowing it was the end of him, the end of his wife, and his wife, a *real woman*, dying, still fighting, a gun in her hands, shooting to kill to protect her family.

"My first wife, you look so much like her, Madeline. That's another reason why your grandma gets confused on who you are. Your grandma Madeline was hiding behind an armoire. She told me what happened later. The Nazis who were still alive, and not hurt from the gunshots, immediately searched the house, and she waited, waited with Ismael—"

Ismael—that name again, always that name. It had darted in and out of my childhood.

"Wait," Annie interrupted. "Who is Ismael?"

"Ismael . . . oh, Ismael," Granddad moaned.

I drew in my breath, so did Annie.

"Ismael . . ." Granddad patted his heart and we both put an arm around his shoulder. "Oh, Ismael."

"It's okay, you don't have to talk anymore, Granddad," I said, worried about his health, his weakening, sliding health. I pictured his life draining out of his body, inch by inch until he was no longer there.

"No. I must speak of this now, before it's too late."

"Rest, Granddad, your heart," Annie said.

"Please, breathe, Granddad," I said.

He breathed, in and out. "Ismael is . . ."

Behind Granddad's back, I held Annie's hand as Granddad took one more rattling breath, as if he was sucking in air to drown the pain.

"Ismael is my son."

I felt Annie gripping my hand tight, on reflex.

"Your son?" I asked.

"Yes, your mother had a brother."

"*Our momma had a brother?*" Annie and I said together. I remembered, again, when I was a girl, how Momma had said, "Ismael and I used to play together, now you and I can play together, Pink Girl." I had asked her to tell me more and she'd said, "Some stories are not to be told for years, until the listener is ready and the storyteller can tell it properly . . . so that no one forgets who we are, who we were."

Here was the story, told properly, the secret, the mystery that had been wrapped up in French, English, and German and carried through three generations.

"Madeline and I had a son, a beautiful son, a wonderful, wonderful son." My granddad did not bother to wipe the tears from his wrinkled cheeks. "We loved him so much, as we loved your mother. Ismael loved sports, loved his microscope, loved being outdoors. He loved animals, like you, Annie, and he loved helping people, like you, Madeline. He had a stamp collection." Granddad's voice broke. "Who did he love most of all, though? He loved your mother, his little sister. Everywhere he went, he took her by the hand. It was he she turned to when she hurt a knee, or needed a hug, or help finding her lost stuffed elephant. It was he who read her stories at night and tucked her in. It was an uncommon bond, strong as steel."

I thought of our momma with an older brother, tucking her in, reading to her, and overnight, he was . . . gone.

"Not a day, not a day has gone by when I have not missed my son, and my daughter. Every day I am tortured by the loss of my children."

I closed my eyes as a torrent of pain shook me. Two children. He had lost *two* children. I had seen firsthand my grandparents' unending, raw grief after losing my momma. It had been horrendous, that would be the word for it, *horrendous*. The wailing, how they muffled their cries, shut doors, screamed at the ocean when they didn't think we were within earshot, screamed into the fir trees on The Lavender Farm. Those memories had scorched my mind for years.

"And, and what happened to that son?" I said, my voice wobbling. "Your son, Ismael?"

"He died."

"But . . ." Dare I open that pain, that endless, eternal pain? Did I have that right? Would he want to talk about it? Would it help, finally, after all these years?

"*How?* How did he die?" Annie asked.

There was, again, a long pause while the leaves ruffled, the trees swayed, the hawk dove again to stab another mouse.

"Your grandma, your grandma Madeline, she held him in her arms and jumped from the second floor as the Nazis were pounding up the stairs. We don't know how she survived. She landed first, cushioning Ismael. Her injuries were so extensive. She was bleeding internally, she'd shattered ribs, hit her head, broke a bone in her leg. Ismael's wounds were equally bad. She crawled, Ismael in her arms, and hid under a rowboat in their yard near their pond."

"Granddad," Annie interrupted. "The pond with the swans, right? The one that Grandma talks about, paints in her books?"

"Yes, it is those swans that your grandma drew hundreds of times for her books. It is why we named the stores Swans. That night the swans strutted around the rowboat, which was partially in bushes. They had never done that. When the Nazis came outside, they tried to peck them, they chased them. But miraculously, as your grandma always told me, the Nazis did not see the boat where Madeline and Ismael were hiding."

I had that image in my head. A black night, a panicked mother with her son, jumping from the second story to escape from morally indefensible vermin who wanted to take her life.

"Madeline carried Ismael, limping and bleeding and broken, to the house of a friend of ours, a doctor who was not Jewish. She had to hide, to dart here and there. Luckily it was dark. The doctor sent his son to find me, then he sent him to get your grandma Emmanuelle and your mother, who were hiding at his friend's house, a librarian, in her basement, with a suitcase and Madeline's violin. I had been frantic with worry, but by the time your grandma and your mother—" He stopped to pinch his nose, but the pinching did not stop the tears. "Your mother, so young, she was wearing a blue coat that day . . . blue shoes . . ."

I rubbed his back, devastated for him, for us, for our whole family in that awful time.

"By the time I got to the doctor's house, Madeline was dying. It was hopeless. Only a hospital could have stopped it, and we couldn't go there. I held her on one side, your grandma on the other. She told us about jumping from the second story, the row-boat and the swans and . . . before she died . . ."

He stopped, his lips trembling.

"Before she died . . ."

His lips trembled again, his body shuddering.

"Before Madeline died she took off her wedding ring and put it on her sister's ring finger, your grandma's ring finger, and said, 'Go . . . go . . . you must go now. Use the papers. She can be your wife.' She was so brave. Even when she was dying, her last thoughts were for us, how to save us. I refused to leave, so did your grandma, but Madeline was insistent. We refused again. She said, 'Save my daughter, save yourselves.' We wouldn't leave her, we refused, and she . . . she . . ."

Granddad choked on his misery, his loss.

"Madeline knew we would not leave her, so she grabbed a knife on the table . . . *grabbed a knife* and stabbed herself in the neck. I have no idea how she had the strength to do that, I don't know, I don't understand, she was critically injured, already bleeding out, but with that . . . it pooled, it rushed out as she died. Her blood drained, her life drained."

Good Lord.

I sank back against the bench again, that horrific scene blistering my mind. Annie leaned forward over her knees and coughed. I knew she was feeling nauseated—and emotionally sick.

Madeline hastened her death to save her husband, her sister, and her daughter, who was my momma. . . .

"She knew that Ismael wouldn't make it," Granddad said. "He was in a coma, hardly breathing. Our doctor friend told us that our sweet child was dying, there was no hope, he had min-utes to live. He urged us to leave. But I wouldn't go, I would not leave my son. But then we saw—" He put a cupped hand to his forehead, as if he could hold captive those tragic memories. "We saw the Nazis coming, at the end of the street, they were going door to door, we heard screams. . . ."

"Granddad—"

"My wife's blood was on the floor, my son wasn't moving, his breath was hardly there, his sunken chest." He sobbed. "His chest was rising, but only slightly, hardly at all, he was bloody, all over there was blood, his wounds were so bad. He was dying, we all knew it. The doctor, my old friend, implored us to leave. 'Save yourselves, save your daughter, your son's soul is already gone, I am sorry, but go go go. Your wife would not want all of you to die, she wouldn't want that. Go, go!'"

That scene branded itself onto my brain. My granddad, a young man; my grandma, a young woman; my momma, a girl in blue, in the midst of two dying people, the blood everywhere, the hopelessness, the desperation, and the Nazis beating their way down the street.

"I . . ." He choked on his own tears. "I leaned down, and I kissed Madeline, and I got blood on my hands, my mouth. Your momma, she didn't make a sound, and she hugged her mother close. Your grandma hugged her sister, pushed her hair back, caressed her face, then the three of us went to Ismael, hugged him, kissed him. I held him close, rocked him back and forth, I thought I would die of pain. His head was back, the blood . . . so much blood, he was so pale, not moving. Dying."

I was crying freely now. Annie's face had completely stilled. It was the mask she always wore when the pain was too much.

"I didn't want to leave, didn't want to, but the doctor grabbed me, pulled me away, and he and his wife, they had risked their lives for us, they pushed us out the door. I grabbed your grandma, but a teenager, and your mother, who picked up Madeline's violin, and we left."

"Oh, Granddad," I said.

He moaned, from the top of his soul. "My son died without us. He died without his family." He wailed, long and hoarse, wretched. "He died alone. I am ashamed. I left him, left my son in his last minutes. I was not there. His father was not there."

"Granddad, please," Annie begged. "You didn't have a choice. He was in a coma, he was dying . . ."

"If you hadn't left, you all would have ended up in the camps. All of you, Momma, Grandma, you...Annie and I wouldn't be here."

"Logically, I know this. It has never, it *will never* make it better. My son died without me holding him, talking to him, praying for him. As a father, I was not there."

We patted him, we soothed him. It did nothing to help him. Nothing could heal that pain. It is foolhardy to think it ever could.

The hawk dove down to stab another mouse as the trees swayed and the leaves rustled, and Annie and I and Granddad were in France, in a ruthless, dangerous world.

"We barely made the train," he whispered. "I showed those bastards, those Nazis, our forged papers, but we were questioned, anyhow. They liked that, liked to scare people, liked to strut. They were criminals, brutal, conscienceless, merciless. But your mother, your sweet mother, in her blue coat and blue dress, she whipped out her momma's violin and played one of the pieces she had made up herself. Even at that age, your mother loved to compose her own music. She had an ear..."

"She had them convinced that, indeed, we were going to a violin competition in Vienna, as I had told them. Those stupid men, monsters, all of them, they listened, and they believed us, even though the violin was far too big for her. They were too ignorant, too drunk on their own power, to know it."

"A girl, at a train station," I whispered. "Playing a violin for Nazis after kissing her dead momma good-bye, her dead brother ...how did she do that...how did she not fall apart..." But that was our momma. Indomitable. Brave. Headstrong. Talented. I sobbed, thinking of her, of all my momma had endured, from the time she was a tiny child.

"There are three tiny dents, on the right side of your violin, Madeline," Granddad said.

I nodded. I knew of those dents.

"After she played the piece, she swung her violin and, three times, it hit the train. It dented the violin. We smiled at the Nazis, your grandma and I, while I hid my hands in the pockets of my coat, which still had the blood from Madeline and my son on them, and your grandma held her coat tight over her dress, because her dress was soaked with Madeline's and Ismael's blood, from hugging them. Even the inside of the violin had blood in it—that's the butterfly stain you see, Madeline."

So that was where the butterfly had come from. *Blood from my family.*

"Within an hour of those bloody hugs, your mother was playing a song for Nazi officers to convince them we were a happy French family, not Jews trying to get out, Heil Hitler, Heil Hitler. I had my Heil Hitler down. We were leaving for a violin competition, Heil Hitler. I had not even asked her to play."

"And you got on the train."

"We got on the train, your grandma wearing her sister's wedding ring, posing as my wife, as our papers indicated. Your momma, as soon as we were settled in the train, went numb from shock. She had lost her mother and her brother and grandparents. They were all gone and she was on a train, leaving with nothing, going who knew where. We got off the train, within the hour, in case the Nazis were somehow following, then we were helped by a loose connection of people the doctor knew. We hid in barns and a church, abandoned buildings, but we were betrayed. The Nazis came for us and we had to defend ourselves once again; your mother saw everything. . . ."

He stopped, his jaw tightened, and I remembered what Grandma had said about Granddad killing three people with a knife, how she had kicked one of them until he wasn't moving.

"We walked over the Pyrenees Mountains. We walked to Spain, then left Spain, after months in abject poverty, for New York. Damn near killed all of us. We tried to start over, but every step I took, I knew I was unworthy of God. Unworthy of speaking to Him, unworthy of any relationship with Him, so I told Him that I would do everything I could to help others, to atone for what I had done."

"But Granddad, God knows why you had to leave them."

He moaned again. "That is only one of my sins, child. There are more. I committed a heinous crime, heinous, but I cannot tell you now. Not now. Not today. This is enough." His voice cracked, the tears streaming down that proud man's face before his hand rose abruptly to his chest. "This is enough."

"Granddad! Are you all right?" The volume of Haydn's Symphony no. 39 in G Minor rose about ten notches.

His face went pale, white and silky, he swayed, his eyes lost focus, and he would have tumbled forward had we not caught him.

Annie is trained in CPR, as am I.

We used our training and ignored the screaming in our heads.

24

Sherwinn's, Pauly's, and Gavin's trial opened to a jammed courtroom. Everyone we knew was there, plus a number of journalists. Annie and I were . . . well, how does one accurately describe it? We were humiliated, scared to death, deeply traumatized, and numb. Our emotions soared and dipped.

I won't detail the whole trial, or the part when the jury was handed the graphic photos of Annie and me, or the testimony of the police officers and the doctors at the hospital, or how the three monsters refused to be put on the witness stand, but I will share Annie's testimony.

Annie hadn't spoken for months. She would whimper, cry, and climb so hard back into herself we couldn't find or reach her, her words at the bottom of an emotional black hole. The defense insisted that Annie take the stand, even though they knew all about her debilitated emotional state.

"Your honor," our attorney, Arthur Benning, protested, tall and rigid, "Annie O'Shea no longer speaks. Defense council knows this, knows she can't be put on the stand. It's a detriment to her fragile health. This will set her back—"

"Your honor," Bing Hicks, one of the three defense attorneys argued, a sneer on his fleshy face, "my clients have the right to hear their accuser. The jury needs to hear her, to ascertain her truthfulness and honesty, to make sure she's not making this up. . . ."

The attorneys went back and forth heatedly arguing, the

crowd getting increasingly noisy, but Annie ended up on that stand.

My momma stood up seething, shaking with rage. "Your honor, please, you can't do this to Annie—"

The judge, a man with thick curly hair and a stolid expression named Marvin Bonds, hit that gavel with a smack; the defense attorneys were up and preening and protesting; Arthur and a couple of his assistant attorneys stood and added to the screaming, too; the gavel smacked again and again, with the judge yelling at my momma to "Sit down this minute, Marie Elise"; and we lost. Annie had to testify.

"What's your name?" Fleshy-face Bing Hicks asked Annie after she sat in the witness chair.

Annie didn't speak, only rocked back and forth, her arms wrapped around her pink sweater, her pink bow holding back her curls. The red seemed to glow brighter that day. I figured it was my dad, somewhere near.

"Do you understand what's going on here today?"

Her eyes had that lost, *I am gone* look to them. *Not here.*

"Who are these men?"

Annie made a muffled sound, like a crushed bird, but didn't look at them.

"Did they do anything to you?"

Annie shook, made an odd sound with her mouth.

I could hear the people in court whispering, shifting. They were getting angry.

"Did they ever touch you?"

Annie started humming Pachelbel's Canon in D Major. I played it for her at night before she went to sleep because it seemed to soothe her.

"Are you lying, Annie?"

My momma about choked on her rage. Granddad put an arm around her and held her down as she tried to stand up. A bunch of people in the courtroom protested.

"Are you lying, Annie?" Hicks asked again.

My granddad made a growling sound in his throat.

"You can't lie, do you understand, Annie? You can't. You

could go *to jail* for lying." Hicks tapped a pen on his palm. *"To jail."*

Our attorneys objected, objected again. "Badgering...intimidating...she's a child..."

The people in court were barely controlled. Shell Dee's husband was so mad, he yelled out, "There's a liar in here, and it's not Annie, you superprick," and was pulled up and out the door by the bailiffs. Trudy Jo's husband yelled, "You should be in jail, not Annie!" and was yanked out next.

My grandma gripped my hand so hard I thought it would break, then she swore in German, her preferred language for swearing.

Hicks smirked. "Don't be a liar, Annie."

That did it.

Boom. Chaos in the courtroom. Grandma, Granddad, Momma, our friends, all were up and on their feet, a mass of outraged voices banging together, the gavel coming down again and again. The judge yelled at Hicks that he had "no more room at all. I will throw you out."

And Annie? She didn't say a word, not a word. She rocked and hummed in her pink sweater.

Finally, when things settled after the bailiffs and other policemen filled the aisles and yelled threats to evict everyone else, Hicks was at it again, facing the jury, pompous, arrogant. "Annie O'Shea won't talk because she doesn't want to say anything bad against my clients. This is a wild young woman, out of control, a rebel. Don't be fooled by her age. She participated fully in what happened here."

My momma yelled, her voice, hoarse, teary, "That is a lie. A lie!"

The gavel came down, etc., etc.

"She liked what happened," Hicks went on. "She liked the photos, she liked the attention. She encouraged it. *Encouraged it.* Who doesn't like their photos taken? She wanted to be famous!"

We had not liked the attention. We had not encouraged it. We did not want to be famous.

My granddad said, in French, "Dammit, I will kill him or have him killed."

Grandma said, in German, "I will stab his heart, twist the knife. . . ."

"Annie O'Shea is involved with all of these men."

Fleshy Face's next words could not be heard over the loud denials in the courtroom. One man yelled, "She isn't involved with anyone, but I'd like your face involved with my fist." That man, the assistant principal at my school, was led out, and the gavel pounded everyone into submission.

"These girls get caught," Fleshy Face pontificated, arms outstretched, "and lo and behold! They say they're victims. Victims!"

The judge yelled when chaos threatened again. "Sit down, shut up, or you'll be evicted from this courtroom, all of you! Order. Order!"

My grandma muttered, "You bastard, you utter, contemptible bastard."

"These girls aren't victims!" Hicks shouted. "They're part of it. They were going to be paid a huge amount of money. They agreed to it for the money. They sold their bodies, for the money. Willingly! By choice!"

Next to me my momma was being physically restrained by Granddad and one of the assistant attorneys, who had turned around and grabbed my momma before she could leap at Hicks's throat.

"I will not have my clients, *innocent men,* going to jail for this. Annie O'Shea won't talk because she feels *guilty* that my clients are here in the first place. She and Madeline weren't hurt, they *liked* it!"

I burst into tears. We had not *liked* it.

That's when Annie started shaking her head back and forth, back and forth, her eyes suddenly with us, as if she'd woken up in the middle of the crime itself, in the middle of hell, and she had decided to fight. She opened her mouth and a scream came out, let loose, a wail from the center of her heart, the same place where her raw, open, seeping pain lived.

My momma and I were both restrained from going to her, me by Trudy Jo and Grandma, my momma by Granddad and Arthur.

I shouted, "It's okay, Annie, I'm coming, I'm coming!"

My momma yelled, her voice throbbing, primal, "Stop it, stop it! Stop hurting her! Stop it! Let me go to her, let me go to my daughter!"

It took all they had to restrain both of us as I kicked and struggled, but to this day, I know our attorneys and my grandparents did right by us. They wanted the jury to see Annie, see her reaction.

Annie continued to scream, then she stood up, her body rattling from head to foot, and pointed to those three evil, demented men, tears racing down her face as if her eyes were leaking. She pointed her finger right at them, and in that tense, quaking courtroom, she spoke for the first time in months. "They made me! They forced us! They hit us! They took off our clothes! They ripped my sweater! They ripped our pink dresses! They hurt us! I'm not lying!"

A communal roar of disgust rose up.

"I didn't like it! We didn't like it! We didn't want to be famous! But they said they'd kill Momma if we told! He killed Mickey! He killed Teresa! They took pictures! I said no no nooooo, and Madeline pushed them away. We tried to fight, but they're bigger, they hit us! They said bad things, mean things to us. I said no no no! All the time, we had to go to Pauly's house. I hate it there! It's cold, it's bad. They're bad and they made us do bad things."

As soon as Annie had joined us, though, she was gone again, I saw it. Her eyes were back at the shack, that ugly, violent place, as if a new movie had replaced the old. "Don't kill Momma," she rasped, staring straight at Sherwinn, Pauly, and Gavin. "No, I'll do it, I'll do it, say you won't hurt Momma! Don't throw her at the wall, Pauly! You don't kick her, stop kicking her! She's bleeding! I'll help you, Madeline! Not that again! It hurts! Get off of me! No camera, no cameras.... I won't smile. I don't want to be on my back. Please let us go home!"

We all froze then, struck, shocked, horrified, as Annie went on and on, gone but with us, lost but there. "Is she dead?" Annie called. "Madeline, Madeline! Is she dead? Wake up! She's not moving! You killed her! Is she breathing? I don't think she's breathing! Granddad, help me!"

The defense attorneys tried to get her to stop. "Your honor, she's not answering the questions . . . your honor, she's insane . . . your honor, this is prejudicing the jury . . . your honor," but Annie screamed over them, and the judge pounded his gavel and told the defense attorneys to "Sit down and shut up!" and still Annie screamed.

The courtroom was in a full-throttle uproar.

My momma hit Arthur so hard he let go of her and she straddled the bench to run to Annie, but was caught by a bailiff, her heels flying in the air.

"Let go of me! Get off of me, Sherwinn!" Annie sobbed. "I don't like that cage. I don't want to go in it again. I don't want to wear that! No, I won't! No, don't touch me!"

Grandma was done. She was in the aisle in a flash and called out in French, "I am coming. I am here, my darling," but was caught by a policeman.

"Oh no, oh no, oh no!" Annie sobbed, her voice pitched high over the wreckage of that courtroom. "No, I don't want to do that again. No cameras! Stop! Don't you hurt Momma!"

Granddad was done, too. He swung himself over the bench, but his attorneys, a bailiff, and a friend held him back. "I'm coming, Annie! I'm coming!"

"Granddad," Annie said, clutching her head. "Get Granddad! Grandma, can you help me, can you help me!"

Annie screamed again, from that miserable place Sherwinn had put her that she couldn't climb out of. I was done sitting. The courtroom had broken down to absolute anarchy with people yelling, some members of the jury standing up and protesting that Annie needed help, she needed help.

"*Help her! Help her!*" they yelled.

The defense attorneys, I was later told, were the only ones not moving. They had fallen back in their chairs, heads in their hands.

I was quick and young, I could dart and twist away from people's hands, and I went straight over one bench, then another, jumped into the aisle, dodged an outstretched hand from a bailiff, and went straight for Annie.

As her cracking voice split that room in half she shouted, "I hate you, Sherwinn. I hate you, Gavin. I hate you, Pauly!" I reached her and pulled her into my arms, tight and close.

"Madeline," she called out, raw and coarse, her eyes at the ceiling, back in the corners of her numbing memories. "Madeline, where are you? We have to get out of here! I want to go home! I want to go home! I want to go home!"

"It's me, Annie," I said. "It's me. We're going home."

She turned her head toward me, so our noses were two inches apart. "Madeline," she choked out. "Madeline!" She wrapped her arms around me. I held her close. We swayed together, and she buried her face in my shoulder.

No one tried to separate us.

My granddad's voice was raw from hurtling threats against the three evil men in that room with no less than three men holding him back, my momma had collapsed in Carman's arms, and my grandma was calling out, struggling against the policeman who I was later told was an emotional mess himself that day, "I am coming, my darlings! I am coming!"

One juror leaned over and vomited, one had to be propped up by another because he fainted, four were still standing and protesting that someone should go and help us, and one woman had her hands up in the air, shaking, as in, Help me, God.

The room was a total, complete disaster, and it became worse as six men, all fishermen friends of my dad's, hurdled benches and people, fought off police and bailiffs, and launched themselves, their muscles, and their lust for revenge at Sherwinn, Pauly, and Gavin.

They beat the holy shit out of them.

As one fisherman friend said later to my momma, "It was

worth being arrested, Marie Elise. I heard my man, Luke, Big Luke, that night in my jail cell. He said, 'Covey, good fucking job,' that's what he said. 'Good fucking job.' Heard it clear as I hear two beer jugs clinking together, yeah, I did."

Now my dad never used the F-word. Ever. At least at home around his Pink Girls but, maybe, *maybe* he would have used it with Covey. Why do I think he might have used the F-word that time, speaking straight from heaven?

Because my momma gave Covey a hug on the deck of our house by the sea and said to him, "I think you did a good fucking job, too, Covey."

And my momma never swore!

I testified the next day into the tight, rigid silence of the courtroom, police and bailiffs all over that room. I was supposed to testify after Annie, but since the courtroom was in total disarray with police and bailiffs restraining this person and that person, including the fishermen who were throwing punches like sledgehammers, the jurors yelling, and journalists snapping pictures, they had to close things down.

Sherwinn, Pauly, and Gavin glared right at me, their faces a mass of swollen bruises and cuts. I tried not to look at them, but at one point Sherwinn drew his finger across his neck.

I kept testifying.

At another point Gavin stuck his tongue out and wiggled it at me.

I kept testifying.

Pauly pursed his lips like he was kissing me.

I kept testifying. They made me feel sick and panicked, but I thought of Annie, and the more I told the truth, Arthur told me, the longer those bad men would have to stay in jail. So I shook, and I kept testifying, for Annie.

I relived all the abuse Annie and I had endured as I recounted it. I could even smell the cigarette smoke, feel their sticky and slimy hands, the old pizza, the must and the rot. I told what they did to us, even though I was humiliated and shamed.

The defense attorney kept trying to break my story up, to

make me cry or stutter, but the judge kept saying, "Overruled," and pounding his gavel, and I kept right on.

Click, click, click.

Later I was told I was crying during my testimony, winding my fingers in and out of each other, pulling on my curls, making strangled gasps and groans, but I didn't remember that.

By the time I was done, Arthur was the color of a sick ghost, and Hicks with the fleshy face was almost curled into a fetal position at his table. His co-counsels were holding their heads, as if they couldn't bear another sentence from me entering their lives.

There were formalities after that, closing arguments, the graphic photos were brought up again, then the jury was excused to the jury room.

They were back out in twenty minutes. They had their verdict.

They found it in our living nightmare.

Guilty. All three, all charges: Guilty.

"May you rot in hell forever," the jury foreman intoned. "Rot in hell." The courtroom exploded in triumph, but there was no triumph for Annie or me or our mother.

This was not a win.

We had already been destroyed.

Momma forbid us from coming to court the next afternoon for the sentencing, for reasons that were later obvious to us. We didn't want to be in a courtroom again, ever, but we were not going to miss this. I knew Annie felt the same as me because I said to her, "I want to see them go to jail," and she nodded.

Momma had a neighbor, Mrs. Donnehey, come and stay with us on that sunny spring day. She was older, with long white hair, and she cried over soap operas, sometimes starting at the very beginning credits, before the story had even unfolded. She brought us cookies every couple of weeks. When she found out what happened to Annie and me, she brought us cookies every day, pinwheels, peanut butter, oatmeal raisin, all in pretty boxes with ribbons.

We loved her, but when she started watching her soap opera that afternoon, bawling much harder than normal, we snuck out in our pink dresses, our white sandals flying us to town. We slid into the back of the courtroom, and when the judge said, "Marie Elsie, you may make your statement," we snuck in to sit with our grandparents. They were dismayed to see us there, but what could they do at that point? They put their arms around us, kissed the tops of our heads.

Momma walked to the witness box, her light pink dress with the embroidered white daisies circling the trim swirling around her legs. Her step was strong in the cotton candy pink heels, and the yellow ribbon she wore that held back her black hair reminded me of what she'd told me. "Yellow means there's still hope in this pickled, wrinkled, warped world, sugar. Yellow means there's a new tomorrow scootin' around the corner."

I could not see any hope that day. I don't think I've seen much hope since then. It died with that yellow ribbon.

"My husband, the girls' father, Luke O'Shea," Momma said, then stopped, and tried to get control of her emotions.

Beside me, Annie clutched my hand. Beside her Granddad inhaled quickly, and muttered, "Now there was a man for you," and Grandma dabbed her eyes.

"Big Luke was a good man." Momma put her head up and faced Sherwinn, Pauly, and Gavin at the defense table. Her back straightened, her gaze almost violent, and I knew she hated them with every fiber of her being.

"He was a wonderful father and a wonderful husband." There was loud agreement in the courtroom, scattered applause.

"He provided for his family, kept us safe." My momma sniffled, tightened her lips together. "He loved us. He loved us so much."

Annie snuggled closer to me. We missed our dad. Damn the storm that whipped up every ugly emotion on the East Coast that night, spun it into the ocean, and drowned him.

"I miss him every day. I miss him more than ever now. Truth is, if that storm hadn't taken him and the other good men on the boats that day, I would still have my Luke and this never would have happened to my girls. No, never. I blame myself. I blame myself for getting involved with Sherwinn. He's an evil, horrible person, and so are Gavin and Pauly. They are sick, violent men who will always be a plague upon this earth."

The courtroom was now silent with respect for my momma, who was struggling not to cry.

"I don't know how my girls are going to get over this. I know that the love of my parents, the love of all of you, will help, but will my girls ever be able to put it behind them? Have they scarred them so badly they'll never get over it? I keep asking myself those questions, and I don't know. But what I do know is that Sherwinn, Pauly, and Gavin will always be a threat to my girls' lives."

She shuffled a few papers with shaking hands. "Sherwinn sent me a few letters. I have them here." She waved them in the air. "This one says, 'Marie Elise, sweetie, you going to be running your whole life, 'cause if I see you in court, I'm killing you after I'm outta jail and you ain't ever gonna see your girls again if you live that long.'"

There were gasps in the audience.

"The second note says, 'Marie Elise, sweetie, you keep your girls' mouths shut tight or I'm going to see they go and visit their daddy soon. Got that, sweetie?'"

There were more gasps, shocked words exchanged.

"One more letter. 'You can run, but you ain't gonna hide from me. I will track Madeline and Annie down, sweetie, and have my fun with them.'"

She lifted her chin.

"You see, folks," my momma said, "I can't have my girls' lives threatened like that. I can't. I can't have them growing up, knowing that these men will get out of jail and come after them with a knife or a gun or their bare hands. Sherwinn is a psychopath. Gavin and Pauly are sick child molesters. If my husband, Luke, were around, he would take care of this problem, but he isn't, so it's up to me. But the problem is, you all know, that I'm fighting this tumor in my head." She tapped her head. "I can't guarantee that I'll be around to protect my girls."

She hesitated for a moment. "Sherwinn, Gavin, and Pauly, I hate you. Hating anyone was a foreign concept to me before you three, but I hate you more than I thought I could hate. The Bible tells me not to hate, but I hate what you did to my girls, what you did to my family, to me. I hate what you've done to their futures. But I believe in God and in hell, and I know where you three are going and that gives me some peace."

She put the letters down as the courtroom burst into applause. "I want to apologize to all of you, to all of my friends out here, whom I've traumatized. You've been good to me, true friends. Luke and I love you all, and so do our girls."

I didn't get that statement—no one got it at the moment, the words hanging in the tension like jagged mysteries—but we all "got it" later.

"Judge, I am done making my statement. Thank you."

The judge nodded at her. "Thank you, Marie Elise. You're right about Luke. I think I speak for all of us when I say we miss him."

"He was a good man, Marie Elise," someone shouted.

"He'd be proud of you, Marie Elise."

My momma left the letters in the witness box so she didn't have anything in her hands, her light pink dress with the white daisies circling the trim swirling around her legs.

When she was about three feet from those viperous creatures she said, in a voice as hard as a chunk of iron, "This is from Big Luke. He's going to escort you to hell. Good-bye." She spread her legs in her cotton candy pink heels so she would have perfect balance, then whipped her gun out from her bra.

It was a small pistol, a lady's pistol, but it did the job fine. You don't need a Herculean-sized UZI or a bazooka to shoot child molesters. A ladies' pistol will do the trick.

She raised it, lickety-split, before anyone could stop her, the white daisies still twirling a bit, and *bang, bang, bang.*

She shot Sherwinn first. His chest arched as the bullet went straight through. Then she shot Pauly and Gavin, who had half a second to react. Their bodies twisted and jerked. My momma took three steps forward and leaned full over the defense table and shot each one of them one more time, as their attorneys cowered or jumped over the bench behind them. My momma wanted to make sure the job was done, and done right. One of her cotton candy heels tipped up in the air for balance, her yellow ribbon slipping over a shoulder.

It is somewhat a wonder that no one else was hit by an escaping bullet, but like my momma said when we visited her in jail, "I shot at a downward slant. You know I have perfect aim. Grandma taught me how to shoot, and I can hit a fly buzzing a bee. And you two! I told you to stay home!"

Indeed the bullets that passed through their bodies were found imbedded in the wood floor.

Were Annie and I further traumatized by our momma's shooting of those three sickos?

Yes, we were. We had seen our momma kill three men.

Bang, bang, bang.

I've heard those shots forever. I've relived that day thousands of times.

But here's the thing: My momma, still lost in a black depression for not protecting her beloved daughters, was taking opportunity where she found it. Where else would she have been able to shoot those three dead? They'd been in jail, they were going back to jail. When they got out, she knew she'd be dead. My momma wasn't taking any chances. No, Marie Elise O'Shea was not taking any chances. She did not leave things to chance. She called chance "wishful wishing."

She killed them to protect us, now and forever.

Bang, bang, bang.

They were dead.

Her girls were safe.

Bang, bang, bang.

She was arrested.

Steve was waiting for us outside the courthouse, in the midst of the panic and confusion, after the shooting.

Trudy Jo, Carman, and Shell Dee hustled Annie and me out of the courtroom, amidst a rush of policemen running in, a crowd of buzzing people, and a sky-high level of cacophony. Out of the corner of my eye I could see Mrs. Donnehey sprinting toward us—I had no idea she could run that fast—and I knew by her crumpled face that she was sobbing.

I dropped my gaze as soon as I caught Steve's eyes. I was dirty. Guilty. Ashamed. I would never be good enough to play with Steve again. He was Steve. He was tall and cute and smart. No, Madeline O'Shea couldn't be with Steve Shepherd.

In my pocket I had the heart-shaped rocks he'd given me.

I turned away from him.

That night, way way late at night, with Annie curled up beside me in bed, our grandparents downstairs reeling in shock over what their daughter had done, our momma in jail, I closed my eyes and saw my dad. This time, he was standing tall. He wasn't crying. He didn't look happy, but he was upright, his hard chin squared, his shoulders back.

I knew that my dad would have met those three on their way down to hell and beaten the tar out of them before escorting them to the devil himself with a smile, like my momma said.

Would he have wanted my momma to go to jail for killing those men? No. He adored her every word, every kiss, every dream. But would he have believed, especially given that my momma was dying, that she made the right decision in killing Sherwinn, Pauly, and Gavin?

Yes. Without a doubt, yes, even though not having my momma around made me feel empty, completely gutted, as if love had left me for six gunshots.

Annie had pulled herself into a tight, tense ball. I wrapped my arms around her, but my hug wasn't enough. It had never been enough. I had not protected my little sister.

I have lived with that forever.

25

⌣

"What did you make him do, ride a trapeze?"

I smiled with relief when I saw Dr. Rubenstein coming out of Granddad's hospital room with a smile.

"He's okay, ladies. We're going to keep him here for a few days, but then we'll send him back to the farm. Here's his list of complaints: Hospitals make him sick. He's bored. He wants to be with your Grandma—she worries easily. He could walk out right now, dammit, this is costing a fortune, why all the fuss, the nurses won't let him rest, all this gobbledy gook and medical slang, it's like we speak from a foreign planet." Dr. Rubenstein laughed. "And, again, he's bored, bored, it's so boring here!"

"That's our granddad." I breathed, then sagged with relief against the hallway. "Thank you."

"You're welcome." He eyed both of us. "What is it? Is something else wrong?"

What was wrong? Let me count the ways: Granddad had stopped breathing momentarily so we had to do CPR to revive him. When he was breathing, we carried him to the truck, sped down the driveway, and called an ambulance. We met the ambulance about a mile down. Granddad had prostate cancer, heart disease, and arthritis. He'd had a heart attack. We'd just heard about how our biological grandma had committed suicide, how Granddad's son had died, and their near-fatal escape. Grandma had dementia. I was expecting a media storm very

shortly detailing events that still made my breath swirl frantically around in my body. I am a lie.

"We're fine," I said. I remembered how my granddad answered that question. "Damn fine."

"Yes, we're dandy fine," Annie said. "Dandy damn fine. All
dandy."

Dr. Rubenstein didn't believe us. We knew he didn't believe
us. He wrapped us in those huge arms of his, anyhow. "Our
families go way back. Call me anytime you need anything."

We nodded.

"It is boring here, though," Annie drawled.

"Nothing to do at all except listen to doctors speaking from a
foreign planet."

"Damn boring," he agreed. "Damn boring."

He was a good man, that Dr. Rubenstein. There are good
men around, you know.

"How are you feeling, Granddad?" I asked, leaning over his
bed.

"Damn fine. And I'm not staying here. Hospitals make me
sick."

I almost laughed. Laughed with relief. Not long ago we were
breathing into his mouth, now we were listening to him complain about how hospitals made him sick. How life can change
in minutes. . . .

"We understand that the hospital makes you sick, but since
you refused to breathe out on the farm, we're gonna have to ask
you to stay," Annie quipped.

"Yes, indeedy," I said. "Annie or I or Nola or the other
nurses will be with you 'round the clock. Won't that be fun? A
jim-dandy good time."

"Hell. Then you all can spy on me," he grumped. "As if I'm a
tarantula that needs to be watched at all times."

"You're a good-looking tarantula," Annie said, "if only a bit
long in the tooth."

"Yes, too furry and prickly, your bite isn't pleasant, but
there's some good-looking-ness in there, too," I said.

He cleared his throat, all signs of the brokenness he had shown us earlier gone. He had toughened back up, chin high, shoulders back. He did not want to talk about his past anymore today. That was our granddad. That was how he had gotten through the broken glass scattered throughout his life. Box up the pain, *move forward.*

"Girls, thank you for the CPR." I did not miss the tone of his wry humor.

"You're welcome," I said. "What a pleasure! A delight! It was glorious."

"No problem. I've always wanted to breathe heavily into your mouth," Annie said. "It added excitement to my dreary day."

Granddad rolled his eyes.

"And I've always wanted to squish you," I said. "Your chest compressed impressively. That's something to be proud of. You have a squishy chest."

"Yes, and you had fresh, minty breath when you finally started breathing again," Annie drawled. "Delicious. I practically wanted to eat it."

"Damnation." He sighed. "Now, listen up. You're not going to boss me around on this. I am my own man and I'll make the decisions about my own health without interference. I will agree to stay one night in the hospital, given the circumstances, but then I'm going home to the farm, so don't put up any of your flop-sided arguments. Spring is coming and I'm not going to miss watching the lavender bloom. Or the tulip trees. Your grandma likes me around during those times, especially."

I coughed. Annie wiggled, as if her laugh was inside her and she wouldn't let it out.

Grandma liked him around all the time. He was her sun. Her lover, too, as she had told us many times. Her "animal lover," or her "insatiable lover," or her "sex-god lover" when she was jacked up and randy.

"We won't keep you from your lavender or the tulip trees. We won't keep you from Grandma, either, that nasty, naughty woman," I said. I paused as I heard Nola's soft, soothing voice down the hallway, then heard Grandma call out, in French, "Dear and dear! Why is my beloved lover in the hospital? Is it his penis? He's never had problems with his penis before. It's always up. Didn't the swans protect it?"

Granddad sat up. "Don't upset her," he growled to us. "She is easily upset."

Annie rolled her eyes at me. As if we would intentionally upset Grandma. "Are you sure, Granddad? I wanted to try out some torture techniques on her."

"Gee, Granddad. That was on my list of things to do today: Upset Grandma. Now you've ruined my fun."

"Darling!" Grandma gushed as she glided in, her blue-green eyes shining. She bent to kiss him on the forehead, then on both cheeks. "I hear that your penis is in trouble!"

I saw my granddad's mouth twitch, smothering a laugh. You see, a man of lesser strength and confidence might get out of whack at such a public comment. Not Granddad. "My dear." He held out his hand and she sat on the edge of his bed. "It is a pleasure to see you."

"And you." She smiled at him, stroking his face. She was wearing a silvery dress, emeralds, and high black heels, as if she were off to the opera. "But, what is it? Why are you in the hospital? Are you sure you'll be safe here? Is there blood?" Her face turned grim and worried, and she lifted up the sheet and peered down it. "No blood, but will they report us?"

"Yes, I'll be safe." He patted her hand, watching her mood carefully. "How is the lavender?"

"The lavender!" Grandma exclaimed, clapping her hands together. Her two impressive, jeweled rings flashed. One would think they were fake, they were so stunning. They were not fake. "Why, it's beautiful! Nothing can hurt us when we're in the lavender. That's why you planted it for us and why the marbles are there! We planted beauty, didn't we, so we could hide all the terrible things that happened before we came here. We didn't want to look at blood anymore, only pink petals, and lavender plants, and apple orchards. We can pretend the ugly never happened."

"Yes, we can pretend." Granddad looked exhausted again.

Grandma giggled. "I have something for you, my love."

"You do?"

"Yes." She giggled, leaned in close, then took a second to peek at Annie, Nola, and me. "We can't let the children see, though. Turn around now," she told us, waving a hand.

We three obediently turned around. Nola grinned. "She's in a frisky mood today. Wait till you see this."

I peeked. Grandma stood in front of Granddad, unbuttoned her expensive silvery dress, sloooowwwly, with practiced seduction, and flashed him.

Underneath her dress, she was naked. Buck naked. Not a stitch. Not a thread. Nothin'.

"Want to kiss this?" she said, very sexily.

I sent a sideways glance to Nola. She whispered, "You know I can't control her. Your grandma does what she wants."

Annie's jaw was working, her body wiggling again. She was trying so hard not to let the laugh out!

"Want to kiss this?" Grandma chirped. "I think you do! I think you want to kiss this!"

I stared up at the ceiling. Part of me wanted to laugh, the other to cry. No matter how far my grandma's dementia went, she always knew she loved, and desired, my granddad. That never changed. It probably never would change. What a love. What an enduring love they shared.

"I wore my naked suit for you, my love!" Grandma said.

Annie, Nola, and I started to shuffle out the door, side by side, like soldiers. We tried not to peek again.

"I am so glad the doctors have fixed your penis!" Grandma giggled. "Shall we see if it gets big like a log right now?"

There are many names for lavender: Morning Mist, Manakau Village, Raycott, Regal Splendor, Imperial Gem, Little Lady, Loddon Blue, Willowbridge White . . .

Lavender comes in the most glorious colors on the planet— dark pinks, light pinks, deep purples, light purple, white, yellow, a blend.

How can a person stand in a field of lavender and not feel joy, peace, a tug of calm.

I'll tell you how: When they're being chased by demons, living or dead.

"Here's an article on Steve," Annie said, handing me a magazine from New York the next evening. "He looks pretty darn hot."

We swung together on the swing of the deck overlooking the lavender rows. Lisa, the cat missing an ear and half a tail, was on Annie's lap. We'd spent hours that day going to Annie's vet appointments, then we'd watched Grandma paint a white swan. It had a swastika on its breast, until she'd taken a knife and shredded that canvas to bits while swearing in German. She prefers to swear in German.

I took the article. I knew I would add it to my collection. "He does look hot." That would be an understatement. He was gorgeous, gentle, manly, weathered a bit, strong jawline, whiskers that gave him a risqué expression.

"I understand why you didn't respond to any of his letters when we were kids, Madeline."

I nodded. "Hurt too much."

"Do you know if he's married?" She picked up her glass of strawberry lemonade.

"I don't know." I didn't want to know. The thought of him married to another woman made me saddened beyond belief. Would that have been me if I had not been forced into a shack? Would we have been in love forever and married out of high school? Out of college? Our parents would have loved that. His parents were smart and funny. In-laws like that would have been a gift.

We swung in the breeze. Annie's dog, Mr. Legs, and his three legs were curled up beside us.

"Do you want to know, Madeline?"

"Know what?"

"Do you want to know if Steve's married?"

I did. I didn't. Mr. Legs whimpered. He was asleep, dreaming.

"He's successful with the Pink books," Annie said. "This says he lives on land in Massachusetts. Has horses, dogs, a bird, a pond."

I nodded. I did want to know. I didn't. It would hurt either way. Tears dammed up in my throat, tears that have been stuck there ever since I wrote poetry with a tall, blond-haired boy in a tree house.

"He's involved in volunteer work with an abused children's group, it says. He's on the board. He speaks about it, fund-raises for them. It's successful. Gee whiz. I wonder why he's involved with that," Annie drawled sarcastically, stroking Lisa. "He was a remarkable kid. Would have made an excellent Special Ops guy, but he was too tender hearted. Remember the pink dresses he had his mom make us? The pressed flowers? The cookies?

"How is it that a boy that age was able to reach out like that, be that brave and gentle? I think it was his parents. And I think it was his love for you, Madeline, and as your sister, that love traveled on over to me, like sparks from the fire. Remember that time he came over and Sherwinn was there and Sherwinn said something rude and Steve snapped, 'That's not a good thing to say, Sherwinn. Don't speak like that to Madeline.' He was made of gunpowder, Steve was. He was no frilly wimp."

I nodded and sniffed. I missed him. I'd always missed him, missed the friendship.

"Remember how he always tried to get us to come to his house after Sherwinn moved in?" Annie went on. "Hell, he knew something was wrong, *he knew it*. He was a kid from a loving home, he wouldn't have even been able to conceive of what was happening to us, but he got that something was wrong, and he did something, he took action."

I nodded, my throat so tight, those tears a lasso around me.

"He told Momma he didn't like Sherwinn," Annie said. "Kick my ass, he was brave."

"I know." He'd told her several times. He was trying to help us, save us. How tight can tears be locked up in a body before they burst like a dam?

"Remember the trial? He was waiting for you outside."

I thought I would lose that dam holding my tears back and I'd drown.

"Madeline." Annie held my hand. "Look at me."

I tried to put myself back together.

"Madeline. Yoo-hoo."

I took a shuddery breath, then met her blue-green gaze.

"Steve has never married."

The dam broke.

"He's never married, Madeline, and obviously neither have you. Maybe you're waiting for each other. Like freakin' soul mates. Ever think that?"

I made Granddad and Grandma, Annie and Nola blueberry pancakes and scrambled eggs the morning after Granddad arrived home. I served Grandma and Granddad in bed. Grandma was in white lace with her white curls down around her shoulders. Granddad was smiling. He so loved Grandma, even though I think she wears him out. Still, romance would keep him young.

I thought about Steve. He was coming to Portland to speak about his book in a concert hall here, sponsored by Powell's Books. It had been announced in the newspaper many times. The event was sold out. He was Steve Shepherd, after all.

I did not have a ticket.

I could call him to say hello, but I wouldn't.

I couldn't.

I could still smell the shack on me.

Boutique Magazine
A Life Coach Tells You How to Live It
By Madeline O'Shea
Things to Think About Before You Get Married

Ladies, I am not married.

I do not see myself ever getting married.

This is not because I can't picture myself in a

white dress (bad color for me, not a virgin) and
I think that a father walking his daughter down
an aisle to her new husband is a bit like leading
a pig to slaughter, although the pig has a very
fluffy veil on and is, probably, by that time,
chugging Valium.

The bride, not the pig. Pigs don't chug
Valium.

My friends, since we are approaching the
dreaded wedding season, think about the
following questions that I shall list. Why?
Because then you can avoid coming to my
office and telling me about how you hate, hate,
hate being married but are trapped for any
number of reasons, including, but not limited
to, children, money, health issues, religious
reasons, and so on. I am a life coach, specializing in relationships in your life. I should not be
doing marriage counseling, and I tell my silly
clients that all the time, but to save you fees
later, ask yourself the following questions
before you get married.

1. Why do you want to marry this man? No,
   honestly. Why? Think and think and
   think again. You're attracted to him,
   right? Your lust is scrambling your brains,
   the passion is overwhelming your
   thinking. Note: This is not a reason to get
   married. Trust me and my other clients.
   The passion will fade, and then you are
   left with each other. Be sure you like the
   "other."
2. Do *not* avoid red flags. This is what I hear
   in my office all the time. "He drank a few
   times a week when we were dating . . .
   sometimes he drank too much." Truth:

He is an alcoholic. "He did drugs, but only occasionally, for fun, with friends." Truth: He is a drug addict. "He watched porn but he said it wasn't insulting to me, or us, he did it to relax." Truth: He is a porn addict. "He had a temper, but if I didn't push his buttons, he wouldn't have flown off the handle." Truth: He is an abuser. He is already manipulating you. "He's kind of boring, I guess, and controlling, but he's reliable." Truth: You will be so stifled by this man you will want to drown yourself in a human-sized pot of chili by the second year of your marriage. "He doesn't listen very well, but no man does." Truth: He doesn't listen because he doesn't care what you have to say unless it is about him. "He gets upset when I ask him to help me with the house or cleaning or errands." Truth: You will be a maid if you marry him. "He doesn't ask me a lot of questions about my day, my life." Truth: He is a narcissist. These are red flags. Red flags mean: Do Not Marry Him.

3. Are you done living your life? Have you gotten the degrees you want? The job? Have you traveled? Have you met lots of different people and lived in different places? When you are married with children, even though you will love your children more than you ever thought possible, much, if not all, of that fun stuff will come to a screeching halt. If you are a woman you will put yourself on the back, back, back burner to care for your family.

Are you ready to be on the back burner? Don't kid yourself that this won't happen to you like it happened to your mother. It will.

4. Is there a significant age difference between the two of you? Doesn't matter now? When you're thirty, and he's fifty, it will. What about religion? Think you can work your two religions out? What about when the kids come? Are you sure on that? Money problems can throw your marriage into a tailspin. Do not think it is fun to be with someone who spends all sorts of money to have fun. Your escalating Visa bill will smash all passion between you before you can say, "We're bankrupt." Do you hate his mother, his family? This is blunt: Don't marry him. You do not want to spend every holiday with people you can't stand. After the third year of marriage, honestly, the man you're sleeping with now will not be worth having a lousy Christmas each year for the rest of your life. Has he been divorced a couple of times already? It's likely you're going to be divorcée number three.

5. Are you 100 percent ready to commit yourself to one man for the rest of your life? Some people say you should have one marriage for your young love, a second marriage to raise kids, and a third for a friendly companion in old age. Not a bad idea, I say, but never underestimate the destructive nature of a divorce. Divorce will smash you from the inside

out and keep smashing for years, and I'm
not even starting in on the demolition it
will bring to your kids.

Ladies, think on this one. We have an
antiquated, almost biological need to get
married in this society. It is from our
puritanical roots. Marriage is a lovely
relationship, I hear from my few happily
married clients, when it works. When it
doesn't, you will reach levels of loneliness,
despair, depression, and fury that you did not
know exist. So, be sure before you get married
that you don't think with your nether regions,
think with your brain. Do not despair that
you'll never get married, think of how you'll
feel if you're on a camel in India having the
time of your life. Do not think in terms of the
perfect husband and kids, think in terms of
pretty good. Because, honestly, that's what you
can hope for out of life: That is will be pretty
good.

Above all, ladies, be strong. Be yourselves.
Like yourself. Be courageous and adventurous
and curious. Be open-minded to people and
ideas and new thoughts and hobbies and
directions. Be *you*. Be the new you. Be open to
changing you. Because when you are the you
you want to be, and you have been that you for
a long time, that is when you are ready to
consider getting married, if this is something
you wish to do, and you find someone who
embraces *all of you* as we humans embrace the
sun for basic survival. And do not get married
one minute before this happens.

Wait for the sun.

When I was done with my article, I walked down to our pond, sat on the dock, and thought about the sun. About my personal sun.

I thought about what it would have been like to be married to Steve all these years.

How many kids would we have? Where would we be living? What would our career paths be like? Would I have a career or would I be at home with the kids full time?

I thought about sex with Steve.

I thought of all those photos I'd saved of him.

Yes, I think I could roll around naked with him, I do. He's probably the only man on the planet I could roll naked with, the only one.

I smiled as the blue heron flew across the water, elegant, strong, independent.

What was Steve's pond like?

26

My momma made the best of her time in jail.

This is not to say that she liked it but, as she told us, "I gathered my hellfire, don't forget that line, Madeline and Annie, sometimes you gotta *gather your hellfire,* and I made the most of a difficult situation. Did you know they don't allow high heels in prison?" She winked at us. "No pink, either! I broke my own cardinal rule: Don't be frumpy! Let yourself shine!"

The warden of the women's jail had a sister who was a customer of Momma's, and she raved about Momma's Marie Elise's Excellent Cuts and Cuticles. The warden asked Momma to cut the inmates' hair and do their nails. You had to earn the haircuts and the manicures, though. You couldn't get one automatically, like a standing appointment on Thursday at four o'clock after mopping or laundry duty. So, using that bribery, the ruckus at the jail went way, way down. It's amazing what a cut and style can do!

"Those girls," my momma told us one day when we were visiting, "at least most of them, have been led astray by the men in their lives. They had terrible childhoods and they were led into drugs or alcohol and made messes of their lives. I tell them, when you get out of jail, practice the I Am Me, Stay Out Of My Way program. I tell them, you go to college and get a degree, you get training, you stay away from those gutter-minded idiots. Keep your hair and nails trimmed and styled all the time, proper and pretty. If you're broke, buy one crisp white blouse and one pink blouse, one pair of beige pants, one pair of black pants, and never be without a black skirt and black heels. Put your chin up, your shoulders back, and walk like you're worth it. That's the Shake Your Confidence and Strut talk I give."

She led hairdo and makeup classes at the jail, which she called "Being a Lady" classes. It was "how to look like a respectable lady and attract respectable people to you, not bad people, not slutty people, not criminals, but respectable people, because you ladies are respectable!"

She told me later, when she was out of jail, "Honey, I had to do something in there, had to help those other ladies, or I'd lose my mind. I missed you and Annie so much, my stomach almost ate me alive. Now let me give you an updo with those curls of yours, and we'll play dress up with Annie. Go and get your sister."

After the shooting, Grandma and Granddad moved permanently into our house. There were attorneys, advisors, and experts coming in and out all the time, like ants. My momma's trial was coming up faster than any other trial because everyone knew Marie Elise was dying.

The enormous amount of publicity from my momma's shooting lent a hand to speed, too. We were on the rocket docket.

Our grandparents gave us the attention they could, but their main goal in life, almost all they could think of, was getting their critically ill daughter, whose headaches were increasing, even with the medical attention the hospital was offering her, out of jail.

I watched my granddad order everyone around. He told the attorneys and everyone else what to do. He was in on every meeting, every plan, every thought, every idea. He yelled. He was intense, driven, focused.

He would save his daughter or die trying.

I watched my grandma handle every minute detail. She was the co-boss. She was the organizer; she was the one with the notebooks, the law books, the phone. She was the one calling on experts all over the nation. She hardly slept.

She would save her daughter or die trying.

Annie and I, we missed our momma so much, we felt like dying.

Nighttime was the worst. Annie and I slept together. We ached for our momma, for our dad. And the replay of the day in court when our momma blew three men away to hell hardly stopped.

My momma's trial started on a clear, blue, nervous day, where even the clouds were skittish and wanted to get out of town. Again, I will only repeat the highlights of this particular trial, not the whole thing.

Momma wore a white, slim-fitting dress with maroon-pink trim that dropped to about an inch above her knees. She wore gold hoops in her ears and two bracelets, one from Annie and one from me, which we made with puca shells and pink and yellow plastic flowers. We made ourselves matching bracelets, too. She wore a yellow ribbon in her hair, for hope.

She was gorgeous, even though she was clearly, to us, worn out, pale, exhausted.

She'd been in jail for three months and she had a tumor in her head. That'll take a bit of a toll.

Her attorneys' defense?

That would be temporary insanity.

I got it. It meant that my momma temporarily lost her mind.

Here's what I also got, as did Annie: Our momma had never lost her mind. Not one inch of it. Every bullet that came zipping out of that gun was premeditated. The only question on the Gunshot Day was if she should wear her darker pink dress that resembled smashed cranberries mixed with lemonade or the lighter one with the daisies. She liked daisies.

The prosecuting attorney's name was Terrence Walters III. Fancy name. Not so fancy family. He'd been brought in from a whole other city. Truth was, there were other prosecuting attorneys who could have, and should have, handled the case against Momma. Why didn't they? It was because of Marie Elise's

French Beauty Parlor. All the prosecuting attorneys in the area had wives, mothers, sisters or cousins, who were clients.

As I heard it later, one of the prosecuting attorneys said, "If I go after Marie Elise, my wife will never sleep with me again. I'm Catholic, I can't divorce, so my life is looking pretty bleak without sex."

"I can't prosecute Marie Elise. Hell, she came to my sister's house every four weeks for a cut and dye when she had mono. No way."

"That is not gonna be my case," Maggie Gee's brother said. "I would have done the same thing that Marie Elise did if someone went after my daughters except I would have used my hunting rifle, because I'd be going hunting."

So we had Terrence Walters III from Boston up against my momma. He had the slickness of a city attorney and the ferret face of a man with a pinched-up personality. His family line had been in and out of jail for generations and he was the first "break out," so to speak. To be fair, his father, a convicted murderer of two whom he popped off in a drunken bar fight, was quoted as saying his son made a mistake in prosecuting "that sweet woman with the beauty parlor."

The jury was seated, the courtroom jammed with everyone we knew, the news reporters and the cameras lined up like sardines along the wall. It was déjà vu all over again, times ten.

"This woman," Terrence the Ferret said as he pointed at my momma at the defense table, as if the jury needed help in locating her, "in cold blood, shot three men who were seated right there, *right there,* folks, not three months ago. She took the law into her own hands." He spread out his hands. "We're not disputing the crime that Mr. Barnes and Mr. Gyrt and Mr. Samson committed. Not at all. What those boys did wasn't good. It wasn't good."

Wasn't good? I shrank in my seat. Grandma put her arm around me and Annie. No, what had happened to us "wasn't good." Grandma was dressed impeccably, jewelry, scarves, a designer dress. Beside her sat Granddad, also impeccably dressed in a suit and tie. I swear they'd both aged ten years in months. Annie and I wore pink dresses and pink sweaters.

The Rubensteins were in the row behind me.

"It wasn't good?" my momma called out, her back straight in her white dress with the maroon-pink trim. "It was criminal. It was a criminal act against two innocent, young girls."

Terrence the Ferret's mouth dropped. "Your honor!"

The news reporters scribbled.

My momma's expensive attorneys put their hands on her arms to quiet her.

The judge glared at my momma. "It's not your turn to talk, Mrs. O'Shea. You will wait your turn."

I knew the judge, Victor Mangiotti, vaguely. He was the granddad of my girlfriend, Sally, at school. Sally always said he was the, "Awesomest Poppa ever. We go fishing all the time. He knew your dad, Madeline."

"Since it is his turn to talk," Momma went on, "it would be a good idea if he did not dismiss the heinous crimes committed against my girls as *not good*."

"Mrs. O'Shea," the judge warned.

My momma waved a hand like, Fine, I'll be quiet, but my momma was livid. *Livid.*

And when my momma got livid, she got smart. She always outsmarted my dad when she was mad at him. When he was late for dinner for the third time, she served him chicken. The chicken was still alive. He was never late again. When he was grumpy with her one night, she packed his cooler for lunch the next day and a live toad popped out. No food.

I was miserable, but a tiny part of me wanted to see what my momma would do.

Terrence the Ferret humphed and babbled on imperiously, facing the jury, and told them what happened when my momma had a ladies' gun in her hand and *bang, bang, banged* it. "People, we don't have the right to administer justice ourselves. That's not what our judicial system is about. It's not what our Constitution is about. It's not what this country is about! We leave the law to the law. In fact," he shouted, "the law worked

in Marie Elise's favor. Sherwinn, Pauly, and Gavin were going to
jail! There was justice here. The system worked. We can't have
women"—it sounded like he was spitting the word *women*
out—"parading about who shoot others in a courtroom with
hundreds of people present. We can't have *women* murdering
other people because they're uptight about a verdict. We can't
have *women* wielding guns and shooting men who make them
mad. We can't have it. We need safety and truth in our justice
system. Truth! Safety! Not *women* taking control!"

The *women* on the jury were not happy.

"She thought it out. She planned it. She executed the plan.
She's not sorry for it. You, the jury, have to tell everyone, in this
state, this nation, that taking revenge, not following the law,
murdering people is not the answer. If you don't convict this . . .
this *woman*"—he sneered at my momma—"we'll have people
shooting each other right and left, with impunity, with a reck-
less, anti-American disrespect of the law. Don't do it, folks,
don't turn America into an anarchist country!" Terrence the
Ferret pointed a finger at my momma. I cringed. Annie whimpered.

"Mrs. O'Shea is claiming she temporarily lost her mind." He
scoffed. "Temporary insanity. Marie Elise O'Shea had not lost
her mind. She was not temporarily insane. She had not lost it to
grief. She wanted to kill those men in cold blood. And—!"

And there it was. My momma was quite clever. She wasn't an
O'Shea for nothin'. She gazed right back at Terrence the Ferret
and . . . *smiled.* She smiled. She knew her beauty. She knew it
would throw him.

Terrence stared at my smiling momma, the words stilling in
his mouth. His mouth opened. It stayed opened, shocked. He
could not move or speak; it was as if someone had stuck him
with a spear. I saw him visibly relax, basking in that smile, that
peace and warmth, that sexiness.

"And—" he said, but he couldn't gather his thoughts.

I saw my momma wiggle her shoulders in her chair.

"And—"

I heard her attorneys snicker.

Terrence's face flushed more. "She—"

My momma, I saw it, she stuck her chest out—she was heartily endowed—and wound a curl around her finger.

"Mr. Walters," the judge rapped out. "You were saying?"

Terrence the Ferret ripped his eyes from my momma's smile and that heartily endowed chest. He pulled on the neck of his white shirt, cleared his throat. He stole a peek back at my momma and I saw his Adam's apple bob. "And this . . . this pink *woman* shot the men with her sex pistol and she—"

He stopped, mortified. *A sex pistol?*

"This woman, Marie Elise," he backed up, as my momma continued to smile at him and wiggle, wiggle. "She whipped up her breasts . . ."

People in that courtroom gasped and tittered.

"I m-m-m-mean," Terrence the Ferret stuttered, "she whipped out her gun from her cleavage and she shot the honkers."

The honkers?

Terrence the Ferret wiped his forehead as my momma ran a finger over her lower lip.

One of our expensive attorneys had a hand over his mouth so he wouldn't laugh with the rest of the people in court.

"She didn't shoot the honkers," Terrence the Ferret argued with himself, "she shot my clients with her . . . with her . . . with her soft guns. I mean, she shot them with a gun from her breasts." He slapped a hand to his face. "With a gun from the inside of hidden . . . in her dress! There was a gun in her dress *big bra!*"

This was almost funny.

The news reporters scribbled.

My momma fanned herself, tilted her head.

Annie snuggled closer to me.

"She," Terrence said, flushed and blotchy while pointing at Momma as she tossed back her hair, "in hot blood, I mean, in cold blood, shot three men naked! No, that's not what I meant! She shot three men and they died and they were angry they died!"

Maybe they were angry they died. I didn't care. Was I supposed to care?

Everyone laughed.

"Are you all right, Mr. Walters?" the judge droned.

"Yes! Yes!" He wiped his sweaty forehead. "But I want to remind everyone that this pinkish woman is remorseless and wears a bra! No, no! She keeps a gun in her bra! Look there, no, don't look. There's a gun! No guns!"

Terrence the Ferret was done and he knew it. He covered his eyes.

"Anything else, Mr. Walters?" the judge asked.

My momma grinned.

"No." He glared, sweating, at my momma. "She's a bad, bad, nasty bad woman who shoots men in the hard groins!"

More laughter. Terrence the Ferret looked pale and sickly, but he had one more argument.

"*Women* should not shoot men they're mad at. *Women* should not have the guns to do that. They should not have their racks up and shooting. They can't take the law"—he turned and stared at my momma and pointed a finger as my momma drew a finger down her cleavage—"into their breasts!"

Laughter filled that courtroom, even the jury box, but I could tell, even as a kid, that this attorney had ticked that jury off. Especially the *women* on the jury.

It was my momma's head attorney's turn to talk.

Dale O'Conner had been raised in the south before moving to Boston and used his drawl to his advantage, through and through. Elegant, but a homebody type. Smart but not snobby. He opened with some down-home information about himself.

"Hello, everyone. My name is Dale O'Conner. My whole family worked in the mines." He smiled softly. "My father couldn't believe I wanted to be an attorney but, folks, there was something about the law I couldn't step away from. I believe in the law, you see. I believe in justice. I believe that people should face the consequences of their actions, but I also believe that the law shouldn't be too punitive. I believe all that. When my dad was working in the mines he sometimes called a dangerous spot the 'dark zone.' "

He paused, pushed his hands in his pockets. "That's what we got here, folks. A dark zone. You've met my client, Mrs. Marie Elise O'Shea. Her husband, Big Luke O'Shea, who owned O'Shea's Fisheries, was the father of their two girls, Madeline and Annie. He died in that ferocious storm a few years back in the Atlantic. That loss 'bout crushed my client. She loved her husband very much. But she kept working at her beauty parlor, kept taking care of her girls, and when she thought love came along a couple of years later, she took a chance on it. She took a chance on love. Who among us hasn't? We're humans, we take a chance on love."

I saw the women in the jury smile wistfully. A man wiped an eye.

"That ended disastrously. Her daughters, Madeline and Annie, were horribly abused by Mr. Barnes and Mr. Gyrt and Mr. Samson. Monsters all of them. I cannot begin to describe the . . ." Here Dale stopped, as if to control his feelings. "I cannot describe, as a parent, how it would be to know the terror, the grief, the desolation that Marie Elise felt when she found out what had happened to her sweet, innocent daughters, what crimes had been committed that those men were rightly convicted of." Dale cleared his throat, then told the jurors, in short, quick form, what had happened to Annie and me in the shack and showed the photos to the jury.

We bent our heads, so humiliated, so hurt, ashamed.

Our momma didn't want us in court, but our grandparents, and their attorneys, knew the impact we would have on that jury. Free the mother! She shot those men for her two daughters! Here they are! In pink!

"I have daughters. Two of them. And I have three sons. You all probably have kids, too—nieces and nephews. Maybe grandkids. How would you feel if this happened to your children, your grandchildren?" He waited that one out, so the jury could build their own graphic images. "Why, it's unimaginable, and if it did, I can guarantee you, you'd feel rage and pain cracking your mind wide open, like a split watermelon."

Most of the jurors nodded.

"I'm telling you, folks, we parents and grandparents lose our cotton-pickin' minds when our kids are threatened, if we think their health, their safety, even their emotional health is in jeopardy. We fly into Papa or Mama Bear mode, don't we? Nothing matters except our kids when we get right down to it. We don't love anyone more than we love our kids, do we? We might love our spouses mighty hard, and our parents, our brothers and sisters, but any parent, when you get right down to it, they love their kids the most, they love those kids to distraction. They love them *completely*."

He had those jurors; those heads were bopping.

"And after all the trauma the girls had been through, the crimes, when Sherwinn, Gavin, and Pauly were being held in jail before their trial, she started getting letters." He read the letters where Sherwinn threatened to kill us, and the jury blanched. "Here's another sad fact, folks. Marie Elise has got a brain tumor. Her days are numbered, sadly enough."

"Oh, no!" a woman on the jury declared, shaking her head.

"That's a damn shame," another said.

"Objection!" Terrence the Ferret snapped.

"Overruled and be quiet," the judge said.

"Marie Elise knew she wouldn't be around to protect her girls. She knew with those monsters out of jail in a few years, her girls would never be able to grow up and become mommas themselves, become grandmas, so she shot them, killed them, right here, by golly. You could call it self-defense. I would."

"Objection!" Terrence the Ferret yelled, on what grounds I don't know.

"Overruled," the judge said.

Dale rocked back on his heels, blinked his eyes to get those tears out of there! "What happened is not in dispute, folks. You're gonna get the details of the shooting, I'm sorry to say. I'm not arguin' it, not at all. I won't lie to you, I've got nothing but honest words for all of you, but Marie Elsie isn't guilty, no sirs, no ma'ams, she's not." He stuck his hands in pockets. "The prosecuting attorney, Mr. Walters, will tell you that Marie Elise was as clear as a bell that day, smart as a tack, that it was all coldly calculated. Premeditated. Planned. And you know what, folks?"

He raised his eyebrows.

"He's wrong. My client—" He turned to look at my momma in her white dress. "My client, Marie Elise, was temporarily insane. Why, she plumb lost her mind. Just plumb lost it." He leaned toward the jurors. "Now y'all tell me something, and be honest with yourselves right here, right now. If monsters like Sherwinn, Pauly, or Gavin had come after your kids, wouldn't you have lost your mind, too?"

The jury nodded.

"Yep," a rangy, muscled man in a red plaid shirt said, slow like honey.

"I would have!" a female juror announced, huffy and puffy. "I would have!"

Terrence the Ferret audibly groaned. "Objection," he said, but it was rote, defeated.

I know for a fact that if my grandparents weren't fighting for the very life of their daughter, they never would have let me testify again. Annie was not speaking. It was determined that we would not even try to put her on the stand.

"You can do this, kiddo," Dale told me privately. "Just tell the truth. Do it for your mom. Keep your eyes on me, don't look away. Pretend it's just you and me. Don't be scared. I'll be with you the whole time."

Over my momma's vehement objections and pleadings, out loud, in court, I testified into that packed courtroom.

I did what Dale told me to do because I wanted to save my momma.

I told about how Sherwinn, Pauly, and Gavin put blue sheets over our heads so we couldn't see then put ropes around our necks and giggled and called us the Blue Ghosts.

I had to stop because one of the jurors said, "Aw, shit and hell," blunt and loud, and I got distracted, but Dale told me to look right at him and answer another question and I did because I wanted to save my momma.

I told how I was embarrassed to be naked and having men touch me and it made me cry.

I had to stop again when two women on the jury made gasping sounds and they distracted me. Dale told me to look right at him, and I did even though I had to keep wiping my face. I did it to save my momma.

I told how the cigarettes burned my bottom and how I didn't like seeing Annie thrown against walls.

I had to stop when Carman said, "For God's sakes, that's enough! That's enough!"

And Shell Dee moaned, "Lord help her, Lord!"

I told everything. I did it for my momma.

"Madeline, what did you tell your momma about a week before Sherwinn's, Pauly's, and Gavin's trial?"

I sucked in my breath as a whole pile of nasty memories sunk down on my head. I closed my eyes. I wrapped my arms around my body. I heard a moan slink out of my mouth.

The judge waited.

The jury waited.

The news reporters waited to scribble.

Everyone in the room held their breath.

"Madeline?" Dale said, gentle.

I wanted to cry. I wanted to die. I wanted to disappear.

For one second, I looked up and gathered my hellfire, as my momma would have said. Annie, my sister, my best friend, was standing in the courtroom. The one who wore tutus with me, grizzly bear outfits and kimonos. She held up her wrist and pointed at it. She was wearing a bracelet like our momma's with puca shells and pink and yellow plastic flowers just like I was.

I put my hand over my bracelet and took the deepest breath of my life.

"Before my momma shot Sherwinn and Pauly and Gavin, I

told her what they did to me in that room with no windows. I whispered it to her." I rocked back and forth again.

Dale took a deep breath. "And what was that?"

"They did the ice-cream truck with me."

No one moved an iota, but the tension flared sky high.

"The ice-cream truck?" Dale said.

I saw my granddad sag in his seat.

My grandma bit down hard on her lip.

My momma kept her eyes right on mine, but that didn't stop her anguish.

"He did something bad to me. It hurt. When I screamed he hit me in the face. He said, 'How do you like the chocolate ice cream?' "

Sobbing was audible.

I heard someone swear.

"He did other bad things with me with ice cream. Vanilla and strawberry." I detailed the bad things and the photography. *Click, click, click.*

"Why is Marie Elise on trial at all?" someone from the back yelled. There was general agreement.

Somebody else called out, "Marie Elise ain't guilty. She ain't guilty."

I heard someone yell, "This trial is a travesty."

"Quiet down." The judge rapped his gavel. "Quiet."

My grandma's whole body was vibrating, as if someone were right inside her, wringing her around.

The Rubensteins were pale white.

"I told my momma everything. Everything. I told her about the ice-cream truck."

"What did she say to you, Madeline?" Dale asked.

I stared straight at my momma.

"My momma." I had to stop because I was crying, memories of the ice-cream truck, and Sherwinn and not being able to help Annie, mixing in with how much I loved my momma and how much I missed her, how alone and lonely I felt without her every single day.

"My momma told me that she loved me!" My voice rung

around that courtroom. "My momma told me that I'm a beautiful girl! She said she was proud of me." I heard my words pitch high. "She said I'm smart and a good girl. She said I'm special to her and my dad loves me, too." I thought of my dad, his hug and his smile. "My momma told me that nothing was my fault and she hated Sherwinn and Pauly and Gavin and she hated herself for bringing them into our lives, but Momma," I said to her, my voice crackling, "you didn't know. *You didn't know.* They told us they would kill us if we told."

"What did your momma do next?" Dale asked.

"My momma hugged me." I shook my head back and forth, back and forth, so exposed, so lost. "I didn't want to play ice-cream truck. I didn't want to be in the room with no windows. I didn't like them taking photos. But my momma loves me. I love you, too, Momma, I love you, too, Momma." I stood up in the witness stand. I wanted to hug my momma so much I ached, my whole body a radiating mass of pain. "I miss you, Momma, I want to be with you. I want you to come home, please, Momma, come home." I leaned over at the waist and yelled at her, "*Come home!*"

"Objection," Terrence said, so weak.

"Overruled," the judge said, rote.

I turned to the jury. "Please let my momma come home! *Please!* Please!"

"Objection," Terrence said, even weaker.

"Overruled," the judge said.

The jury members were in tears and comforting each other.

"I want you to come home, Momma! I want you to come home! Please, Momma! I miss you! I miss you so much! I love you!" My tears streamed down my face, like water from open faucets.

"Okay, I've had enough," the judge said, the best poppa in the world, as he swiped at his eyes.

Dale came up to get me, took my hand, and walked me back to my seat. I was not allowed to hug my momma, but I said to her, loud so she knew I meant it, "I love you!"

She blew a kiss back at me, her face a mask of misery, of desperation.

There were formalities to follow that one would expect over the course of an excruciating trial. The attorneys for each side were up and down, up and down, and there were closing arguments.

Terrence the Ferret's argument was short. He'd sunk into himself during the trial, stuck down in the seat like he was glue. He did not look at our momma, or at us, only at the jury. "You can't take the law into your own hands, even if it seems like you should. Mrs. O'Shea can't do it, either, even if she believes that the men who kidnapped, abused, and photographed her girls deserved to die. She thought they would get out of jail and come after her girls and kill them because of the letters she received, and she was probably right, but she still can't kill them. You have to find Mrs. O'Shea guilty even if you would have shot those men if they did the same thing to your kids or grandkids. Thanks for your time." He sat back down in his chair, back hunched.

Dale said, "Close your eyes and picture the faces of your kids and grandkids. See their freckles? Their gap-toothed smiles? Their messy hair? The time they were covered in mud, remember that? What about the way they eat snow cones? It's all over them, right? Think about their first day of kindergarten, how excited they were to go to school for the first time."

I watched the jurors' faces, their eyes closed. Each one of them had a sweet smile.

"Now, folks," Dale said, his voice bunny soft. "If someone played ice-cream truck with your kids, your grandkids, what would you do?"

Instantly their expressions whizzed to fury.

One juror, a man who was the size of a logging truck, started sobbing and didn't even bother covering his face. "Oh no, oh no . . ." he moaned. "Oh no . . ."

A woman hissed and raised herself halfway out of her seat.

Another juror stood straight up and yelled to Dale, jabbing his finger in the air, "I would kill him, man, I would *kill* him!"

His reaction seemed to surprise him, and he blinked a couple of times.

The judge banged his gavel.

Dale ended with, "At the beginning of this sad trial, I told you that Marie Elise plumb lost her mind. Heck, with that tumor she has in her head, who knows what that did to the poor woman. She was temporarily insane with rage and grief and fear, wouldn't you have been? Folks, let's not keep these girls from their mother for one more day."

The jury was dismissed.

The jury filed back in under five minutes. It was, and probably still is, the quickest determination of guilt or innocence in the history of this country.

"Jury Forewoman, do you have a verdict?"

"We do, your honor."

"What say you?"

"In the case of Massachusetts versus Marie Elise O'Shea, we find Mrs. O'Shea, *of course,* not guilty."

The courtroom exploded, deafening cheers and clapping, as the judge pounded his gavel, the reporters scribbled, cameras flashed. The jury forewoman had something else to say. She glowered at the prosecutor. "We do, however, find the prosecutor guilty of being *stupid.*" She shook her finger at the prosecutor. "Very stupid. Case never should have been tried, young man. You're responsible for bringing more pain to Mrs. O'Shea and her family. Shame on you. *Shame on you!*"

The courtroom exploded again, and I jumped over two rows to get to my momma's hug. She caught me midleap, her face wreathed in smiles, her yellow ribbon flying.

A photographer caught that photo, my excitement, my momma's radiating joy, my grandparents' euphoric happiness, the Rubensteins' fists in the air in triumph.

Annie didn't smile, but she had her momma back. She had her.

"I love you, Pink Girls," Momma said, her voice wobbling as she held us close. "I love you so much. I will love you forever and ever. Now give me a kiss."

*   *   *

How did Momma's French Beauty Parlor save her life? Everyone loved her. That's why none of the good prosecuting attorneys would take the case. That's why we got Terrence the Ferret. The attorneys had to go through tons of jurors before they could find twelve who weren't close friends of my mom or dad.

My momma shot three men in cold blood. That would be murder. It was clearly premeditated. She hadn't lost her mind. She was totally sane.

She came home a free woman.

Later that night, snuggled into my momma's bed with her and Annie, I closed my eyes and waited for my dad to appear. He did. He was smiling, his arms in the air, hands clenched.

Victory.

27

"That reporter, Marlene, called," Georgie said. She was wearing yellow rain boots, a white skirt, and a yellow sweater. "She wanted to know about your relationship with Steve Shepherd."

I slammed a book on my desk.

"Whoa. Bad feelings on that one, huh, Madeline? Anyhow, I asked that she-witch why she wanted to know and I got to talking to her and she said you and Steve grew up together and she was pissed off, I could tell, because she said that Steve Shepherd had his attorney file papers against her, too, like you, to stop this article, and Steve told her, himself, over the phone to 'Back the hell off' and told her that the article was 'inappropriate and hurtful' and 'What is wrong with you, Marlene?' "

Georgie tapped her boot. "Yeah, Marlene wasn't happy. She said that everyone in Cape Cod, and now this 'famous writer,' was down her throat, and she was upset because she has a book herself she's trying to get published, and she thought that Steve was going to get in the way of that because of who he is."

Georgie pulled on the ends of her hair, which were dyed yellow to match her outfit. "So. Is Steve an old love of yours or something?"

An old love.

Yes, that would be right.

My only love, too.

* * *

Steve and I used to write stories and poems together. We'd run off into the woods, or scramble down to the ocean, or tie on life jackets and paddle a canoe to the middle of a pond and write in journals (me) and notebooks (him). We'd take turns sharing with each other.

He liked snake stories for a while, then he moved on to snake families and all the problems they had with each other. He also wrote informational papers about snakes. I wrote about swans, like my grandma, only my swans were always wild and rode motorcycles and shot arrows and gave advice to all the other swans on how to live their lives, like my momma.

Sometimes I would write a paragraph of a story, he'd add a second paragraph, I'd add the next, switching back and forth, and we'd end up laughing till we were rolling on the grass. Other times I'd give him a silly sentence like, "My name is Frog Man. I like to eat..." and he'd have to write a story. He would tell me to write, "If I were a bee I would..."

"You're a good writer, Steve."

"Thanks, so are you. Do you want to read the fourth chapter of *The Snake and Me* now?"

Sometimes we'd read books, too, back to back under a tree, or lying on our stomachs in the tree house my dad built us. It was odd how many things we both liked to do.

We liked to tease a dog named Frisky. He was a bad, brown dog and liked to bite people. If you could leap over the fence wrapped around his backyard, run to the other side, and leap over the fence again without getting bitten, you won. I tried this run one time; Frisky ran out and bit me on the arm. While the other kids screamed, Steve leaped over the fence, stuck his hands in the dog's mouth, yanked it open, yelled at me to run, then took off himself when I was over the fence, my pink dress ripping as I leaped off it.

He was like that. He would take the bite for me.

What would have happened if, over the years, I had called him back, or thanked him for the flowers or funny gifts he sent periodically? What would have happened if I had accepted one of his humorous, kind offers to meet him for dinner or fishing or canoeing?

What would have happened?

I sniffled.

What if?

"I'm being blackmailed."

Annie stilled across the table from me under the gazebo. It was drizzling teeny raindrops, as if the skies wanted only a scattering of attention. Door and Window were with us, white and fluffy, sitting by Annie, their mother.

"By who?" She clenched her jaw: Scream in.

"I don't know for sure, but I have an idea." I put my violin, with all its dents and scratches and butterfly blood stain, which came from the blood of my family, back in its case. "I'm sorry, Annie. I'm sorry. I didn't want you to know. I didn't want to involve you, didn't want to upset you," my voice wobbled, "but I think—"

"I think we're done with you trying to protect me, that's what I think," she snapped. "I don't need it and I'm sick of it."

I sat back, verbally smacked.

"I think we're done with you feeling guilty about what happened to us and you believing that you have to make it up to me for the rest of our lives. I think we're done with you treating me like a fragile kid sister. I'm trained in hand-to-hand combat, explosives, and weaponry. I know how to poison people, and I can kill anyone with my bare hands. I am not fragile. I am your equal and you need to remember that we were children, *children*, Madeline, when everything happened and you were absolutely heroic in what you did to save me, to help me. You hugged me every night when we were kids, you hit all three of those sickos so many times I can't count, and when we were in that shack, you held my hand constantly, so let it go." She grabbed both of my hands. "*Let it go.*"

"My whole life I've felt like I failed you."

"You didn't. You've never failed me. Never. We were kids.

They were shits. They're in hell being prodded by a pitchfork and I'm here on The Lavender Farm, with my family, my explosives, my chain saws, and my animals. I've got a job taking care of animals that, in their most violent moments, are still tame and polite compared to mankind. So," she said, businesslike. "Who is it? Who's blackmailing you?"

"I don't know." I was still reeling a bit from what she'd said. Could I let the guilt go?

"I see the envelope you've got. Give it to me."

I handed it to her. She slipped the photos out. Her expression didn't change much, but she was grim. "This isn't all of them, is it?"

"No." It wasn't even a quarter of them.

"Who are you thinking it is?"

"Do you remember that Pauly had a creepy son who lived with his mother most of the time? He had reddish hair, he was fat, and he pulled down his pants twice in front of us?"

She glared, not at me but at him, the creepy son, the vision in her mind. "His name was Sam."

"Yes, Sam. He may be living in that house, although it was so run-down, it'd be hard to believe a rat would live there."

"I'll take care of it." Decisive. Done.

"Annie, I want to call the police."

"Absolutely. Call them. But I need to go to Fiji first and make sure those photographs, whatever is still there, are incinerated, then you can call and we'll make sure Sam's going to jail. God knows what he's doing to other people, so let's lock the scummy flasher up. Do we have a deal? You can call the police when I return from Fiji."

I paused. "Yes. But don't kill him."

"I'm not going to kill him. It's not my style. But the photos are going to get a sunburn."

"Can I come with you?"

"No."

"Please."

"Don't even ask, Madeline. Remember my specialty: Explosives. And I work alone." She snapped her fingers. "That line, 'I work alone,' that's from a movie, isn't it? Sure sounded good."

We laughed. She leaned over and hugged me. "I love you."

"I love you, too, Annie."

"Let the guilt go, Madeline. Please. Explode it. It's killing you."

I bent my head and nodded. Door and Window crawled under the table and licked my hands. I would try. The guilt was killing me, day by day, constantly. It lived beside my lies to myself.

"It wasn't your fault," she said. "It wasn't mine. It was theirs, and you can't let them continue to rent space in your head like this. You have to block them out, shoot them, decapitate them. They have to go. The guilt has to go with them." She hugged me close. "I love you, sister. With all my heart and all my explosives, I love you."

Annie left the next day for Fiji because she is a wee bit off her rocker. She was back in two days. She did not have a sunburn.

I scoured the papers from my hometown. It did not take long to find the article. "Home owned by former convict burns to the ground. Inspectors believe the home may have been hit by a rogue lightning strike. . . ."

I stared at the ashes of what used to be the shack and the oak tree behind it. The tree was taller than I remembered. We had spent hours studying the knotty trunk, the interlaced branches, and the wind-brushed leaves of that tree. The trunk had burned in the explosion, but it was still standing. I did not miss the analogy there.

"Did you find anything?" I asked her over a pile of nachos with avocado and sour cream at the kitchen table about ten o'clock at night.

"Yep, I did. Pauly's son, Sam, is the one who's blackmailing us. There were stacks of photos of us in there, two envelopes addressed to you, one to me, and letters cut from magazines for the notes. I think Marlene tipped him off to who you were during her reporting—she told you she was going to interview Pauly's, Sherwinn's, and Gavin's families—and he went through his dad's stuff. The police were supposed to gather all that as evidence before his dad's trial, but obviously there was more. Pauly probably had some under the house or hiding in storage or at the photo shop."

So Pauly's son was living in his father's shack all these years. Disgusting. He was disgusting, his father was disgusting. But there had been no hope for him with a father like Pauly.

"The photos are gone. They're in Fiji."

"Thanks for sending them to Fiji." I envisioned that fiery explosion. "I'm impressed, as always, with your Blown to Kingdom Come skills."

"Thank you. I pride myself on my talents with explosives."

"Cheers to that." We clinked glasses. "Not every woman can blow up houses repeatedly and get away with it."

"Nope. Takes a lot of skill and training, thank you, and a salute to the United States government and various agencies."

We ate our nachos, extra cheese for me. "It makes me sick thinking of you even being in that shack again."

She was quiet for a while. "I waited till he left. He's fatter now with an odd tuft of hair on top of his head like an upside-down bird. I sat in that back room where they kept that cage. I stood in the living room where they did those terrible things to us. I looked out the same window at the oak tree. I smelled the pot, the mustiness, the dust, and all these horrible visions pummeled me, like I was being hit and hit and hit, but after about five minutes, I put my head up and I beat the hell out of those memories."

"Excellent. Did you beat them hard?"

"Yep. I hated being at that shack. It still smelled like infected and crazy male brain. But it was freeing in a weird way, too. We were attacked as little girls by three heinous men. We couldn't have prevented it. We were victims then but we're not now. *We are not victims.* Sherwinn, Pauly, and Gavin are all dead. Look what we've done with our lives. Look who we are. We've overcome what happened to us. We've overcome them and their shit-ass ways."

"Yes, I suppose we have. Or at least I'm working on overcoming them."

"No one can walk away from that and expect their whole life to be glorious and perfect, but we're here, Madeline. We're here and we're not letting what happened to us for a few months as kids dictate the rest of our lives. We've never done that, even if we've been chased by nasty visions." She had another nacho. It crunched. "I'm a vet, you're a life coach. We work hard, we're healthy. We have Grandma and Granddad and each other. Good things have happened to us. Many good things.

"And, those three," Annie went on, "they're all rotting in graves, maggots in their eye sockets, their bones cracking, while we spend a lot of time walking up and down rows of lavender, helping animals, hiking the property, and you tell everyone from your fancy schmancy downtown office what to do with their lives."

"That's true, but I don't like my fancy schmancy office. I don't like my fancy schmancy house or my fancy schmancy car. I do like these nachos." I had another one. I love the crunch of nachos.

"You're cracked, so am I. If you want to uncrack yourself you should let the lease go on the office, get rid of the house and the car, and start over. Live here permanently." She dipped her chip in a hunk of guacamole. "But we have the choice to start over. *We're* still here. No maggots anywhere."

"Starting over sounds good. A reset. And I'm pleased we have no maggots anywhere."

"Take your own advice, Madeline. Move. Change. Alter your freakin' path. Don't you use words like that?"

"Yes, I do." I thought of my upcoming speech for the Rock Your Womanhood conference, then dunked my nacho in salsa.

"I also went to the beach when I was there."

"You did? How was it?"

"I sat there for hours, watching the waves, back and forth, in and out."

"And?"

"And, I loved it. As you know, like you, I haven't been to the ocean in years, but maybe it's time, Madeline, maybe we should go."

The idea made me sad a bit, but excited, too. Our whole family had loved the sea until it had eaten two members. "I miss the sea."

"I've always missed it."

"So have I. I thought it would make me crack if I saw it again."

"You're cracked, anyhow."

"I am."

"Maybe we should dare, Madeline."

"I could take that dare. Maybe."

We sat for a bit, eating our nachos, cheesy, salsa-y, yummy.

"Love you, Annie."

"Love you, too, sister mine."

We put a nacho in each other's mouth.

They crunched.

Why is it that at nighttime we usually get most honest with ourselves?

Is it the cover of blackness?

Is it because what's bothering us—loneliness, frustration, anger, worry, regret, ambition, greed—keeps us up at night and we're alone with our thoughts?

Is it because night is quiet, the moon is staring at us, the stars are far away, and there's more truth in the air, more clarity, without the hassle and stresses of daytime?

Is it because people are asleep around us so we feel more alone as they skitter and toss through their own dreams?

Nighttime, way late at nighttime, is when I think best.

It was so darn dark and cold out that night. So darn dark. My dad would have said the weather felt threatened.

In my head, through that darkness, I heard Mozart's Great Mass in C Minor.

It was appropriate background music for my curiously methodical thoughts.

*   *   *

"That reporter, Marlene, called here today," Granddad told Annie and me the next night after a spaghetti and meatball dinner on the deck.

"Dammit," Annie muttered.

I stood up and paced, trying to find my breath, which felt like it was hiding in my lower back. I wanted to kick Marlene. I wanted to scream at her. I wanted to shove her against a wall and pummel her.

Annie got up and paced, too. We paced and passed each other, turned on our heels, kept pacing.

"What did you say to her?" I asked. Damn, but I hated Marlene. What was she thinking, talking to an old man who had had a heart attack after I told her not to?

Granddad didn't say much at first. He continued to swing on the swing. "I told her not to write the article."

"And she said?" Annie asked.

"She said the article was being written. She had a melodious voice."

"Did you tell her that you wouldn't speak to her?" Dread entered my body and whirled around, freezing cold and threatening.

"I did. We talked about how I wasn't going to speak to her. She was very pleasant."

"And you hung up?"

He nodded. "I did. But first she asked me if my parents were from Holland."

"Which they are not," I said.

"Granddad, where is she getting Holland from?" Annie asked. "Why Holland?"

Granddad went on as if he hadn't heard. "Jews have been running around the globe forever. Scattering to all corners, persecuted, hunted, destroyed . . . prey for others."

"Did she ask anything else?" Annie asked.

"She told me she had been looking at Holocaust records. She was very conversational."

The word Holocaust sunk heavily between us. "Why did she ask you that?"

Granddad's face crumpled for a long minute until he visibly pulled himself together, head up, shoulders back. "She asked because Anton, Emmanuelle, and Marie Elise Laurent died in Auschwitz after being in Drancy. So did their two other children, one boy, one teenage girl."

"*What?*"

"What the hell?" Annie muttered.

"Yes, the Laurents died in Auschwitz," Granddad said. "They died."

"So, a different family of Laurents?" I asked, completely confused, that sense of dread eating at me like a disease.

"Yes, they were different Laurents," Granddad said.

I sagged with relief. Not that I was grateful another family died, but there was something ominous here, frightening, that I didn't understand.

"So, she's confused," Annie said. "The reporter is confused and is including another family in her article?"

"No, she's not confused," Granddad said, leaning his elbows on his knees, head bent, before he pulled it up, as if he was pulling up a lead weight, his eyes tortured. "The Laurents died in Auschwitz. Their names were Anton, Emmanuelle, Marie Elise, Aaron, and Johnna Laurent."

"I don't understand," I said. "That's your name, Grandma's name, Momma's name. Help me, Granddad, what's going on here?"

"Why is she digging like this," Annie asked. "What is this? Why are we even talking about it? Who are Johnna and Aaron?"

"My dears."

I swear my granddad aged another ten years in front of us, as if the white light of the moon had sucked those years away.

"We are not the *real* Laurents."

28

Momma came home from jail, and three days later we had a bang-up, rocking-good party. "We have to celebrate life," she told us. "You Pink Girls, you are my life." She kissed and hugged us, then together we made chocolates brownies with mint, like our dad used to make us.

Most of the town came, and Momma was deluged in flowers and gifts. Granddad and Grandma brought in crab, shrimp, lobster, salads, and a cake in the shape of a sailboat. Tents were set up, a band arrived, twinkling white lights were hung.

My momma smiled, she laughed, she hardly left our side. We linked our arms around her waist and held on. Steve was there, but I couldn't meet his eyes, couldn't smile back at him, couldn't go with him and the other kids to run around our property, I couldn't. I was bad. I was less than him. Not good enough.

We had spent almost all of the past three days together with our momma, in our house by the sea. My momma, Annie and I, and our grandparents. We played games and laughed and talked and tried to recover from the disastrous wreck our lives had become.

My momma cut our hair and did our nails. We did her and Grandma's nails. Even Granddad let us polish his nails, as our dad had before us, and he proudly showed them off at the party.

The sun shone, the rain sprinkled, rainbows appeared everywhere, like magic—Marie Elise's magic. I heard triumphant violin music in my head as my momma and I played our violins together out on the porch for everyone at the party, with Annie inside banging on the piano.

But my momma was fading, we could all see that.

Fading quickly.

She went back to work at Marie Elise's French Beauty Parlor, that beacon of pink, but only when Annie and I were in school. I think she did it to keep her mind off herself and her terminal illness. She left early to be home when we got home. On Saturdays we went with her.

The hair spray poufed in plumes, the scissors snipped, the dryers blew, the chandeliers glittered against the pink walls, and the women chatted and laughed and passed bottles between them in the resting room overlooking the sea, which my momma ignored.

Carman burst into love songs, poured champagne for all and offered up toasts.

Shell Dee regaled us with information about the human body, how waste is made, and her frustration about losing weight. "Calories in, calories out. What I wish is that we had a bug we could swallow that would eat up all the extra food inside of us and make us skinny. Honestly, you know how many women would be scarfing those bugs if they knew they could be a size six? What's an itty-bitty bug inside your gut when you have a tight boom boom?"

Trudy Jo talked about her kids. "Steph is a teenage girl. That means her hormones rule her brain. She has a boyfriend now. So he rules her brain. She has lost hers. There is no fluid in there or anything else. There is the word lust. Lust rules her brain. What would Shakespeare say? 'We should be woo'd and were not made to woo.' "

We did our homework or read or brought the ladies pink cookies on platters with Red Hots or poured pink lemonade and helped clean up.

Maggie Gee brought Grandmother Schiller in for a Marie Elise Dye and Cut to Die For. Grandmother Schiller hugged my momma, her white hair swinging fashionably about her shoulders. "You nice lady, Marie Elise. Good shot, too. You got good shot. Bad men gone. Good job. How you like my hair today? I brush."

Jessie Liz's boy was still painting naked ladies on bare walls in town, but this time he'd painted a fat naked lady on a wall and the woman had half red and half pink hair. It was rumored that Tilda Smith was not pleased and threw a fit. Jessie Liz and Momma laughed so hard, Momma had to cross her legs so she wouldn't pee on her pink skirt with the ruffle.

LaShonda had not conquered her bra addiction, but she did bring three for Momma. "You're stacked, Marie Elise, I know that, and I think these will fit you fine. I'm so glad you're back, honey." The bras were purple, pink, and bright green with lace.

Momma asked our grandparents to stay permanently at our house by the sea. She did not need to ask again; they wanted to be with their daughter every day. They spoke French or German to us most of the time. Grandma taught us how to paint, Grand-dad taught us basic economics and how to run a business. We played by the sea, took the boat out and watched the sun set, ca-noed and hiked, laughed and sang French songs.

And, one day, a day with generous sunshine, a yellow circle of fire hanging politely in the sky, and a cool, melancholy breeze, our momma could not get out of bed.

Like that, overnight, our momma took a turn for the worse around a deadly corner.

She became pale, fatigued, wretchedly sick, her head aching so badly from that thriving tumor she couldn't move.

She went to the doctors, she went to the hospital.

There was nothing they could do.

The tumor was eating her.

The next Saturday Momma gathered up her energy and the five of us took the boat out. We sailed for hours, and we sat, cuddled up to our momma as she tipped her head back to the sun that shone on all of us like a warm blessing. We ate shrimp and crab sandwiches and lemon meringue pie.

My momma weakened further as the weeks wore on, the

pain in her head, constant and excruciating, and Annie and I cried on her many times, soaking her pink shirts, pink dresses.

"Girls, remember that we're a family," she told us, cupping both our faces with her soft hands, her nails painted pink. "Your dad, me, you two, Grandma and Granddad, your dad's parents. Take that love, take the love that we've always given to you, and hold it in your hearts, never let it go, believe in it, bask in it, build a future on it. Love transcends everything, even death. That means our love is always around you."

"But we'll miss you, Momma," I said, broken, a child who had lost so much and was about to lose more.

"I'll miss you, too." Her eyes flooded. She didn't hide the tears.

To this day, I am glad that my momma didn't lie to us, didn't deny the truth of her upcoming death. She didn't dwell on it, didn't bring it up much, but when she did, she was honest, she was frank, and she offered up her wisdom and advice for the rest of our lives: "Honey, you must go to college . . . you must not smoke or drink . . . do not have sex before you are married, earn that white wedding dress . . . you must choose a man who believes you are the sun, the moon, and the earth and will treat you every day as the precious woman you are . . . don't use too much hair spray, it'll give you helmet head . . . unless your house is on fire, there is no excuse not to wear lipstick . . . show compassion to others and don't you dare judge anyone harshly or, you mark my words, God will bring you down a notch or two . . . don't forget you're an O'Shea and a Pink Girl . . . high heels are a must, a *must,* because a woman must feel powerful . . . don't wear too much makeup or you'll look like a streetwalker . . . keep your breasts covered unless you are with your husband in the bedroom and then you may prance around in nothing, or cover yourself with only a red boa and flick it at him . . . don't ever forget that your dad and I love you more than anything and we will always be with you."

"What's going to happen after you die?" Annie asked one

night, finally speaking a little again, her body quaking in her blue owl pajamas.

"What's going to happen?" our momma said, a bit drugged out from the prescriptions that didn't do enough. "Why Big Luke, your dad, he's going to come down and get me. He's going to open his arms and I'm going to float into his, and we're going to fly over the sea because we all love the sea, all the O'Sheas love the sea, and we'll float over you, because we love you two so much, and we'll be together again, Dad and I, up in heaven looking out for you girls."

"Can he take us?" I asked, sobbing, my hands kneading my own blue owl pajamas.

"No, Pink Girl, he can't." Her voice was down to a whisper, her strength going, that fire-whipping pain radiating to every pore in her body. "We can't. We won't. You two girls have your whole lives. Decades ahead of you." She stopped and put a hand to her head. The pain was killing her. "But when you are very, very old, and it's your time, Dad and I will come and get you, with our arms out, and you'll float to us and we'll fly over the ocean because we all love the sea and we'll head up to heaven together in the clouds."

"I want to go now," Annie said. "With you. I want to go."

She kissed us on our foreheads and pulled us close, all three heads together, only one head being killed by an alien tumor. "I'm sorry, baby, I'm sorry."

We fell asleep in her arms, the three of us, Annie and I in matching blue owl pajamas, abject fear and grief spiraling through our dreams.

The next night, very late, our momma took our boat out.

By herself.

I woke up in her bed, Annie asleep beside me, and I knew our momma was gone.

I heard Vivaldi's *The Four Seasons* in my head as I tumbled out her French doors to the deck. Way off in the distance I saw our boat. I saw it under the white light of the moon, the sea soft and calm, barely a ripple, and I knew what our momma had done.

"No!" I screamed. "No!"

My screams woke up Annie, who started screaming, too, and she leaped up and hid under the bed until she realized we weren't at the shack amidst a sickening crime, we were at our house by the sea. The screams woke up Grandma and Grand-dad, who pounded into our momma's bedroom. I pointed to our boat, way out in the ocean, under the light of the moon, on that soft and calm sea, and Granddad took off running.

He tried, he tried so hard to reach her. He took Steve's par-ents' boat onto the water. Another neighbor heard our cries and took his boat out, too, speeding over the waves, but they were too late. Too late. Too late.

Too late.

It was what my momma wanted. She dropped herself into the sea. She ended her life, and the debilitating pain in her head, when and where she wanted to. She didn't want to suffer but, much more than that, she didn't want us to suffer further watching her. I knew our dad would come down and get her. He would hold out his arms and she would float to him and they would fly over the sea, because they loved the sea, all O'Sheas love the sea, and they would fly over us.

Out on the deck, still watching our boat, and way off in the distance, seeing Granddad and another neighbor racing out, I felt it. I felt a hug, I felt them, my momma and my dad around me. Annie felt them, too, because she tilted her face up and kissed the breeze, twice. I put my arms up and I felt my momma's kiss, my dad's whiskers. We had our last moments, our last hug, our last touch.

I felt them fade away, and Annie and I held hands, our grandma hysterical beside us, on her knees, keening, wailing in French.

I put my hand out, to catch my parents, but all I felt was the breeze, light, cool, swirling. I closed my eyes and saw my dad standing next to my momma, his arm around her waist. They were not smiling—in fact I could see tears on their cheeks—but I felt their love. I felt their strength. My momma was wearing a pink dress and pink heels, my dad was wearing his jeans and the painted cardboard whale around his neck. His nails were polished.

"Come back," Annie yelled, through Grandma's racking sobs. "Come back! Come back, Momma! Please come back! Momma, come back! Please! I love you, Momma, don't leave me. Don't leave me again, Daddy! Don't leave me! Please!"

I put my arms around her, and in my head the violins shut down, bows off strings, and I heard this, "We love you, sweet daughters, our Girls in Pink."

Steve's whole family tried to help us. All our friends tried to help us. Meals, flowers, gifts, offers of their cottages to go to during summer, ski chalets we could borrow, anything. Let us help you, they said. We want to help. We're sorry. We're so sorry about your momma!

But grief is a walk alone. Others can be there, and listen. But you will walk alone down your own path, at your own pace, with your sheared-off pain, your raw wounds, your denial, anger, and bitter loss. You'll come to your own peace, hopefully, but it will be on your own, in your own time.

Steve cried with me. Every time I cried, he cried.

He used all his allowance money and with his momma, a gentle woman, he went shopping and chose material for pink dresses for Annie and me and a pattern for his momma to follow. His mother sewed them up. They were vogue and straight lined, not fussy.

She must have been up all night for days because Annie and I wore the dresses at our momma's funeral. Everyone wore pink. All the ladies in their pink dresses and skirts, even the men had on pink ties, pink shirts. The wreath of flowers on her coffin was pink, a pink piece of satin underneath that, pink flowers packing the altar. Women talked about how much they loved my momma, how she'd changed their hair and changed their lives, how Momma's advice made them stand up and stick up for themselves. They talked about Marie Elise's French Beauty Parlor and the friendship and kindness they'd found.

Two weeks later Grandma and Granddad and a whole host of people helped us pack up our house. I'm not sure where a lot of the stuff went. My guess is that my grandparents gave much of the furniture away to people in need. Carman, Trudy Jo, and Shell Dee helped Annie and me gather two huge boxes each of our momma and dad's special things to keep, like china and teacups, photographs, gifts, pink outfits and pink heels, Momma's violin, the yellow ribbons, her jewelry, a tackle box, a few of his ties, and a couple of fishing poles. When we arrived in Oregon, those boxes went in the attic at The Lavender Farm.

Carman gave Annie and me tapes of Momma's favorite songs. Six tapes each.

Trudy Jo gave us a set of Shakespeare books.

Shell Dee gave us models of the human body and framed pictures of our momma with her arms around us at Marie Elise's French Beauty Parlor.

On a day when the clouds looked hysterical, ripping across the landscape, we climbed into the back of our grandparents' rented car and headed out of town. We took Bob the Cat with us in a carrier. She was still limping.

"Why is everyone outside on the street?" I asked my grandparents as we rounded the corner into town. I was wearing the dress Steve's mother sewed for me, my violin with the butterfly stain beside me on the seat.

My granddad stopped the car and stared at all the people lining the road, both sides. Grandma reached for his hand, and gasped.

I saw my teachers from school, our neighbors, the priests and ministers, all of our friends, and Steve. There was Steve, my snake-finding friend, with his parents, standing tall.

"Is there a parade?" I asked. I hadn't heard of any parade.

My granddad cleared his throat. My grandma grabbed a lace hanky and dabbed at her eyes.

"There's my violin teacher," I said. "And Mrs. Cooks, the librarian. And Sheriff Ellery. There's Shoney and his mom and Maggie Gee and her grandmother and Shell Dee, Trudy Jo, Carman . . . and all their kids . . . what's going on?"

My grandma's voice cracked. "They're here for you. For you and Annie."

"What? Why are they here for me?" I glanced at Annie. She was confused, too, but only mildly. She'd retreated pretty far back into her head again.

"They're here," Granddad started, then wiped a hand over his face. "They're here, my darling granddaughters, to say good-bye to you."

"Good-bye?" I said.

"Yes, honey," Grandma said. "They're here to say good-bye."

We drove through town slowly, windows down. Everyone waved. No one was happy. I saw people with handkerchiefs wiping their cheeks. They had signs that read, "We love you, Madeline and Annie" and "We'll miss you, Madeline and Annie."

I stared right at Steve. He stared back, then ran to our car and handed me heart-shaped rocks, his face miserable.

I watched him and all our friends grow smaller and smaller until I couldn't see them anymore and that was it and good-bye.

Good-bye.

We drove past the ocean. I thought of the storm that was furious that night, how it drowned my dad and sunk him. I thought of our boat, how Momma had dropped herself into the waves. Two people, gobbled up by that ocean. "I don't want to see the ocean again," I said. "Never."

Beside me, Annie shook her head.

Good-bye, everyone.

Good-bye, Dad.

Good-bye, Momma.

Good-bye, Steve.

I love you.

Good-bye.

29

As I drove to The Lavender Farm that night after seeing a crushing load of clients, the lights of the city and the suburbs fading and giving way to the orchards, farms, and barns of the country, I thought about my and Annie's conversation with Granddad on the deck.

"What do you mean, we're not the real Laurents?" I asked.

He stared straight out into the darkness, an owl soaring from one tree to another, a dark moving shadow. "We had to get out of France or die. In my quest to save my family, I did something terrible. This reporter, Marlene, I am sure she knows what I did. She looked up the records at Drancy, at Auschwitz, on a whim, on a gut-level hunch, by chance, I don't know. But now she has it."

"Has what? What did you do?" Annie asked, pushing her hair behind her ear, not a curl showing, like me.

"I got us papers. All five of us. Your mother, Grandma and I, your grandma Madeline, and Ismael. I had tried for weeks to get us papers, to get us out secretly, in trunks or trucks, through different channels, and I hit a dead end. Try, that's all Jews could do then, try. Try in the face of hopelessness and a marauding, murdering band of German thugs and a traitorous puppet government that turned their backs."

"How did you get the papers?"

"Were they forged?" I asked.

"Yes, they were forged. A few people were trying to help Jews get out before they were rounded up like cattle and gassed. *Gassed*. Human to human, one human to another: Gassed." He shook his head, the shock of that atrocity never going away.

"How did you get them?" Annie asked. "How did you get the papers?"

"How?" He looked at Annie and me, in turn, those old eyes a morass of raw pain. "I stole them."

"You stole them? From—" I stopped.

"From who?" Annie asked.

Please, no.

"From a man who did not deserve what I did," he said.

Please, no. *He didn't.*

"From a family who did not deserve their fate."

He did. *He had.*

Understanding dawned in Annie's eyes.

I could hardly believe it. My granddad had never stolen anything in his life. Never. He gave millions of dollars away a year. He was kind and respectful to everyone, his generosity was established . . . he couldn't have. *He couldn't have.* He wouldn't have . . . and yet, and yet.

He had.

He had stolen the papers for his family. For himself and his wife, Grandma Madeline, their two sweet children, our momma and her brother, for his wife's sister, a teenager, our Grandma Emmanuelle . . .

"I stole them from the Laurents," he said, his voice ragged. "The real Laurents. His family had been in France for hundreds of years. He had two brothers, Meyer and Sagi. They were good men. I knew them. Her family was from Holland. She was one of eight children. They had three children. Those Laurents went to Drancy first, then Auschwitz."

His eyes blackened with guilt and shame. "I stole from one family so my family could live."

I coughed, feeling like I was being strangled with shock.

"We almost missed the train that day. I had to go by their house, after I knew"—his voice broke—"after I knew that Ismael and Madeline would not need their papers, because they were dead, *dead*, I put the papers under the Laurents' door so two of them could get out, but it was too late. Too late. The Nazis had already been there."

"Granddad," Annie said, putting an arm around his neck as he wept.

"They died. They all died. I checked, from the safety of my farm and home in Oregon, from the safety of my fortune, from the safety of my business and the safety of my new American citizenship, I checked. I wanted to repay them, I wanted to give them all of my money, but they didn't make it. I killed them. It was me. I killed them."

"No, the Nazis killed them," I said, aching for the Laurents, for their family. "They killed them."

"I did. It was my family for theirs. I chose mine. I love my family, family is my everything. But was my family more *worthy* of survival? No. We were not. We were not better, we were not more exalted. We were not more loved by God. We were equals. And I chose my family over theirs. I chose. Like God chooses, only I did it for Him. I pushed the father to the ground, I hit him in the head. I knew he would have the papers on him and he did. The blood that poured from him. Poor man, poor man, and then I ran. I ran with his life, with the life of his wife and children. I ran and I left them there to die and I kept their name in my new country so we could start over, when they had no country at all, only barbed wire, barbaric living conditions, and ovens that never stopped burning."

I envisioned a fallen France. Invaded. Overthrown. Jews trying to get out, Jews rounded up, shoved in cattle cars . . . and Granddad's family, *my* family, knowing they would die, the children would die . . . and he going to this man's house and . . .

"Granddad," I said. So wrong, so wrong what he did . . . but . . .

That darn owl hooted again, haunting.

"You've lived with this forever—" Annie whispered.

"Every day of my life, I have thought of the Laurents. I see them in my dreams. I see them everywhere. It is the strangest thing. I see them *smiling* at me. All five of them. The family I murdered smiles at me. It makes it worse. They were good people. Smart. Kind. The father welcomed me into his home that day. 'Come in, come in, friend, quickly.' He hugged me and I cracked his head open. I have never been able to get rid of my guilt. It has stalked me, every day it has knocked me down." He was openly crying, a man who did not like to cry. " 'Come in,' he said." He groaned, fisted his hands together. " 'Come in, friend.' "

We hugged him close. What to say? How to comfort? A vision of a man, a good man, being smashed by my granddad . . . all frantic, all needing to get out, to get out *right away* . . .

"Granddad, that's why . . . that's why you donate so much money, isn't it? All the time."

"Yes, to atone. To make up for my crime. Every time I give money away, I write it down in my leather journal."

I knew that leather journal. Old and weathered, pages bent, it was in his office, in a drawer.

"I write down the name of the organization, I write, 'For the Laurents. For the Laurents.' Sometimes I list their names individually. Anton Laurent. Emmanuelle Laurent. Marie Elise Laurent. Johnna Laurent. Aaron Laurent. 'Come in, come in, friend,' he said." He broke down again. " 'Come in, friend.' "

We let him cry. We sat and let him cry while that darn owl hooted again and we crumbled on the inside.

"Everything I give away, it is for the Laurents. I am not worthy to even be here. It should have been them, but I stole their lives. Stole it. As my entire family was stolen from me."

Annie and I exchanged a glance, more confusion.

"As Grandma Madeline and Ismael were stolen from you," I said, needing to clarify as I sensed another secret.

He kneaded his fingers together. "There are more, granddaughters."

"More?" *More* secrets?

He inhaled, but it sounded like a mini, mangled scream. "Yes. When I say our entire family was stolen from us, I mean the *entire* family. I was born in Germany. So were your grandmas, Madeline and Emmanuelle. But all four of our parents left large

families in Germany for France. We visited as children, back
and forth the families went, from Germany to France and back.
But things were so bad in Germany, years before they were bad
in France. We tried to reach them and one by one, starting in the
late nineteen thirties, we couldn't. Some, I know, tried to get
out, but they were too late. I heard through a friend that one
family, our cousins, hid for about six months. They were betrayed, rounded up, sent to the camps. Another uncle and aunt,
their three children...they went to a hidden cabin in the
woods. No one heard from them again after the Nazis went
through. Others were arrested. They were intellectuals, always a
threat. Professors and artists and scientists. Many musicians.
There were six violinists in the family in Germany. They were
gone. Gone. When the war ended, there was no one left. *No
one.*"

"You checked."

"As best I could." He wrung his hands. "I hired a man there.
We had the names of our family members. My uncles and aunts,
cousins, the grandparents. Young children, old people, teenagers.
They were shipped off to various camps all over Germany. And
that was it. They were gone. Disappeared. Eradicated." He
wiped his eyes. "You know how they got out of the camps?"

I didn't move. My lack of breath wouldn't allow it.

Annie clenched her jaw to keep the you-know-what in.

He pointed a trembling, old finger up to the sky. "That's how
they got out. They were burned, their ashes shot through the
sky, then scattered, and out they went. They went by ash. Their
bodies, their bones, their blood, their minds, their talents and
skills, their love and compassion, their memories and dreams,
all burned. They floated in the wind, all over Germany, all over
Europe. Who knows where they floated to after that. Who
knows? Did their ashes land in Berlin? Did they land in another
camp, where another relative was starving to death, being ex-
perimented upon, digging a ditch to fall into? Did they land on
a Jewish friend's shoulders as they were moving rock, as they
were packed into cattle cars, as they were marched through the
snow? Did they go farther, to Russia, where the soldiers were

freezing to death on their makeshift battlefields? Did they travel to Poland where the Nazis treated all Poles as subhuman? Or did my relatives catch a current of air and make it to America? Do they see my life now, this home, my business, our family? Are they glad for me? Do they miss me? Do they resent me, that I lived but their children did not? Are they ashamed of me? Have they disowned me for what I did?"

I squeezed his hand, wordless. What do you say to this?

"My relatives, your relatives, they became ash." He held his head. "And I caused the other family to become ash, too, the Laurents. Jews were turned to ash."

"Granddad, I've never seen you . . . you've never practiced your faith."

"No." He shook his head. "We came here and I told God I would no longer practice my faith. I am unworthy. I am unforgiveable. My guilt has near killed me." He laughed, no humor. "We even bought Christmas trees, bought into a holiday that wasn't ours. I tried to put the past behind me, not talk about it, shut it out, because the pain was going to kill me, kill your grandma. Kill us both. Some pain is so grievous that talking about it does not alleviate it, only exacerbates the physical agony. But your wonderful grandma and I shared our love for Madeline, for Ismael, and we were determined to provide a happy life for your momma."

He was tormented, so tormented.

"Did our momma later, when she was an adult, know about the papers, about the Laurents?"

"No, she didn't know about the Laurents. When she was older, and asked about our escape, I told her I had the papers forged, but I didn't tell her I stole them. Why would I do that? Why would I burden her?" He groaned. "She was burdened enough. She had lost her mother and brother, her grandparents, her homeland, her family in Germany, her home."

I thought about our momma, playing her violin outside, speaking in French to someone. "Did our dad know about this? About your escape from France? About Grandma Madeline and Ismael?"

"Yes, he knew. Your momma told him. She had to. It explained why she cried at unexpected moments, why she talked to Ismael, why your name had to be Madeline, after her mother"—he nodded at me—"and why your name"—he nodded at Annie—"had to be Anna. Your momma's real name was Anna. Before she wore a blue coat with blood on it and became Marie Elise Laurent."

Anna. My momma's real name was Anna, not Marie Elise. What was her last name, then? Her real last name? What were Granddad's and Grandma's real last names?

"Your momma needed your dad to help her," Granddad went on, "to understand, to hold and comfort her, and he did. He was a real man, strong enough to carry your mother's losses."

I put my arms around him on one side, Annie on the other, those broad shoulders bent, almost doubled over.

I remembered what Grandma had said, though. She did know, she had always known about the papers, about what her husband had done. She had kept that from him, so her knowledge would not be another weight for him to carry. "I love you, Granddad."

"I love you, too," Annie said.

"How can you?" he rasped. "How can you possibly now that you know who I am? A murderer, a taker, a betrayer, a coward, a man who sent a fellow Jewish family to ash." His shoulders hunched, his sobs wrenching.

"Granddad, I have always loved you, I will always love you. No matter what," I said.

"Me too." Annie rubbed his shoulders. "How could we not love a man who is a sex-god lover to Grandma, who thinks hospitals are boring, boring, boring, chops wood each year like a maniac, and has good, minty breath when given CPR?"

Despite himself, he chuckled.

So did I. Laughter and pain, they do go together sometimes.

We held our granddad, a bowed man, as the owl offered its final piercing, haunting hoot, the luminescent light of the moon shone down, and the lavender readied itself to bloom.

* * *

Was stealing the forged papers that belonged to another Jewish family wrong?

Yes.

Would you have done the same thing?

No?

Yes?

Are you sure?

Can you even begin to conceptualize what it would be like to have your entire family's life at stake? To be chased down by, as Grandma called them, the black ghosts? Could you truly look into your child's eyes and not do everything possible—everything—to save her?

And even though we speculate how we would react, how do we know? How does anyone know, in a tragedy, under threat of a beastly, ghastly death, in a state of raging fear, how they're going to react? No one knows unless they've been there.

You wouldn't have done what my granddad did? You wouldn't have stolen those papers? Are you absolutely sure about that answer?

I'm not.

My guess is that I would have done what he did. And, like him, I would have been haunted the rest of my life by the smiling faces of the other family.

The real Laurents.

I was up all night. I hiked the property, sat on the wrought iron bench on the hill, lay on top of the table in the gazebo, spun a cartwheel over the rows of lavender, watched the sun come up and over the hills, the sweet pinks, tangy oranges, a slash of purple, a hint of maroon stretching across the horizon, everything fresh, new, dewy. I listened to Mozart in my head and thought about scratches and dents, and butterfly blood.

Annie saw me as she was walking her dogs. They circled her, ran forward, then back, as if to make sure she was still there, their tongues lolling about, tails wagging. Life was splendid for those dogs, an adventure to be had every day. Trailing behind her was Cat, who thinks she's a dog. I'm surprised she didn't try barking.

She came and sat by me. Door and Window, white and fluffy, cuddled into my lap, Mr. Legs kept running in circles. Three legs, but he didn't let that stop him. He was happy. Happy to be in the country, happy to sniff, happy to be. Nope, losing a leg was nothin'. He was moving on. Where was that squirrely squirrel? He'd get him, by golly, no squirrel was going to outsmart him!

After a few minutes of friendly, sisterly silence, I said, "Annie, you were right."

She nodded. "Let's walk."

We talked as we walked through the rows of lavender. Several times I bent down and picked up a colorful marble between the plants, dropped by our momma as a girl, dropped by Annie and me, and our grandma. I tucked them back into the lavender and let them be.

As the sun rose high, it shone down in yellow stripes through the clouds. It shone on our friendship, a friendship that I treasured more than anything else. It shone on the sister love that only sisters share.

"So, what do you think?" I asked.

"What do I think of your wild-ass plan?" She threw a ball and Mr. Legs chased after it. "Rock it out, Madeline. I'm with you."

I told Granddad of my "wild-ass" plan later.

We were in Grandma's studio. He had pulled out a few canvasses, as he often does, to admire Grandma's work. He has always been her most ardent supporter. "She is an artist of artists. Imaginative! Creative! Such emotions in her paintings! Such truth! The children love her paintings, but not as much as their parents!"

The artist was lost in the dips and caverns of her mind, but to him, she was always his Emmanuelle or, perhaps I should say at this point, his *Dynah*, the woman he loved.

This time he was admiring her sister swan series. On one canvas two white swans jumped rope together, dressed in matching purple hippie outfits. In another a black swan with a green flowered hat was playing the cello, the other black swan, in a yellow flowered hat, played violin. Another painting showed two white swans dancing together in twenties-style gold dresses, ropes of pearls, and high gold heels.

Annie and I don't dance. We haven't danced since the house by the sea.

"What do you think, Granddad?" I had asked the questions I needed to ask; I had the answers I needed to have. "If you don't want me to do this, if you have the slightest objection, I won't do it. I understand." I held my breath.

"You own the story of your life, Madeline, no one else." He put his chin up and reached for my hand. "Tell the story. Tell it the way you want it told."

"Okay," I whispered, petrified.

He wrapped me in his arms and, amidst Grandma's sister swans, we stood and hugged.

Life is so much better when you have someone to wrap your wings around.

I worked like a fiend for days. I saw clients, had meetings with the Rock Your Womanhood chiefs, long ones, short ones, rushed and hurried, laugh filled, problem filled, we hammered things out. I worked on my speech, finished my column, the title being, "Giving a Speech: Don't Wet Your Pants."

I felt like wetting my pants.

Steve Shepherd would soon arrive in Portland to talk about his latest book in the Pink series. Another evening had been added. It sold out, too. He would give his speeches not too long after I gave mine.

At my office I received a bouquet of wildflowers in a twelve-inch-long canoe. Yes, the vase was shaped like a canoe.

"I'm going to be in Portland, Madeline. Can I take you to lunch? If you want, I'll build you a dinosaur made out of rocks." He left his cell number.

I wouldn't call him. I couldn't.

In my head, though, I heard my momma. *Gather your hell-fire.*

I ran my hands through my stick straight hair. I wasn't feeling very hellfirish.

Put your heels on, Madeline!

All I had was boring heels.

Don't you dare be a frump. Don't you dare! Let yourself shine.

Okay, Momma. I'll try. I'll try to shine.

You can do it, Pink Girl.

I heard the symphony in my head the night before the Rock Your Womanhood speech. They were playing Brahms's Hungarian Dance no. 5. At the end, I swear I could hear clapping.

I thought about the lies I'd told to myself, to others, and the past I'd secreted away like a prisoner behind bars.

I thought about my momma and my grandparents, all living under their own lies and secrets. My momma had left Anna in France and become Marie Elise. My granddad had left Abe, my grandma had left Dynah. They came here and buried who they had been. My granddad had tried to bury what he had done to the Laurents. None of them had been able to bury the grief they felt for Ismael, for Madeline, for the rest of their families.

I do so love the liars in my family.

I thought next about a sailboat, a beauty parlor, a dad who wore funny hats, a momma who doled out advice in pink heels. I thought about lavender. The healing power of lavender.

When I was done, I thought about the sea.

30

"Helloooo again, ladies!" I shouted into the raucous cheers and hoots, the women on their feet, spotlights flying, rock music blaring in the background, my voice echoing around the conference center.

I wriggled, I did not *dance,* waved my hands, grinned, bowed, grinned more, showed my canines. The video screens on either side of me flashed out, "Madeline O'Shea! Rock Your Womanhood!" in loud colors.

"Have you been rocking your womanhood today?"

Whooee. You betcha they had. Their womanhood was on full blast speed.

"Who has brought their O'Shea's Inner Fight-Kicking Spirit?"

They'd done that, too. I had told them how to gather their O'Shea Inner Fight-Kicking Spirit during my first speech, at the beginning of the conference. "Let's see it, ladies!"

Though I was nearly blinded by spotlights, I saw those high heels flying as women kickboxed the air or held up their heels above their heads.

"Who is gunning to Release Yourself From Whack Job Men and Memories?"

The women made fake guns with their hands and yelled *pow, pow, pow,* like I'd taught them. It was deafening.

"Who is here to Rip-Roaring Enjoy the Hell Out of Life?'

Their screaming 'bout blew my head off.

I went on like that for a while. The rock music roared in and out, the lights changed colors, purple, blue, pink. Pink. How ironic. What a circus. All I needed was a decorated elephant and a lion tamer.

"Okay, ladies, have a seat on your fantabulous bottoms." I didn't think that Carlotta would mind me borrowing her word.

"What I want to talk about now, today, this moment, is truth."

I took a deep breath. I'd made my decision. It was my wild-ass plan. Once all was out, all was out. I'd probably be finished in this career, but hell. If I didn't ever have to wear a soul-crushing suit like I was wearing today, this time in boring beige, I think I'd be okay.

"I want to talk about honesty, about being *who you are,* and embracing *who you were.*" I strutted across the stage. "I want to talk about dealing truthfully with your past, not hiding from it, and understanding how it embraces or suffocates you still today. I want to talk about being truthful with yourself. I want to talk about facing the lies in your life and replacing them with bald-faced, raw, rumbling truth. In fact"—I paused, knowing I was going to be way, way over a ledge in about one minute—"I want to talk about me."

Whew. *Did I just say that?* I swallowed hard. I heard a *click, click, click* in my head. I felt slick, sweaty hands. I smelled fear and cigarettes.

Then I heard a fiddler. *A fiddler.* Right then. Boot-stomping, heel-kicking, fiddle music.

I breathed in, not a good breath, but breath.

"I want to talk about my truth. I want to talk about my lies. The lies in my life, the lies I've told myself, the lies I've perpetuated to everyone else. I want to talk about my past, my childhood, my secrets."

I could feel all those ladies lean forward in their seats.

"You see, friends, I'm a lie."

Silence.

"I've been lying to you."

Cavernous silence, quite gripping, actually. Out of the corner of my eye, I could see the chiefs of the Rock Your Womanhood conference freeze up. I had not discussed with them my lies!

"I've been telling you all what to do and how to run your lives, yet I haven't even been following my own advice. I'm like the financial planner who is bankrupt. The psychologist who ignores his mental problems. The roofer who denies that a river is flowing through his house through the roof. I'm a life coach whose life has collapsed."

Backstage the chiefs were now clutching each other in fear.

I paused, gathered my hellfire. "I've told you not to get mired in muck, but I'm so mired in muck I can barely move. I've told you to leave your past hurts behind, to make a new life, but I am so stuck in my old life I'm surprised I'm not attached to a time machine. I've told you not to allow any borders to delineate where you can go in your life, yet I have borders so high you could not scramble over them with a fire ladder and a personal rocket. I have told you to create a home that is a frame for your joy, but I hate my house. I have told you to dress like you are on the fashion runway of life, so that your clothes reflect your blossoming. I hate my clothes. I hate my suits. I have told you not to buy into the material things of life because you'll never be happy, but I have an expensive car and expensive clothes, all bought to convince myself that I'm someone. It has never worked."

I stalked across the stage, my face up on those ginormous video screens. "I have secrets that I have desperately, with every fiber of my being, tried to hide, and yet . . . I can't hide them anymore. Someone else has taken control of my past and is going to reveal those secrets very soon."

I felt so calm suddenly. So very calm. Annie was somewhere out there. In my head, I reached for her hand.

"In the last months someone else has taken control of my life. I have told you a thousand times not to allow that to happen. You. Take. Control. Do not be a guest in your own life, do not let someone run your life, do not stay offstage. Be onstage, and be the star of your life. But I have not taken that advice myself.

Someone else has decided that now is the time to reveal who I am to you. To everyone."

I stopped and tapped a heel. "I'm not gonna let them do that. No, I'm done. I'm taking the control back. Ladies, I want to tell you about my childhood."

I told them about Marie Elise's French Beauty Parlor, and they belly laughed and smiled at my stories of plumes of hair spray, Grandmother Schiller, Shoney's paintings of naked women in town, my momma's blunt advice, her pink outfits, the chandeliers. I told about Carman's champagne drinking while reading love scenes aloud from bodice busters, Trudy Jo's ranting about her children and Shakespeare, Shell Dee's fascination with the human body. I told them how I played violin with our momma, how Annie played piano with our dad, how we made up songs together and danced on the grass by our house by the sea.

I told them about Big Luke, and how we painted his nails and made him funny hats that he wore and how he encouraged us to be ourselves. I talked about the storm that killed him and watching my momma on the cliff with her pink shawl flying behind her. I could hear women sniffling in the front rows.

And, finally, I talked about Sherwinn, Pauly, and Gavin.

I did not become too graphic. What would be the point? But I told about what happened in our own home with Sherwinn, the dilapidated shack, the slimy feel of the walls, the metallic taste of the water, the old pizza lying about.

I told them what we had to do for the *click, click, click.*

I heard their gasps, moans, more tears. In fact, I put several photos up on the video screens. They weren't the most graphic, but you got the point. I did not leave them there long.

I tried not to cry. It didn't work, but I did not let my tears ruin the rhythm, the message of my speech. Soon it began to feel like a group cry.

I spoke about the trial, and how my momma shot all three of those sick monsters and said, "This is from Big Luke. He's going to escort you to hell. Good-bye," and how I've heard those six gunshots my whole life.

I told them about her tumor, her terminal illness, how she had to guarantee herself that her girls would live to see their own grandchildren. I told them about her trial, the cotton candy pink heels and the yellow hope ribbon, her excruciating physical pain and how she dedicated the last months of her life to us until it was unbearable and she took the boat out, dropped herself into the sea, and met our dad in the clouds.

I had to pause there and wipe my face. I noticed the Rock Your Womanhood chiefs out of the corner of my eye. They were riveted.

I told the ladies how I had tried to bury everything, and how it hadn't worked.

"I'm damaged." I admitted that truth into the caverns of the conference center, knowing Annie was there. "I. Am. Damaged. I am damaged down to the core of my soul and, currently, unfortunately, I'm being blackmailed for the photos that were taken of my sister and me as children."

I heard the gasp. Thousands of women sucking in air at once.

"Blackmailed. Some creep sent me the photos and told me if I didn't hand over an insane amount of money, he would hand those photos out like candy. I don't want the photos out there, but more than that, I do not want to be held captive by this man. I can't. I can't have one more man ruining my life, controlling any part of it. I won't have it."

"Good for you, Madeline, you ass kicker!" One woman stood and raised her fist in victory.

Another woman, about twenty rows back, stood and yelled, "That's right! Don't take any shit!"

A third. "Captivity is not for us, Madeline! We're women!"

"So I took action." I let my voice rise.

"Yeah! Yeah!" those noisy women yelled, then applauded.

"I called the police." They applauded louder. They got on their feet!

"As we speak, that man is being arrested."

"Yeeesss!"

"He will pay for what he's done." I did not mention how Sam's house had been exploded.

Woo-ha! Hee-haw! Ear-splitting noise.

I did not repeat the comment from the woman in the front row who yelled, "I hope they cut his penis off!"

Or the comment from her girlfriend, which was, "Boil his balls! Boil his balls!"

I then made a short rant on porn—how it's an infectious disease in our country, how children are being abused, how I would stand for children in this terrible business, how it would be my new mission in life. "I'm out of the closet, and I will drag other people out of the closet who are committing criminal acts against our kids!"

Whooee! They fisted their hands in Woman Power victory, like I'd taught them.

As they were screaming, I remembered my visit with the Portland FBI days before.

They came to my house in Portland. Annie was there, too. We showed them the photos and the blackmail notes. The latest: $350,000. Or else.

Even the FBI guys looked a little green as they stared at the photos.

Keith Stein, my bulldog attorney, whom I had asked to be with us, started bawling like a baby.

I showed them the latest note. I told them who I thought it was. Pauly's son, Sam.

"We'll fry him," the FBI guy said.

"And the pictures," I said. "I don't want them released. I don't want anyone to see them."

"We understand," the agent said. He had white hair and eyes that had been around the block a thousand difficult times. He cleared his throat. "Miss O'Shea, I'm sorry this happened to you and your sister. I remember the case. I was a young rookie in Boston then and I'm . . ." He cleared his throat again. "I'm sorry."

"Me too," another agent said, her hair pulled back in a clip. "Tragic. How are you ladies doing?"

Annie and I glanced at each other. "Not bad," I said.

"We're not feeling explosive anymore," Annie said.

I tried not to laugh.

Keith the bulldog kept bawling like a baby.

I waved all the clapping, hooting women back down.

"I also recently found out that I am not who I thought I was. You see, my momma's maiden name was Marie Elise Laurent. That's the name under which she was traveling from France, then to Spain, after walking over the Pyrenees and traveling to America when she was a young girl. That was the name on her papers. Her father's name was Anton Laurent, her mother's name was Emmanuelle Laurent. But those weren't their real names. Their real names, I have come to find, were Abe Bacherach and Dynah Rossovsky. My momma's real name was Anna Bacherach. They were Jews. My grandma is not my biological grandma, she is my great-aunt. I'll wait until you can get ahold of all this. It took me a bit."

I waited. While I waited, I breathed. My breathing was easier. The air didn't seem stuck so bad.

"My biological grandma's name was Madeline Rossovsky Bacherach, I am named for her. My grandma Madeline jumped from a second-story window, her son in her arms, while being chased by the Nazis. Her injuries were extensive. She dragged herself to a doctor's home, someone willing to help, but was too injured to escape. When my granddad and my grandma Emmanuelle refused to leave her, she killed herself with a knife."

I did not miss yet another gasp in that audience. A collective inhale.

"My family, what was left of it, fled from the Nazis. They fled to live."

I told the rest of that complicated story, but I did not tell about how Granddad stole the papers. I couldn't cause him more pain, especially in his condition, at his age, and not here. It wasn't my place, and it would do no good for the smiling Laurents.

"I sensed, when I was a child, that my grandparents and my parents knew something I didn't know, that there was a secret. I knew there was someone named Ismael, but I didn't know who Ismael was. Now I do. Ismael Bacherach was my grandparents' late son, the brother of my momma. They have spent their whole lives missing him, loving him, feeling him in their hearts. My momma used to talk to him outside by the sea as she played her violin."

I stopped so I wouldn't sob. My dear momma, longing for her brother, talking to him into the cool sea air.

"What I've learned from all of this is that we can't move on from our tragedies until we deal with them, until we face them. I need to move on, fully, from my tragedies. Here's what I know: I am Madeline O'Shea. Flawed. Wracked with a lot of pain. Struggling. Wrestling with life. *But I am trying.* I am trying to be better, trying to be authentic, trying to be me. Trying to feel clean after what I went through as a girl, trying to feel pure, trying not to let my emotional dirt smother me, stamp out my breath, crush my soul. I have been driven by my emotional dirt for too long."

I wiped the tears from my face, but darned if this whole thing wasn't feeling cathartic.

"I want you ladies to close your eyes. Think of the emotional dirt in your life. Cry if you want. But think about what's been wrapped around you tight and hard and hurtful. Think about something that happened. Maybe something you did, something that was done to you, a terrible mistake, or many terrible mistakes that you made. Think about your losses, your hurts. I'm giving you time."

I waited for two minutes. There were a lot of women there, and those tears and sobs came. I was a mess. They were a mess. We were all a mess.

"Now, ladies, stand up. Put an imaginary pencil in your hand and write in the air about your emotional dirt. Write it all down. I'll wait."

I waited for two more minutes. We were all a mess as those pencils went flying.

"You want to cry? You cry then!" I shouted at them. "Cry. Get it out. Scream it out, yell! Let it out, ladies. We can't keep this inside anymore, it's killing us. Let me hear it!"

A woman in one of the front rows yelled, "You failed me, Mother."

Another announced, "I'm lonely and I think I'm gay!"

"I still love my ex-husband, the pig ... I haven't had sex in eight years! I'm addicted to pain killers ... I'm unhappy ... My mother was never there for me ... My father is in jail ... My brother brags all the time and I wanna strangle him ... my childhood sucked ... I was abused by ... I'm broke ... my daughter's an alcoholic ..."

I waited another two minutes for that internal muck to be released, then I changed course.

"Now you ladies listen to me," I boomed out, ferocious again, my hellfire gathered up and burning bright. "You listen. You drop that pencil on the ground, that pencil that spelled out your hurt. Drop it." I watched hands drop that pencil. "Stomp on it! I mean it, I want to hear you stomping!"

I heard it, they stomped.

"Rip down that piece of paper you were writing on in space. Rip it! Rip it!" I saw women waving their hands through the air. "Set it on fire! Get those flames whipped right up! It's on fire, right? The ashes are floating down? Stomp on those ashes." I heard 'em stomping again.

"Scream at those ashes!"

They screamed.

"Yell, 'Never again will I let my emotional dirt hurt me!' "

They yelled it.

"Yell, 'I am done with it, I am done with the dirt!' "

They yelled again.

" 'I am clean, I am pure!' "

Man, those yells hurled round and round the convention center walls.

"Scream it again! Scream it again!"

Those ladies almost brought the roof down.

"You know where my transformation is going to start? Do you know? Right here." I pointed down at the floor, then out into the audience, up into the balconies. "Right now. I'm starting with how I look. I don't like my suits. I don't like how businesslike they are. I don't like the boring colors. I don't like the matchy-matchy look to them. I don't like that I feel as if I'm in a linen straitjacket and a chastity belt at the same time. I wore them to put armor over myself so I could believe *I was someone.* What a joke! A suit cannot make you someone. Only you can make yourself someone. And the suits aren't me. Not me at all. You want to see the new me?" They clapped. They hooted. "Are you sure?" They screamed that they did.

I envisioned my momma, arms up, cheering, reminding me it was a "cardinal sin" to be frumpy.

"Let me show you." I nodded at the sound guy, who turned on a funny strip tease number as I took off one piece of clothing, and another, and another.

When I was done I was standing in my new favorite outfit: A shiny pink and black cheetah print skirt. A black lace shirt. A black leather jacket with a yellow ribbon for hope tucked into the pocket.

Georgie and I had gone shopping together. She said, "You have put a screech on your hormonal layer of cataclysmic inner turpitude."

I did not know what a hormonal layer of cataclysmic inner turpitude meant. "What does that mean?"

"It means, my rad boss, that you like yourself now and you are roaring."

Yep, I was getting there, getting to like myself.

The finishing touch? I kicked off my dull heels, grabbed a bag onstage, and slipped on the cotton candy pink heels my momma wore.

The spotlights beamed down on me as I yanked the rubber band and bobby pins out of my hair and fluffed it. My curls cascaded to my shoulders—no more flat ironing for me. No more killing my hair because of what Sherwinn had done to my curls. "I have trapped my curls like I have trapped my life because they reminded me of something sad that happened to my sister and me, something sick. But I will have no more trapping in my life. None. Here's my curls, here's me! *Here. I. Am.*"

They cheered. My, how they cheered.

"This is me. This is Madeline O'Shea. No more lies. No more burying my past. No more secrets. This is me and you, all of us here together. I am me and I rock! Rock your womanhood, ladies! Rock your womanhood. Say it with me!"

Pandemonium. Groovy, yeah. They loved it. *Rock Your Womanhood!*

Loved it.

"No more lies, ladies, no more muck. Be you! Be yoooouuu-uuu!"

I *almost* felt like dancing.

Annie and I scrambled out to the limousine after I'd been on-stage three times with standing ovations.

When we pulled away from the curb, she opened a cabinet, pulled out two champagne glasses, poured the champagne, and handed me one.

"Cheers," she said.

"Cheers."

"You rocked my womanhood."

"Thank you. Back at ya."

The days after my speech were jammed with calls, e-mails, reporters.

I was a story.

I had circumvented Marlene's article, not only with my speech at the convention center but *Boutique* printed my speech, in full, in their magazine. Newspapers covered it, too. I took some vengeful glee in cutting her off at the knees. It's not personal.

Her article came out. It received scant publicity. There was nothing in it about Granddad, the stolen papers, Auschwitz or Drancy and the real Laurents. Perhaps Marlene couldn't prove it. Perhaps it wasn't relevant to the article on my mother and the trials. Perhaps she was so steamed I beat her to the punch, she gave up and wrote the thing without further ado. I don't know.

In future articles I took the opportunity to rail against child porn. "It's illegal, it's immoral, it's hideous. People who traffic in this, who produce or distribute this smack, should be jailed. No, it is not okay to buy it. No, it is not okay to have it in your collection. It's not harmless. Without a market for child porn, we wouldn't have children in porn, being abused, raped, and attacked. *You are guilty if you are looking at it.*"

Click, click, click.

Somehow, though, when I announced that I'd been black-mailed, it triggered creepy men to say online in their perverted chat rooms that they had the images of Annie and me in their collections, too. How they boasted. How proud they were. How special. They had photos of Madeline O'Shea! Famous lady! Naked! Did you see the one with her dressed in high heels and nothing else, bending over to touch her toes? Did you see the one with the rope? What about the one with the guy in the blond wig and her. . . .

I had Keith Stein, that bulldog, hire a computer forensics guy. The FBI ran stings with local police. They went to pornography-loving men's homes. One of them was a prominent attorney from a wealthy family. He had a trust fund.

I am now suing him for that trust fund. His wife has left him. She will take half of what is left.

Another man had a massive collection of child porn, including photos of Annie and me.

He was a U.S. senator. He, too, had a fortune.

I am now suing the U.S. senator for that fortune. He has resigned under an onslaught of publicity.

A third man sent us a letter and said he had stacks of our photos. "Mountains of them. I've got a price. Give me a call." Dumb man. A friend of Sam's. He lived above his mechanic's shop on the Cape.

Annie went to Fiji. She is a little off her rocker. He does not have a home anymore, or a mechanics shop, or photos. He has been arrested. The newspaper noted that a gas line leaked and sparks from a machine led to the fire. Troubling, it was, two fires in such a short amount of time on the Cape.

It is my new life's mission to eliminate the production and distribution of child porn. I will do whatever it takes to prevent any child from going through what Annie and I went through. I owe it to those children. If I can prevent this relentless misery for one child, it is worth it.

Maybe that's why I went through what I did. Eventually, I would get myself together and become a vengeful, whip-ass former victim who would come up swinging for vulnerable kids. There was the "good" in it, right there.

I am done hiding. I am done cowering.

Keith Stein called me the other day about these lawsuits. He is a bulldog, as I have mentioned. He gets very mean, legally speaking. "They're threatening back, Madeline." He laughed. "All sorts of things, defamation of character, they'll counter sue you, you'll be liable for court costs, etcetera. What do I tell them?"

"Tell them . . ." I thought about my life and what men had done to me, how they'd hurt me, how these other men-monsters were hurting other children, and I said what I thought, and I meant it all the way through to my bones. "Tell them I said, *Don't fuck with me.*"

I received a package from Torey. Inside was a letter.

"I read your speech, Madeline. I have let my emotions out for you, for the kid you were, for three days. I sent you an animal hug."

I opened the box.

Inside was a long, furry (fake) tail.

"Aurora King is here, Madeline," Georgie said via the phone.

"Excellent." I put aside an offer from a speaker's bureau to go on a national tour. "I've been thinking that I need a handful of glitter in my hair."

"She says that she can feel your spirit and it is . . . what color, Aurora? Gold. She says your spirit is gold and she is not sensing any black swirling around you. She says she was so worried about you recently that she meditated for you, at night outside . . . what? She said she lit candles, too, for you and made a special tea with mowi wowi. You know what mowi wowi is, right?"

I rolled my eyes. "Did she bring any of the tea?"

"No, she didn't. She says she's seeing shelves, a red hat, a boy/man, I don't know what she means by that, and an old wedding ring with blood."

"Good. What is she wearing?"

"Gold. Ruffles, fairy wings."

"Show her in. Tell her not to throw glitter at me."

"Don't throw glitter at Madeline," I heard Georgie say as she rang off.

I opened my door to Aurora and closed my eyes.

She threw gold glitter at me.

But this time, I was prepared. I threw silver, glittery stars back at her. Two huge handfuls.

She was surprised, but then she announced, staring at me in my blue pencil skirt with a ruffle and a pink, silky, Japanese-styled blouse, with awe in her voice, "I believe you've found your soul."

"I have eight clients now, Madeline," Ramon told me. "Eight clients lined up that I'm building stuff for like decks and arbors and trellises. Most of them in your neighborhood. I have other people who have called, I called them back, and I'm going to meet with them later. Plus, I had so many people who needed their lawn mowed that now I've hired a guy to do it. He was in jail with me. He's a hard worker. Made a mistake when he was twenty-one and sold drugs, but now he's going to minister school."

"Good job, Ramon. And, I love my yard. I hate my house, but I love the yard. My realtor said that I'm going to be able to price it higher because of what you've done."

"Thanks, Madeline."

"You're welcome."

"Want to hear the best news?"

"Sure do, Ramon."

"I'm getting my brother back."

I had to grab tissues for the tears leaking from my eyes.

"Thanks, Madeline. You know all those kids you give life coaching to down at Youth Avenues? Everybody thinks you're awesome. I think you're awesome, too."

"Back at ya, Ramon. Back at ya." I sniffled, accidentally snorted. He hugged me.

Folks, reach out a hand to help others in need. You'll never regret it.

A'isha Heinbrenner, the woman with the five kids and a husband she divorced after thirty years of marriage, came to see me. She was wearing stylish jeans, a thick red sweater jacket that simply screamed "Scotland," and bold jewelry made of stone. She had dyed her hair a zippy auburn brown color and grown it out a couple of inches. She wore bright red lipstick. She had returned to Oregon to sell / donate / give away almost everything she had, including her home and cars. "I love Scotland, Madeline." She was a whole different person, at least ten years younger, twenty-five pounds off her body, energy radiating in waves. Maybe it was the Scottish whiskey. "And Scotland loves me. Come and visit, will you?"

I nodded, hugged her.

Maybe I'd go to Faerie Glen and make a wish.

The Giordano sisters stopped in, swinging their cat tails, twiddling their whiskers. They showed me the front page of the living section of the paper.

"Meow! Here we are, Madeline," Adriana said, pulling on an ear. "Don't we look catty?"

"It's us and our good deeds! The reporter wanted to know our identities, but we wouldn't tell her!" Bella said, swinging her tail. "Shhh . . ."

"We're the secret cats, and we prowl around town and make people's lives better," Carlotta said, scratching her claws.

I glanced at Princess Anastasia. She made that spitting sound. Bee La La rolled her eyes, I swear it. Candy Stripe yawned.

"Daddy left us so much money!" Adriana said.

"Every time we do a good deed for someone, we send him a photo!" Bella said.

"And, across the bottom we write, Meow Meow!" Carlotta said.

"Fun and fun!"

"Wicked naughty!"

"Fantabulous!"

"We brought your suit, Cat Madeline! We're leaving in five minutes, so hurry up! A good man who has leukemia is going with his wife and five kids to Disneyland!"

"You've been sent a terrarium." Georgie strutted in, holding a box. Knee-high black boots, black short skirt, tights in purple stripes, one purple streak in her white-blond hair. Her muscle was flexed where her grandma was smoking a cigar. "Look at this!"

Stanley barked and we went through the bark, shake, and hug routine.

From the box she pulled out a humongous glass sphere. Inside the sphere were plants, moss, and white glittery sand. The glass sphere had been painted with two white birds on a delicate tree branch. On top was a hook so you could hang the terrarium from the ceiling.

"It's amaaazzzzing," Georgie said.

"Who's it from?" I held the sphere in my hand. Inside the sphere were pink and blue plastic butterflies; a tiny, yellow spotted frog; two purple snakes; miniature blue jays; and a six-inch-tall blue cottage with a red front door.

"It's from, can I have a drumroll?" Georgie said, then imitated that drumroll. "Steeeeeeeve Shepherddddddd!"

I sucked in my breath and almost dropped the sphere with the painted birds.

"I'll read the card," Georgie said. "Greetings, Madeline, from the snake finder. I'll restrain myself from pestering you anymore, fair lady. But, remember, I'm always available for frog

catching, puddle jumping, writing stories back to back, or canoeing down a river. Cheers and good luck. Steve Shepherd."

I sank into my leather chair.

"I think he likes you, Madeline, yep, I think he does. What do
you think, Stanley?" Stanley barked, waved his paw.

I could not wave back because I was holding a sphere.

I wouldn't call him, I couldn't.

But he was speaking tonight. . . .

It was sold out, but one of my clients was the head of the box
office at the concert hall. . . .

I sat in the balconies, way high up in the back, Annie beside
me.

I was wearing a black pencil skirt; a blue jean jacket; a blue,
red, and yellow scarf with fringe; huge hoop earrings; and some
killer high heels. I had bundled up all my suits and given them to
Goodwill, so there was no chance of wearing a straitjacket/chas-
tity belt again. My curls were down and curling all over.

"You look hot," Annie said. "Love the new you."

"Me too," I said. "If I have a suit on again in my entire life,
I'll know it's because someone is stuffing me into a coffin."

"Don't worry. For your coffin outfit, I'm going to dress you
in a bikini and have a tattoo artist draw Mr. Legs on your stomach. It'll be your final gift to animal-kind."

"Thank you, Annie. I know I can count on you to help me
make a dignified exit. I do have a fondness for Mr. Legs, too."

The lights went down, someone from Literary Arts made an
introduction, and boom.

There he was.

Steve Shepherd, way down there, onstage.

I was back on the Cape, running through sand, sailing on the
ocean, laughing in a plume of hair spray, passing out pink cookies with Red Hots. I was skipping through the woods with
Steve, climbing trees, exploring ponds . . .

I was back there, back in time, with Steve.

And though I was way, way up at the top, at one point, he

saw me. He stopped talking, midsentence, for loooonnng seconds, until people turned and stared. He grinned, a charming, sweet smile, and he was young again and so was I, and it was the two of us, with Annie tagging along, and we were playing in the lake, the sun hanging softly in the sky, benevolent and kind, the wind cooling our hot foreheads, that sweet innocence boomeranging between us.

31

There was a very, very happy, *enormously* happy *thing* that came from my revelations of child abuse and the real names of my momma and my grandparents.

I received a call in my office, on a rainy, blustery, but strangely soothing afternoon, as if the weather were feeling maternal. It was from an older man. Georgie did not understand his French, so she transferred him to me. "I got the *bonjour* part, but nothing else, Madeline. I think you better yak with this one."

"*Bonjour.*"

"*Bonjour, bonjour,*" he said, then burst into tears.

It was hard to understand his French through his tears. I heard other people in the background, speaking a language I did not understand.

"*S'il vous plait.* Is it true that your mother's name is Anna Bacherach? And, *s'il vous plait,* is your grandfather's name Abe Bacherach, his first wife's name Madeline Rossovsky Bacherach. Please, please, is this the truth?"

It was the truth.

It was a miracle.

It was a gift.

It was hard to understand my French through my tears.

We enlisted the aid of a private detective, a former Israel special forces guy in Tel Aviv who Annie knew from her "mystery years." After doing some checking, to make absolutely sure we had things right, because we could not afford a mistake, Annie and I told Granddad very carefully, very slowly, with Dr. Rubenstein by his side, just in case, in the gazebo, on a day when the happy sun slanted at angles and lit everything up with gold sparkles.

I wanted to tell him in a hotel five minutes from a hospital, or even the lobby of a hospital, but we thought it would stress him out even more, so we told him the truth, the lavender starting to bloom in rows, purple, white, and bluish flowers bursting into life.

"I don't understand," he said, his voice down to a hoarse whisper, his body rigid, as if he couldn't let go or piece by piece he'd fall apart.

We waited. It was so much. So much to process. Maybe too much.

"I don't understand. Are you telling me..." His hands shook.

I grabbed a hand, so did Annie. Dr. Rubenstein leaned forward, watching all physical signs to make sure Granddad was not going to have another heart attack. He'd even brought a bag of medical supplies.

"What you're saying is..." Granddad's eyes filled with huge tears. It is so hard to see an older person cry. There's something that much more heartbreaking about it, and this news. This news!

"I don't believe...you're sure..." He started to sob.

Annie told him about the private detective, the research, while Dr. Rubenstein burst into tears. He was not a quiet crier.

"You believe that it's true then...."

"We know it to be true," Annie said. "Damn true."

"You are telling me that my son—" A tremor ran through his whole body, rocking him.

I kissed both his cheeks, held his face in my hands.

"My son Ismael, Ismael!"

"Yes, Granddad, your son Ismael—"

"You are telling me..." He called out again, guttural, loud.

I was so broken for him ... and yet, so happy, so immensely, roaringly happy.

He shook his head, back and forth, back and forth. "You are telling me that Ismael, my son, *he is alive?*"

We were telling him that. "He's alive, Granddad. Ismael's alive. He lives in Tel Aviv."

He covered his face, and he shouted, that shout echoing through the gazebo, around the rows of lavender, down the land quilt of hills and valleys, and over the blue mountains to the sea.

His whole soul poured out, raw and wounded, then he stood and spread his arms out, up to the sky, his head throw back. "Thank you, God," he thundered, every word splintering with grief, with joy, with the miraculous miracle that was now his life. "Ismael! Ismael! My son, my *beautiful* son! I am coming! *I am coming!*"

My granddad is suffering from prostate cancer. He is also suffering from arthritis and heart disease and had a recent heart attack. He is extremely old, has worked full time for decades establishing his stores, and has lived a life of such tremendous, overwhelming grief, loss, and guilt, it is a wonder he is not long dead.

Within a day and a half, we were in Tel Aviv.

"I will go to my son," he told Annie and me, his voice cracking, a fire blazing in those old, kind eyes, eyes that had hardly stopped spilling tears since this most incredible news. "And if I die one minute after seeing him, *one minute* after I hold him in my arms, I will die grateful. I will die happy. I need..." He stopped, his voice choked. "I need only one minute," he whispered. "One minute with my son. Do you understand? *One minute.* That's it."

I hugged him close. The trip might very well kill him. In fact, it probably would. It was long, it was stressful. Anything could happen. It would be worth it. "You'll get that minute, Granddad, I promise you."

* * *

The question of how to travel with Grandma was one we spent a little time on. We never thought to leave her at home, even though the flights would be grueling and how she would react unpredictable. She needed to be there, but how best to do it? Where should we fly to first? Should we spend the night in Boston before flying over? Two nights? What time of day should we fly?

Nola and Dr. Rubenstein had already agreed to go with us. "It will be my greatest pleasure," Dr. Rubenstein said. "I will do it for the love of your family. For my parents and your grandparents' enduring love and friendship."

Nola said, "I will come. Your family has brought me so much happiness, I will be with you in your happiness, also."

Grandma heard us talking that night when we thought she was in bed.

"Ismael!" she said, rushing into the room in a lacy yellow negligee with a yellow lace skirt and high bedroom slippers with a fluffy white plume at the toe. She had not bothered to put a robe on. "You said Ismael! You've found him! He's with us now! Is there still blood?"

"No, Grandma, there's no blood," Annie said, soothing, hugging her. "There's none."

She clapped her hands, then leaped into my granddad's arms, her face aglow. "We will go to him tonight! Tonight! Where is he?"

We explained to her that he was far, far away. She clapped her hands again. "I will pack my bags and we will leave on the backs of the swans and they will fly us away to my nephew, Ismael!" She paused. "Madeline is there, too, isn't she? In the Land of the Swans?

"No, Grandma," Annie said. "She's in heaven."

"Not yet, not yet!" Her face crumpled, fists tight. "What about Anna in her blue coat with the violin?"

"No, Grandma, I'm sorry. Anna's gone, too. In heaven." I swallowed hard.

"Luke?"

"In heaven, with his arms around Anna." Yes, he would be hugging our momma.

Grandma clapped her hands to her cheeks, arching her back in grief. "I miss them, I miss them!" she wailed. "Oh, I want them back!" We waited for her to compose herself, to dig through the grief that punctured the dementia, and I slung an arm around those tiny shoulders.

"But we can see Ismael," I said.

Abruptly she stared at us, the fuzz lifting.

"Madeline's in heaven with her daughter, Anna," she said. "They are with the swans. They are in the Land of the Swans now, in the garden, by the pond, over the bridge. Okay!" She hugged my granddad, then kissed him on the lips. "Now don't you get all horny with me, young man! We don't have time for any of your sexy shenanigans! You'll have to wait until tonight, a proper time to make love to me! But I'm busy now. I have to pack a bag for Ismael! I knew we would find him! I've always felt him right here." She pointed to her heart, then rushed off on her heels, her lacy skirt flopping. "Always!"

Dementia works in interesting ways. Our grandma was done packing in minutes. When she skipped out of her bedroom in her negligee to give Nola a hug and "help" Nola pack, Annie and I opened her suitcases.

She had packed almost perfectly. Sweaters and blouses. Pants. Shoes. Scarves. A tiny bikini, who knew where she got it, and her two most wild lingerie pieces, one in animal print, the other black lace, and a pair of pink fluffy handcuffs. I did not want a visual image of those handcuffs with Granddad. She also packed another suitcase with fancy dresses, sparkly heels, her jewelry case, and long white gloves. Grandma was ready!

Tucked inside the pocket of the suitcase, there were several swans, one carved from wood, another ceramic, a third made from glass, a menorah I'd never seen, and old, old pictures. Annie and I went through them, later asking Granddad who they were. He could not control his emotions. He did not try.

One photo was of Grandma Madeline and Grandma Emmanuelle as girls with their parents, the parents who shot the

Nazis and died in their own homes, their father in a wheelchair. Another was of Grandma Madeline and Granddad, our momma, and Ismael, as a family, in front of a pond, all grinning and holding instruments, and a third photo was of Grandma Madeline and Grandma Emmanuelle together, holding Ismael and Momma on their laps. We found a ring box at the bottom of the suitcase. Inside was a diamond ring, the diamond small but pretty. It was Grandma Madeline's, from Granddad, the ring that Grandma wore to escape out of France, the blood from her sister soaking her dress.

Granddad held the ring to his heart, then kissed it, putting it carefully back in its box, tucking it in the suitcase.

Beside the suitcase Grandma placed my violin and told me, "No more dents and scratches now, Madeline. We have to show Ismael. He'll want to see your violin. His blood is in it. You call it the blood butterfly. There's a story there. A story in the violin."

Later, after I packed, I played my violin by the piano, Bach's Partita no. 3 in E Major.

Annie sat on the bench. She did not play.

Lavender is a gift.

It offers beauty, and it offers practical uses.

That night, I did not sleep. We were leaving early for the airport, so I walked up and down the rows of lavender. I bent to touch a leaf, inhale the scent, pull a weed.

I didn't know when we would be returning to The Lavender Farm. I didn't know when I'd hear the owl hoot again, see a flash of a coyote, pet Mr. Legs or Door and Window, or when I'd bark at Cat. I didn't know when I'd see the sun set right over those purple blue mountains or watch the clouds change the colors of the land quilt as they floated over. I didn't know when I'd come back and drive through the blooming tulip trees that Granddad planted for Grandma because he loved her more than life itself and wanted to make her happy.

I put my arms out, like a plane, and spun around, slowly.

I didn't know when I was coming back, but I knew this: I

would make a change in my life when I returned. I would spend more time with the rows of lavender that marched over our land like purple flames.

I heard three violins, together, fast music, dancing music, clapping music, boot-tapping music, fiddler's music . . .

Dancing music.

Ben Gurion International Airport in Tel Aviv airport is light, bright, modern, and swarming with security.

Granddad, Grandma, Nola, Annie, Dr. Rubenstein, and I went through customs and picked up our bags, then Annie and I held on to each of Granddad's elbows as he hobbled through. "I will not use a wheelchair, so don't even suggest it," he'd growled. "I will meet my son . . ." His voice caught again, and the tears streamed down, sticking in the lines of his face, the lines brought on by despair and despondency, by sunshine and smiles and a farm and family. "I will meet my son standing, that I will do, dammit."

When we had our bags, we saw a huge group of people not twenty feet in front of us. Old people, middle aged, teenagers, children, toddlers, babies. I noticed that many of them were crying, tissues flying, shoulders shaking, arms around each other, gasps audible when we turned to face them.

Granddad stopped and stared, stunned, overwhelmed.

They stared back, stunned, overwhelmed.

A man with thick white hair, like Granddad's, and soft brown eyes, like Granddad's, with a thin frame, like Granddad's, and only a little taller, stepped forward shakily. "Mon père," he rasped out, his face crumpling. "Mon père, mon Dieu, mon père." He put his arms out. "Father."

As if propelled by a force greater than his own, our granddad took three long, wobbly strides and met his son, his son Ismael Bacherach, whom he thought died in Paris as the Nazis surrounded them, whom he had missed and mourned for his entire life, whom he had prayed for and loved. Granddad stepped into his son's arms with a raspy cry, low and scratchy.

The two started to crumple together, and other men rushed

forward to hold them up, but they were upset, too, and the tears flowed, from all of us, from Nola and me, from Dr. Rubenstein, and from the family we never knew we had, whom we embraced as if we'd known them forever.

Our tears streamed out, not the tears of life's inconvenient difficulties, but the tears of unspeakable grief and astounding relief.

Even Annie cried.

My granddad had found his son.

His name was Ismael.

Grandma had insisted on wearing a silky red jacket and a skirt with a ruffle and a jaunty red hat with a red feather on the plane rides over. "Ismael loves the color red!" she declared, smiling broadly, her face, which had aged with such graciousness, alight with happiness. "It's his favorite! He'll know me, Aunt Dynah, when he sees the red."

She told everyone she was going to see her nephew and the blood was gone. *Gone!* She snapped her fingers when she said "gone." The blood was gone! Snap, snap!

As Ismael and Granddad hugged, Grandma watched from the side, the tears falling down her cheeks. When Granddad and Ismael finally parted and Ismael wiped his eyes, he focused on my grandma.

"Aunt Dynah," he croaked out, in French, then hobbled over, his emotions overwhelming him. "Aunt Dynah!"

Grandma threw her arms out. "Ismael! My Ismael! How I've missed you! I have felt you right here." She pointed to her heart. "I have brought you swans, and I have worn your favorite color! Red!"

Ismael had a wife and *seven* children.

They were all there with their spouses and children—a total of twenty-eight grandchildren. The spouses of Ismael's children had brought their parents and siblings and those siblings' children. His neighbors and friends were there, too.

Ismael's children's names? Abe for his father, Madeline for his mother. Dynah for his aunt, Frieda and Eli for his maternal grandparents. Anna, for my momma. Ismael after himself.

After a great deal of chaos, Ismael motioned for silence. "My family," he said, broken. "My friends. I am so glad you are with us today to celebrate this most momentous, this most miraculous event." He broke down, more tears. We were all in puddles. "I want to say something special, something novel to mark this event, something profound, but I can think of nothing but two words. Two words only!" He paused again, gathered himself together. "To my father, my aunt, my nieces..." He shook his head, and his voice came out through the rolling tears, the decades of anguish, the incomparable joy, "Welcome home."

Welcome home.

Can you imagine the party we attended at Ismael's house?

Enormous. People everywhere. Tables and tables of endless food. It lasted all night, *all night long*.

There was a rockin' band, too, and at the first song, the entire mob, as one heaving, laughing group, tumbled to the middle of the great room and danced.

We were pushed along—Grandma, who immediately threw her arms in the air and started shimmying; Granddad, who hobbled in and managed to bust a move, which got him huge applause; and then Annie and I.

We resisted, we laughed, we tried to leave the mob, but hands grabbed us, pulled us back in, pooh-poohed our refusals.

Finally Annie and I took a gander at each other. What to do, what to do? We didn't dance anymore. We hadn't danced since we lived in the house by the sea with a momma who wore pink and a dad who told us we could be whomever we wanted to be.

"Shake it, Annie! Get down, Madeline!" Our cousins (our cousins!) yelled at us, shakin' it hard, twirling around, boogeying away.

Ah, what to do.

Annie started it. She did one of those slinky moves, tip of finger to tip of finger, as if music was rolling through her body. I was next, and I put my fists above my head and wiggled my fanny.

Annie made a groovy roll with her whole body.

I spun around, to the beat. We grabbed each other's hands, and that was it.

We danced.

For the first time since we had lived in the pink, we danced. Granddad, Grandma, Annie and I, Nola and Dr. Rubenstein. We danced with each other, with our cousins, with Ismael and his wife, Devora.

We danced with our family.

We danced.

Annie and I finally put Grandma to bed at three in the morning. "Tell Abe to come right on up, dear." She winked at me. She had been determined to wear her cheetah print nightgown. She attached the fluffy pink handcuff to one wrist. "Tell him I'm ready to chain myself to him."

"I'll tell him, Grandma," Annie said. "I think he's gonna like that handcuff. It'll make him feel dominated."

"He is such a good man," Grandma said. "The swans had to help us walk over the mountains, but then we lived with hardly anything to eat or drink. Anna in her blue coat was hungry. We took a big swan to the place with all the lavender after the place on the corner with all the food. I was but a girl, an innocent girl, and Abe, he was my sister's husband. We were lost, together lost, wanting Madeline, wanting Ismael whose wings had been smashed. Abe had me go to college. I studied swans when I was there. Swans and painting and marbles."

She drew a shape of a swan with her hand, as if a paintbrush was in it. "And Abe was so proud, he put my swans in his stores and we worked in those stores, always working, and one day, after a long, long time, on a day filled with centaurs and giants and talking beavers, we fell in love. It was on the deck near the lavender and the marbles. I kissed him because I had fallen in love with him. I loved him!" Her face brightened. "Love!"

Love, sweet love, the brightest beacon, the warmest hug, the desire above all else.

"Abe said to me, after the kiss, he said, 'No, no, Dynah... we can't,' and I said, 'Why not, Abe?' and he...the lavender magic was there that day, and he knew. He knew what was between us, the passion. We never had that passion when Madeline was alive. He was my sister's swan then, but he knew that our new love was pure, that Madeline would flap her wings and understand. He kissed me back, held me in his wings, and I held him in my wings forever." She laughed, sighed. "Forever and ever I have held him, and when I am in heaven I will share Abe with my sister, Madeline. I love my sister! She is right here, in my heart, and I will share him, and we will all be together in a nest filled with sticks and cotton with Anna and Luke, who are in the nest already."

The mention of my momma, of Marie Elise, née Anna Bacherach, and the mention of my dad, had me all choked up again.

"We will fly together and land on the pond and play our instruments in an orchestra!" Grandma announced. "All of us— you, too!" She kissed us both, on both cheeks, like the French do. My tears ran into her kisses.

"Abe found our Ismael, didn't he, Madeline? Didn't he, Anna? *He found him!* And he was right here, in the Land of the Swans, the whole time."

She clapped her hands.

"We have our love, don't we? Our family love!"

"I thought I had lost my entire family," Ismael told Annie and me the next afternoon on his rooftop. His face was so like my granddad's, younger, but even the lines grooved into the angles and planes were the same. "My mother was dead, the doctor told me, and my father, my aunt, and my sister were on the run." He closed his eyes. "I was alone in a world that had gone mad, lost itself, its morals and value for life obliterated. It was as if all the goodness had left, disappeared, and in its place was only hatred and killings and tanks and guns."

Ismael had woken up in the crawl space under the doctor's home, where they'd hid him when the doctor and his wife saw the Nazis moving toward their home. He was in and out of consciousness for days, too critically injured to move. For weeks the doctor and his wife cared for him until his strength ebbed back.

Ismael, when healthier, made plans. The doctor knew everyone, he had connections, and after being hidden here and there, Ismael eventually joined the French Resistance. The doctor and his wife were sent to the camps as "traitors" and died within weeks of their arrival of typhoid. "They saved my life. Knowing the risks of hiding Jews, they literally gave their lives for others. What more can be said? Their actions were heroic."

Ismael, even though he was barely a teen, became an expert in explosives.

"With unimpressive caches of explosives we had to be creative," he said, winking. "My specialties were trains and train tracks, with some side work done in intelligence. I was young, quick, much taller than most children my age, but older by grief. I took my anger, my aloneness, my pain, and focused on my explosives and what I could do to bring down the Nazis."

"I like explosives," Annie said.

"Tell me about that," Ismael said, leaning forward, grinning. "I understand you were with the government."

"I was. For years. Now I take care of animals, but tell us more, Uncle Ismael, please."

"I will, but only if you promise me that we can talk explosives later."

Annie actually laughed. "Deal. It's one of my favorite topics."

"Me too!" Ismael's face lit up. He settled back into the past, a turbulent, horrid past. "Europe was in chaos and we were part of it. I determined that I would do whatever it took to bring down the Nazis or die trying, but I could not stop worrying about my family. Had they made it out of France? Were they lost in the camps, dying, sick? Had they been shot trying to escape, their bodies buried somewhere in Europe, covered by snow, rained upon, walked over? Sometimes I drove myself crazy, wondering if I had walked over their graves in the years I spent crisscrossing France in the Resistance.

"Toward the end of the war we were caught by the Nazis. We were betrayed. I was with six other members of the Resistance. The Nazis shot two of the men on the spot, point-blank. They took the two women, I don't know what happened to them. Poor Bridgette, poor Mara." He bit down on his lip and we waited until he composed himself. "We were sent to Dachau. We were stamped, like cattle, permanently branded." He tapped the numbers on his arm. "I gave them a fake name. I was defiant. I fought wherever I could, in any way I could. We were starved, beaten, and worked almost to death. Disease was rampant. There was no sanitation. It was inhumane, vicious, the result of the sickest, most violent of men.

"Finally, the Americans came to liberate us. They came right through the gates and we stared, we could not believe it. We cheered, we cried. . . . Then shots, machine guns . . . The Americans killed SS and guards, they were livid, these hardened U.S. soldiers crying when they saw us, the walking dead and the dead piled up in train cars, like one might pile up beef. The inmates killed some of the guards, too, most often with their hands, a shovel. . . . I killed a guard myself, a man who had tortured all of us. He deserved it. Some people do not deserve a place here on our planet. I am not proud of it, but there it is."

There it was.

"I received medical care. I was starving, I had trouble swallowing, I had tuberculosis, I was infested by lice and bugs, and I had unhealed wounds. When I could stand up, walk, move, I stayed and helped the other victims. Some, even after care, died. They were too far gone. I will not tell you now the other horrors I saw in Dachau, it is too much. Too much depravity." He caught back his cries. This took about five minutes. We waited for him once again, holding his hands in ours, our own hands trembling with the visions he cast.

"When I was better, I tried to find my father, my aunt, my sister before leaving France. I hoped, I lived in the hope that someone, *one* of them even, would be found alive, but no. I could not find them. There were no Bacherachs. They had disappeared. I later hired an investigator to look for my family, but he turned up nothing, because Bacherach was not the name being used anymore. I had to assume that they had died, too, in the blasts of the war, in the rubble that Europe became after madness overran it." Ismael ran his hands over his face. "To me, all was lost."

And lost to us, too. The family, our family, in Germany, in France, gone. We never had a chance to know them at all.

"But I knew I could not stay in Europe any longer. France had turned against my family. The Germans and the Nazis had turned against my great-grandparents. The Russians had turned against my great-great-grandparents. Everywhere, forever, Jews have been persecuted, assaulted, scattered. I came to Israel to help create a place where Jews would be safe, safe forever. That is why I am here, that is why I will never leave."

He took a deep breath, and I knew he had taught himself to not travel too far into the memories lest the memories kill him. "So I had many children. I love all of them, I love my wife. I love family. I had to have a family again and now you, my sister's daughters, my father, my aunt, all here." His face scrunched up and he breathed in and out. "You are the daughters of my beloved sister. I have missed her since the day we parted. Always a loss I can never run from."

Our granddad, along with Annie and I, had told Ismael about Momma, about her beauty parlor, the pink, the house by the sea, our dad's death. We had told him briefly about the trials, and how she had dropped herself into the sea. He listened carefully, but never once had the tears stopped streaming from his eyes.

"You must call me Uncle Ismael. I am your uncle, the brother of your mother." He hugged me, reached for Annie. "You are my family," he whispered, his voice hoarse. "You are my family. Forever and ever we will be together. We are family, my red-haired nieces."

I knew my mouth had dropped open, a gaping hole of surprise.

"You can see the red?" Annie asked.

"Absolutely!" Ismael gushed. "It's glowing all around you. It's the luck of the Irish in you! From your father. I hear he was a great man."

"Yes, he was," I said.

"Great man, a most pure and gentle mother, grand and lovely daughters," Ismael said, so emotional again. "He would be proud of you."

I should have attached a tissue to my face with glue to catch all the tears spurting from my eyes.

On the second night, after another raucous family dinner, Grandma gave Uncle Ismael the three swans she had brought with her, including the blue glass swan she had keened over that night in her bedroom, as she moaned, "Now, I remember. I'll never forget it."

She stood in her full-length, satiny black evening gown, her white curls piled atop her head, and tapped a wineglass with a spoon and a grape at the same time. When she had everyone's attention, she said, "Ismael loves swans. So I have brought him swans. Don't let them fly away, Ismael! You have to hold on to them tight because of their wings. Don't break their wings."

Ismael stood up as soon as she started speaking, to respect his aunt, his face tight as he fought for control, even before she reached into her gold silk purse and, with great fanfare, handed the wood, ceramic, and blue glass swans to Uncle Ismael.

"These, I have saved for you, my nephew. I knew I would see you again in the Land of the Swans."

Uncle Ismael took them with solemn ceremony, holding the three swans in his cupped hands, then kissing Grandma on both cheeks, twice. "Thank you, Aunt Dynah. Thank you."

"And now, I have another gift for you, Ismael."

My cousins brought out a huge canvas, easel, brushes, and paints, and Grandma, with those talented hands, painted, truly, the most realistic, awe-inspiring swan she had ever painted, the feathers white and fluffy, the lines elegant, the palm trees of Tel Aviv in the background. The swan cradled a violin in its wings.

"For you, Ismael," she said when she was done. "May our violins never be apart again."

"Never," he rasped. "Never again will we be apart."

"I love you, Ismael," Grandma said, her hands cupping his face, and I could almost believe the dementia, for a moment, had left. "I have never stopped loving you."

"It is the same for me, Aunt Dynah," he choked. "I love you. I have always loved you."

Uncle Ismael cried again so hard, he had to sit down.

"We are together again, Ismael," Grandma said. "Together. A family of swans."

All the rest of the family cried, too. Hankies flying, napkins shared, how they bawled.

The next day Uncle Ismael had the picture framed and hung as a centerpiece in his home so he could look at it every night and study the lines, the texture, the color, the love.

On the third night, Grandma, resplendent in a purple, off-the-shoulder ball gown and a diamond necklace, stood with the ring box in her hand. She hit her wineglass with a spoon and a slice of apple. When she had everyone's attention she said, "Ismael, now we will be married!" She opened the box in front of her elegant, white-haired nephew who had, like the gentleman he is, stood again out of respect for his aunt.

Inside the box was the wedding ring. "My husband, he gave this to your mother, my beautiful sister, who jumped like a swan and had her wings broken when she saved you from the black ghosts. Now, it is yours."

Uncle Ismael, once again a mess, could hardly hold his hand still when she pushed the wedding ring on his pinky finger. "Your mother, she and my husband loved each other. Then, when she was gone, and I was no longer a girl, I fell in love with your father, and he loved me back. There!" she announced. "Now we're all married together!"

Uncle Ismael's children are so emotional. They were a blubbery mess, and they made blubbery messes out of Annie and me and our granddad, too, and Granddad wrapped Uncle Ismael and Grandma in a huge hug, and that was a blubbery mess.

It was only relieved when Grandma shouted, "I can't make hot love to you now, Abe! You have to wait until later! Then, I'll take you to the stars!"

She pulled away, smiled seductively, and shimmied her chest at him.

On the fourth night, late, when the moon was soft and waiting, I saw Annie sit down at the piano in Uncle Ismael's living room.

She ran her fingers over the keys, played scales, up and down, up and down.

She played one piece after another by Mozart as if she had been playing in her head for years, waiting to let it out through her delicate fingers. I lifted my violin. We played together.

Somehow, the family knew this was a special moment. They were quiet, that noisy bunch. They listened, they watched, they joined us in a bubble of wonder.

I was startled when I heard a second violinist join us, and Granddad, *Granddad,* who I had never heard play before, who had refused to play, stood beside me, then Ismael joined us.

For long seconds, Annie's fingers froze, my hands didn't move, struck again at the head-banging surprises one finds in life, the surprises that leap and jump and twirl around, alighting at the most unexpected moments.

We dove back into our music, after Annie and I grinned at each other, confused and surprised, but hey. What the heck. There would be answers later as to why Granddad had never played his violin for us. And, if we did not receive answers, that would be okay. Life is not going to answer all my questions. I can rest in that. I can hold on to it, and be at peace with it.

We played together, my granddad, Uncle Ismael, Annie and I, Grandma waltzing around the room, resplendent in yellow, singing a song of love and lust about my granddad.

*   *   *

"It is a miracle," Uncle Ismael said to me. "A most happy miracle."

"Yes," I said, as the sun set, purple here, orange there, yellow, a bit of pink, embracing and hopeful. "It is a miracle."

"It was a pleasure to hear you play the violin last night," Uncle Ismael said, those eyes so warm. "You are very talented."

"Not like you, nothing like you."

"You get it from your granddad."

"I'm sorry?"

"Your talent. He was one of the finest violinists, ever, in France."

My mouth dropped open. I had heard him the night before, I knew he was talented....

"I was so proud of him...." Ismael told me about the orchestra Granddad played in, how Grandma Madeline also played the violin.

"It is the strangest thing. I..." I paused. "You will think you have a crazy niece on your hands but..."

"Tell me. I want to know. Please." He leaned toward me, eager, trusting, so kind, despite the insane horrificness of his past.

I looked into his brown eyes with a touch of gold, so like my momma's. "Uncle Ismael, I hear..."

He blinked at me, and something dawned in his eyes, excitement, disbelief. "You hear?"

"I hear... I'm so embarrassed, but ever since I was a little girl, in my head, no one else can hear it, but I..."

He stared at me intently. "Madeline, do you hear violin music in your head?"

I caught my breath. *"I do."* I paused, worrying about what he would think. "I've heard you play the last couple of days and I'm sure... Uncle Ismael, I am sure that I am hearing *you.*"

He closed his eyes, then opened them, and grabbed my hand. "It is you I hear, too."

"You hear me?" I ran a hand through my curls. "How... how do you know?"

"I have heard violin music in my head for over thirty years.

First I heard a child, a talented child. I knew because of the skill level it was a child, but the child became better and better. She improved in every area, and she became a master. Listening to you, I knew it was true, but I thought I should not bring it up so soon." He laughed. "I thought you would think I was crazy. But you are a rebel violinist, aren't you?"

I was shocked once again. "Yes, I am."

"You play everything. From Mendelssohn, Mozart, Bach, Beethoven, Jewish folk music, Texas-style fiddling, Western swing, Irish jigs and reels, Stéphane Grappelli, bluegrass . . ."

"Yes. I'm all over the place. I like the change, the moods, the . . . tunes!" I laughed again.

"I've played in the orchestra here for years."

"I swear I've heard clapping."

"I've practiced alone, duets and quartets . . ."

"I've heard you."

"I could hear someone practicing, starting and stopping . . . finished pieces, eloquently played."

We watched the light play on the hills, the shadows, basking in the miracle, a miracle that should not have been, that had no reason, no explanation, but it was there, between us.

"We have heard each other," he said, wonder in his voice. "We have heard each other for decades."

"Over an ocean, over land, over thousands of miles . . ."

Uncle Ismael stood up with his violin.

Before he started, I knew what he would play. I stood next to him. He looked in my eyes, nodded. Together, in perfect timing, we began.

It was one of my favorites: Mozart's Symphony no. 40 in G Minor.

Grandma began her ritual of giving Uncle Ismael a swan on a regular basis.

"We are in the Land of the Swans," she told everyone. "I must make sure he has enough. He loves swans!"

Nola and other members of that massive family would take her "swan shopping." The swans she bought were made of all different materials: woods, ceramic, glazed pottery, steel, natural elements, glass. She also drew him swans.

Sometimes at night, after dinner, she would smile serenely, with such love in her eyes, and she would present Uncle Ismael with a swan. "This is from your mother," she would tell him. "She loved you so, like I do!" Or "This is from your sister. She loved you so, like I do."

And Uncle Ismael would take the swan, and he would sob, for his mother, his sister, for life, and others would cry. This was a very emotional family we had entered into. The men did not try to cover their emotions, and the women were equally bad. Very bad. They cried and laughed all the time, often at once.

When the gifts of the swans started to arrive, Uncle Ismael had shelves built in his living room, floor to ceiling, and the new swans joined the ones Grandma brought him from Oregon. They were displayed as one would display great art.

"Ismael," my grandma would say to him often, smiling, but reprimanding, "no more hiding!"

"Never," he would answer, bringing Grandma's hands to his lips and kissing them.

"We are staying in Israel."

"You're . . . what? Did you say you're staying?" I asked, struggling to understand.

"What do you mean, staying?" Annie asked. "You mean, you're staying for a week? For two? We can extend our vacation. . . ."

"No, dear. We are staying. Your grandma and I are not leaving. I am not leaving my son again." Granddad's face started to crumple. "I can't leave him again. I love you both, you know that—"

"Granddad, we know that." I reached for his shaking hand. We were in one of the lush gardens around Uncle Ismael's home, out on the patio, under a green umbrella, two palm trees swaying.

"And we love you," Annie said, "but, what do you mean, you're staying?"

"We are not leaving. We will be buried here in Israel."

I cleared my throat. Every day in Israel had been a day of emotions. We were hugged and held, our hands caressed, our cheeks patted, our shoulders linked by others' arms.

Annie, *Annie,* who avoided human contact except from Grandma and Granddad and me, actually embraced our family. She hugged them and didn't look like she was under forced oppression. One of our cousins said, "Annie is such a warm and generous person, so affectionate, Madeline, like you."

I was watching a miraculous miracle.

"You . . . ," Annie said. "You mean, you mean you're not going back to Oregon?"

He shook his head.

"You . . . ," I said, tripping on my words. "You're going to live here?"

He nodded. "Ismael and Devora have invited us to live with them here, and Nola has accepted, too. She will stay with us. We will fly her sons over three times a year to visit. Their house has plenty of room."

That was true. Uncle Ismael and Devora, his cozy, comfy wife who had fought in a war and was a crack shot, were very successful. They had a thriving import–export business that reached worldwide.

"But even if there was hardly any room," Granddad said, his lips tightening together, "or my son lived in a shack, or a one-room home that he would not leave, and he invited us to stay, we would stay. I would stay with them in a hut. I would stay with them anywhere." He turned to us, gripped our hands hard. "Stay here, Madeline, Annie, please. Stay with us. Let's make a new life here, all of us, together."

I leaned back in my chair, as did Annie.

"You're kidding," I said.

"No, my love, I am not. You girls, you are my life," Granddad said, anguished, breaking. "I love you more than my own life, I always, always have, but please understand, I can't leave my son again, I can't. It will kill me."

"But Granddad—" I said.

"But Granddad—" Annie said.

Then we closed our mouths and were silent.

But what? What argument was there? None.

"My brain is almost exploding," Annie said, "but I can't think of any good reason why you shouldn't stay here."

"I have only met my son again, after all these years," Granddad said, a hand brushing his white hair back.

"We understand," I said.

And we did. We got it.

Annie leaned over and kissed him. "Granddad, you can't be away from Uncle Ismael and the gang. Not for one day. Not for one minute."

Nope. He couldn't. No can do. I would react the same.

"Will you all stay, too?" he asked, eager. "We can sell The Lavender Farm, or keep it, whatever you wish to do. You can build houses here, start a new life, be with your family. Seven children, Ismael has. Seven. All of your first cousins, and they have children, too. They are your family. . . ."

I loved Israel. I loved Tel Aviv. But I wanted to live on The Lavender Farm and, maybe, perhaps, I wanted to call the snake hunter. I choked up when I looked at Annie. I didn't want her to move to Israel, but it was her choice.

"Granddad," Annie said. "I'm not going to live here, but Israel is . . . it's beautiful. I feel like it's part of me, part of the missing part of me. So, I'll make a deal with you, Granddad."

Our granddad leaned forward.

"Madeline and I, we'll stay for a while, then we'll come and visit all the time, okay? We'll visit. You stay with your son."

"Is that a promise? You will visit often?"

"It is, Granddad. It is a promise."

More tears.

Our new family was not pleased about Annie and my leaving for Oregon. They argued, they pleaded, they cajoled.

Why, Annie could work as a vet! Plenty of people in Tel Aviv needed life coaches! If we didn't stay we would miss Kelila's wedding, and Maya's fortieth birthday, and Rivka and Yudel's anniversary, and two bar mitzvahs! Two! All in the next few weeks. We couldn't go! *We couldn't!* It was a bad idea to return to Oregon. Bad! We were family! We had time to make up! Please! Don't go!

They all came, as a noisy mob, to see Annie and me off at the airport when we left.

Granddad gave me a hug and left tears on my cheeks. Grandma hugged me tight, then slipped something into my pocket. It was a bag of colorful marbles. "For the swans in the lavender."

They are an emotional group. The men all show their emotions and the women are equally bad.

Very bad.

We had found our family.

I loved them already.

32

~

When we returned to Oregon I bought Annie and myself Jeeps. They were pink. I ordered vanity license plates. They said PNK GRL 1 for me, because I am the oldest, and PNK GRL 2.

We drove my pink jeep to Anacortes, Washington, and rented a sailboat. For a week we sailed in and around the San Juan Islands. We saw porpoise, killer whales, seals, a bald eagle, and deer. We stopped off at Olga and hiked up to the café and had raspberry and boysenberry pie. We bought pottery. We walked through Eastsound and bought paintings and photographs of the sea. We went to San Juan on the horn-tooting white ferry and had peppermint ice cream. It was so delicious we went back and had strawberry ice cream. Both pink ice creams. We were not afraid of ice cream anymore.

We sailed and sailed, sometimes in silence, sometimes laughing and chatting, often allowing tears to roll, as we reintroduced ourselves to the ocean again, its depth, its personality, its freedom, as our dad used to say. We watched the colors glint off the water, and Annie declared, quoting our momma, "The only color the ocean is missing is pink."

"I love you, sister," I told her. I shook my hair in the wind, all the curls flying around my face, tight curls, loose curls, frizzy curls.

"I love you, too." Her curls flew, too.

We had tossed our flat irons in a steel bin together at The

Lavender Farm, and Annie had used a wee bit of explosives to blow them up. "Never again," she'd said. "No flat ironing."

We both agreed that our hair was looking a bit redder lately.

"Must be Dad," Annie said. "I'll bet he was impressed when you had all the Israeli family doing Irish jigs. You're a boot-stomping fiddler."

"Thank you. You're a hellion on the piano. Your hard rock tunes were especially popular."

Her face became contemplative as she studied a distant is-land. "It would be very cool to bang down on piano keys one day and somewhere else an explosion would fire into the sky."

I rolled my eyes at her. She laughed.

I pulled the hood of my pink sweatshirt up, as Annie had done with hers, our sailboat creating a cool wind.

"It feels right to wear pink again, doesn't it, Pink Girl?" she said.

"It sure does, Pink Girl Sister." We had even bought matching pink tennis shoes. Geeky, we knew. In the distance I saw a fin. Yep. Killer whale. It was surrounded by the pinks and yellows of the sunset. There is hardly anything prettier than the sunsets you see when you're in a boat on the Pacific Ocean, the green emer-ald islands of the San Juans sticking up like tips of mountains that had been scattered and dropped by a giant hand.

"I think I'm ready to let him serve me chocolate cheesecake without cringing."

I nudged her with my elbow. "Now you've got me puzzled. Baffled. Lost. Speak on, sister."

"Bertie."

Ah, Bertie. Lovesick Bertie.

"He always remembers that my favorite dessert is chocolate cheesecake, that I love artichoke chicken soup and the fluffy rolls from Chitty Chang's bakery. He buys me flowers and chocolates and cards and those sorts of silly things."

I thought of the lanky, longish-blonde-haired, tough-ass, ro-mantic Special Ops man with the alpacas who were so often "under the weather." What a man. "He's got a good memory."

"Yep. He does. Persistence, too."

I let the waves fill the silence for us, colored fire shooting across the sky.

"I think I could . . . I think I might could maybe . . ." She took a deep breath.

"You might could maybe . . . ," I prodded.

"Hold his hand. Go to dinner. Maybe watch a sunset with him on the top of the hill."

"I'm sure he would be deeelighted." I laughed thinking about the hope that sprang eternal on Bertie's face whenever he saw Annie.

"He's sent me so many gifts since your speech, Madeline, including chocolate cheesecake and a flower pot shaped like a Labrador, and he's called, so he knows and still . . . still he wants to be with me."

"He wants to be with you, *and* he's a sex god," I mused.

"Yeah, he's definitely hot. I think the hotness scares me a bit, though. It's hard to take a leap into hot."

"I know about those hard leaps. I can barely get my feet off the floor."

Another fin appeared, dove back down. So much is going on in the ocean that we will never see. But we know it's there, powerful, beautiful. Even animals have relationships.

"We should take the leaps, though, Annie. If we don't leap, we don't live."

"Think we could do that? Like normal women?"

"We've never been normal. It's not something I strive to be anymore. It just isn't gonna work for us. But I think we could give it the ol' heave-ho and see what happens."

"The ol' heave-ho?" She finally exhaled, winked at me, and grinned. "A leaping heave-ho?"

"A leaping heave-ho."

"A leaping heave-ho for love."

We high-fived each other, then took sips of our beers. Two geeky geeks.

Well, whaddya know. The O'Shea girls were gonna take a dare on love and life. I picked up another slice of pizza, after pushing my curls out of my face. Annie was on her third piece. I figured I'd have four and quit then. But I might not. The pizza was amazing—thick crust, thick cheese, thick pepperoni. We could eat pizza and ice cream again. Wasn't that something?

I know I am *becoming* whole. I am not two people in one, trying to hide my real self. I am no longer a lie. I am not pretending.

I am part of a huge family. I am part lavender farm, part house by the sea and French Beauty Parlor. I am part beat-up violin, part swan, part heart-shaped rocks. I am the daughter of an Irish fisherman and a Jewish pink woman. I am the sister of a vet who likes her explosives.

Together they fit. It was all very American.

"I'm going to say something cheesy."

Annie pulled a long piece of cheese off her pizza. Perfect timing.

"Good, shoot it out. I hope it tastes good."

"To me it does. I think, Annie, as overly dramatic as this sounds, that today, right now, on a sailboat, eating pizza, wearing pink, with that killer whale out there goofing around . . ."

"Yeeeesss?"

"Today is the first day of the rest of my life. I'm starting over. I'm redoing myself."

"Super-duper," Annie said. "It is cheesy, but I'll start over with you. It'll be the first day of the rest of my life, too. My first goal: Give up my trips to Fiji."

I whipped my head around to confirm that strange declaration. "You're kidding?"

She smirked. "Duh. Yeah, it's a joke. Where there are animals with abusive owners, there will always be explosives."

We clinked our beer cans and watched the sun sink between the islands, like a sleepy blob of melted gold, the waves turning purple and orange in the light. "To explosives," I said.

"To starting over," she said.

"Cheers."

On a night when the clouds billowed and roared with regret and sadness, Annie and I opened, for the first time, our granddad's leather journal.

There was his guilt. His regret. His atonement.

Millions and millions of dollars.

To the Laurents.

To Anton Laurent.

To Emmanuelle Laurent.

To Marie Elise Laurent.

To Johnna Laurent.

To Aaron Laurent.

In the margins, all over, I am sorry.

I am sorry.

"Come in, friend," he said. "Come in."

I didn't call him until I had things together.

I had bought into our materialistic society's definition of success because I had felt like nothing, "less than others," and felt I had to own all the "stuff" in order to prove my own worthiness. Stuff never brought me worthiness or esteem, never helped me to like me. It was a losing battle, but I had to fight it, and lose, before I understood that part. Slow learner I can be.

It didn't take me too long to shed all that crap. I sold my house that I didn't like. Living in a modern spaceship, that was completely opposite from our house by the sea, hadn't blocked out those crushing memories, as I'd hoped, it had simply magnified my loss.

I gave my car away to be auctioned off at Youth Avenues. The house and the car reminded me of how I've tried to be someone I'm so not, to project an image of me that is patently false. I closed my office downtown, added an office to Grandma and Granddad's house with a view of the lavender rows, and started seeing my clients there. I thought I'd lose a bunch of them because of the drive.

Nope, didn't lose any. In fact, they love it on The Lavender Farm, and they all come about an hour early and walk around to get some peace in their lives.

My office has two sets of French doors and lots of windows. I have a comfy L-shaped blue couch with fluffy pink pillows, a number of lights with flowered shades for gentle effect, a leather chair, a compact kitchen where I can make my clients tea or coffee and we can sit at the kitchen table or, in warmer weather, head for the deck and the view of the blue and purple mountains west of us. There is absolutely no modern art.

The Giordano sisters said being out at The Lavender Farm was "nature touching their feminines." Adriana said, "The farm helps me quell my inner and outer mood swings." Bella said, "Menstrually, this is a far better place for me." Carlotta said, "In spirit, I believe I am a tree." They brought their cats.

Corky (mean lady) does not throw chairs when she comes out. In fact, sometimes we sit on the deck and drink lemon tea and watch birds. That's what she likes to do. "See, when you hate yourself, you hate everyone around you," she said. "I had a lot of hate. Thanks for telling me to volunteer. Holding sick and premature babies has made me not so obnoxious. Don't you think?"

Georgie still works for me. She does a lot of work from her house, via computer. I can hear Stanley barking at me when we talk on the phone.

Going to the dock over the pond and playing my violin brings me peace. I can still hear Ismael, and we laugh about it over the phone. The gunshots are so quiet now, dim and dull, as if covered by a noisy Israeli family, a quiet bench on the hill, and Annie's friendship. Sitting in the middle of rows of lavender rejuvenates me. Touching it, smelling it, creating wreaths and potpourri and other crafts, I'm happy. I do not want to leave The Lavender Farm again. This is home.

I was sitting in the middle of the lavender rows when he arrived, two marbles in my hand that I'd dug up, one purple, one pink, both with silver flecks.

He climbed out of his truck and saw me right away. For a minute, we stared across the purple streaks as I heard Mozart's Piano Concerto no. 17 in my head, rising up, up, and up further still.

He was very tall. He was wearing jeans and a white, button-down shirt. I was wearing jeans, too, and a white shirt, and my cowboy boots. For some reason, a vision of May's "We'll charge you up" silver sequined bra and thong came to mind. Maybe I'd be wearing them soon.

I had spent ten days reading his books and drinking lemon tea. I started with his first one, *The Girl in Pink,* and moved on. He had written five books. I had been petrified of what I would read, the memories it would bring back. I knew that Steve had not written about the trials, the photographs, the abuse, or me. He had too much character to write about that.

No, these were touching, tear-jerking love stories, two lives, a boy and a girl, best friends, who grew to be a man and a woman, their lives never meeting at the right time, the right moment. Georgie was right, there was magic to them somehow, humor, a touch of heavenly miracles. Each character dealt with the challenges, disappointments, and joys that can be expected in life, but it was the prose, the rhythm, the words that described the pulse of each character, and their everlasting hope of finding love, that kept me reading.

I headed down the hill toward him, stepping over the purple and blue lavender. He smiled at me and we were kids again, except he was very tall and had shoulders like a bronco. In those eyes I saw warmth, kindness, and wisdom.

"Madeline," Steve said, when I was about three feet from him. "It's good to see you again."

"You too." I smiled back at his smile, couldn't help it. The words "I missed you" slipped right out of my mouth.

He laughed, but I felt the longing, the friendship that still bloomed, the promise of more. "I missed you, too."

"You're a little taller than when I last saw you." And, oh, he was truly gorgeous in an "I can hug you the rest of my life" type of way.

"Your hair is redder than it used to be."

I gave him a bouquet of lavender, then stood on my toes and kissed his cheek.

He even smelled the same, like the ocean, pine trees, butterscotch, and a hint of spring.

He smelled like home.

I took a deep breath.

Yep. I could breathe again.

THE FIRST DAY OF THE REST OF MY LIFE

Cathy Lamb

ABOUT THIS GUIDE

The suggested questions are included to enhance
your group's reading of Cathy Lamb's
The First Day of the Rest of My Life.

DISCUSSION QUESTIONS

1. Was Madeline an effective life coach? If you made an appointment for a life-coaching session, what do you think she would tell you to change? Improve? Or would she say that you have "gathered your hellfire" and are on the right course?

2. A'isha Heinbrenner, a client of Madeline's, says, "You know, Madeline, . . . I'm not lonely at all. It's bothered me that I'm not lonely, because I thought that I should be. But I'm not. Alone means I'm with myself. Alone means I answer to myself, I do what I want for, literally, the first time in my life. Alone means that I can think what I want. It means I'm not burdened with the constancy of doing things for others." Can you relate to this statement?

3. If you were on the jury at Marie Elise's trial, would you have found her guilty or not guilty for killing Sherwinn, Gavin, and Pauly? Did Marie Elise make the right choice? What would you have done?

4. For many readers, the scenes in the shack and in the courtroom where Madeline and Annie recount the abuse they suffered may be very difficult to read. However, if those scenes had been softened, the reality of what happened, and the impact on Madeline and Annie, would also have been softened. Did the author strike the right balance?

5. Madeline said, "Annie relates better to animals than people, and she cannot abide abuse of any kind. She decided to be a veterinarian during her 'mystery' years. Annie said, 'I saw too many human limbs in places where they shouldn't be, and I decided I wanted to be a part of putting things back together, not destroying them. But I don't want to work with people. I love animals. They don't frighten me, they don't need anything from me but medical care, and they won't hurt or betray me intentionally.' " How do you picture Annie? If she lived next door to you, would you be friends? What do you see happening in her future?

6. In many ways, this was the story about a scratched and battered violin and the lives of the people who owned it over three generations. How did the author intertwine history, both during the Nazi occupation of France and back and forth to Madeline's childhood, to propel the story?

7. What did the lavender field symbolize? What did the swans and the Land of the Swans symbolize? The marbles? The "emotional weather"? Pink? The ice cream and pizza?

8. Was there a particular scene that best exemplified Emmanuelle and Anton's love for each other? Which one?

9. How did Madeline and Annie change from the beginning of the book to the end? Would they have changed if they hadn't been forced to change because of the article and the blackmail? What would they have lost if Madeline hadn't made her speech at the Rock Your Womanhood conference?

10. Madeline says, "I can only compare life to being shot from a cannon into the middle of space and being bombarded by all sorts of debris—pieces of satellites and shuttles, asteroids, shooting stars, maybe an alien spaceship. We're hit all the time and sometimes we can't find Earth. We can't even find the Milky Way galaxy. We're lost. Running around, dodging this and that, trying not to get hurt or killed, and all the while we're looking for home. That's how life is. It's a meteor shower." Is this true? What does it tell you about her?